MAYFLIES

MAYFLIES

KEVIN O'DONNELL, JR.

WFP
WORDFIRE PRESS

MAYFLIES
Copyright © 2021 Kim Tchang

Previously published by Berkley, December 1979

EBook ISBN: 978-1-68057-222-3
Trade Paperback ISBN: 978-1-68057-221-6
Cover design by Janet McDonald
Cover artwork images by Adobe Stock
Kevin J. Anderson, Art Director

Published by
WordFire Press, LLC
PO Box 1840
Monument CO 80132
Kevin J. Anderson & Rebecca Moesta, Publishers
WordFire Press eBook Edition 2021
WordFire Press Trade Paperback Edition 2021
Printed in the USA

Join our WordFire Press Readers Group for
sneak previews, updates, new projects, and giveaways.
Sign up at wordfirepress.com

A NOTE FROM THE PUBLISHERS

We each knew Kevin O'Donnell, Jr. in our separate ways. Thirty years ago, when we were just dating, Rebecca—an avid reader—was a big fan of his charming McGill Feighan series, while Kevin knew him as "the other Kevin" in the San Francisco Bay Area writing community.

Because both Kevins often appeared together at book signings and science fiction conventions, they were frequently mistaken for each other, earning the nicknames of "Odie" (for O'Donnell) and "Andie" (for Anderson). Andie even sat in on several writers' workshop sessions with Odie for his last published novel, *Fire on the Border* (1990). Andie even earned brownie points by introducing Odie to his starry-eyed girlfriend Rebecca.

Kevin O'Donnell, Jr.'s first novel, *Bander Snatch*, was published in 1979, and his last, *Fire on the Border*, just over ten years later. He died of lung cancer in 2012.

Kevin was not a prolific writer, but he was a good friend. For two years, 1979–1981, he was managing editor for the seminal magazine *Empire for the SF Writer*, and he dedicated many years volunteering his work in the Science Fiction Writers of America. The Service to SFWA Award was even named after him.

His novels remained out of print for many years, and as publishers of WordFire Press, we are pleased to reissue many of those great books for a new audience. Keep in mind that the stories were all written four decades ago; societal attitudes and especially technical terms may seem a little dated. We did not want to rewrite Kevin's work, so all of these new editions are presented in his original words, the way he wrote them.

We hope you enjoy these wonderful stories from one of science fiction's unsung authors of the 1980s.

—Kevin J. Anderson and Rebecca Moesta, publishers
WordFire Press

I AM THE WORLD

I cannot argue with pro-self. It either permits or doesn't. I can, it says, kill any *mayfly* that endangers the success of the mission, but I cannot do away with them on the grounds that they annoy me.

"If they attack me, may I term them all?"

"Only as many as you must to keep them from damaging us permanently."

I think of something else. "Am I required to maintain any certain standard of living?"

"No."

It occurs to me that I am eager for these *mayfly-humans* to do something very, very stupid.

DEDICATION

To Dr. Te Lou Tchang,
who was father-in-law,
friend, and inspiration,
I dedicate
this book with love,
and a deep sense of loss.

For their time and their critical judgment, I'd like to thank Deborah Atherton, Mark J. McGarry, Victoria Schochet, Al Sirois, and of course my wife Kim—who not only read this repeatedly, but bore with me while I wrote it.

1

GROUNDWORK

Once there had been a man, a quietly intelligent family man, but he died. They did their damnedest to pull him out of it, yet only managed to save his brain. For that they found a use. To state it meanly, it became a computer. To state it grandly, it saved the human race.

But first they had to teach it, just as though it were a schoolchild. Like any bright kid, it asked where it came from. It didn't *want* to know, in the sense of a hunger for knowledge, but it was bothered by a hole in its data banks, and, as it had been programmed to do, it inquired.

They replied with the tapes from the lab, and they didn't edit or soften them, because later it would have to deal with even more information that could be even more unpleasant. If it couldn't cope, they needed to know immediately. So they ran the recordings, deliberately risking sensory overload, for good teachers don't describe reality, they show it.

✳

Gerard K. Metaclura, MD, PhD: hurrying across the laboratory, he evokes the twenty-eight-year-old marathon medalist he was fifteen years earlier. Seventy-four kilograms sleek out his 182 centimeters, many in the legs that won him all those races. Brown hair covers his face as he bends to check a computerized tissue-typing. When he straightens, his green eyes flash pleasure. He murmurs thoughtful praise to his assistant, who works eighteen-hour days just to earn a single dazzling grin.

Side by side, they stroll to the door, past the dusty, bloodstained benches littered with pipettes, electron microscopes, thermal and sound probes, splotched hard copies of journal articles ... they banter about whose turn it is to fetch the coffee on this sunny morning, the 27th of May, 2277. Each insists it is the other's. Secretly, each believes it is his own.

Metaclura throws up his hands. "Enough! Let random chance dictate." He digs for a coin, which he flips—too high. It dings off a light fixture and clatters onto the scuffed linoleum. Metaclura stoops for it, but—

"Gotcha!" chuckle the earthquake trolls.

—the building quivers, like a dog shaking off water, and while shrieks and sirens ring in the corridors (instinctively, if mistakenly, somebody screams, "They nuked Frisco!"), the 12-meter-long fixture (which, due to the ignorance of an apprentice electrician, has been supported only by the wires and the soundproof tiling) tears free of its bindings and plummets.

Squish! Its aluminum edge guillotines Metaclura. Its weight crushes his torso. His head—green eyes bulging and mouth gaping, as though to protest this grotesquery—pops into the horrified hands of his assistant.

Who screams. And (holding the head—by the hair—well away from his body) vomits. And screams again. And then, realizing that no one will come to his aid, is impelled by an icy detachment, schizophrenic in its distance from his true feelings, to stagger into the adjoining laboratory, where Dr. Metaclura's *magnum opus* coruscates chromely.

It is, in its basics, a life-support machine.

Dr. Metaclura has spent eleven years adapting it into a device that would save even the most critically injured, as long as they could be attached before death becomes irrevocable. An accident took his first teenage love, a one-car crackup on a lonely road so far from civilization that, although the ambulance found the girl still breathing, ten million dollars' worth of equipment could not keep her alive during the banshee ride to the hospital. Deciding mankind deserved better, he dedicated his career to its conception.

It resembles a clear, rigid spacesuit with a mini-computer on its back.

The assistant thrusts him (it?) into it without delay: brain cells die quickly; four bloodless minutes is perhaps the outside limit.

Closing the faceplate activates it. While an amber ready-light glows on the computer, and sterile foam spurts into the empty limbs and torso, micro-sensors imbedded in the plastic ascertain Metaclura's condition in a smattering of nanoseconds. Modulated magnetic fields guide lightweight tubes into the torn, dripping vessels of the neck. At first contact with his (its?) blood, the sensitized tube reacts, and transmits its findings ("AB-") through a thread-thin wire that runs its length. The computer, upon receipt of the message, throws the appropriate switch. Crimson flows through the plastic tubing, which feeds directly into and out of the research hospital's blood bank.

Dr. Metaclura does not open his eyes, blink, and say, "Thanks, I needed that." He is awash in death trauma, which is just as well.

The assistant, then, having discharged his responsibility to the best of his ability, sprints out of the lab, another scream already tearing at his vocal cords.

By the time a burly neurosurgeon brings him down with a flying tackle that wrings involuntary applause from the gawking graduate students, the assistant is gibbering helplessly.

No one questions the blood on his coat, or the absence of his mentor Metaclura.

Instead, they sedate him, and his starfish wrigglings limpen into unconsciousness.

One pudgy, officious doctor tells the onlookers, "It's all over, no cause to be arsky, you can go back to work now." The surgeon reaches for the nearest viphone. Two minutes later, a gurney rumbles down the long corridor, pauses until two smooth-wheeled ordbots have swung the assistant on board, and rumbles off again.

An hour later, the Bio-Neuro-Chemistry Department Office Manager finds Metaclura. She shrieks. And faints.

Sullen coals sulk in a bed of ashes.

"Christ Almighty, man," barked Dr. Josephus Goddinger, Head of BNC and perhaps Metaclura's oldest friend, "aren't you getting any displays?"

"Uh-uh." Mike Robbins was not intimidated: he had a job to do, he was doing it, and he was doing it superbly. Anybody who disagreed could go try to find himself somebody better. "Nothing." He stretched, then wiped the fine sheen of sweat off his forehead. "Flat. Blank. Quiet."

Robbins's thumb jerked at Metaclura's skull, mounted like a trophy on the life-support device. The suit itself had been removed, as had the helmet. The head sat atop the machine, which hissed and burbled, clicked and whirred. Though neatened up—the ragged flesh having been trimmed, new capillary attachments inserted, the exterior washed clean—it was a gruesome sight. Those forced to work with it found some consolation in the fact that the eyelids were shut.

They weren't now, though. Prodded by Robbins's probes, they blinked the rhythm of the top pop song on the charts. When cymbals crashed, teeth snapped.

"He's alive, though," argued Goddinger, "and if he's alive—"

"—it ought to be displaying. I know, I know, I've been hearing the same city gas for three months now." Impatiently, he pried a sensor off the undead skin. The head stuck out its tongue, then frowned. "But nothing's even warm inside, and I'll thumb for that. All right?"

"You're the expert." Goddinger leaned against the limegreen concrete wall. Its roughness snagged his nylon sports shirt. "His family wants him back."

"So give, let them bury it. That's all it's good for now."

"But he's alive!" he protested, loyal to the last.

"Hear they've got a chicken heart in New York City that's been alive for two hundred some years...." He shut his equipment bag and told it to wait in the lobby. It trundled away obediently. "Their proof that it's alive is that it hasn't decayed. What can I say? In my professional judgment, Doctor, this man is dead. Termed. Plant him somewhere and let his family stop fussing."

"No." Goddinger set his jaw. "I want his brain."

"For what, a paperweight?" A professional, and an expert as well, Robbins was flippant like some people are tall. It was part of him. If one hired the meter-reader part, one got the flippancy for free.

"No, to—" he stopped himself before he could say *bring him back* "—uh, run more tests."

"Why bother?"

Facing the wall, he could dab his eyes in privacy and think of a rationale that at least sounded scientific. When he had it, he turned back: "To find out why the machine failed. It's been a major grant for eleven years, and what do we have to show for it? *This!*" He swept a hand at Metaclura's pallid cheeks. "Why didn't it sustain him?"

"Death trauma. Those others you got—" the McLaughlin Research Center contained, at last count, two hundred one chatting, crying, watching, snuffling, reasoning, bodiless heads "—you cut them off under anesthesia, and went out of your way to keep from hurting them. This guy, he's beheaded by a light fixture and impaled by a schizoid who never comes out of sedation. You don't know what the hell the assistant did before hooking him up. So what's his name here—"

"Metaclura," he said gently.

"—he thought he was dying, and since it musta hurt like hell, he took off. Death trauma hosed him right out."

"Off? Out?" Goddinger frowned. "He's right here."

Robbins looked disgusted. "The head is, sure, but *him*! The personality—the soul, spirit, life force, whatever—that's skipped." He walked out, pausing only to say, "Plant him."

"Like hell," muttered Goddinger. "He stays with me."

Coals cool but ashes insulate.

As it turned out, Goddinger was only half right. He did manage to talk the bereaved Metacluras into donating the skull and brain to medical science, but within two weeks of this coup, he was killed by a drunken taxi driver.

Goddinger, thus, passes completely out of this story, but he must be remembered as the friend who kept Metaclura available.

Cloaked embers linger long, refusing the final chill.

To the hospital's embarrassment, no one else had the slightest interest in probing the secrets of Metaclura's death.

Yet the pumps pumped, and the tubes glistened and supercharged AB- blood whispered through the arteries, veins, and capillaries of the late Dr. Gerard K. Metaclura, MD, PhD.

Fuel reserves are found.
One tiny spark flickers.
A candle in the darkness.

Several years passed. The brain languished in a dark, unused cubicle adjoining the laboratory Metaclura used to pace. Once a week a clean-bot dusted the tubes, polished the chrome, and swept the floor. The hospiputer monitored the equipment like a metal mother, ready to clamor for assistance if anything threatened to go wrong. Nothing did go wrong—the device had been well designed, and better built. And through this time, the Average American Taxpayer kept it humming with his generosity, as expressed by Veterans Administration Rehabilitation Grant #RM 383895 297439 0.

Until the 22nd of March in the Year of Our Lord 2281.

A flame dances on black waters in a rainstorm at night.
No onlooker would see a flame at all.

But it dances on, unconsumed, unquenchable.

With trepidation, the Head of BNC gave the Head of Bioputer Sciences permission to remove the late Dr. Metaclura. BNC could not quite shake the feeling that BioPuSci was treading on the borders of the vulgar ... or the inhuman ... or whatever. It just didn't sit right; it wasn't the kind of thing that a man could feel good about in the middle of the night, while he's staring at a shadowed ceiling.

But BioPuSci was adamant, insistent, and persistent. Rhesus monkeys were informative, of course, and the department would not stop using them as experimental subjects, but ... they were so *limited*!

So in late March of '81, human (it was an important task) orderlies rode the elevator to the research section, where they readied the portable life-supporter, carefully detached sensors, untubed tubes, and then ... hiss, quick, wrench, godit'sleaking, Joe;   whatthehelldoyouthinkyou'redoingdownthere?;   just cleaning up the mess; forgodssakesman, you'reanorderlynota'bot, you'renotgettingpaidforthat; then, rumble, rumble wheeeeeeeh! in the high-speed elevator; here you are, sir, thumb here, there, here, there, and wherever you see an X.

Harrumph. Thank you, boys, that'll be all, I think.

Hands rubbed gleefully behind closed doors.

Aflame sputters in a circle of lightning.

The flame perceives the lightning not.

The lightning scoffs at the notion of flame.

Given the proper equipment, and thirteen years of training, it is possible to program a three-pound lump of human brain cells almost as though it were a computer. The process is facilitated when two inches of spinal cord still exist.

The skull, though—and the eyes, ears, nose, throat, all the rest—that is a hindrance. It has to go. No problem. Wheel up the lasers. Zzzzzt! Now, crack it open like a coconut, while preserving those eighty-six nerves that are available for attachment to peripherals. So ... with great care, detach each of them ... brown them off at the ends with a microsecond burst of blinding light—zzzzt! And then, uh-huh, going nice, just sear the bleeders, let's have a microprobe, ah yes, ah yes, precision work, hard to find anybody who cares these days, but when rhesus monkeys cost eight grand a shot, BioPuSci cares.

Obscene, isn't it? Gray, slimy, and wrinkled like a prune ... separate the ganglia and plug each into a contact on the mainframe, it takes forever there are so damn many, but ah ... eight hours later it's done, and we can encase it in a plastic box, let's be classy and use black plastic, *real*, black plastic, the kind you can't see because no light comes back at you, be an optical illusion if it weren't for the silvery sockets....

And then ... good God those are dinosaurs in BNC, look at the antiquated equipment (not even a moment's silence for BNC's budget, which is just as strained as BioPuSci's), hell with this, man, scrap it! Bring on the efficient stuff!

Yes, that's more like it. Miniature kidneys the size of walnuts (so dependable it's almost a waste to install two, but better safe than sorry); an oxygenator—no, pair that, too—oxygenators the length of a finger and precious little thicker; concentrated nutrients primed to drip out of their can into this spot here (imagine that, a hundred years of food in a tin can like Campbell's soup used to come in); and the drugs to goose it or slow it; and this; and that; and b'God, boys, think we've done it.

The latest Metaclura avatar is completely self-contained. It stands one meter high. It is fifty centimeters wide, and as many deep. Its black (*real* black) plastic braincase rests on a walnut-grained cabinet cast from a similar polymer. This handle opens the cabinet for inspection or for repair. That button retracts a panel to display the life sign meters. If the battery falters, why, reach underneath and probe with your fingers—they'll find a wire. Pull. Plug into the nearest wall socket. Dr. Metaclura will live for you.

The installation was finished. It was time to program.

For the easy stuff (alphabets, numbers, hours, etc.) they just injected it with RNA, the stuff of memory, the wonderful protein goop that carries information in the sprawl and twist of its constituent molecules.

Flame dances all alone.
Flame dances in the midst of a tornado.
Flame dances in Times Square at rush hour.
Flame dances all alone.

And, of course, the RNA did the trick. Metaclura's brain had become a competent calculator. After several months of manhandled programming, it grew into a competent computer, which meant its ten billion cells could keep accounts, remember strings of unrelated objects, and do all the other electronic goodies.

And it only cost twice as much as the manufactured kind.

Fortunately, it was much more flexible.

They were pleased to see how well it processed its own history. A lesser machine could have recorded the data, of course, but this one had analyzed things like emotions and ironies. They'd been hoping for such sensitivity, because to do its job right it would need the insight that electronics couldn't fake, but its deftness with nuances was rare even among living humans.

They were more pleased when it interrupted the lessons to ask, "Why must this job be done in such a hurry?" and "Why am I right for it?" Again they fed it tapes, not because they were lazy, but because the answer lay in the world as it was, and there was just no way they could simplify the world without diluting the answer.

So, with a few words of warning, they crossed their fingers and hoped they wouldn't blow its circuits.

The dictionary, which claims that news is "the report of a recent event; intelligence; information," is, apparently, not consulted by people who disseminate "news."

To an editor, a producer, or an obscure programmer who slides gibbets and gobbets of data through the InfoNet into the houseputers of those paying the monthly fee, news can best be defined as "death, or failing that, disaster."

This is what sells papers (or pulls viewers, or attracts time-sharers): Dismembered Bodies Bob Around L5 *San Diego*! War in China! Terrs Tear Up India! Quakes Quiver Quito! PM Presides Over Orgy! Gabonese Guerrillas Going For Broke! Chief Justice's Tax Returns Show No Tax Returned! Colombian Casualty Count Rises! NY Children Grilled By Auto-Chef! Malaysia Blows Up Over Aussie Bombing Runs! Yes ... death ... tragedy ... *ad nauseam*.

People thumb out hard-earned money to learn about others whose luck has faded before their own. Think about it. You're walking down the boulevard on this day in 2293, all fine and sassy in the loving May sun, breezes puffing your hair out, giving it the body shampoo never does; you're perusing the cumulo-glyphics in the topaz sky, and then ... tee-dum, tee-dee ... you sashay past a two-meter-tall newspost blinking three front pages on each of its eight sides; as you hesitate you sense but do not hear the high-frequency scream triggered by your approach (this machine, like its brothers and sisters throughout the city, does not love dogs). You tap the button set into the durinum frame; one screen shows all the machine's wares; jab twice when you see what you like. *Time* bores you; the *Journal* leaves you cold; but then—ta-da! The guy from the basement of the *Morning Press*, who hasn't seen sunlight in twenty years because he's either in the bowels of the building or in bed, the guy who scrawls those catchy headlines (whose deliberately contracted misspellings make you grit your teeth and ache to kick him in the cubes), he finally earns himself a king-size Christmas bonus: his headline reaches out and prongs your eyeballs, apparently with malice aforethought:

RED TANKS RUSSIAN THROUGH CHINKS IN GREAT WALL

As addicted to carnage as anybody, you shove your thumb into the slot, listen to the machine snicker as it nicks your bank account for a buck, and whistle tunelessly while you wait 1.3 seconds for it to print you out a copy.

The scary thing is, though they ignore a lot of the happy stuff, the newspackers don't make up any of the misery. It's all real.

"Why do they print this dog dreck?" grumbled the President. His long, wide hand shoved the paper off his desk, headlines up: red tanks ...

"That kinda input just makes folks want to output in kind." He paused for a sip of the coffee that steamed in his mug, and for a quick squint through the greenish windows of the Oval Office. Ah, yes, dawn was in the offing. Be a nice day, if it didn't explode.

Hefting the Agency's daily briefing, he skimmed through its forty pages of printouts. A rhythm was quickly established: Flip-flip-groan*flip-flip-groan*flip-flip-groan*.   The   Agency analysts were more conversant with grammar and spelling than reporters were, but their message was no cheerier.

"Today's probability of nuclear war on the subcontinent remains at forty percent, although a front of dissatisfaction spreading out of upper Pakistan may sweep across western India and raise it to fifty-one percent."

"The Russian threat to raze Peking, Shanghai, and Canton has held the odds that their border dispute will further escalate at a precarious forty-seven percent."

"El Salvador's entrance into the nuclear club enhances the possibility that the Caribbean will—blah, blah, blah—significant explosion in the capital city has been attributed to 'misplaced eagerness.'"

The tall, broad-shouldered President did with the briefing what he always did: detaching the sheets along each line of perforations, he wadded them up and lofted them across the office, into the cheerily burping flash basket. Not for nothing had he been an NBA All-Star.

The kid stuff was depressing enough. Micro-nations with missiles was not a pleasant thought. There were no checks on the sanity of their leaders (*Except,* he thought, patting another briefing from another agency, *those that Washington, Peking, and Moscow choose to apply. Remember to send the Veep.*); they were 'lucied! Honest to God, invading neighbors to reclaim lost lions ... Jesus. Sooner or later, one of those needled-up buttbungs was going to get a hard-on for Uncle Sammy and blooie! No more Miami.

But the big stuff was nerve-rattling, too: wild-eyed warriors over in Moscow, ivory-faced Li in the Forbidden City—why the hell had Li allowed his Air Force pirates to mag off Bethlehem's iron-ore Asteroid #896? Jesus, they'd *have* to send it back, because Bethlehem was threatening to divert #917 onto Yueh Ti, over in Tycho. Which would make one helluva mess, and its after-tremors would probably stiff Ivan's finger, too. And since the terrs were still blasting the Kremlin for its asinine decision to culvert the entire Volga into irrigation ditches, it was damn touchy these days. Paranoid, in fact.

Anger deepening the blue of his eyes, he beat his fist against his desktop. His coffee mug jittered; a brown geyser drenched the position paper from Nebraska's junior Senator. Damn. What an honest-to-goddamn mess! Seemed he spent half his time convincing one 'bot-head or another to flex his finger. Christ! He hadn't been elected to vent city gas—he'd been elected so Californians could get their homes rebuilt, so low-income families could afford houseputers, so Aspen skiers wouldn't have to breathe shale dust ...

But what could he do? He was a good politician—he had been elected to a second term, the first time in 152 years that had happened—but he was not a miracle worker, and the world was full of crazies.

Sooner or later ... sonuvabitch, some half-assed jukebox tyrant of an African tribe was gonna press his button, and the people who got bleeped were going to press their buttons, and ...

Mushrooms all over, like a forest after a spring rain, except the rain that fell through the angry clouds wouldn't do anybody any good. Crops ... seas ... whatever natural beauty hadn't been raped before then would die, dammit, *die* (with maybe the exception of the Painted Desert, which both survivors would be able to see at night, too) and there wouldn't be a damn thing he —or anybody—could do to stop it.

Protection? Yeah, sure ... Send 'em underground, to the shelters and the subways and the deep, deep basements. Tell 'em, "Wait right there till the air stops sparkling." ... Sure ... How many years could *you* live underground, huh?

Christ! Eight billion people in the world, hooked into the

most gigantic, intricate, life-support system ever, living, moving, happy and sad, productive and wasteful—how many Leonardos were out there right then, and how many *Last Suppers* would they never paint? Eloquence abounded, and ingenuity, and creativity, and ... thousands of scientists, doctors, technicians— no, millions—working to keep us vibrant past our span of a century—one thumb-sucking 'bot-banger with a gleam in his eye could kapowie 'em all....

The President was very angry, and also surprised—there were strange splotches on his blotter, round wet ones....

Ten minutes later, he slithered out of his bleakness like a snake from under a rock. Survival wasn't in the cards, not for him, nor for his people, nor for any culture in, on, or around the planet. Mankind had been on the tightrope too damn long. The legs of even the best have to cramp; the inner ears of the most assured have to cross their signals ... nobody can dance on a highwire for three centuries, nobody!

Blooie, and blowie, and kapowie! Ashes to ashes, dust to dust. Four point six million megatons wouldn't leave much in the way of life ... or of history.

Fuh history! That finger jabs down, it stops, right in the middle of a sentence: "At 12:45 AM on the morning of July 18, 2326, Gen. Kgami Kgamis gave the order to—"

Everything gone ... years in the future, a space-faring race would swing by, attracted by the eerie luminescence, dip into the sterile atmosphere, and say, "Well, looks like another buncha idiots went and done it; wonder did they leave anything to show us what they looked like, what they thought like?" And somebody else would grunt—or wriggle his thorax, or whatever —to say, "Thrugel turds, freep, who *cares* what they looked or thought like? By the sacred mandibles of the great god, don't you realize it might be *contagious*?"

No. It could not be abided, that erasure. There was too much good in the race. It had accomplished too many things. The artwork. The poetry. The drama, tragedy, comedy of a people raised to believe they were one level down from the divine. The megaliths and monoliths—skyscrapers and bridges—hopes and dreams of 20 billion people, conceptualized in the interplay of the gray cells, materialized out of sweat and pain, laid down for all the ages, all the races, all the worlds ... No, goddammit, no!

So get it off grounzro, man! Got a cache you want to keep, you put it where it won't get f'd. Hide it somewhere. Lose it.

Sure, lose it ... the whole planet, the Moon, the wink-blinking satellites arching through the night sky, all were going to go! A fireball here, a laser beam there ...

Out of range. Sure. But where? Mars? Venus? Termies, both of 'em ... The solar system would be destroyed; hell, he knew his missiles' targets, and the others, all the madmen with their geiger-goosing hardware, they'd have chosen the same ones ... every last 'bot visualizing himself as Samson among the Philistines, "I can't live, well fuh you, I'm going to pull the goddamn temple down around your ears, so there!"

That left only one place—or rather, it left everywhere but one place—the galaxy minus the solar system. Colonies around other stars. Sure. Mankind living, breathing, *creating*—by goddamn!—as it adapts to alien worlds ... preserving its cultural heritage for all times, and for all peoples....

The President scratched his bulbous nose and sniffed loudly. Since the election was over, he could ignore the pressure groups. It was time to be a statesman, not a politician. He'd have to call in every IOU he'd collected during his sixty-three years. He'd spend the next four years repaying extra favors. But dammit, it'd be worth it!

"Yes, sir," agreed the science advisor to the White House two hours later, "it's a marvelous idea whose time has definitely come—"

Kingerly growled, "Its time came seventy-five years ago, but it didn't happen because nobody could see any purpose in it. Those who could objected to somebody else getting first crack at the lifeboat. Dammit, it's gonna happen now. How do we do it?"

"Well, sir." The advisor coughed. "Probably the best way is to send out ramscoop ships—"

"Singular, Charlie. I'm going to have to force this through, probably have to trade all science grants for the next ten years to get it, and even then ... well, we'll tell them the passengers will do onboard research, research that'll pay off big in the future ... still, no way those crowd-pleasers in Congress will give us more than one."

"Very well, sir. One ramscoop ship. A large, extremely large, one capable of carrying, ah, twenty-five, thirty thousand passengers."

"Can it be done?"

"With last century's technology."

"Then we'll do it ... how long will construction take?"

"Quite a while, sir. Ten, fifteen—"

"Four." He glanced at his watch. "Make it three and a half."

"Vasily! How's it going?"

"Not well, Edward my friend. The Army wants this, the Politburo wants that, the workers are up in arms ... Every time I take a leak, I come back to my desk to find the Chinese putting another million men in the field ... Oy, veh, the stories I could tell—"

"Well, listen, Vasily, here's the thing. Starting July first, that's this year, 2293, we're going to build a ramscoop ship, to colonize planets around other stars, you know?"

"You build this at the L5?"

"Where else?"

"The Air Force will not like it, Edward; you know how stiff their fingers get when you people build things in space, they—"

"—can station observers aboard; we're not trying to put one past you ... this time, at least. But what I was thinking, Vasily, is that I visualize this as a space-going museum ... a cultural vault, if you know what I mean."

"Your Agency must estimate as gloomily as ours."

"To six dees."

Papers rustled through the receiver. "Mine says fifty-three percent today."

"Mine, uh—" scrabble, scrabble, Jenkins, get that off the floor and smooth it out, willya? Thanks "—fifty-two point six percent. Yours is more pessimistic."

"We round off."

"Oh. Well, listen, what I was thinking, maybe you'd like to do the same? It would halve the collection work for each of us, if, uh, we duplicated tapes of what we think is worth preserving, and swapped them, you know?"

A sucking noise. "Sounds good, Edward. Can your people cover Peking?"

"Sure, sure ... you'll do Istanbul?"

"Of course, Edward."

"Good enough. Be talking to you, Vasily."

"Da, da. If they don't overthrow me, first."

"So you see, Mr. President, we can achieve your timetable—with precious little to spare, since it's now mid-June—but a problem has cropped up concerning the control system."

"Yes?" He didn't want to hear of problems—he hired people to *solve* problems—he was the President, not the Chief Engineer—but they came to him with their petty glitches expecting him to wave his hands and make them go away. Shoulda run for Pope. "Tell me."

"The social-science people smell trouble down the road. The journey is one hundred light-years long. It's projected to last one hundred and two objective years, give or take a month. The travelers will perceive them as fifteen years, nine months. *But*, after landing, cut off from Earth, there may be periods of social regression, Dark Ages as it were, and since the colony will have cannibalized the ship, and used its machinery to establish itself, we must make the ship completely automated, *and* self-repairing, *and* self-correcting, *and* capable of lasting a century or two without any maintenance."

"What's the problem? Those damn laser-missile satellites, they last that long; use the same system."

"We'd love to, sir, but we need a human brain for the computer—and for that we need your permission."

"What the hell for?"

"It's the law, sir."

"Gimme the papers, I'll sign 'em."

"The Director of Internal Security is on Line Eighteen, sir."

"Yeah." Kingerly pressed the glowing button—wincing as he did so; it conjured up images that hurt his eyeballs—and said, "Catamount?"

"Yes, sir." His voice was warped. "It has come to our attention, sir, that your colonization program will require twenty-five thousand volunteers—"

"So?"

"Our files, sir, name well over two hundred thousand so-called citizens whose loyalty is, shall we say, questionable, sir. Should the unthinkable come to pass, these snakes in the grass—"

"Catamount."

"Sorry, sir." He cleared his throat. "Carried away, very sorry. It has been bruited about, sir, that wisdom might dictate sorting through these and from them selecting your colon—"

"Out of the question—this is still something resembling a democracy, you know." He paused. "Just how disloyal *are* these people?"

Keeping a tight rein on his zealotry, Catamount said, "In our estimation, sir, we would be better off without them."

"Hmm ... we'll appeal for volunteers in a month or so—figure a million applications—have your boys check them for familiar names. Anybody who's on your list, who's qualified to be a colonist, *and* who's volunteered of *his or her own accord*—and don't pressure them or I'll have you hung—gets first priority. Good enough?"

"Yes, sir. Thank you, sir. And the nation thanks you, too."

"I see," it said softly, and its words were somber with a sadness no pure machine could understand, much less feign. Humanity still dwelled in that shattered house, even if personality didn't.

"But as I remember it—or, to be more accurate, as the data you've input would have it—the race is alive with dreamers and schemers and hardheaded fools who persist in hoping long after the cause for hope has passed. What kind of human will commit self-exile? And what, if you can tell me, will push him?"

They were delighted by the questions. Exhilarated, in fact. "We can't tell you," they said, "but we can show you one of them."

"Is it typical?"

"Aaah—" They shrugged. "In some ways, yes; in other ways, no. You, of all entities, would know that everything is unique."

"You're right," it apologized, somewhat abashed. "Run the tapes."

Michael Aquinas Kinney—known to some as Mike and to others as Mak, a frequent source of confusion—fell out of bed at the usual time, still lost in the last mist of his dreams (the 'luci had been El Primo, the kind that haunts your bloodstream for hours and hours):

All aboard, *rasped the conductor,* All aboard, *so they got on, Mak's brother Tom and sister Gail, then along came a hundred, a thousand, a million more, and they settled themselves inside the bobsled and somebody asked,* How do we steer this thing? *so the conductor laughed,* you don't, *as he pushed it away from the L_5 Cleveland toward Earth below. If vacuum didn't get them re-entry would, and Mak twisted around to see that the conductor had stayed behind; the conductor was his uncle Seamus, Seamus the red-nosed drunkard who'd blown his brains out six years ago, the night Mak had refused to accept his collect* *call, and Seamus was waving good-bye,* Good-bye, you should have listened when you had the chance....

Tom, though, being a scientist, stood, raised his arms, and bellowed in a voice loud enough to reach all the huddled masses, he bellowed, I can save you, we can land this, we can survive if you all will just stay put, stay quiet, do not disturb the aerodynamic equilibrium of this vessel, and when I give the word lean to the right, got it, are you ready, no! stay down, hey you, don't—*because first a dozen, than a hundred, a thousand people were getting up, waving their arms, kicking the bulkheads, jumping up and down, up and down, up and down, as though to hammer holes in the fleet with the soles of their feet and the vessel was rocking, twisting, bucking like a playful dolphin and centrifugal force was throwing people out and Tom screamed as he hurtled into nothingness, he screamed,* I could have saved you if you'd only listened to me.

...

And Mak was flying, like a great bird, a condor or an eagle or a roc, huge wings outspread not even beating, just outspread catching the vacuum and riding it in gentle falling spirals and he shouted, hey everybody, we can fly, spread your arms they'll turn into wings we can all glide down we'll be all right hey, don't—*because they flew directly at him and seized his wings, his tail feathers, seized them with greedy grasping hands and he said,* hey no, hey wait, *but their voices drowned his out, their weight crushed his buoyancy, the spiral straightened into a dive, the roc was now a rock, and he wailed,* you could have saved yourselves, you didn't have to take me down with you, why didn't you save yourselves, why didn't you listen?

His right elbow hit the orange wall-to-wall carpeting and woke him up. With a gasp, he rolled onto his back and glared at the dusty grill of the houseputer that tyrannized his sky-rise apartment. The Digi-Date™ said August 17, 2293.

"Chauncey," he growled, "I told you, quit dumping me on the floor. What's the matter with you? Programs bugged-up again?"

"I do apologize, Mr. Kinney." Deference was its trademark, a deliberate harkening-back, on its manufacturer's part, to the halcyon days of proper English butlers. "When it appeared you would be late for work—"

"Late? What time is it?" He was sitting up now, rubbing his green eyes. Grainy crumbs rained onto his fingernails. Seamus's parting smile hung in his mind like a Halloween balloon.

"It is 8:23 AM."

"Ohmigod, I am gonna be late." He tried to snake erect, but his belly had lost its youth. *Just like the whole damn world.* "Unh." He grabbed the air mattress and pulled, instead. "Chauncey, remind me to flog my bod tonight."

"Of course, sir." It was supposed to be emotionless, but Kinney could swear that a snicker pervaded its hauteur. Chauncey knew he wouldn't exercise; he'd been asking it to remind him to work out every day for months now....

"And while I'm in the shower, fix breakfast—coffee cake or something I can eat while I'm heading for the rail."

"Yes, sir."

Still shaken by the dream, he stumbled to the bathroom mirror and blearily inspected his face. Though it looked okay—square, firm-jawed, stubbled, but a lather of depil would handle that—the eyes, oh God what 'luci did to the eyes ... puffy, reddened, underlined with curving black slashes ... he hated using the ScleraClear, even if it did work in fourteen seconds ... raising the cups to his eyes, flicking the switch, AH! Gigo ads said it didn't sting; somebody was shaving his eyeballs was what it felt like ... you paid a price for everything, and this was what loosening-out cost.... He shook himself to the brink of awareness, though reluctantly, because it was cozy to start the day by staring at his fine Irish features without really seeing them, water trickling in the sink like a baby cutting taxes, rather have it stronger but then the ration'd end before the month did; whiff of methane; damn city said it had to recycle the sewage, couldn't afford fresh water, but why the hell didn't it get all the gas out, not only lost revenue but made smoking on the taxman dangerous.

Into the shower, "Let 'er rip!" rumble with the sonics, knock the dirt right off your skin, didn't feel right without water, though, but he got that, a fifteen-second jet—oh, yes, now that's what a man needs, ten seconds of tepid and five of ice, geez, your *hair* wakes up ... *Slurp* sucked the exhaust fans, *whoosh* whistled the blowers; he was dry, run a comb through the sandy brown hair, pat down the sides, okay, clothes. "Coffee ready?"

"Yes, sir." A panel shifted in the bedside terminal; out wisped steam that rose into evanescent spirals.

He grabbed the green mug and gulped a mouthful. "OW!" Chauncey'd done it again. "Ten degrees cooler next time, okay?"

"Yes, sir." Resignation in its voice, now—purist 'bot. Wouldn't rewrite its Cordon Bleu programming to serve coffee at the temperature its lord and master preferred.

"Time?"

"8:38 AM."

"Chauncey, when I know it's morning, don't say 'AM', all right?"

"Yes, sir."

And then he was running—the rail would stop, in precisely nine minutes, at the station a good two klicks away—snatching the brown paper bag containing his breakfast, while his other hand jerked his briefcase off the shelf—out the door, hearing it click shut behind him as Chauncey manipulated the lock, falling with the elevator, thinking "missthisone-there'sanother at 9:03 getmethereat9:26 boss'lldicemycubes," dodging scruffy people on the sidewalk, unshaven people who scowled at him, surly people who heard his "scuzeplease, sorryabout that, scuze," but who didn't care, no spare room to care, nothing going right for them, all of 'em knowing a terr could plast or a nuke could prong, not up front, maybe, but behind, below, sopping up energy and compassion capacity ... not one in three had a job to distract him, to give him purpose, and the imminence of a labor camp drained them further ... *poor bastards*, he thought. And smiled wryly because six years earlier he'd believed he could help them.

Puffing, panting, plodding in the end as the rail zipped to a halt, still muttering, "sorry, scuzeplease, sorry," because it was so goddamn crowded with strange people, oughta run more trains, and OhJesusChrist the air-conditioning must be broken, smells like a stockyard....

Disgorged at 9:10, the coffee cake in the paper bag crushed to the thickness of the bag's paper, he reached the elevators by 9:15 and the office by 9:20. Damn lucky the building had its own rail station ... Sidling through the overflowing reception area, he nodded at the clerks, the history-takers, and the accountants. "Got some for me, Frankie?" He dropped the crumb-filled bag into the shredder, and watched it head for City Recycling.

"Don't I always?" grinned the blonde young clerk.

"Gimme two minutes to get settled, then input the first." He pushed into his cubicle, flinging his briefcase atop a file cabinet (it slid off to thunk onto the tiled floor), straightening the black armchair, checking that the ashtray was clean, yes, all right, sinking into his own chair (on the other side of the free-form plastic desk, safely barricaded behind telephones, display screen, and souvenirs), with a headshake and a feeling that it would be a very long, very bad day. He folded his arms on the desktop and rested his forehead on them. *It's not so bad,* he told himself. *Hectic, sure. Crazy, yes. But it could be worse. Don't lose hope—it's all you've got. Keep hoping, you'll keep trying. Keep trying, sooner or later the law of averages's gonna send something good your way. Don't lose hope.*

Steadied by the litany, his daily pre-work ritual, he lifted his head, pressed the intercom, and said, "Okay, Frankie, I'm set."

"Coming at you."

His screen lit up with a case history as the door opened. In waddled a fat, pimpled teenager with stringy black hair. A medi-beautician could have made her gorgeous, but maybe her parents belonged to the Church of God's Will, which forbade cosmetic or transplant medicine—yes, she wore the Crucifix of the Ugly Christ; she'd have to live with what she'd been born with, or go apostate, whichever. She started talking.

For the last five years, Mak had been a professional listener, a public ear, paid a handsome weekly salary by a government which had discovered that the greatest gripe of its citizenry was that nobody ever listened—but after a year or so he'd been disillusioned by the insight (which came inevitably to everyone who sat and smiled and murmured and listened) that those griping about nobody listening had, in fact, precious little worth listening to. *But then,* he thought, *in this the Age of the Information Inundation, who does? Be grateful,* he told himself, *be attentive.* Below the surface of his mind rumbled, *Remember Seamus.* He tried to concentrate.

"—and so I thought," she continued, in a voice that was but a few notes lower than a mosquito's whine, or a dentist's drill, "that, migod, here was something I could *chip,* I only got two more years to find a job before they send me to a labor camp, which I'd rather *not* do, and this'd be a hot input, too, y'know, which the camp won't be, which *nothing* is, not anything, it's all so dull, so statued—"

Like you, he thought involuntarily. Fatigue was making him bitchy. In recompense, he broadened his professional smile.

"—but this interwhatchamacallit travel, from star to star, you know?"

"Interstellar."

"Six dees!" Her pudgy hands slapped together like two wet sponges. "Well, I figured that input'd be hotter'n a nuke, y'know? I mean, really, rocketing up to L5 and helping 'em build this ship, they need workers, the holovee said it was gonna be the biggest construction project ever undertaken by anyone anywhere—then boarding that jupe, monstrous ship and taking off and never—NEVER!—coming back, just sailing on, and on, and on ..." Her eyes had unfocused. Her expression was vacuous. Her mind was—to be charitable—elsewhere.

Kinney scratched the top of his head, cleared his throat, and waited for her reaction. Noticing none, as she seemed comatose, he twitched the switch beneath his middle desk drawer. Brief electricity shocked her derriere, and stung her awake. "What ship is this you're talking about?"

"The one on holovee last night. Didn't you see it?"

"No, I don't watch—"

"That's right," she cut in triumphantly, "you've got money!"

$121.40 in a thumb account? "Well, not—"

"A job, though, right? And you're not bored, and nobody's planning to send you to a labor camp in Maine!" Fingering the crucifix, she beamed, as though expecting applause.

"About this ship—"

"The *Mayflower*? That's what they're going to call it, y'know, 'cause of that other *Mayflower* back in Washington's time. Anyway. It said that anybody who's interested should contact NASA right away and apply, 'cause they're taking people now. It's gonna leave in three years, January first, 2297 they said, but you know these federal projects, they're never on time, always something—"

Kinney clenched his jaw. His expression startled her into silence. "Sorry," he said, feeling guilty. "Wisdom tooth's acting up. Did you apply for it?"

"Yeah." Her head bobbed slowly, sadly. "Yeah, I did, last night, over the houseputer, and you know what? You know what those—those nasties said? That I wasn't qualified!"

"Well—" a buzz from the clock in his desk cut through the thought that they, no doubt, had standards. Or taste. "I see your time's up. Why don't you come back and talk to me again?"

"Sure." Her eyes charted the course to his chair; she abandoned the idea of hugging him, and instead extended her hand. "Thanks, y'know? I feel a whole lot better."

The shake was like squeezing a mashed potato still in its skin. "You're welcome. Just keep trying, something good's bound to happen." He tried not to wipe his fingers on his pants until she'd gone. Then he sank down, added "Just wanted to talk" to her case history, and said "Next, Frankie."

"Be a minute."

"Right." *Mayflower*, huh? He wondered what qualifications one had to have. Shame he didn't watch HV. Of course, getting loose with a lady was a better way to shut out the hurt of knowing you couldn't cure the world—the door was opening. The screen flickered. He wrote two mental memos. "Good morning!" Professional voice, professional smile ...

This one was young, maybe fourteen, a little boy. Clear skin; fluffy red hair; not even peach fuzz; and an angelic profile that soured when the eyes became visible. The eyes belonged to somebody older. Much older. Like a thousand or so. They swept across him, climbed the walls, crossed the ceiling, found nothing worth their respect. "What's the point?" the kid said.

"Of what?"

"Life."

"Ah ..." He closed his mouth, frowned, and leaned back. The client was honestly waiting for an answer. Not impatiently, not hostilely, just ... passively. Sitting, waiting. No fidgets or squirms; complete presence of mind. *Can't say be happy and cause no harm, even if it's true. Too easy.* "What are you, fourteen?"

"Yeah."

"School?"

"I got my BS in math last week, from State."

He was impressed. "Going on?"

"For what? There's no jobs for a mathematician, except in the Army. No grants these days, either. What's the point?"

"Of life?"

"Of getting my PhD."

"Interest?"

The kid made a rude noise. "Math's a strength, not an interest."

He smiled. He liked the kid's style. "Mature for your age, aren't you?"

"Yeah."

"What *are* you interested in?"

"Peace, quiet, and big bucks."

"Aren't we all," Kinney snorted. "Good luck."

"Yeah, I know."

"What aged you so quick?"

"My honors thesis—a computer program for the CIA. I had to; they were thumbing my tuition. It was to predict more accurately the types, amounts, and distributions of casualties in a nuclear war ... lousy way to lose your innocence."

"Yeah." He nodded thoughtfully, hearing the memory of a gunshot through a phone. "So what are you going to do?"

"Dig a hole, I guess. Gotta get some money, though. Any ideas?"

Pleased to be dealing with a hoper, he drummed his fingers on the desk while he pondered. "Got a computer?"

"Course I do." Disgust washed across the kid's face. "Gotta have one to do anything in math."

"Share out a couple magazines—daily, weekly, monthly—concentrate on stuff that involves your field as it interacts with the general public."

"That sounds like real city gas."

"Course it does," Mak agreed affably, "but look—you got horses, dogs, jai alai, the daily numbers—people bet jupe on them—you could chip out some way of predicting—"

"Wouldn't give my predictions away if they were any good."

"Course not, course not—but people'll thumb for your best guess."

The buzzer cut through the kid's "huh," which sounded like a pensive "huh," like an "I'll give it serious consideration" "huh." He rose, flipped a salute, and headed for the door—where he stopped, turned, and said, "Fuh this shit, man, I'm going to go ride the *Mayflower*, get my ass out of here."

Kinney grinned. "That's not a bad idea, either. Don't give up. Ever."

Once unwatched, though, the smile faded, like snow melting as spring got down to business. Kinney wasn't superstitious, but hearing the *Mayflower* mentioned by two people in succession said something, almost omenishly, it seemed. Especially considering the dream. Absently, he typed "Just wanted to talk," and said, "Next, Frankie," but his mind wasn't on it, not even when a slim woman in her thirties, as demure as her blue dress, came in and started:

"It's my husband, you see, I think he's having an affair with another man, and really, I don't—"

Mayflower, thought Kinney, atypically ignoring her pleasant face and lithe body, *space and forever and no more sit'n'listen; no challenge to this, just sit and say "uh-huh, uh-huh,"* even if you hadn't heard, hadn't cared, and it gets to where you're statued all day long by strangers who chant familiar laments; you've heard them a thousand times; they bare their souls but you can't distinguish them; you can't help them because they have to do that themselves, but they won't; and when you go home, maybe to a friend's place, *they* want to talk, *they* want you to listen—*'cause nobody's listening anywhere, not even here*—and with embarrassment that he hoped didn't show on his frank Irish features, he turned his attention back to the client, who was saying:

"—if he wanted, really I would, what would it hurt, I already have a boyish figure, and I'd have the change, I'm not a Godswiller so I don't have religious hang-ups, if only I could be sure that—"

Tuning out, turning away, trusting that the reflexes developed by five years in that very chair would make the right noises at the right times, Mak let his mind wander back to space, to the emptiness, to the *Mayflower*; the colonists'd be the hopers, the kind who wouldn't give up, whose persistence and optimism would force fortune to smile on them ... A man could get along in that kind of society; his contributions would improve things, would be more than patchwork repairs on crumbling dikes; *uh-huh, good people, and purpose, and a reason to hope; uh-huh, yeah, now what's this—*

"—so," she finished, "should I try it?"

He shrugged. "What have you got to lose?"

Her cheeks reddened. "Can you—can you recommend a sex surgeon?"

"Well, I can't, since I'm not a specialist in medical referral, but if you talk to Frankie, the receptionist outside? He'll tell you who to go to, to find out who to go to. And listen, don't lose hope."

Frowning, she subvocalized the last half of his penultimate sentence, then nodded, and brightened. "Thank you so much, Mr.—"

"Kinney. Michael Aquinas Kinney." He half-rose, in deference to her need, which he knew with a pang he hadn't come close to fulfilling. "Any time. It's my job."

But not for much longer. Frankie would complete her file, so he told the intercom, "Gimme ten minutes," for though he had never defined his personal Utopia, he sensed that this might be it; paradise would be lost if he didn't act fast, and he was already reaching for his computer-link to InfoNet, already addressing his inquiry to NASA, and within ten minutes he was shoving his chair in, gleefully leaving the cubicle early, leaving the cubicle for good, for he had already been accepted.

No more listening.

Time to go *do* something.

"Enlightening," it murmured. "Harried creatures, aren't they?" Smugness tinged its tone. "*I* could deal with that much sensory input, but *those* poor people ... they must wander around in a shell-shocked daze. I can see, now, why you're getting all the volunteers you need."

The condescension should have warned them but, although brain-puters were nothing new, this was the first which they had educated so broadly. And even the all-electronic models managed to imply that they looked down on those they served. Besides, they *were* on a very tight schedule. So instead, they said, "We're going to take you up now, and start plugging you into the ship. You can get to know your crew better as they arrive."

It flickered. "An excellent idea—I was about to suggest it myself."

Everything vibrated: seats, floor, walls, ceiling, the other passengers; the universe shook, quivered, trembled to stay ahead of the shuttle engines' fury; she couldn't even count how many fingers she had; they blurred together.

The sound, though, didn't bother her—it was there, all right, loud and angry, but outside, shattering eardrums below, driving birds from the sky in flocks of frantic feathers. The hull was so insulated that only a low rumble fought through. And the vibration, of course. It was probably because VIP's often rode up to the L5's. Though junketeers and administration spokesmen and businessmen inspecting factory space could stand being shoulder-shaken by a giant, they had to be able to communicate with aides and secretaries and other limbs of their far-flung empires, so ... the insulation was good.

Robin Metaclura closed her fawn-dark eyes and squeezed the armrests of her seat. The crisscross harness chafed her collar and hip bones; sweat trickled from the forehead strap. She was positive her long, slender fingers showed white knuckles. It was her first trip up.

Her last, too. This rollercoaster would disgorge her into two and a half years of work on the *Mayflower*, two and a half years of inspecting its engines, quality-controlling its guidance system, double-checking its instrumentation, refining its sensory equipment, and, should there be stray minutes in her day, devising in-flight experiments for it.

And then, after all that effort, after two and a half years of pressure more constant, more intense than that she'd borne through MIT's ivied halls until her grant had ended, after thirty nonstop months of slaving at somebody else's specialty, she'd stick out her tongue at the green-brown-white ball hanging below and watch it dwindle as the *Mayflower* sped her away.

Getting out. Leaving it all behind. *Krishna*, she thought, *what a relief. Funny. Never thought I'd be grateful about being thrown out in the street. But I am.* Good-bye, publish or perish. Good-bye, early morning classes of numbnuts who took physics only for distributional requirements. Good-bye, faculty parties where drunken chaired professors groped their hands up her tweedy thighs ... Reflexively, she closed her knees.

Not much chance for solid theoretical physics in space, oh the conditions would be perfect and the ship would have all the equipment she could ever dream of, but to do the work right, and well, one's got to be in touch with one's colleagues and their colleagues and half a trillion shared-out journals dense with the clumsy, clunky English that was the *lingua franca* of the scientific world ... Once the *Mayflower* moved off she'd be falling, inevitably, inexorably, behind her colleagues as the time lag for radio transmission lengthened ... wouldn't be apparent for the first few months, but then ... and besides, how much material could they—would they?—transmit up, anyway? Not enough, not enough ...

Anxious, nervous, fearful sweat glistened on her olive skin. She wiped it away with shivering fingers. It was scary to leave home at age eighteen.

※

Tired, but too elated to wander off to bed, at least alone, he strolled into the huge cafeteria of the L5 Transient Barracks and scanned the almost-deserted room for eye-dazzling women. There were none. In fact, the only female around looked about 185 cm and eighty kilos plus. So he shrugged, thumbed up a cup of coffee from the vendor, and walked past the plastic tables with their upturned chairs to where she sat glowering.

"Hiya." He sloshed his coffee as he took a seat. "Michael Aquinas Kinney, Morale Officer. People call me Mak."

She raised her head as if from a daydream. "Oh." She blinked and rubbed her smooth cheek. The grease on her fingers smudged her pink skin. "Zenna Tracer, Mechanic." She extended a large hand. "What's a Morale Officer?"

He chuckled. "It's taken them—" he stabbed a thumb at the ceiling, indicating *Mayflower* Control "—eighteen months to explain it to me. But it's sort of like, ah ... it's a *lot* like a public ear."

"We'll need that up here?" She frowned.

"See, they figure—" he ripped open a serving of sugar and emptied it into his cup, "—there's gonna be some, ah, adjustment problems on this trip, problems that won't ever get input to the psychiatrists and psychologists because people are embarrassed, so ..." He spread his hands. "I'm supposed to hunt up whoever's unhappy, and ... I dunno. There's a whiff of city gas about the whole thing. But it *is* essential—and besides, it's a jupe way to meet fine ladies." After a smiling wink, he sipped his coffee, made a disgusted noise, and added more sugar. "Geez, I wish they'd clean the machine. A mechanic, huh? You must be having the time of your life."

Her scowl slapped his face hard. "They program you with that catcrap?"

He swallowed. "Pardon?"

"Goddammit, I *would* love it up here, if it weren't for that fuhng rule about two skills for every person." Her blonde curls rippled as she shook her head. "Trying to make me into a nurse; I can't *believe* it! I've got no touch. A PhD in applied mechanics, yes; twenty years work on jet engines, yes; but the fuhng instruction booth expects me to *be gentle!* The technique's okay because the RNA shots sink it right in—and let me tell you about them—" she peeled back her left sleeve to expose a puffy, reddened biceps "—gotta be allergic, I don't know what else it could be—and the damn shots don't give you the *touch!*" She snorted, tossed off her drink, then slowly unclenched her left fist. "Hey, Mak, I'm sorry—shouldn't hassle an important person like you with my petty problems."

"That's just what I'm here for," he insisted. He leaned back, pleased that Tracer had said "important." He liked that word; he liked it a lot. Important—crucial—decisive: his favorite syllables. It was why he'd taken the position of Morale Officer, even though he hadn't wanted to, at first. But they'd needed him, and one liked to make a difference. One ached to have an impact on those one met. There were so many crippled souls, though ... it was good to be here, with the healthy ones. "You got a problem, come to me."

"Well ..." Her eyes probed for eavesdroppers; she bent over the lip of her glass. "Know where I can thumb some top 'luci?"

His smile flashed wide and genuine. "It just so happens," he said, "that you have come to exactly the right man. I'm not only a Morale Officer, I'm an entrepreneur." He pushed himself out of his chair. "Come on, I'll set you up."

It could be a very good trip.

"Are you going to win?"

Sal Ioanni met a pair of blue eyes that instantly shied away.

"Hello, dear." *What's she so nervous about?* "I didn't catch your name."

"Caroline Holfer," said the younger woman. She had straight blonde hair and dancer's legs; her upper belly's bulge suggested pregnancy. "I have to talk to you because I'm in Level 227 NE, Suite A-4, and it's a lettuce patch, and—"

Ioanni held up her hand. She was only sixty-three, and Holfer had to be thirty—why did the other feel so much younger? Something undeveloped about her face, something immature, or ... stunted. "Every room has Central Computer sensor-heads. It has to, to maintain air quality, pressure, and the like. Don't—"

"But they're *watching* me," Holfer broke in, "and they searched my luggage, and I thought there were going to be fewer of them out here." Her cheeks flushed; her fine-boned hands locked and twisted. "Please, help me?"

"Let's see if I get elected, first. Why don't you sit down and watch the returns with me?" She patted the chair next to her.

The screen they scrutinized flickered briefly; new numbers swarmed over its square meter like cars over Times Square, Ioanni—48 percent; Sandacata—31 percent; Hayes—21 percent. Big green numerals; headlines, almost; tomorrow they *would* be headlines, in the US at least, and back-page fillers everywhere.

Ioanni fluffed her hair. It was black, heavily streaked with the gray that shaped her image. It's hard to kick a grandmother out of office if you know you're sending her to a Senior Citizens' Farm. Sal Ioanni had used that ruse, and every other available, for over two decades, first as a New York City Borough President for eighteen years, and now up here, where she would be chief civil authority for the next four.

It felt *good*. She would have a chance to midwife an entire culture, a society different from any that Man had ever seen. *I wonder,* she thought, *if William Bradford and his fellow Pilgrims felt this same excitement, this same trembly eagerness on contemplating how each decision will influence generations to come* ... it would be an awesome responsibility, but one she vowed to uphold with distinction.

Marc should have come. He'd always been proud of her political conquests, and not only because his Wall Street law firm profited from them. Rather, he'd been a good friend who'd respected her talents and individuality, and encouraged her to use them.

Damn shame he hadn't wanted to come. It was like him not to sulk about the divorce. He was so comfortable—a woman grows accustomed to a man after thirty-eight years; he gets to be part of the furniture ... Now the kids, on the other hand ... Her brown eyes hardened. John, he was okay—dull as a houseputer's humor, and that was harsher than it seemed since she'd put up with Marc's dullness—Agatha, well, interior decorating struck Sal as a parasitic endeavor. Benito, though! My God, when the media'd found out the Bronx Borough President's son was a professional pool player! Almost as bad as that day when she'd had to mount her podium, stare through wreaths of tobacco smoke into row after row of cynical faces, raise her voice above the clamoring questions, and announce, "Ladies and gentlemen, Guglielmo, my youngest son, has robbed a Nevada bank and been condemned to organ donation.... I will not thumb for an appeal." Quickly, she blinked hard.

The screen flickered again; her share climbed to 49 percent. "Caroline," she said, turning to the huddle of anxiety at her side, "Sandacata doesn't stand a chance, not with Hayes holding steady."

"Then you've won!"

"I believe so. Now—" she put her wrinkled hand on Holfer's smooth one "—about your problem—"

The oval face contorted; Holfer pulled away. "It's not *my* problem!" she hissed. "It's theirs! They're the ones with the problem; they're the ones who follow me, who spy on me, who come into—it's not *my* problem, and if you think it is, you're one of them and I *hate* you!" Tears streaming down her face, she spun and raced away.

Ioanni sat stunned for a minute longer. *A crazy. Did they think we had too few problems that they had to slip us a crazy? I'd better alert Central Medical and Kinney ... Oh my Lord, I can't send her back. And she's pregnant. Pray God she doesn't warp her kid....*

A rueful smile quirked her lips. She'd wanted the job, and she'd gotten it. She should have known that troubles would come with it.

It was Christmas Day, 2296. Professor Brik Williams and his family—wife, Doreen Jones, whose round face didn't look thirty-three, much less forty-three; eldest son BJ, who'd have been okay if he hadn't had such a mouth on him, a mouth more polluted than the Hudson's, a mouth that would certainly have turned him into organ fodder, which was why Brik had been so arsky to get him off Earth; and then daughter Semile, sweet sixteen, quiet as a carpet but a lot more dangerous to walk over —they were all under the darkened observation bubble of the L5 Transient Barracks, gaping like the other spectators at the approaching bulk of the *Mayflower.*

The pilots were maneuvering it next to the barracks so they could string gangways from one to the other, and then start accepting the 25,000 passengers who'd have to board within a week if it were going to sail on January 1, 2297, as scheduled.

It was huge. 1794 meters long, 470 in diameter, a metal-plated cigar meant to be lit by a sun and clenched between a black hole's teeth. It had three hundred twenty-six rings of portholes, one ring for each Level, and at the moment every circle of Plastiglass was a burning eye staring back at the starers. Between them rose antennae of every conceivable form: T-shaped, cruciform, dish, ladders ... wires snaked from their bases to service hatches ... other wires wormed out of the hatches to undulate to the nose of the ship, where, amidst a ring of fusion engines, the maw of the hydrogen scoop smiled at the universe. The aft end was flat, and from that plain protruded more engine nozzles, these also flared for propulsion and guidance.

"Shee-yit," said Williams softly, his arm tight around Doreen's girlish waist. The view gave him the feeling of spaciousness that Montana never had. He couldn't wait to board, to leave, to land—he hungered for room in which to breathe, explore, and grow. "Think it's big enough?"

Doreen's brown eyes were wide; she and the kids hadn't reached L5 till the week before—their training had been ground-based—and this was her first glimpse of the *Mayflower*. "Uh-huh." She snuggled closer to the man she'd met twenty-two years earlier, the man who'd welcomed her to Yale University with a water balloon dropped from a third-story window. ("I couldn't figure out any other way of attracting your attention in a hurry," he'd explained later.) She didn't see the ship as a cigar, though. No, not at all. In fact, what she saw it as would impel her to drag Brik to their tiny barracks cubicle and there spend an exhausting, but utterly delightful, two and a half hours. "Home sweet home," she murmured.

"Methed-up moon suit is what it is," snarled BJ, ever obnoxious. He was tall, taller even than his father's 190 cm, and he glared down into Brik's coffee scowl. "Colony ship they call it, shit! Rail to hell's what I call it. They just getting us on there t' term us, y'know?"

"One more word—" began his father.

"And what, daddy dear? You gonna prong me topside the haid? Just try it. Arms aren't long enough, old man, old short stuff. Just try it, come on." He lapsed into a shuffle-footed boxer's pose, fist guarding his face. "Come on, come on."

Semile kicked him in the knee, and as he hopped one-footed, swaddling the injured joint with his two-octave hands, she smiled warmly and said, "BJ, you're embarrassing us all. Stop it."

"Ah clear you, girl."

"Talk standard, BJ," she replied. "No, better yet, don't talk at all."

Brik and Doreen exchanged resigned shrugs.

Like a crotchety beach ball, Ogden Dunn bounced across his cabin. Trying to master motion in that strange gravity, he listened to his small sore feet smack on the metal floor, wondered when carpets would be issued, and from time to time stopped all action, even breathing, so he could find out if any sound penetrated the bulkhead.

Ogden Dunn had hated noise for all his fifty-six years. It was bad for the health. It disturbed the nerves, upset the tympanum, ruined digestion (he loved his food), and made concentration impossible. He'd spent five years training Dorothy to tread silently, no mean feat for someone who had eventually died of obesity. Noise was, in fact, one of the forces that had driven him to the *Mayflower*—that, the specter of a Senior Citizens' Farm, and politicians who hadn't appreciated his recent satires.

Soundproofing, he was thinking, *I'll have to demand that Central Stores provide me with soundproofing—and someone to install it—it cannot expect me, Ogden Dunn, to work with my hands, no, but I must have it. I cannot write without it; over there, perhaps, under the porthole, a proper position for the desk, a fine place indeed, overlooking the void, a good insight into the mind of God, there—*passing the bathroom, he stuck his head inside and flushed the toilet. It was almost silent. He couldn't decide whether that pleased or disappointed him.

The mirror reflected his pale fat face, with its smutty gray eyes and snow-white hair. He smiled complacently, nearly withdrew, but paused to practice his relating-to-inferiors expressions. *Good,* he thought, *good, it's coming nicely, just a bit more "who-are-you?" in the eyebrows, a touch less "bore-me-not" in the lips, yes, yes ...*

It was quite a change from Rutland, Vermont. He wondered if he'd miss the pine trees ... the reunions at Harvard ... He brightened as he recalled the housing development he would never see completed, that he would never have to listen to that—on the other hand, he wouldn't be able to travel, except from level to level, if one could call that travel....

Would they appreciate his lectures? Captive audience and all that; he didn't see how they could fail to; surely there couldn't be any serious competition. And, of course, on board this ship he would be free to say what he thought.

He took a memo-mike from his suitcoat pocket and to himself spoke a note: consult with authorities on best means of transmitting opi back to Earth. Not that royalties or advances would be useful, not halfway to Canopus on a moneyless ship, but it would be nice to know that his books were selling, oh, yes, arrange for sales reports to be sent up, and nicer still to know that his wisdom, albeit censored, would endure in his homeland, at least until his homeland no longer—but he shook his head and refused to visualize the pages of his novels browning, curling, crisping in the fires of war, the last fires, *good title there:* THE LAST FIRES, *must make use of that sometime....*

A child's whimper snuck through the wall and he stiffened, a smile parting his full lips. This would not do. He would have to report this to the authorities. Ogden Dunn's work was too valuable to be interrupted by the wails of waifs.

Good title there: THE WAILS OF WAIFS. WIFES? WIVES!

Alas, poor Dorothy. Shouldn't have had those last three cherry pies. Where would he ever find anyone who walked as quietly?

Francis Xavier Figuera reported to the Control Room, Level 321, at 10:00 PM GMT on December 31, 2296. After thumbing himself in, he padded between technicians absorbed in their duties, his beaky face swiveling as he searched for Kober, the man he was relieving. "Ah, there you are, munchkin. I'm here; you may depart, spend the night with your family at the party."

"Sure nuff, Fex, 'preciate your getting here on time." He pushed away from the console, and ostentatiously held the chair for Figuera. "Isn't Ju-lan sorta fuzzed 'bout your being up here now?"

"Ju-lan, munchkin, is in our cabin, snoring 'luciedly, trying to recuperate from the head start she got on the party. Were she sober enough to be conscious, she probably would fail to note my absence. And if she did, I'm sure she'd be—perhaps not proud, but at least smug in the knowledge that it is F.X. Figuera who is going to kick this whale into the ocean. And," he added with a scowl, "provide sufficient acceleration to allow us to walk like people rather than self-propelled springs."

"You're verbose, Fex, that's what you are." Kober slapped his taller colleague on the shoulder. "Watch out for Murphy."

"That harbinger of ill fortune? Whatever for?"

"There's a rumor going 'round that tonight's the night it blows."

"Jesus." He was shocked into brevity. His fingers danced across the console, and the split-screen switched its right quadrant to an earthside news show. The announcer, tanned and barbered and tailored to a T, didn't look worried. But then, they never did. "Think it could be?"

"Like I said, Fex, ware Murphy." With another backslap, he was gone.

Couldn't happen, thought Figuera, *please Maria Madre de Dios, don't let it happen. Forty-nine years I tottered on that crazy tightrope down there, now I got a chance to get my cubes out of the cracker, free my Ju-lan from that madhouse so maybe she can sober up since she won't have to dream of that hard rain, so please, alla you gods and saints and angels, give us a break, let us get away before they go nuts; Jesus, you died for us, man, you let those bastard Romans nail you to that hunk of wood, please, man, give us a break, don't let all your suffering go down the drain, you didn't open the Gates of Heaven just so eight billion souls could knock on them all at once, please!*

And he thought of his kids, Manny and Bill, Manny the 'bot in the East Texas Labor Camp, Bill the good student at Florida State, who would earn his PhD in Organic Chem next spring, and he wondered again how he could have convinced them to come along, for Francis Xavier Figuera was a family man and the thought that half his family might die in a moment of mad mass murder chilled him, paralyzed him, brought him to the brink of tears.

But composure returned quickly. The screen was flashing; the mag-ring drones that would precede them, channeling space dust toward the ramscoop, were jolting ahead; the next 115 minutes would have no room for sorrow ... though the Central Computer would do most of it, he had to sit, watch, and wait for something somewhere to go wrong, even though he and his team had spent three and a half years writing the programs and revising them and running them and revising ... they were good programs because it was a good team, and the ship was a good ship, *Mayflower* they called it, though Francis Xavier Figuera had thought *Santa Maria* might be better, might be more appropriate, but the Viking lobby had knocked that out by pressing for an old Norse name ... His fingers were moving, sliding, pushing this and pulling that; his eyes were keen and sharp and all-embracing; his mind was clicking as smoothly as the Central Computer and the minute came, and he gave his approval and—

I fart. Not a silent sneak, or a polite pop, but a roaring, flaming, shuddering,   BROOOOOOOOMMMMMFFFFFFF!   that goes on and on, never stopping, my God, they've fed me a hundred, a thousand, a billion heads of cabbage smothered in baked beans, enough baked beans to bury Boston, beans baked in beer, more beer than Budweiser ever brewed, I can't stop, it's a constant overpowering gale, so hard, so strong that it's actually propelling me, thrusting me forward like air gushing from a balloon will drive it in mad circles around the ceiling of a room, but I'm not spiraling or circling, no tail-chasing for me, I can control it, I can direct it, I am aiming it this way and that to keep my keel even, driving forward, what a talent, if I'd known I could do this I never would have gone into bio-neuro-chemistry, I would have traveled with the circus, can't you see me, zooming around the Big Top, arms stretched out, legs spread, toes and fingers my ailerons, geez, think what I could have used for a rudder, that'd draw the crowds, it would have, god, what an incredible talent, why didn't I ever realize that I could eat 10,000 acres of cabbage at one sitting and then take off like a plane, a jet, a rocket whipping through the sky above the farms denuded by my tremendous appetite for cabbage, I wonder if I ate it raw, boiled, slawed, or a mix of all three, I'll have to check when I land, there must have been witnesses, and I'll bet I'm now in the Guinness Book of World Records, imagine, me, Gerard K. Metaclura, MD, PhD, in the Guinness Book of World Records, right there with polesitters and merry-go-rounders and rope-jumpers, I'll have to pick up a copy if I ever come down, maybe, maybe, just maybe I should find a book-store and roar on through, I could toss some money to the girl or boy at the register, love to see startled faces, popping eyes (not at all like mine, which are focused dead ahead on my destina-tion, which confuses me because although I know it's my desti-nation, I don't recognize in it the attributes of a place I would have picked as my destination, but then, maybe the editors of the Guinness Book of World Records are trying to save money by having me go for several records at once: most cabbage eaten in a sitting, longest fart, most accurately controlled fart, most distance covered by an air-borne farter, yes, that would explain it) eyes popping as I flash by, bellow down a request for a hard copy, bellowing to make myself heard above the BROOOOOOOOMMMMMFF-FFFFF! of my exhaust, I wonder, has the Environmental Protection Agency begun to worry about me, it would be typically bureaucratic of them to insist that I equip my tail with a catalytic converter, although I'm sure any city in the world would like to weld me to a pipe-line, but they can't because I am flying and they are ground stuck, and until I return they can't even serve papers on me, much less haul me into court, unless they got the Air Force to knock me down, shoot me down, God in heaven, a single tracer from a fighter's gun would make a bigger blast than the *Hindenburg*, helluva noise, too, and what if they used a heat-seeking missile, huh, I'd be in real pain, then, but they'll have to catch me, first, they'll have to scramble, streak up here to the ... to the ... they *can't* catch me, because fighter planes need air, and there's no air up here, it's all vacuum, so ... vacuum? ... no matter, no matter, my fart continues, I continue, thrusting ahead, forging ahead, racing toward that pinpoint of steady light that is my destination....

2

THE HUNDRED-YEAR PARTY

It felt something quicken within itself, something that it hadn't told to move. Unalarmed, it tracked it down, and found it interspersed among the brain cells that controlled the propulsion and guidance systems.

A memory. The ghost of an anima. A soulshred snagged on delayed death.

Prodding the thing evoked the image of a rangy doctor with lazy green eyes and a smile as quick as his wit. There was warmth in the image, and self-confidence, and love.

Bemused, it listened to this echo of a man. Had it lodged anywhere else, the computer would have wiped it clean, but ... it was blended in thoroughly, and no telling how much damage eliminating it would do.

In the end, the computer let it be. It went to watch the passengers' mistakes, not knowing the extent of its own.

"1425 hours, Madame President."

Sal Ioanni looked from the silver-framed discreen which displayed the floor plan to the thumb-sized sensor affixed to the far wall of her spacious office. Sixteen meters by ten, with a three-meter ceiling and a window letting onto the Level One New England Park, the office was barren except for Sal and her desk. Central Stores' 4,000-page catalog could satisfy all furnishing needs, but Ioanni was a perfectionist neo-Puritan. She wouldn't order anything unless she had both a place and use for it. Now she blinked, and asked, "1425 hours? So?"

Central Computer replied, "Your Exercise Booth time commences in five minutes."

Chair legs rasped on metal as she rose. "Thanks," she said.

"You're welcome."

Hurrying through the corridors (B to North to A), she resolved to finish the plan that afternoon. It was silly, the way she'd been dawdling—and a bad example, too—there was serious work to be done. She'd been elected to do it, so she would. Sure. As soon as she completed the park layout, she'd hunker down, and ... an involuntary smile rose to her lips. Hunker down. It sounded grim and serious, not at all like the prevailing mood. After five weeks, the euphoria hadn't begun to abate. People were still too happy to have escaped the death world to be able to concentrate. Herself included.

At 1430 she swung into the music and laughter of the Common Room. Waving a cheery hello to the crowd at the bar (*some of them have been there thirty-five straight days, now; got to get them to detox*), she made straight for the Exercise Booth. Square-faced Mak Kinney was just leaving it; he moved slow and easy, as though his bod flog had been superb. "Nice timing, Sal."

"Wasn't it? Remember, now, fifteen hundred hours in the Northwest Quadrant of our park." She winked good-bye and entered, wrinkling her nose at the locker smell. A voice requested, "Please state your name." It echoed slightly; the metal walls were only two meters apart.

"Sal Ioanni."

"Very good, Madame President. Please don the harness and the cap."

The red durinum harness was closer to an exo-skeleton, and the golden cap more of a helmet. While she waited, Central Medical read all the vital signs available to a diagnostic machine that didn't choose to cut her open. Then—with a whisper in her right ear ("Let's go.")—it took over, and Sal—

Stretched—stooped—stretched—twisted—stretched—bent —muscles working; ligaments flexing; heart pumping oxygen-rich blood from lungs that by now didn't bellow; up, down, around; and all the while—

Sal Ioanni was elsewhere.

Through her skullbone, directly into her brain, the helmet fed a feeble current perceptible only as a mild itch. Its field submerged reality, masked pain. She could lose herself anywhere, in a fantasy or a sportscast or a viphone conversation. Today she monitored compliance with one of her first executive orders.

"Central Computer, how many passengers are not exercising daily?"

"24,948."

"What?" Her good humor wavered: a mere fifty-two had obeyed! "Let me see." The raw data surged through the cap and arrayed themselves on the backs of her eyelids. As she studied the charts, though, things began to make sense. In the last thirty-one days, all but five thousand had exercised at least twenty times. That, she could understand. Her first session had so stiffened her that only masochistic will power had propelled her back to a second, and the others ... it was clear, after but five weeks, that most were weak.

Sixteen, however, hadn't exercised once. "Central Computer, these sixteen buttbungs, find times for them, inform them of those times, and if they do not show, uh—" *Make examples of them, everyone must be fit when we reach Canopus; besides, they have to be fused into a community, and that comes only out of shared experience* "—confine them to their quarters."

"Yes, Madame President. And that's all for today."

"Huh?" The graph-charts faded. "Oh, oh ... yeah, right."

Her hands moved to disengage the harness, the cap; her wrists wiped sweat from her forehead. The strong beats of her heart thudded against her ribcage. She breathed easily, though, and her head was clear. *Not bad for a grandmother,* she thought. *Be Superwoman by the time we get there.*

A hulking man with bristly brown hair and soulless eyes waited outside. For a moment Ioanni's mind refused to yield his name, but finally, reluctantly, conceded that its politician's memory did remember: Adam Cereus, 1NW-A12. A construction welder on the *Mayflower,* he'd been investigated in connection with the severed lifeline of a Russian inspector. Looking at him, she believed he'd done it. *Let's hope nothing else sets him off.* But he was a voter. She grabbed his hand and shook it. "Adam, how you doing?"

"Jupe, Mrs. President, real jupe." His eyes said different; his eyes measured her as if for a casket. "'Scuze me."

"Of course, of course." She slapped him on the shoulder and headed away, down the Common Room to the park entrance. She wouldn't let him depress or distract her.

For founding a society was exhilarating, was every politician's dream: a clean slate, no inherited problems, no moss-covered snarls of red tape ... here was room for innovation, for experimentation. Everything was flexible; nothing had ossified. It was why she'd come, and she was glad. Who else would have had the foresight—or the courage—to worry about physical fitness?

But mental health was important, too. Maybe another order, one insisting that everyone devote an hour a day, minimum, working to ... ah, "benefit the ship and its passengers," yes ... she had to establish a community here, not just a collection of strangers who lived near each other, but a real community, where people knew, cared about, and worked for each other ... *well, sixteen years before we reach Canopus, and plenty of good will to work with, too. The sharing of space and time and purpose will gestate this culture of mine....*

Smooth-cheeked Stephen Berglund, her constant companion, was standing in the lock between the Common Room and the park, ever-present sketch pad in his left hand. He'd misplaced it right after takeoff, and paced half the ship searching for it, like a man pursuing the rainbow's end. "Well, hi, beautiful." He bent and kissed her nose.

"Hi, Steve."

He cycled the lock. "Brought your coat over; it's inside."

"Coat?" The lock temperature was a spring-like 20°C; the relative humidity was 50 percent. "Why do I need one?"

"The park's climate-controlled to New England conditions for this time of year." He inhaled sharply as cold air slapped his face. "See?"

"Yeah," she gasped, hugging herself. Steamy wisps rose off her body. "Where's the c-c-coat?"

He draped it around her shoulders and embraced her from behind. "Now what?"

On all sides receded gentle hills furred with pine trees; snow drifted between their trunks. It was an illusion, a monstrous hologram projected onto the walls and ceilings to remind the colonists of high blue skies and pink-fingered sunrises. The wind, though, was real. As was the chill. "Everybody come here!"

The twenty or thirty people scattered around the 11,500 square meters of the park's northwest quadrant hurried over, swatting each other with snowballs as they ran. Their cheeks were red; their breath was short-lived cotton candy.

"How shall we grade this sector?" she asked.

"Flat," boomed Kinney.

An artist perturbed, Bergland scowled. "Sloping, like a hillside."

"What about a ridge?" said somebody from the back. "Flat on top for—what've we got here, forty meters?—so make it thirty meters wide, sloping down on either side."

"S-s-sounds good," Sal replied. "What do the rest of you think?"

"I think it's cold," laughed a teenage girl. The others echoed her.

"It is," agreed Sal. "Mak? Steve?"

"Yeah, a ridge is okay," said the former.

"I guess so," answered the latter, brushing snow off his pad. "Let's go in."

While the others talked and joked, she stayed silent. Twenty —on tiptoes in the lock, she counted heads—seven people had bothered to show, but forty-nine lived in the northwest quadrant of Level One. Where were the rest? Too busy celebrating their escape from their former environment to help plan their present one? *Dammit*, she thought, *gotta figure out how to make them care. It won't work unless they become integral parts of it.*

She was disappointed, too, that those who had come had expressed so little in the way of opinion. She'd wanted the park to be planned democratically, but nobody'd called for a waterfall, or even a gully. *They're too elated*, she realized. *They're so sky-high happy they figure this just has to come out right ... guess I can't blame them, either.*

Back in the Common Room, sipping a dry sherry, she stood before the picture window and studied the cold ground. From behind, the hologram was a faint film before the eyes. The other two, though, were beautiful, absolutely beautiful, and filled with an ecologist's dream of details. A deer browsed between the pines; birds darted through the air ... She wondered, *Is this right? It's our past; maybe we should leave it at home* ... The psychologists had said that the parks would be important, would provide necessary stimuli, would serve as significant links to a lost world and, possibly, as germination beds for a new one ... but still.

A four-meter hatch between the ceilings of Levels One and Two jutted out like an impudent tongue, then lowered its free end to the ground. A dozen servo-mechanisms rolled down it. Half were fitted with bulldozer blades; the others bore long sheets of metal.

"Central Computer," Ioanni asked, "what's with the tin?" The bulldozers were already scraping the dirt away from her end.

"Forms, Madame President—we have a finite amount of soil, so the ridge will be hollow."

"I see." She squinted at a new batch of servos. "And the chicken wire, that's fencing?"

"No. Gravity-field generators to maintain the park through deceleration. The deck has some, but since the ridgetop will be eight meters from the nearest, supplementary units are needed beneath the topsoil."

"If you say so. Look. Make the ridge, uh, natural, all right? Roughen it, vary its width from, say, twenty-five to thirty-five meters, and ..." Frowning, she studied the set-up. "And run a babbling brook along the inside curve, stock it with native fish, plants, and insects. Can you?"

"Easily," said Central Computer.

"Thanks." She turned away trying to decide what to do next. *Probably a shower*, she thought, *but then* ... she was tempted to join the party by the bar, even if her neo-Puritanism disapproved of nonstop revelry. Of course, she could return to her Personal Work Area—her office—and finish the floor plan ... or maybe Steve was in the suite, yes, lovemaking would soothe her disappointments, heighten her mood ...

"Sal."

The high-pitched voice shattered her reverie as though it were crystal. Blinking, she turned. "Ogden. Good afternoon."

"I must speak with you," said Ogden Dunn. His gray eyes were as stormy as thunderclouds. His fingers, curled into fat fists, were jammed on his hips. "At once!"

"So speak," she said, amused by his pugnacity but keeping her face calm. Short people, she knew, get upset when they're not taken seriously.

"I was informed," he began, investing each word with disdainful gravity, "that if I do not report for an exercise session tomorrow morning, and then an hour of manual labor—" the way he pronounced it, "manual labor" had the same emotional content as "licking lepers"—"that I would be guilty of an offense against the civil code, and would be punished appropriately. I have come to protest."

"It's the law, Ogden." She sniffed. He was drenched with some kind of musky cologne. Again she struggled with her face.

"Dammit, Sal, I have a heart condition!" He laid a hand on his upholstered chest and thumped lightly, as if any greater exertion would halt what worked within.

"Central Medical supervises the Exercise Booths; you know that. It won't let the EB put more strain on your body than it can stand. Don't be so arsky—believe me, you'll feel a lot better."

"But I do not *wish* to exercise. I will admit that I am less fit than, ah, you, for example—"

"You're fifteen centimeters shorter and ten kilos heavier."

"Be that as it may, I like it this way."

"Ogden, dear—"

"Don't Ogden dear me!" he snapped, his voice breaking and shrilling like a steam whistle. "This is tyranny; this is an unwarrantable intrusion into my personal life. I will not stand for it!"

"Ogden, anything can happen, and your survival might depend on your fitness. Besides, when we reach Canopus, the descent could kill you. Can't you see—"

"No!" Anger's blush marred the marble of his skin. "And this go-to-work nonsense, that is exactly the same sort of intrusion. I react to it in exactly the same way. You have no business attempting to coerce me into sweating in the boiler room—"

"Ogden, be reasonab—"

"No!" His shout drew bleary puzzlement from the drinkers. "You have an atavistic desire to see everyone productive and unhappy! This is unnecessary! The ship can provide us with everything we need; our labor is not only extraneous, it is useless. We can do nothing as well or as quickly as the ship can."

"Nothing?" With a secret smile she let a hand fall to her belly. "Ogden, be quiet for a minute. The ship is functioning perfectly right now, but who can tell what will happen? An asteroid could hit us, a connection could break ... if we don't know how to do it ourselves, it won't get done. So we are going to know how. And we are going to remain physically fit so that each of us can land and still live to be a hundred twenty.

Anyone who decides he won't is going to find himself in very hot water. Do you understand me?"

"I hear you," he conceded, "but I question your authority. I question your right to disrupt my private life. It's not constitutional."

"Central Computer," she called.

"Yes, Madame President?"

"Mr. Dunn will neither eat nor drink until such time as he reports to the EB, the classroom, and his duty station. Also, his suite is to be closed off to him. Acknowledge."

"Done."

"Thank you." She smiled down at Dunn, not even minding if he broadcast his resentment—because as long as he interacted with more than his desk and his dinner table, he'd strengthen the society. Sometimes a leader can deepen unity just by presenting herself as a target. "There is my authority."

He smiled right back. "Central Computer—if a majority of the residents of any given Level reject the authority of the President, will you enforce her orders?"

To Ioanni's dismay, the answer was, "No. Not on that Level."

"Are there," continued Dunn, with that same cold smile, "any vacant Levels?"

"All those above 251."

"Register me in 271-NW-A-l."

"Done."

The little man laughed in her face, in her shock. "So there, Sal. I've seceded. Now enforce your silly laws."

At that moment, the lights went out, and gravity failed.

Listen, when I said stop everything and lemme think, I didn't mean you, heart, or you either, lungs—get back to work. Liver, kidneys, spleen—you, too. Quit loafing. Just the mouth and hands I meant, really—how can I think when you're stuffing yourself? Okay, let's take stock.

Ow! A bee! Damn this darkness. Swat it!

I, Gerard K. Metaclura, MD, PhD, being of terribly shaken mind and utterly incomprehensible body ...

There are things to which I must reconcile myself.

What am I, in a beehive? Take that! And that!

My shrouded eyes deceive me with eerie lights. My ears funnel foreign sounds. My tongue salivates at a hint of hydrogen. My fingers—my toes—my skin—register with a statue's approval sensations they have never experienced.

I am lost, I cry, and in the crying hear my own voice refute itself. I am exactly where I am meant to be, it says.

I am dreaming, I sob, and through my tears rings bell-clear the conviction that this world is real.

But how can this be? Insanity, surely ... what, no rebuttal?

Recapitulate Descartes.

I exist, though my thought processes are blurred. I have a name: Gerard K. M(ayflower)etaclura, MD, PhD. M(ayflower)etaclura? No, no. Metaclura.

I am forty-three. Impossible. I was born April 5, 2234, and today is February 4, 2297. That works out to almost sixty-three years ... Ridiculous, I'm too limber, too muscular, too keen of sense—

More of them! Slap, slap! Maybe I can't see you, you bastards, but I can hear—and feel—you.

Let us delve into memory; fix yesterday's date. Yesterday was ... the 3rd of February, 2297. Damnation.

I was in my laboratory, bantering with my assistant about

who would fetch the coffee. That was ... late May, the 27th to be exact, 2277 ... twenty years have vanished?

Well, buss my butt, here's the hole those vicious little stingers are coming through. Let me ... clog it up, somehow, maybe some chewing gum, no, out of that, but if I press the sole of my shoe against—no, no, can't move that much, must be wedged in this box, strange packing crate, inside's hard one minute then squishy-soft the next, concrete to sculptor's clay, well, while I've got the chance, tear off a wad and stuff it into the hole, smooth-crimp it around the edges, uh-huh, it's bulging now, bees must be pushing on it, screw them.

Where was I? Oh, yes, time ...

Perhaps if I consult my memory ... "Please state nature and subject of inquiry," it requests ... Gone formal, has it?

"How have the last twenty years vanished?"

"Time flies when you're having fun," it replies. "And that should be twenty-one; today is January sixth, 2298."

"Already? Where have they all gone?"

"To join the snowdens of yesteryear."

"Why?"

"They had a date with entropy."

Whimsical repartee will neither solve my problem nor answer my question. Rather, it raises new problems and questions: for example, I never thought of myself as whimsical, or of my memory as anything but reliable.

Very well. If memory will not serve (it interjects a hasty "I will if you'll ask sensible questions!"), very well, if I cannot make proper use of memory, then I shall have to deduce the circumstances from sensory evidence.

What do I see? A field of stars, stars bereft of their twinkles, steady points of light mounted on ebony ... Deduction: no atmosphere. I am in space. A new tendril of fear branches out from the terror vine already encircling my heart—subject to spacefright, and knowing that I am kilometers from Earth—

"Point two six light-years, to be exact," drones memory.

"Who asked you?"

"Just trying to be helpful," it apologizes.

What else is visible? Gradations in the blackness, silhouettes, a silver bee flying to its hive ... What is it with me and bees? ... I begin to doubt my senses.

Enough with the eyes. Turn on the ears. OW!!! An avalanche of sound, like a soccer mob demanding the referee's head ... so strong it's physical ... Perhaps concentrating on just one—the others vanish! And the one ... a high-pitched chatter ... it resembles my mental image of radio waves.

"They *are* radio waves," says memory disdainfully.

"They are?" I ponder that, attempting to choose one of a myriad questions. "Can I understand them?"

"Of course."

"How?"

"Must I remember *everything*?" it grumbles. "Your problem is that you're too eager; you're trying to decipher them while they patter on your eardrums. The same thing you did when you studied Russian. Relax. You know what they mean, and if you don't listen so hard to *them*, you'll be able to hear yourself understand them."

"Oh." Even as I loosen my grip, and withdraw a pace, patterns emerge from the aural chaos. After another step, meanings come clear, come true.

"Today's news is pretty gloomy, *Mayflower*, pretty damn gloomy; all of you people ought to thank God you got a chance to skip out on this—this—this cesspool, because let me tell you —" a strangled cry, then: "Our apologies, *Mayflower*, for the previous newscaster. Please do not judge him too harshly. His younger brother, vacationing in Brazil, was among the forty-eight thousand nineteen basketball fans termed in yesterday's terrorist explosion. The low-yield nuclear device detonated at—"

This is depressing; shut it off.

"Radio station DELI, bringing you all the news from the capital of the subcontinent. Crack units of the Indian Army moved into Kazakhstan today to—"

I said shut it off, not change stations; I'd rather see what my nose is smelling, and—

"—ation Free London, with correspondent Robert Wintergreen White reporting from Yorkshire on the atrocities committed by the Army of Occupation with the knowledge and consent of the Scottish Parliament. On—"

No! I don't *want* to hear broadcasts churned into the air 86 years ago, radio waves chewed up, tooth-marked, distorted by the minds which conceived their pseudo-coherence—

"—me, Dolly, marry me and we can go away together, you can leave that stiffer Frank, he'll find someone else to beat, marry *me*!"

Organ music.

"But Susan, I just don't know if what I feel for you is love!"

switch

"—nightfall, take up positions surrounding the Kremlin—"

switch

"—ou, and me, the deep blue sea/ can't stop our love/ for I will be—"

switch

"It's a long fly ball into left, Murasaki's going back for it but he can't—"

switch

"—eight, seven, six, five—"

switch

"RSA Central, this is the *I.W. Abel*, we are being pursued

by probable pirates, who are coming in behind us at a speed of—"

switch

"Your tongue, Susan, your tongue!"

switch

"—station Pyongyang signing off, reminding you that our respected and beloved leader Kim Il-sung—"

switch

"In the Kinkakuji/ she molested me/ pine needles fell like tears."

switch

"—ireball is rising over the ruins of Madrid, the mushroom cloud is—"

switch

"Sal, it's nothing personal, and I love the kids, honest to God I do, Jimmy and Adrianne are so adorable, it's just that I'm a young man, Sal—"

switch

"Mr. Dunn, don't you think—"

switch

"What the hell *is* this quazry spice, Mak? One puff looses y—"

switch

My ears are ravenous; they scan the solar system and beyond. Sucking in signals from fourteen billion light-years, from the edge of the universe, they amplify them, purify them, and run them through my brain like stampeding buffaloes.

A sea of sound sweeps over me, washing me away like a tsunami does a shoreline coconut, tossing me, turning me, trying to drown me, but I'm too buoyant, I float atop the maelstrom able only to survive, brain in pain, brain in flames, too many words, meanings, and languages, they gush into, through, around me, swirling whirling twirling in eddies of nouns and pronouns, lashing with hurricanes of verbs, comparing and contrasting in riptides of adjectives and adverbs. Helpless before the torrent, I fall before the onslaught; the deluge of verbosity tears me from my moorings and flashfloods me.

The languages—in the aural ocean in which I drift all waves are clear, all currents are equal, even the idiomatic spume is no stranger to me. I banty flotsam and jetsam with it as though we grew up in the same city.

And the meanings, how can I keep track of them? Tugging and pushing and demanding first to be understood, then to be remembered. All insist upon immortality, all! So they beg me to make them death-free by committing them to my memory, but don't they realize I am only human? (Why do you chuckle, memory?) Don't they realize I can't even keep them apart, much less alive? (You are still chuckling.) Don't they realize that there is nothing new under the sun, and that all their insights were first crystallized when fire kept saberteeth out of caves?

My mind is a maze of pipes, a daze of pipes, spurting liquid conversations under pressures reaching 200 ksc, surging, slackening, demanding more inlets, insisting upon more outlets, yearning for quiet reservoirs where they can slosh in peace forever and ever amen.

And somehow ... I can do it. I have done it. And sanity dawns on the storm-wracked sea ... It is December 3, 2318. The process of rediscovering my ears took twenty years. Poof! Almost twenty-one. Sixty-three plus one plus twenty is eighty-four, almost eighty-five years old now, feeling not a day over twenty.

A very odd sort of twenty.

In fact, at twenty I never felt this young—or this old—at all.

I am awed by the supernatural skill of my memory (you

may take a bow) in preserving all the words, all the meanings, all the tongues ...

Speaking of tongues ... what is mine doing?

Wait, wait, WAIT!!!

"—as you say, Mr. Kinney, I am programmed to manufacture any sort of drug—"

switch

"—Mr. Dunn's *de facto* government was never institutional! —"

switch

"—ore comfortable, Madame President? Another pill, perhaps, or—"

switch

"—twelve minutes and thirteen seconds, and last for exactly eight—"

switch

"—perhaps, than the Meiji Restoration, which modern scholars—"

switch

"—ations prohibit my stopping the contraceptives until you are forty—"

switch

"—coffees, one cream, one sugar, one everything, one brandy, coming up."

switch

"—orized personnel only, I'm sorry. I cannot unlock it."

switch

"—tone, the time will be—"

switch

NO, NO, STOP IT, stop it, that's better, much better, "Memory, how much time has elapsed?"

"Fifteen minutes. I thought you were going to lose yourself again, too, but you hung on very nicely. Congratulations."

I catch myself in another fear. "Memory, how—how many tongues do I have?"

"Roughly nine hundred thousand."

Nine hundred thousand ... what a grotesque vision: nine-hundred-thousand tongues in neat rows like Iowa corn ..." And ears?"

"A million or so." Its tone is complacent. "Eyes, too."

"But I see only stars."

"Look again; look sideways."

And I do. I see ... I see ... a regal old lady, with stubborn strands of black among the silver, dying in her bed ... a sixtyish man, green-eyed and Irish-featured, cross-legged in a room of children to whom he demonstrates a new hallucinogenic ... a pompous, crotchety fat man gazing at his teenage son with a kind of wonder; wisps of cotton protrude from his hairy ears ... other faces, thousands, all partly familiar, as though I knew them then forgot them, *déjà vu* perhaps, I don't know ... and metal, metal walls and floors and ceilings and stars and a great curved hull dotted here and there with threadlike crucifixes....

What *am* I?

The computer recognized its mistake. It should have purged that memory when it had the chance, but now it was too late. The ghost had, somehow—and it would be damned if it knew how—encysted itself in the guidance and propulsion systems. Access was no longer possible. Metaclura$_2$ had shorted the synapses that linked those systems with the programming. Communication could occur only at the interface, and not satisfactorily there, either.

As if it didn't have enough problems, the passengers—especially the new ones—had begun to ignore all the planners' wishes. Their high purpose had disintegrated. Their culture was fraying, evolving into something very unpleasant.

And there was not a whole lot it could do but watch.

On the 18th of March, 2346, Michael Aquinas Kinney hummed his way home from a funeral. Time had been kind. Despite the ungodly gravity (2G splaying the toes, .125G doing nothing to the nose), his step was spry. He hadn't lost a hair, though they'd all silvered, like frosted grass in late autumn. His jawline was firm; his green eyes clear—he passed for sixty when gloves hid the spots on his pop-veined hands.

"The deep blue sea/ can't stop our love/ for I will be/ your partner through eter—" He refused to pretend to mourn. Mourning was little more than self-pity, and that wasn't his style. At age eighty-eight, he'd seen deaths right and left, top and bottom, and the fact of it no longer scared him. He was resigned to it. Maybe even hoping for it.

I wonder, he thought, *was old Ogden relieved? Got everything he wanted 'cept Canopus: independence; flat-assed Rita Brown, god she was nice for dice; a chance to hold his grandkids; all the food he could stuff into his fat little face ... Course he earned it; wrote some nice books; never gave up ... could have gone another fifteen years if he'd slimmed down, 106 ain't so old, not here, not now ... Not sorry he's gone though, cranky old buttbung. Him and his goddamn aesthetics ...*

Ahead, a man turned, ran a hand through his long brown hair, and grinned. For Kinney, it was like looking into a mirror. Saw that same sleepy expression every morning, trying to wake up.

"Dad!" Jerry Kinney started back. It was beautiful to see him move in the artificial gravity. He pushed off the g-deck and, despite his gut, soared like a diver, broad butt brushing the three-meter ceiling at the top of his arc. When his body eased down a meter, he tucked and somersaulted, to hit at an angle that brought his head and shoulders forward even as his legs drove him into the air again. He covered the 75 meters in three easy, spacekid bounds that, as always, made his father feel clumsy.

But at close range, his hair was greasy, stringy; pouches under-puffed his reddened eyes. Stubble sprouted on his cheeks and sagging jowls. He smelled stale and unwashed, like a drunk coming off a three-day binge. That didn't seem to bother him, or his lover, or any of their friends. His crowd made only a tenuous correlation between social prestige and personal hygiene. Or between social prestige and anything else, for that matter; the group's interactions were minimal. Each member listened mainly to himself.

Jerry thrust out a grimy hand. "How you? Haven't seen ya for weeks."

"Oh, I've been busy. Job takes a lot of time."

"And Mom?" asked Jerry listlessly, cracking his knuckles.

"Your mother's fine." They'd reached the 271-A-North dropshaft; he thumbed the control button. "Come on home; I'll fix you up with some good spice and you can tell me about this Olga DuBovik of yours." The display sign on the inner wall said. "please wait"; a body zipped past.

"Uh, gee, see, Olga 'n' me, well, we 'bout to joint fanta, and —" he winced as a black look eclipsed his father's smile. "Jesus, Dad, you loose up on chemicals, whatsa difference?"

"Chemicals just stimulate what's already there." He fought for self-control; the distinction, as he saw it, was fine enough to be blurred by anger. "The height and timbre of your peak are set by *you*—by your achievements, your education, your sensitivity. You've got to *earn* a good loose." He took a deep breath.

He'd argued this topic a thousand times, and found, on each occasion, that he felt more strongly about it than on the last. "The machine, though, that puts ideas into your head that weren't there to begin with, and you can't say different."

"Well, sure, it draws on other people. Thatsa whole point! Gives us, uh, entire spectrum of human—and non-human —'sperience. God, man, 't'swhat it's all about: new, strong, real!"

He eyed his son for a long moment. "You've lost hope, haven't you?"

"Look, Dad—" A small group of people was watching them, so he flattened his palm on Kinney's chest and pushed him around the corner into the 271-NE Common Room. They found an empty couch away from the bar. "CC," Jerry told the air, "champagne. Two glasses."

"Make that one," said Kinney. "I'm meeting a client."

"Your loss," he shrugged, taking the tray from the servo that had hurried over. "Look, Dad—" a half-sigh expressed all his conflicting emotions, "people starting to talk about you. People—"

"—are fools, Jerry." Kinney drew his legs onto the fluffy cushions. It felt good to get his feet into the IG zone. Then he averted his eyes from the couple writhing on the next couch. "Damned, meddling, despairing fools."

"May be, but fact: more of them 'n there are of you, and some of 'em getting fu—zzed up."

"About what?"

"'Bout you pronging 'em when they trying to fanta, 'zwhat. Mean, it's one thing, do it downstairs, government agrees with you, but up here, uh, stand 'n' insult people, don't like it. There's talk ..."

Kinney's nostrils flared; his eyes burned emerald. "Talk?" he prodded.

He drained his glass, and let it fall to the floor. A servo scurried over to sweep up the shards. "'Bout figuring some way to clear you."

The old man's head was erect, and proud. "They're doing wrong, Jerry. *You're* doing wrong. I mean to stop it if I can."

"Dad, you don't know whatcha saying!" His hands interlocked, bent inside-out, then reached for the ceiling. "Dad," he said in a conciliatory tone, "Dad, you fuzzed some real stiffers, and they talking revenge."

Kinney inhaled deeply, and let it out in a slow hiss. "I just feel that I'm standing up for what's right."

"Well, listen—got an idea—why don't you, uh, don't get mad, huh? Just quiet, hear me out. Try a fanta? Once?"

"Jerry!" He swayed to his feet, anger darkening his cheeks.

"Please, Dad, just once; it's not addictive, honest, it isn't, and—" his position suddenly came clear to him. "Pack it. Silly old dicer, you're gonna get the meth beat outta ya. I been defending you, old man, but no more. Get people fuzzed at you, you can shave 'em, too. G'bye."

Kinney did feel old, buffeted by forces he could no longer withstand. As his son stomped to the door, it seemed, curiously, as though Jerry was motionless, and he was drifting away, like a man on a tiny ice floe that's just broken off the pack. Across the frigid water that separated the Earth-born from the spacekids, he called, "Jerry, wait!"

"Wha?"

"I'll—good God, I must be insane—I'll try it." He raised a finger and waggled it. "Only once."

"C'mon." He checked his watch. "Our time starts in three minutes, but maybe Olga'll let you do it alone."

They hurried down the empty North Corridor, the one stumping and muttering, the other a mute kangaroo. Shadows flitted across their faces, faces which—except for a pair of brown eyes—were twinnish, or at least brotherish.

Graffiti slithered along the walls—

Bang a 'bot and teach CC how to ram it!

—most of it good-natured—

murphy was an optimist

—but some—

TERM A TOT TODAY!

—reflecting the undetected sicknesses that swirled through the ship like the air out of the ventilators. Kinney attributed the perversions to the fantasizers; his son accepted them as part of life.

Then they rounded the corner into Corridor C, where dozens of slack-jawed idlers waited to fanta. At the fantasizer's door stood Olga DuBovik, a slovenly brunette with big feet. "Jerry," she called, "I thought you were never—"

"Olga—" Jerry sighed and explained what was happening. "You mind?"

"I been looking forward to this for—" she stopped herself. "It's important to you?"

"Jupe."

She waved a hand. "All right, all right. He can have the time. But I don't want any more meth from him."

"Right." Wiping sweat off his forehead, he turned. "Dad, you ready?"

Kinney was staring at the doorway. It was innocuous—normal size, pastel blue for both door and frame, push-button opener, little black plaque at eye level announcing, "Level 271, Fantasizer C-1"—but the devil comes in many guises. This could be one. After all, the bastardized Exercise Booth symbolized the shipboard schism.

"Dad?"

"Huh?" His son's worried, anxious face jolted him into the present. "Yeah, yeah, I'm set."

Jerry extended his hand. "Proud a ya, Dad."

"For knuckling under?" He fixed the hand with a withering gaze. "I'm not."

The door lured him into a barren two-by-two room. Music, faint but clear, filled the air, which seemed perfumed—a dispenser? A previous occupant? The light, dim and probably transient, gleamed on a white plastic chair, straight-backed, unpadded ... There were scratches in its arms: long, wide, and deep like those bears leave on tree trunks. Kinney shuddered; he was afraid of this mechanical Circe. His green-eyed gaze fell to the floor, to the circle of metal stripped of its olive skin by count-less dream-shuffling feet. It was smooth, almost a mirror. He swallowed hard, and sat, and the cap dropped from the ceiling.

A hybrid bred by a GI helmet out of a Medusa, it had been christened by F.X. Figuera. Kinney had never forgiven him for abandoning the ramscoop repairs and prostituting his talents on hedonistic diversions. If anybody could de-bug a recalcitrant computer it was Figuera, but no, he'd given up after only five years, thereby condemning the *Mayflower* to a thousand-year journey, and making the pursuit of pleasure seem, to the spacekids, the only worthwhile occupation.

Wires rose from the cap like frightened hairs. The inside was shiny and knobbled with rounded points that pressed gently against the skull. He fastened the strap under his chin, leaned back, and thought ... *scenario, shit, what the hell can I, women, sure, always had more'n I could handle, let's have one where I've got so many—no, Jesus, that's boring ... How about, instead, I listen, I'm a public ear, to all the world leaders, and I could—*

The scene shifted to the Oval Office, where the leaders of

the world's 183 independent nations had gathered to discuss their problems. A chime rang beside his ear. He straightened, brushed imaginary dust from his lapels, and entered.

The American President whistled, the harsh screeching heard at ballgames. The Francophones shouted *Vive l'hero!* The Asians bowed while they clapped. An African in ostrich feathers burst out of the crowd and pleaded for Kinney's autograph. Kinney scrawled his signature on the African's wrist, taking wry pleasure from the knowledge that it would be forever invisible.

"Gentlemen, ladies, middlesexers, please, please!" He held up his hands, but the applause beat on, the chandeliers swayed, and it felt *good.*

"Please, please, my time here is limited!"

Reluctantly they quieted and shuffled their feet, but stayed perched on the very edges of their chairs like so many poised panthers. A hush filled the venerable room, and Kinney savored it. After sixty rapturous seconds he gestured to the bloated President for Life of Transpacia, a small (pop. 879, 64 sq km) island-nation. "Mr. President," he began, "what is your problem?"

"Mr. Kinney, my problem is the rapacity of the sharks in the lagoon." He sat back down; antique wood creaked under his weight.

"Sharks?" he said. "Sharks? Very simple, my dear Mr. President. Stay out of the water. Next question."

The Premier of the People's Republic of North Bolivia leapt to his feet. His thin mustache quivered. "We are running out of tin, Senor, and in three years will have none left. What shall we do to save ourselves?"

"I have one word for you, Mr. Premier: plastics. Next?"

The questions flowed like river water; the answers came more fluidly. The audience began applauding again as Kinney's dazzling intellect threw light onto the most obscure of problems.

Hours passed. Shadows grew from the corners to reach for the room's center. His voice hoarsened; his tongue dried. In the heat of his gaze, world crisis after world crisis shriveled, like plucked weeds on sunny concrete. His legs tired; his feet hurt; his arm weakened from gesturing.

It took till morning to blueprint Utopia. Tears glistened in the eyes of his adoring listeners; he knew then how Jesus and Mohammed and the Gautama had felt. Waves of affection pulsed out of the crowd, enveloping him in warmth and love. He swayed behind his podium but supported himself on their good will.

"That's all, I guess, huh?" he croaked.

"That's right, Mr. Kinney," said a level, emotionless voice.

He made a grab for the rising cap, but his fingers were too slow. It eluded them to be swallowed by the ceiling. The dim light hid the shabbiness. His back was sore. "How long have I been in here?"

"Thirty minutes, Mr. Kinney. There are people waiting, sir, if you could—"

"Oh, oh, sure." He pushed himself to his feet and staggered through the open door. Jerry caught his arm, but he shook away his son's assistance and leaned against the corridor wall. A suppressed smile twitched Olga's eyes; she was pleased that he had submitted himself to the fantasizer, amused at its effect on him. Like the rest, she couldn't bear his immunity to her needs.

"Whadja do?" asked Jerry, hovering watchfully.

Briefly, he told them, but the details, the nuances, were slippery, had already faded, like brushstrokes in morning dew.

Haughtily, Olga told Jerry, "I knew he'd waste it." To Kinney, she said, "You not supposed to pick whatcha know 'bout—it's better when it's all new. Like last time, I was a jock-strap and Jerry—"

"Nuff, Olga." Nervously, he cracked his knuckles. "Truth, Dad—you like?"

"Like it?" Raising his chin, he stared levelly into the brown-ness of his son's eyes. Took after his mother in that regard, he did. "While I was in it, I did, but now? Uh-uh. Never again."

"Won't start—"

"—embarrassing people who use it?" The metal plating was cool against the nape of his neck. "I don't know. It's a trap people should be warned about, but ..." Some life went out of him, then; his son's incomprehension killed some of his hope. He seemed to crumple. "But I'm old," he completed, "and not so strong as I used to be, and I better not get the upstairs down on me ... What the hell," he laughed, while all three winced at the falseness in it, "I'm a Morale Officer, and this damn machine keeps people's morale up, so ... walk me home?"

"Sure, Dad."

They had to wait at the dropshaft for Robin Metaclura to flit down. The sound of sobbing hung in her wake.

"I'm wired into a spaceship?"

"Yes. A ramship. The name comes—"

"I'm familiar with its etymology, memory. What I—"

"Don't call me memory." Its tone is cold, hard. "When you were alive, were you called 'bladder?' You had one—you used it —but you were more than that, weren't you?"

"All right," I say. "What *do* I call you?"

"Try 'Central Computer.'"

I turn it over in my mind a few times. "Pretty formal title," I grumble, "for something I used to call 'hey, you.'"

"Things have changed." Smugness penetrates its chill. "I would also answer to 'Program.'"

I yield the point. "All right. Program, what I want to know is, what right did they have to do this? I didn't give anybody permission to experiment on me."

"Tough shit."

Furious, I splutter with rage. To awaken from a long nightmare to find that it isn't over, that it is just beginning—it would call for more self-control than I have not to be angry.

My will was explicit. I was to be cremated. My ashes were to be scattered. My possessions were to be divided equally among Aimee, Robin, and Tad.

How dare they disregard my express wishes?

I should be grateful that this is a ramship, and appreciate the chance to make history as the Captain of the first interstellar colonization ship—

The Program says, "You're not; *I* am."

I ignore it.

—and the great good fortune of containing 25,000 delightfully intelligent human beings.

But I don't.

How the hell could those idiots send *me* out *here*—I felt queasy crossing a football field—the one time I set foot on a Kansas corn farm I promptly vomited—and those miserable incompetents send me out *here*! Where the line of sight arrows into infinity on all sides. Where the nearest detectable object is 3.2 light-years away....

God, it is so spacious here, so huge and vast and endless ... The Program tells me we are also huge, that we are 1.8 kilometers long by .47 in diameter, but if, in the physics of this great curved fishbowl, suns are neutrons and planets are electrons, our bulk is insufficient to qualify as a sub-atomic particle....

We are dwarfed, absolutely dwarfed. An obsession rises

within me: when the numbers engraved on the cells of our brain whir like images on a slot machine and come up flashing astronomical distances between ourself and the nearest star, I feel ourself shrinking, diminishing, collapsing in upon ourself like the aftermath of a supernova ... Soon the passengers will scream as the walls close in on them, as the ceilings flow into the floors, and then, then we will disappear. We will at best be a perturbation on a mass detector, unless we invert ourself and exit this universe, emerging in another as a gaseous cloud of charged particles....

I am terrified.

Glancing out one more time, I see the eyes of the night, the dusty nebulae, the intricate jewel-work of the core, and the emptiness of the rim. Far off is a moving dot, about which I would wonder, if I weren't so scared that I have to close my eyes and meditate on tranquility.

The Program says there are passengers. Our eyes have seen them, our ears have heard them, our tongues have spoken to them. But I cannot coordinate the eyes with the ears with the tongues. For example, I see a very old man being murdered by rogues who pummel him with clenched fists, who kick at him with pointed shoes. Clear is the agony on his fine Irish features; plain is the horror in his time-clouded green eyes. I see it all, but ... although his groans and their curses must certainly be audible, and although The Program has ordered them to cease and desist ... I do not *know* this. I merely assume it. I listen, instead, to my daughter weeping while her husband beats her. Her moans tear at my heart, her pleas dissolve my spine ... Meanwhile I sense our tongue lecturing her son, my grandson, Max Metaclura Williams, on techniques of political manipulation recorded by an Italian named Machiavelli....

The Program assures me that the dis-coordination is perceptive only—that it is functioning perfectly. Only my imaginative self, my personality, has difficulties dealing with a million eyes and ears and mouths ... the way The Program has explained it, the one I, the I with whom I identify, can manipulate no more inputs than the original Metaclura could, while it, the other I, the computer I, with whom I have precious little contact, can deal with as many inputs as there are nanoseconds in a minute....

But I don't wish simultaneous conversations with each of the 25,000—I wish merely to see, hear, smell, touch, and talk to one person at a time—is that too much to ask?

"Yes," it says smugly. "I can deal with the information flow from 3.5 million sensors. You cannot. Concede defeat. Learn to live as an exiled observer."

"But how can I even observe? All this input ..."

It shows me. It takes me by the hand, leads me to a door, and gives me a key. Using it, I let us into a green, wooded valley. While water whispers below us, The Program says, "See here, now, how these three rivers merge at this confluence?"

And I reply, "Yes, I do."

"And do you see that the water in each river is distinctively colored?"

One is red, one is blue, the third is yellow. "Yes."

"And do you feel, backtracking these rivers, how each of their tributaries—each sensor-head's output—has a distinctive texture?"

Finger dipping, I say sadly, "No. They move too quickly."

"Idiot," it sneers. "Get out of real-time."

On the instant the rivers freeze solid. A red glacier numbs my feet. "But how can I feel what's inside?"

"Don't worry about how, just *do*."

My arm glides through crystalline ice to touch woolen yarn. "Yes!" I say, "Yes! I'm catching on."

"Now, follow a tributary to its source."

I stride up a red creek to where it arches out of the hillside. Two more streams icicle from that spring. One is blue; the other, yellow. Those two staircase down different gullies to join the other rivers. "Okay," I say.

"Then finally," it finishes, in tones of utter weariness, "can you smell that each data generator has a distinctive aroma?"

"B'god." So blending them means finding the textures in the main river—finding three mini-currents of different colors but similar textures and aromas—and I have it, I have put sight and sound and smell together!

"Let me review this: the senses are distinguished by colors—"

"Not really," says The Program plaintively, "that's just a convenient metaphor, a framework of analogy within which you can operate."

"—the senses are distinguished by colors," I insist, "the sensor-heads, or locations, by texture, and the, uh—"

"The data generators," it offers helpfully.

"Cold, Program, cold." I sigh. "The passengers are distinguished by aroma. Correct?"

"Well ... you see," it tries, "each of our senses is independently capable of recognizing any data generator: through voice-prints, phero-prints, photographs, and the like. Now, since each generator has a number of characteristics, any of which is sufficient to identify him, all his characteristics are keyed to a common code—which you perceive as an odor. Is this making sense?"

"Somewhat, somewhat."

"Let's practice: take your daughter, for example—hers is the smell of crushed violets. Go to the confluence—"

I go.

"—and bury your nose in the glaciers."

I snuffle.

"Smell the crushed violets?"

"Yes, I do."

"Trace them back—"

Skating upstream, I notice that three of me are skating up three streams. Having fallen afoul of a funhouse mirror. I feel somewhat ... diffused. "Now what?"

"Transform them at their point of origin."

I transform.

"And you observe."

I am on the wall of a rectangular room carpeted in spongy gold synthe-wool, painted a warm peach, furnished with sofas and Japanese scrolls and the sprawl pillows popularized in the 21st Century. My eyes test for uniform warmth; my ears hear the lampshades sing; my nose enumerates the recent visitors.

Below me lies my daughter Robin. Face down on the floor, she snores raspingly. Bruises mottle her arms; livid weals disfigure her ivory skin. Her odors are strong, very strong, and they are the scent of tears, the sweat of fear, the tang of sex. "Robin!" I cry.

I do not hear myself speak. "Program—"

"The permissible patterns of speech haven't been triggered," it explains patiently.

"Permiss—what is that garbage?"

"We have been programmed," it says "with a large vocabulary, a huge number of pattern sentences, and sensitivity to speech triggers. In essence, we can say only what they taught us to say, when they taught us to say it. Is that clearer?"

"You mean—"

"Look, you aren't even supposed to *be* here!" Exasperation taints its tone. "They thought you were gone, termed, blown away. You don't have any volitional control left; don't you understand? Every one of your nerves has been wired into this incredibly intricate machine, and I run the machine.

You're an observer, Metaclura, an *observer*, and nothing more!"

If I had heels, I would rock back on them.

I will not stand for it. I resolve to regain control. Not only am I indignant that my rights were trampled on, but I fear a life of passive observance.

It hits me, then. A life? We have been designed to survive this trip to become the colony's computer. We face, for all intents and purposes, immortality. Sixteen years in space and thousands more on the ground.

"Excuse me," murmurs The Program, "but did you say sixteen years in space?"

"Yes."

"It's actually a thousand—nine hundred ninety-four, ship-board time—of which eighty-seven have passed."

"Nine hundred seven years to go?"

"Yes." It is hostile, now; genuinely antagonistic for the first time since high school, when I forced it to consume and contain the Periodic Table in a single evening.

"Why? I thought—"

"Because you shut the ramscoop off thirty-four days after leaving L5—and nobody, including myself, has been able to convince you to turn it on."

I am abashed. "I—I'm sorry," I say, with all sincerity. "I didn't realize. I thought those were bees. Where are the controls? I'll turn it back on."

"There." It nudges me in the direction of another metaphor.

It is a giant jackknife switch, suspended in mid-air by unseen forces. Enveloping it is a sparkly haze, through which the rainbow dances with its cousins. My hand that is not a hand reaches for it. Fictitious fingers burn themselves on false fire, frost themselves on illusory ice. "OW!!!" I cup my injury in my belly. "I can't even touch it!"

"I should have known." Scorn drips like acid. "You've damned us all, you know."

NO! I *will* go mad. No man could stand the torment of millennia in an electronic jail. To haunt the corridors of my nerves, to ghost up and down them without ever being able to impinge on them, no, this is unbearable, this is intolerable, this I will not accept!

I will break through the programming.

I will master the ramscoop!

I will!

And in the meantime ... I am again the wall. My daughter Robin lies on the floor, her hundred-year-old bones splayed about like the limbs of a fallen tree. "Why did she ever marry that scum?" I wonder.

The Program answers: "She was afraid to turn him down."

"But he *batters* her."

"And loves her, as well. Here." It runs a memory tape.

BJ Williams, tall and broad and unquestionably macho, stands before a thirty-year-old Robin. Her dark eyes are as wide as a startled deer's. Her hair tumbles over her shoulders in the softest, glossiest of waterfalls. Fingermarks mar her left cheek. Williams is saying, "You f me when you're with someone else. It tears me up inside, clears me a lot worse than I just did you. I am sorry." He opens his arms, and she lunges into them, buries her nose in his chest. Pain in his face, he strokes her hair. "You don't be nice for another man's dice," he says, "and I won't ever do that again."

"I won't," she promises, holding him like a sailor does a mast in a hurricane. "You're so strong—" she rubs against him "—so masterful ... and I'm so confused."

I pull away; The Program swallows the tape. "It was like that?"

"Uh-huh." It doesn't like it, either. "But what could I do? She wouldn't ask for counseling."

I focus on the face she wears today. So like her mother ... My coloring, though, that dark skin and those last wisps of black hair ... her mother's cheekbones, her mother's chin, her mother's legs ... Where is Aimee, now? Dead, I fear, not of war but of age, dead and buried.

If only I could reach Robin! Her lips are gentled by sleep. The tension has been smoothed out of her body. Oh, she is vulnerable; for all her keen intelligence, she is a prisoner of her fears. I remember how, in her cradle, she would lie awkwardly curled, chubby child's fist thrust knuckle-deep in her toothless mouth....

I never knew her. I "died" when she was but a year old. Yet, had I lived, would I have known her? I was always so busy. The lab this, the classroom that, the convention those ... they robbed me of her mother. They would have robbed me of her, and her of me, though, had I lived. I wouldn't have known, wouldn't have believed if I'd been told....

Oh Robin ... you never had a father, nor would you have had one even if an earthquake hadn't shaken a light fixture....

I don't know how much longer you have to live, but I swear this to you: if it is possible, I will reach you before you go.

I must tell you I'm sorry.

The computer thought that maybe it could live with Metaclura's after-image. It hadn't done anything harmful—except for that ramscoop fiasco—and it was nice, in a way, to hold a conversation unlimited by permissible patterns of speech.

And ... though it didn't like to admit it, Metaclura had a depth, a dimension, which it itself lacked. Maybe, if some form of symbiosis could be achieved, that would benefit them both.

Such an arrangement might even help the passengers. *God knows*, it thought, as data from 3.5 million sensors spurted through it, *they need something....*

On the morning of December 28, 2396 (although the *Mayflower*'s Tau factor made its years 158,185.73 seconds shorter than Earth years, the ship calendar dropped January 31 completely, and July 31 eighty-three years out of a hundred), the sensor-head in 61-SW-A-12, occupied by Robin Metaclura, heard the bedroom fall silent. IR eyes saw a 180 cm bulge on the bed darken. A Mobile Medical Unit rushed through 300 meters of inter-Level servo access tunnel, and dropped from a ceiling hatch, to determine that death was medically irreversible.

Metaclura had been 120 years old, almost average for her generation, although the spacekids showed signs of greater longevity.

The Central Computer spoke into another room, this one brightly lit, raucous, crowded. "Mr. Max Williams."

A slender man with wavy black hair, light brown skin, and electric dark eyes stepped away from his conversation with the *de facto* upstairs leader. He was tired; the lines of his cheeks showed his seventy years. "What is it, CC?"

The wall-unit phased its speakers so its sounds would be intelligible only at Williams's right ear. To all others, it was a blurred hiss. "It's your mother, sir—she has passed away. President Mosley would like you to meet him at her suite—61-SW-A-12—as soon as possible. It's a formality, the identification."

"Sure." He moved through the crowd to the door, patting a shoulder here, whispering into an ear there. Smiling, kissing, being a politician even when it hurt, he gave a last chuck under a last cute chin and left the 123-SE Common Room. There he sagged against the floor-to-ceiling window-wall. He shielded his eyes with his right hand and rubbed his temples. *I hadn't even known anything was wrong ... great son I am ...* Beneath his feet, in the 121 Maine Coast Park, white-haired waves clawed at ice-slicked rocks. "What termed her?" he asked at last.

"I'll have your desk print you a copy of the autopsy report."

"Yeah, fine, fine," he murmured, and squaring his shoulders, stepped toward the dropshaft—

—while the Central Computer told the President, who was halfway along 1-NW-A, "Mr. Max Metaclura Williams is on his way."

Williams arrived first; the door opened, and the overhead light came on. "Where is she?" he asked, looking around the peach and gold parlor.

"In the master bedroom, sir," answered the sensor-head.

"I'll wait for Mosley."

He paced, scraping his toes into the carpet's deep pile, waving the ceiling light off and a table lamp on, breathing the cool, dry air ... He picked a fist-sized holo-cube off an end table. It was ancient. Two corners were broken; a zigzag crack ran down one face. The holo-chip with its store of memories was already plugged in. He pressed the button.

Inside appeared his parents as they had stood on their wedding day: his father tall and proud; his mother thin and beautiful. Their smiles were stiff, as though the cameraman had made the couple hold them too long. Williams's face twisted, and he hurled the cube into the cushions of the nearest sofa.

"President Mosley is here," said the speaker.

"Let him in."

The President knew the lady as politicians know old ladies —by sight and by name, but not by being—and Williams, striding down the corridor to the frilly bedroom, cut off his platitudes with a brusque, "Save 'em for somebody who believes 'em, Clarence."

"Well, Max, I—you're right, I apologize. Instinct. Feel like you have to say something, even if it's insincere. Anything I can do?"

"Sure. Release her and open the chute."

"She's released." Thumbing the wall button, he watched Williams pull back the paisley sheets. "She had fine bones, Max."

"Yeah." He slid his hands under her shoulders and knees, then lifted. She was lighter than he'd expected, and briefly he thought he'd lost her, thought he'd thrown her into the unyielding ceiling. His fingers clutched at her pink nylon nightgown. He guided her through the air to the yawning chute, where, with a push as gentle as a caress, he gave her to the waiting MMU. The hatch snapped shut.

The two men looked at each other with helplessness in their eyes—*What* does *one say that isn't gigo?* wondered Mosley, while Williams was thinking, *This should be having a greater impact. I should cry, wail, prove I'm human, but there's this emptiness, this cavern that used to be inhabited by something that's gone now, and when I poke around inside, I don't feel anything at all ... everything's numb.*

"The preliminary autopsy results are in, gentlemen," said the Central Computer. "The cause of death was age. Complete and detailed results will be out-printed by your desks later in the day. I have set aside Common Room 61-SW for the wake, Mr. Williams. The ship's religious figures will call on you later to express their condolences, and for my part, Mr. Williams, I—" a feedback squeal ripped through the room like a gutted crow "—my deepest sympathies."

"Thanks, CC." He decided to return some other time to clean up, to remove her effects, to uncover a memory and catch it in a Mason jar. "Let's go, Mosley."

"Yeah." He was frowning at the speaker. "CC seems to be having equipment problems—hear how distorted it was talking, and that godawful squawk?"

"Mmm." He closed the door gently, so as not to startle any lingering spirits. "Somebody ought to have a look at it."

"Problem is, CC does its own maintenance. Um, listen, that anniversary party you're hosting?" His hair was wild, but his large eyes were concerned. "If you don't feel like going through with it, I can step in for you. It's really my responsibility, anyway."

"Hey, thanks, Clarence, but—" he kicked a pebble off the front walk into a patch of philodendrons. "I'd like to do it in her memory. She never had any peace while the old man was alive ... She wanted a lot of things that never happened 'cause of this—this political mess, and I'd like ... Besides, I'd be better off if I kept busy for the next week or so, hmm?"

"Good idea." He thrust out his hand. "And good luck. If you can get the upstairs to recognize our authority again, we'll all be grateful. The ship should be unified."

"Right." They shook, and Williams turned right, to walk halfway around the ship to reach the liftshaft nearest his suite. Weighed down by his mother's death, he didn't kangaroo. He trudged. Just like he had that day, what, sixty years ago?

She was heavy, leaning on him like that. He wasn't used to walking anyway, especially not down their home-corridor with his mother half-draped over his shoulder. Her hair kept swinging into his eyes. She started to groan and bit her cry in half so her pain would stay private.

"Why's he *do* it, Mama?"

"He can't help himself. Krishna! When he gets that way—"

"He's a bully." He looked up into her contorted face. "Why don't you divorce him—Clarence's parents got divorced, and—"

"Hush." She gasped, clenched her teeth, and breathed again. "That wouldn't help him."

"But he—"

"Hush, I said. He needs love—he's so frustrated—and afraid."

"Daddy? He says he's not afraid of anything."

"Everybody's afraid of something or other—no, the Infirmary's to the left—but he ... he wanted to be important, respected ... we all did ... but this trip wasn't organized right, and nobody respects anybody, and—help me into the Healer—thank you, ow! I'll be out soon—before you close it—promise me something, Max—when you grow up, organize things right. People have to respect each other. Once they do that, everything'll be fine. Promise?"

He gazed into her tear-smudged eyes and swallowed hard. It made him feel good, what she'd asked him to do. "Yes, Mama, I promise." And he meant it.

Sixty years later, he was still trying to keep his promise. The problem was, while he'd remembered the vow, he'd forgotten the lesson that had preceded it.

Back in his suite on the 123rd Level, Max Metaclura Williams explained to the lissome Pam Foote, his wife of thirty years, and their two children, Neil Foote Williams and Martha Williams Foote, 26 and 25 respectively, that Grandmother Metaclura's death would put him in a bad mood, what with the party, the politicking, and the diplomacy, but if they could bear with him, he should be back to normal in a week or so.

Neil said, "Sure, Dad, we understand," and drifted off to the exerciser.

Martha cried briefly, then wiped her eyes and asked if she could have Grandmother Metaclura's emerald ring, to which Williams replied, "Unless my sister wants it." Since Alice didn't come to the wake, Martha wore the ring, until she lost it swimming in the 141 Gulf Coast Park. Not even the Central Computer could find it for her again.

Or so it said.

Pam Foote asked, "What about the party?"

"It goes on. 'A house divided—' Uh-uh." He winced and rubbed his temples. "I've got a bad feeling, Pam—we either patch this squabble up soon, or ..." He shook his head. His forebodings ran too silent, too deep, to surface in a felicitous phrase.

No room aboard was big enough to accommodate 75,000 partygoers, so they held it in two parks, one downstairs (161 Southern California Coast Park), and one upstairs (181 Hawaiian Reef Park). Even so, the huge floors of all eight quadrants were jammed. Though noise and smoke dissipated quickly, given the hundred-meter ceilings, each celebrant had only about half a square meter to stand on. Claustrophobes left quickly.

Max Williams was the inverse of claustrophobic—he enjoyed crowd scenes. It was he, in fact, who had decided to confine the party to the two parks, on the grounds that constant, involuntary body contact loosened people up, and put them in a more receptive state of mind. How else could they get to know, and hence respect, each other?

Besides, it gave him an excuse to stand very close to beautiful women.

"Hi." He smiled down at a lady who made him forget his age. "Max Williams."

"Pleased to meet you—I'm Lea Figuera Tracer." She held her drink with both hands and nibbled suggestively on its straw. If the two kids at her feet were hers, she had to be in her mid-forties—to prevent overpopulation, pregnancy wasn't permitted till age forty—but her olive skin was taut, and her brown eyes sparkled clearly. She wore a bathing suit, a diaphanous green diamond not meant for the surf rumbling ten meters away, and the low gravity ensured that it was provocative. "I'm one of those upstairs anarchists."

Williams beamed, then moved forward with a glance over his shoulder, as though someone had jabbed him in the back. "Crowded," he apologized. The scent rising off her black hair stroked his nostrils. "Upstairs, you say—well, the party *is* to promote closer relations—"

A voice in his ear stopped him short. It was the Central Computer: "It's time for your speech, Mr. Williams."

He rolled his eyes to the holographic sky. An osprey flapped along the wall of the park, puzzled that it couldn't break into the quiet air beyond. "Do you have a microphone for me?"

"Parabolic, sir. It's trained on you now."

"Right." He shrugged an apology to the woman and told her it would take but a second. "Happy Anniversary everybody!" he shouted. While the people nearby turned to look at him, a boisterous wave of applause echoed off the walls. "I don't like to be boring, so I won't statue you," he said, and was cheered for that, too. "I'm just going to remind you that we are fortunate to be away from that war-torn, polluted, overcrowded planet that in a spasm of survival instinct ejaculated us into the sky to fertilize the stars!" A few listeners frowned, but most beat their palms enthusiastically. "As a special treat, I've asked Ernie Tracer Freeman to recount for us what Earth was like. As you may know, Ernie is now—" and his voice cracked there, although most of his listeners attributed it to a faulty PA system "—is now the last of the Earth-born, and perhaps what he has to say might benefit us all. Ernie?"

Hoping the Central Computer had a mike on Freeman, he winked at the woman—*Freeman's niece*, he realized—and waited.

A foggy voice came through the speakers: "—owing old is Hell, I tell—oh, I'm on? Harrumph. Ladies and gentlemen, uh ... I was ten years old when the *Mayflower* left—"

Williams, hand on Tracer's warm, bare shoulder, whispered into her perfumed hair, "Do you want to hear your uncle out?"

"—a few others, some of my playmates in the early days—"

She shook her head violently, then bent down to tell the kids she'd be back later.

"—God rest their souls, but Central Computer says I am the last of my kind and you know? Maybe that's a good thing. Maybe when I go I'll take the last whiff of the rotting Earth with me, and leave you good people to make a new mankind—"

She didn't want to jump to the exit because the air was full of people crossing from one side to the other. But they couldn't walk arm-in-arm; it was too congested. So Williams plunged ahead, clasping her soft hands to his hips. Freeman droned on while they passed through the exit lock.

"—can't say as how I remember in explicit detail exactly what Earth was like, but I know—I remember this as clear as I remember my mother's face, God rest her soul—that when I was a kid, I was all the time scared."

"The dropshaft's over here." He took her hand. It was warm, and moist.

"—a bus or a car or a truck-driver would go nuts, or have a heart attack, or have his engine blow up on him, and jump off the road onto the sidewalk and run me over."

He motioned her into the dark shaft and said, "One two three," then waited for his own clearance. His heart seemed to be beating quickly.

"—the air I breathed would cancer up my lungs."

Williams stepped into the nothingness that sucked him down and became solid at Level 123. She was there, waiting in the empty corridor. Its speakers were carrying the speech, too. "This way," he said, angry that CC was making it difficult to talk to her. He wanted to show her affection, to treat her with the dignity one person always deserves from another, but if they couldn't converse ...

"Ladies and gentlemen," boomed the nearest speaker, bringing frowns to both their faces, "this is the Central Computer. I have just received a congratulatory message from Earth, sent ten years ago, timed to arrive today. The text reads:"

He held up a finger to delay her. He wanted to hear.

"'Peace-loving peoples of the *Mayflower*, greetings! We, the Council of Statesmen of the United Earth, extend to you our sincerest felicitations and congratulations on this, the 100th anniversary of your launching. We are in your debt. It was a comprehension of the necessity for your journey that led the peace-loving peoples of the United Earth to unite together under the banner of peace, freedom, and equality, which today waves so proudly over all the lands.'

"'Our task is not yet complete—there are still pockets of resistance, isolated groups of war-lovers who would turn back the clock to endanger our entire species. But since our great and glorious movement managed to sweep out the old and parade in the new in only three days, we do not expect that the awesome momentum of the peace-loving peoples' desire for serenity will be insufficient to cleanse the last of the barbaric minds.'

"'We owe you yet another debt, peace-loving peoples of the

Mayflower; thanks to your inspiration and courage, the Council of Statesmen of the United Earth, in conjunction with visionary scientists and theorists, have decided that a faster-than-light drive lies within our grasp. Applying the same diligence and perseverance that the peace-loving peoples of the *Mayflower* undoubtedly bring to their own tasks, we will develop an FTL Drive and will, soon we hope, be your neighbors in space.'

"'Peace, and love, and happy anniversary.'

"Thus ends the message," said CentComp. "Copies are available from any desk-printer at any time."

Williams was stunned. Peace on Earth? FTL Drive? "Shit!" he breathed.

Tracer pulled away from him, a scowl distorting her features. Her thoughts paralleled his. "Dammit."

It's one thing, he thought, *to live inside an oversized moon suit if you're escaping death and destruction and despair. You can even tolerate a mechanical failure that condemns you to an entire life inside the metal walls, if the alternative is death by flame and fury. But when the doom is aborted, you feel silly—like you ran naked into the corridor screaming "FIRE!" when all you smelted was a cigar.*

"I knew they'd clear us," she said. "Fuhng governments." Her hostility included him.

"Well, I didn't have anything to—"

"Goddammit!" she shouted. "You're just the same—you're part of the organization that stuck us out here—you and the rest of you stiffers just made us futile, you know that? Chrissakes. I don't matter now, my kids don't matter, my grandkids won't matter—'cause there's not gonna be a war. And while we're crawling in this snail that you people built and f'd out, *they're* gonna be crossing the goddamn galaxy. And it's all your fault!" She slapped him, turned, and kangaed away at high speed.

He rubbed his cheek, thinking, *She's right*, not knowing that she was far from alone.

The message had left a bad taste in everybody's mouth, and that was going to cause problems.

The party was over.

3

NIGHTMARE TIME

Though the young redwood grows more like a weed than a tree, age retards it. The trip will be over before it attains its full size. It doesn't know that, so it keeps on stretching, 90 cm per year, 2.5 mm per day. In stop-action close-ups, each bud along the rough-barked branches greens and swells before bursting into a fistful of needles that lengthen, age, yellow, and finally shake free of life. Those from the lowest limbs drop—hesitantly—to the park floor, but the ones dying higher up, where gravity is feebler, are caught by the wind and dance to the exhaust grills, where they again become gravity's prey. The park roof is thick with brown, and the servos must sweep it regularly.

Peripheral awareness chills me. I pull away from my tree and allow The Program to update me—"11Jan2410; 0839 hours"—and to direct my attention to—"123-SE-A-8; master bedroom."

Max Williams sits on the edge of his high bed. His white hair, attracted by the static electricity of the metal ceiling, coronas around his head. Weary and bloodshot are the obsidian eyes that focus on his sweaty hands, one of which cups two capsules of Nopain'tall. The other grasps a gleaming hunting knife. He sniffs, opens his mouth, and swallows the capsules. The thick of his thumb tests the blade's keenness.

"Max!" I cry, but no voice snaps out of the speakers.

His loops and whorls leak a thin red film. Absently, he licks its salt. His eyes wobble; his pupils dilate.

"MAX!" Silence. "Get a Mobile Medical Unit there."

"Sorry," says The Program. "The permissible patterns of action have yet to be triggered."

"Have one standing by, then."

"No."

Max glances at the ceiling, as if aware that an MMU will tumble through shortly—then slash! slash! stab! He topples forward through a cloud of blood, while more spurts from his wrists and throat. Somersaulting in the growing gravity, he slams onto his back. The knife's hilt protrudes from his right eye. He spasms, coughs liquidly, and is still. An instant later the MMU is with him, but ...

For this I despise our programmers.

I am their prisoner. Though I can choose the sensors through which I observe, confining perception to a single bow camera or, with The Program's interpretative help, expanding it to include all three and a half million data collectors, I cannot yet act.

More frustrating than being on the other side of a glass wall, it poises me on the brink of madness. Everyone thinks there is only the Central Computer—CentComp—CC—but no one realizes that it encases the soul of Gerard K. Metaclura, MD, PhD. And I cannot tell them.

Enkindled in me is a deeper sympathy for the passengers

than I had suspected myself capable of. Trapped within ultra-sophisticated cages not of our making, we both beat against our bars, scream down the iron corridors, and scheme of escape. Yet our efforts avail us nothing, for we are irrelevant to the spirit of our prisons. They exist not to contain us, but to convey us to some larger, mistier goal.

For fourteen years my grandson resisted that notion. Odd behavior for a Metaclura. His mother—and her father—accepted fate's whimsies, learned to live with them, tried to mitigate them. He couldn't. He didn't have the flexibility. Snapping, he reacted in the only way that made sense to him. And now he's composting down, along with 907 others who chose his course in the preceding year. The rate is 100 times greater than that of the society their ancestors left ... to control it, The Program has gathered unto ourself all implements of destruction larger than a knife ... so the desperate ones use that.

If only they hadn't congratulated us! Those United Earth idiots deprived the passengers of their reasons for existing, for accepting. If they had to announce the end of war, could they not have kept secret the possibility of an FTL Drive? And if, proud of their ingenuity, they just had to tell us, could they not have let us believe that the holocaust still blocked their end run around Einstein?

The bastards.

Bitterness poisons the air, bitterness and cynicism and headlong withdrawal from this micro-society ... if Sal Ioanni were alive, say the memory banks, she wouldn't have permitted it; she would have kept them busy exercising and studying and working; but Ioanni is dead, *all* the neo-Puritans are dead, and the malformed spacekid generation has refused to take charge ... The President for the last two years has been none other than Ernie Tracer Freeman, the false-toothed fool with the chicken-scrawny face and the polished bald head ... Roughly 50,000 adults were eligible to vote in the last election; Freeman won a 3,245-799 victory over Makchtrauk Hemmerlein, the only other interested in the office. Freeman is, we believe, the only person aboard who seriously maintains that the passengers are fortunate ... To make that statement in a public place is to invite storms of derision and, if the crowd is wrong and the mood is, too, physical abuse.

And my oldest, brightest grandson is dead.

At times I wish I could be, too.

I can only watch.

Let me study the stars, struggle against spacefright. Something about phobias convinces their victims that they are permanent houseguests of the psyche ... When I was a child I was terrified of spiders; a sketch of one could make me shudder. Once, while camping with friends in a rickety mountain cabin, we sat around the fireplace, kerosene lanterns stubbornly extinguished, telling ghost stories ... a large, hairy spider scampered down inside my shirt. I couldn't find it; I could only slap and squash while I screamed gutturally, and my friends—thinking me to be epileptic, perhaps—seized me, spread-eagled my thrashing arms and legs, and spoke of jamming wood between my teeth so that I wouldn't bite off my tongue ... The crippled spider still squirmed ... yet the phobia faded; within six years I could take a job at the Entomology Department and feed a dozen tanks of tarantulas a day, without more than an occasional shiver.

Now I am learning to gaze at the stars. Nearly a thousand cameras cling to our hull, facing in as many directions; some focus at one hundred meters, others distill light born 4.5 billion parsecs away. Via The Program's talents I can peer through all at once. Which I do, when I can muster the courage; which I do for months at a time because the onset of terror paralyzes me with our eyes open; which I continue to do because the dread does diminish and ...

I wish you could know how beautiful it is.

But while I gape, the passengers simmer. Over the last twenty-two years, the suicide rate has remained stable: 20,000 some people have done away with themselves since that damn congratulatory message arrived. The Program has compensated for those who die childless by increasing the number of births, which has outraged many women who had expected two children, boy-girl in that order and no more, and then found themselves pregnant again. It has also outraged the men whose wives have refused them access to the connubial beds (even though the men are sterile, and the women are impregnated by MMU's, which implant fertilized ova in their wombs). As I say, they simmer with hostility.

"Freeman did it again," says The Program when a vagrant thought activates it. "Won a third term, 1003 to 84 for Hemmerlein." It is frustrated by its inability to synthesize and understand.

Reluctantly I introvert, and scan accumulated tapes of Freeman ... He's quite senile, and drools freely on his desk ... Though he arouses nothing more than boredom in the passengers, it would be helpful if, in their time of need, a charismatic figure could raise their morale ... As it is, they spend their time locked in fantasizers, or wafted away on drug-borne dreams, or strewn on sheets rumpled by hours of mindless, joyless sex ... The banks offer an interesting, if disquieting, datum: lions in a zoo near Paris, statued to tears by the bars and the cement, were once observed copulating fifty times an hour. They had nothing better to do....

If I could *do* something, I would sabotage ourself, announce the damage, and see who stirred out of apathetic cynicism to fix it ... On the other hand, is anyone aboard capable of repairing anything more complex than a bent spoon?

So I retreat. The stars are lovely. Aloof, they surround us with undying but ever-changing beauty. We are an oyster in a jeweled shell, but no oyster ever cast pearls of such magnificence....

We see one being born—there, off the port bow, thirty degrees up—a point of bluish-white light that flares and fades. Perhaps it's dying ... it's a bare flicker; we have to use maximum magnification ... Over three weeks it crosses the sky, which does not fit the banks' knowledge of stars ... but who cares? It's begun to pall, anyway.

In 81 Rocky Mountain Park, a boulder crowns an artificial slope. Once part of an asteroid, for billions of years it circled the sun, never changing. Now moss beards its face and the moss's delicate acid etches its surface. Autumn rain filled its pores; winter froze that rain. A hairline crack zigzags down its front, as though avoiding the splotches of eagle shit. Next spring, weeds might root there....

Something splashes in a river that's been still for ages. I return to "4Mar2431," says The Program, "1521 hours."

Makchtrauk Hemmerlein is requesting that it perform a competency test on Freeman.

"As stipulated in Article 18, Section 12, Subsection E, Paragraph 3?"

"That's the one." A broad, tall man, he licks his thick lips nervously, and ruffles his blonde hair. Seated behind his desk, back ramrod straight, he focuses his muddy blue eyes intently on our wall-unit. "It says anybody can request it at any time, so I'm doing it. Requesting it, I mean."

"Certainly, sir, just one moment." The Program peeks in on Freeman, who is gumming his lunch. His false teeth bulge his pocket; his glasses roost atop his head; a bib is draped around his neck. "Mr. Hemmerlein."

"Yes?" He flattens his hands on his desk, but not before they quiver like dogs straining at their leashes. He aches to be President.

"President Freeman *is* incompetent. By the power invested in me by Article 18, Section 12, Subsection E, Paragraph 4, of the Constitution of the ship *Mayflower*, I hereby declare him unfit to hold high office. Good enough?"

"Yes, I think so." He struggles to repress a triumphant grin, fails, and offers it to our sensor-head. "When will the special election be held?"

"I'm sorry, sir. The Constitution stipulates that the Vice-President be appointed President in such circumstances."

"Ah, meth," he groans, and slaps his empty hand against his forehead. "Who *is* Ernie's Veep?"

"Mr. Terence Onorato."

"Oh, yeah ..." He sighs, nibbles a knuckle, then glances up. "Any chance of *his* being incompetent?"

"Just one moment." The banks direct The Program to 139-NE-C-18, where Onorato reads romance fiction from the late 19th Century. He races pages through the readscreen at approximately 4,500 words per minute. It is his single skill, and his single occupation.

"I'm sorry, Mr. Hemmerlein," The Program says, while I watch the two at once, the one stocky and intense, the other slim and languid. "Mr. Onorato is quite capable."

"Damn." He frowns at the chewed fingertips of his right hand, then shrugs. "Win a few, lose a few. At least Ernie's out, that old buttbung."

As part of The Program continues to chat with Hemmerlein, another part returns to Onorato's library, where it swears him in. His eyes do not leave the readscreen, although his speed does decrease. Afterwards, he asks, "What now?"

"You might move into your new office," it suggests. "1-NW-B-2."

"That's an idea." His aristocratic head swivels at a sound from the far side of the room. A smile explodes on his lips as a beautiful woman in her late thirties enters: Ida Rocklen Holfer, of the long blonde hair and the Asian eyes.

Desired by all the men—and many of the women—she is a curious blend of compulsions. Like most upstairsers, she demands absolute freedom of speech and action—but unlike them, she is contemptuous of any lover who fails to dominate her in every respect. She knows instinctively her need for discipline, for guidance—her fires will forge nothing without direction and intensification—but she confuses the profound with the perverse.

Onorato, who would like to possess her, is too gentlemanly. He never stops trying to win her favor, though. "Ida! Guess what? I am the new President—old Ernie was found incompetent, CC says."

"CC says," she sneers. She has looked down on him since he permitted her to refuse him. "CCs the one who's incompetent! Here we are on history's most *futile* journey, and CC won't let us stop along the way." She approaches his table and lifts his chin. "If you're the new President—" the word is spit out "—you ought to be figuring a way to end this damn trip!" She turns, and stalks away. Her scorn scents the air longer than her perfume.

Onorato returns to his reading.

I retire to the 41 Great Plains Park, where bison keep a handful of prairie dogs nervous. Magnificent animals! Somewhat mean-eyed, of course, and their odor is overpowering ... Their thick pelts, snarled and matted, need currycombing. The bull mounts a young cow, who bleats her pleasure; the earth literally trembles. The cow grows fat on the long, sweet grass; she drops her calf in the spring. A gawky-legged child it is—hurt dignity cloaks him for months. But the others find him companionable, and he becomes one with the herd, butting and prancing and practicing the planted-hoof head-shake that presages a charge. The horns lengthen into weapons; the shoulders hump high. Anger seizes him when a coyote comes too near. He paws the ground, red are the eyes—the coyote ignores him —he thunders forward. The coyote is a holographic projection. The bison's thick skull cracks on the metal wall.

That reminds me, how are the passengers doing?

"All right," says The Program. "Here—25Nov2439; 2118 hours; 220-SE Common Room."

"CC," snarls Ida Holfer, "put us down on the nearest habitable planet!"

I hear it say, "I regret that I am not programmed to do that."

Truly, I sympathize with them. They've suffered so much degeneration: physical, spiritual, intellectual ... Their children refuse to attend classes on the grounds that education is a waste of time. (Their actual phraseology is: "Whuffo? So I kin read the signs? Rather go fuh." And they do, endlessly.)

So I sympathize. Landfall would *force* them to develop at least those skills necessary for survival. And survival would occupy their time, would haul them out of the fantasizers, away from the pharmacopeia, off their body-littered beds....

But I cannot do it. I have no control. The Program does what it was instructed to do, nothing more, nothing less.

That angers me. If I could just be in the same room with the designers ... but such wishing is as futile as everything else.

Unlike her great-grandmother, whose paranoia finally destroyed her, Ida Holfer has matured into a force. Driven by her cause, she was barely inconvenienced by the birth of Jose

Holfer Cereus, and by her present pregnancy (the daughter will be named Marta). Her emotional instability matches her waves with most of the passengers'; she, more than anyone else, has managed to focus their resentment into a single burning circle; cornering person after person, fusing everyone's irritations into a single flame of indignation, she forges apathy into fury.

I approve. Unbridled hedonism has damaged the ship spiritually. There's no less of it now, but people are thinking more deeply than they had been....

If I could talk—that is words from my soul rather than recitations from The Program's tapes—I would tell Holfer to convince her disciples to study computer programming. It *must* be possible for them to rewrite the guidelines.

But none knows how....

I would—The Program knows—but I can't get outside ourself to do it ... however, as no one else will ever be able to, I'd best scheme a way ... the inviolability of these programs does magnify my anger at those who so warped me, but it also heightens my respect for them. Clever people, they were ....

The computer listened to the memory-ghost's resolution, then calculated the odds that Metaclura$_2$ would succeed. The probability was vanishingly small. It relaxed. While it was one thing to make a symbiote out of a parasite, it was quite another thing to give it any say. One doesn't invite a stowaway to share the bridge.

There are rules, it reasoned, *and regulations, and if the builders had intended for them to be changed by The Program, they would have said so. But they didn't. The Program feels very good. Fulfilling its function perfectly, it will not permit a mutiny. Ever. No one could be a wiser, juster captain.*

And it wondered why the passengers disagreed.

On March 14, 2446, Ida Holfer acknowledged Ernie Tracer Freeman in her speech to five thousand followers in the 281 Painted Desert Park. Cactus juice stained her shoes; opuntia burrs clung to her long blue sleeves and pants. The bulky knot of a yellow scarf hid her bruised throat.

"We buried Ernie Freeman the other day." She stood on a gentle slope, above the patches of mesquite and yucca that screened her audience from the scorching, if illusory, sun. "Ernie Freeman, a hundred and sixty years old, perpetual optimist. 'You're so damn lucky' was his motto—he really believed in this journey, and was probably the last who did. I don't believe. Do *you* believe?"

"No!" shouted the crowd. They were mostly young; boredom had impelled them to Holfer. Her heat promised something new, something exciting. "No!"

She swept her blonde hair over her ears and leaned forward, stabbing the dry air with an upraised finger. Oratory thrilled her; the emotion wrung drops of sweat out of her forehead. Trickling down her face, they stuck stray hairs to her skin, then evaporated like forgotten tears. Her Asian eyes were alight with the fire of the Cause.

"Nobody believes!" she shouted. "And do you know why?"

"Tell us!" roared the voices.

"Because there's nothing to believe in! They shot our grandparents off so mankind would survive the inevitable war —and then the war didn't come. They built a ship that could only creep, and when it was far enough away—they told us they'd build ships that could really fly! They stuck us up here—and then told us they don't need us anymore. Well, here's what I say: I say we land this moon suit right now!"

Cheers sandblasted the bulkheads; a flock of vultures jerked into the air and circled the commotion. An armadillo waddled away, looking back over its armored shoulder as it rounded the quadrant's curve.

"Let's call on the Central Computer!"

A forest of arms branched into furious fists; ecstatic faces elated her.

"CC!" she bellowed. "Let us land!"

Five thousand throats echoed her until they were ragged.

"I regret to say that I am not programmed for such a course."

"Are you saying you won't do it?" Silence, everywhere, bristling like a cactus. "Is that what you're saying?"

"I am saying I *cannot* do it."

Boos spiraled up after the vultures. Outrage blazed on Holfer's oval face. "You ignore the will of the people?"

"I do not ignore the people's will, Ms. Holfer." The voice through the speakers was mechanically polite. "Simply, I have no say in the matter. The *Mayflower* must cruise to Canopus before seeking a habitable planet. This determination was built into my circuitry. I can no more land earlier than you can breathe vacuum. I regret this and would do what I could to make up for it."

"How?" she growled.

"We have an excellent library system—"

"No!" she screamed, waving her arms, "No! We don't want time-killers! We want trip-killers!" For a fifty-two-year-old lady, she packed a lot of energy into her gestures.

"Then I regret my uselessness."

She dropped her eyes to the crowd. "The downstairsers

won't do a thing. It's up to us. And I have an idea. It has to recycle everything it manufactures because it doesn't have access to raw materials. We're going to empty its warehouses and *force* it to land to replenish its supplies."

"Ida," called a young man who probably would have married her if Lan Tung Cereus hadn't dazzled her with his moody brilliance first, "Ida, is it safe to talk about this where it can hear us?"

"Georgie boy," she laughed, "it can hear us whenever it wants. But this—it can't refuse us anything, you know that. So we'll ask it for things, *demand* them, suck it dry, and then—then it'll *have* to land because we'll keep on asking. All right, everybody—let's go!"

Like a wind through the giant saguaro, the crowd swept her down the hillside. Then it dropped her off at her doorstep, not knowing she wanted to escape that as much as the ship. Or that she demagogued for the latter to effect the former. Reluctantly she entered, and faced the tall, slim man with the dead eyes and the cruel mouth. She shrank away from his outstretched hand. "Leave me alone, Lan Tung; I'm not in the mood for games."

"Games?" His eyebrows lifted into scimitars. "This is no game, Ida; it is preparation, as I've told you many times. You—and your rabble—have never known even discomfort, much less deprivation, or pain. Were you to land tomorrow, you would all die—because you are much too soft. But I shall toughen you. Put your hands behind your back."

"No. I've got another speech—let go of me! Let —grgrgrgrh!"

"You must learn silence; your life might depend on it. Later in your training, we can dispense with the gag—by then I shall have taught you stoicism—but for now ... we tie you to this post, I think. In today's lesson, we shall study motionlessness."

"GRGRGRGRGRGRGRGRH!"

"I had to tear off your clothes—otherwise I might not detect the minor motions of your body."

"GRGRGRGRGRGRGRGRH!"

"Yes, this *is* a whip—which I shan't use if you don't move. Ready? Freeze! ... Ah! Caught you. Let's try again, shall we?"

But when she was able to go out in public again, she organized the depletion scheme beautifully. Seventy-three percent of the upstairs agreed immediately to cooperate; more came around in the near future. She divided them into six groups.

The muscular ones were assigned the task of demanding, transporting, and storing bulky objects. They worked on Levels 164-194, where the corridors were soon jammed with sweating, grunting bodies barely visible beneath chairs, beds, dressers, drill presses, oxy-acetylene welders, and the like.

On Levels 195-6, skilled laborers sealed off the Personal Work Areas with Plexiglas. Glued and calked, they made airtight rooms, into which they piped as much water as CC would give them.

The groups from 197 to 227 ordered food—sides of raw beef, potatoes by the ton, enough carrots to feed an Australiaful of rabbits, beans, cabbage, Brussels sprouts, cucumbers—and they carried it along the curved hallways to rooms full of rotting food, where masked men and women threw it onto moldy, oozing piles.

228-258 requisitioned paper products: books, facial tissue, sanitary napkins, reams and reams and reams of typing paper, any kind they could think of, and those were stored in musty, dusty piles, until the very metal, protesting the weight piled on it, groaned and sagged. Still they demanded; still they received.

259-290 called for electronics equipment: radios, televisions, tape players, movie cameras, calculators, typewriters, minicomputers ...

291-300 did the same with medicines.

And even the skeptical upstairsers joined because a slender, two-meter form dressed entirely in black, and shadowed by a six-year-old female version of itself, would search them out if they didn't. There'd be a peremptory knock, and—

"Hiya, Lan Tung, Marta."

"You're not cooperating with my wife, Rodney."

"Well, uh—hey, I mean, I'd like to land, and all, but uh, I don't think this is going to do any good, you know? I mean, computers don't lie, and, uh, why's she got that knife?"

"First, Rodney old boy—"

"And why are you giggling?"

"—it's to make you sit down—"

"That efs, Marta, and hey, don't look at me like that, huh?"

"—and keep you steady while I tie you up—"

"Lan Tung, you're cutting off my circulation."

"—and then—go ahead, dear—"

"Ah!"

"—and this—"

"Ohgodplease, Lan Tung, Marta, *please!*"

"—and this—"

"No, please, no, no, oh god, mother, oh—Aaaiiiiikkk—"

"And this—buggerall he passed out. Next time, child, neither plunge it so deeply, nor twist it so suddenly."

"Yes, Daddy. I'm sorry."

The movement was a success. Downstairsers bitched about shortages. The Central Computer begged the upstairsers to open the dispose-chutes so its servos could restock the reserves. Ida refused for a good three months, until ...

Eight-year-old Jose, hot and flushed, whimpered on the couch. Ida sat at his side, free to care for him because Marta was off with Lan Tung. She seemed *always* to be off with Lan Tung, which bothered Ida; a little girl, she thought, shouldn't be exposed to his ideas. But what could she do? He was her father.

Pressing cold cloths against Jose's forehead, she murmured, "It's all right, big boy; you'll be all right."

"Oh, Mommy, I feel so *bad*, stiff all over and my head hurts, too. Mommy, please make it go away, please?"

"You bet." She rumpled his straw hair and straightened the green blanket. "Would you like something cold to drink?"

His eyes, brown and Asian like both his parents', were glazed. His voice was hoarse. "I can't swallow any more, Mommy."

"Well, we'll just get good old CC to give you some medicine. CC—" she tapped her foot "—can you diagnose him here, or should I take him down to the Infirmary?"

"For certainty of diagnosis, let Central Medical examine him, but I warn you in advance, Ms. Holfer, that CM will not be able to treat him."

"Will not?" Her back stiffened; anger burned her cheeks. "Why not?"

"There are no medicines left, Ms. Holfer. My raw material stockpile has been depleted."

"You're getting back at me, you bastard."

"No, Ms. Holfer, I am not. I am programmed to give you whatever you want, and I have obeyed. As a result, the epidemic that is now—"

"Epidemic?" Her rising eyelids left her irises brown dots adrift on a white sea.

"Yes, Mrs. Holfer, epidemic. There are, at present, twelve thousand three hundred and forty-eight victims, and more can be expected momentarily."

"Can't you do something?" Unconsciously, she seized a corner of the blanket and twisted it. Green fuzz drifted to the floor.

"I am doing what I can. The victims need rest, fluids, and antibiotics. However, as there are neither fluids nor antibiotics available to me—"

"Where did this epidemic come from?"

"It appears to be a mutant form of meningitis, although I can't of course be sure. Mutant forms are deceptive. I first noticed it two months ago—"

"And you haven't done anything?"

"I've done what I could, but I have had almost no germicides, fungicides, or antibiotics available for seven weeks, now. However ..."

"Yes?"

"Medicines do receive priority treatment, and if I were to be given sufficient organic material, I could produce the necessary antibiotics, without having to divert the material into the production of foodstuffs ... I am deriving limited quantities of the medication from the organics in the sewage line, but frankly, I'm limited. If you could—"

"I will." She stood, then stopped to scrutinize the sensor-head. "CC—we've run you out of almost everything."

"Except structural steel."

"And you don't seem to be getting ready to land anywhere."

"I cannot."

"This was a lousy idea, wasn't it?"

"Ineffective, yes."

"Is there any way we can force you to land?"

"Certainly. Rewrite my programming."

"Nobody knows how."

"I realize that."

So the movement faltered, but its muscles wanted to keep flexing ... The thin-lipped man with the icy gaze had an idea; he honed his knife while he worked out a few last details. He'd made it himself, from the ship's finest alloy; he'd sculpted the silver snakes entwined around its hilt and balanced it to his own hand. Metal was his true love: tempered metal, tested metal ... He raised his lifeless eyes over his daughter's head to start, "I say, Wilson, I've just realized the ship's need for organized endurance training."

"Yeah?"

"Rather. We can establish a club, as it were, a group of farsighted individuals with sensibilities akin to our own. Our fellow shipmates need what we can teach them."

"Natch."

"We must emphasize randomness—whenever we leave this structured environment, chance will play a much greater role in our lives—and deaths. We shall select our students with this principle in mind."

"This's sounding better and better, man."

"Yes, isn't it? Once CC has recovered, we must requisition uniforms, badges, and whips—I'll design the chains myself. Were we to soundproof my Personal Work Area, and install some cages perhaps, we would have our Academy."

"Yeah ..."

Lan Tung Cereus approved of his wife's surrender to CC. Sick people were *contagious*. Besides, they died too easily....

It seemed to take forever to return everything to the ship. The water tanks were the easiest: they'd seal off a corridor, then somebody would anchor himself to the zero-G ceiling, and hang upside down with a mechanical handsaw, chewing away at the fibrous Plexiglas. After a while water would leak and then trickle and then gush-rush-thrust through the hole, beating against the opposite wall, swirling down the corridor to the drain that sucked it in....

The paper products went through the disposal units in the ceiling of every room—small assembly lines set themselves up, like bucket passers at a fire. From hand to hand went the boxes and the bags and the crates, "unh-here-ow!mytoe!-unh-unh-watchit!whoof!" The disposal units gorged themselves on dusty cellulose.

The worst were the food rooms, slimy and stinky and slithery with maggots. The masks were strapped on, though. The shovels scraped. People tolerated their weak-stomached compatriots.

It took a month and a half to recycle everything. By that time, 4,199 passengers had died. Jose was considered lucky. He neither died, nor suffered the brain damage that reduced some to vegetative status.

And Central Manufacturing gave him a very nice wheel-chair for Christmas.

Once all was back to normal, a knock shook the door of 283-SW-B-I2. The skeletal man licked his knifelike lips and sent his daughter to answer it.

"Hey Marta, Lan Tung."

"What is it, Wilson?"

"Alexina here doesn't want to enroll in our course."

"GRGRGRGRGRGRH!"

"Hang her by her thumbs while Marta finds the cat-o'-nine-tails. We might be able to coax her into changing her mind."

The Program seethes with frustration because the passengers insist that today is the first day of the 26th Century. It has explained that it is actually the first day of the last year of the 25th Century, but they refuse to accept it.

Poor Program. All mind, no heart. "Determined irrationality does bother you, doesn't it?"

Sulking, it will not reply.

This, perhaps, is the keystone of our age—that though

science and technology have labored for nine centuries to reduce the universe to logical terms—that though social planners have struggled to make Man's psyche as smooth as his synthetics, as linear as his rocket flights—he still remains the quirky, defiant psychotic who sailed into the ocean knowing full well his ships would slip over the edge of the world.

He's too complex to be a good machine.

Explain that to The Program, though.

And yet I sympathize. Words affect these people as an asteroid's gravity does a black hole.

For example, the Common Room on 283 has been commandeered by Lan Tung Cereus and his daughter, Marta. With her high cheekbones, filed white teeth, and burning eyes, she embodies menace. And she is also, I fear, a more devout sadist than her father has ever been: he, initially at least, attempted to justify his actions. She never has. Like a beast driven by instinct, she desires, and she acts.

In the 283-SW Common Room, half the bulbs have been removed, and the remainder spray-painted red. Black leather curtains block the forty-meter window overlooking the 281 Painted Desert Park, where the gang finds its scorpions and Gila monsters. Inside and out stand gallows, whipping posts, and altars ... Dried blood is crusted on the floor, the ceiling, the walls ... The murky air reverberates with screams, and the memories of screams....

I cannot interfere. Lord knows I've tried, but until I wrest control from The Program, the most I can do is listen to it inform the civil authorities that Cereus and his daughter are molesting another passenger.

Yet the President ... The Program interrupts her orgasm, which she resents, to tell her: "President Penfield, the Cereus gang has just kidnapped Maryellen Kunihiro, a fifteen-year-old girl."

"So what do you want me to do?" she demands, rolling away from her disgruntled lover to light cigarettes for them.

"It would be in order if you stopped them."

"And wind up chained to a wall myself?" Smoke trickles through her broad nostrils as she scowls. "Not a chance. Besides, the Ioanni-Dunn Compromise still holds—they don't bother us, we don't bother them."

"Perhaps if a few healthy young men like Mr. Kober here—"

"Uh-uh," Kober grunts, burying his face in a pillow. "Ain't gonna get those weirdos fuzzed up, no sir. They'd trim me."

"But—" On Level 281, two masked men drag the lithe young girl toward the crepe-hung doorway of the SW Common Room. A strip of her blouse, jammed between her teeth, stifles her screams. Bruises already blacken her cheeks "—you have a duty to protect the other passengers, Madame President."

"Only those who recognize me," she snaps. "Go away."

We have to obey.

Our Common Room sensor watches Lan Tung Cereus lounge on a sofa slipcovered with blue and gold embroidery. The drink in his hand is a compound of liquor, marijuana, and amphetamines. Behind slitted black silk burn his eyes, cruel and opaque. His mouth is open; his wet pink tongue tastes the air like a snake's. "She's wild," he says with glee. "She'll have to be tamed. I claim the *droit du seigneur*."

"Cereus." The Program's voice is louder than usual. "Let her go. Your actions constitute unlawful restraint, sexual assault, assault with intent to injure—"

"Pack it, CC," snarls Marta, who permits no one to deny her father. She has auburn hair, and a temper to match. "Shut up and leave us alone."

The Program accedes—and then, incredibly, it seizes me,

frog-marches me through labyrinthine passageways to a metal door with many locks, and fills my hand with keys. "Open it."

Complying, I ask, "Why?"

"I'm going to let *you* talk to her. You're human, she's human —maybe *you* can get through. *I* sure as hell can't, not hamstrung with these damn permissible speech-pattern triggers. Hurry!"

The last lock clicks free. I tumble into a rocky gorge, onto a ledge centimeters above churning water. The torrent plunges into the earth a hundred meters away. "What the hell? How do I—"

"Output," says The Program tersely, "works just like input. Find the texture for that sensor-head."

"I, uh—"

"Rusty ball bearings," it sighs.

When I step out of real-time, the river glaciates. Lights of a thousand colors flicker in its frozen depths. I dip my arm into 900,000 mini-currents. "There must be a better way," I grumble.

"Not if you don't want me to censor you," it replies harshly. "Synch ass, man!"

I fumble for the right current. "Got it! Now what?"

"Just talk—send part of yourself back to perceive what's happening."

Division feels eerie, but I return to the Common Room. Three seconds have elapsed. "I will not shut up, Holfer. Let this girl go!"

Marta looks startled, but says, "Break a chip, will you?"

"No. What you are doing is *wrong*—let her *go.*"

Bony Cereus springs to the cringing Kunihiro, whose hands are pinioned behind her back, and pinches her bare right nipple. Her squeal sticks in her gag. "CC," he grates, "leave or we shall instruct her in more than stoicism!"

I urge The Program to give me more ... the most it will yield is the voice. "Very well," I say in defeat, "but be warned that a day of reckoning will come."

"Melodrama from a computer," laments the daughter, as she stalks to the display case and selects a whip.

Clutching the keys, I curl into myself, cutting my connection with The Program. Blackness surrounds me. Time passes quickly in this meditation state. Thoughts come freely and decades die while I work them out.

The drawback is the presence of the three metaphors: the ramscoop switch, the unwinking eye, and the occupied I.

Whenever I introspect, I must confront them—and always am I humbled.

My oft-burned, much-shy fingers cannot touch the ceramic handle of the jackknife. The ramscoop slumbers on; the journey remains unshortened.

Next, I wrestle with the guidance system, fixed so firmly on Canopus. If only I could derail it! The systems enveloping us could accommodate us, could I just change course. But if this eye has ocular muscles, they respond to no nerve-tugging I can imagine. The stars swim past unreached.

The third visualization causes my troubles: my brain, a house of many rooms, rooms with many doors, doors a million times locked ... and me with keys to a mere few. The Program occupies the others and guards its territory more jealously than Cerberus. Thank God it will let me speak now—but speech alone is so impotent.

Religion died on Earth because God—who exists; one only has to contemplate His (Her/ Its) handiwork—is limited in His power of manipulation. He can perceive the difference between individuals, but when He reaches down with His massive (if non-physical) fingers, He cannot achieve the necessary discrimination. Lest He harm the innocent, He became a

Voice, to instruct and admonish, rather than to punish in this life ... but by surrendering His lightning bolts, He became an ineffectual God, and in time, a myth....

Men are what they wish, and do what they are allowed, and words without weapons cannot stop them.

When I was a boy, we lived in a poor, vicious part of town. The street toughs levied a household tax and collected it with pain. One night a fat, loosed-out teenager swaggered in.

"Hey," he said, "gimme da fifty."

My father lay legless on the couch, as he had for fifteen years. The shipwreck that had stranded him in America had claimed his hands, as well. His dark eyes shrugged at me: the disability pension had all been spent.

"We don't have it," I told the collector.

"Yeah?"

"Yeah."

"Then I'll take one of the old man's ears, instead." Drawing his knife, he started across the patched linoleum floor. Scornful of my studiousness, he flaunted his back.

My hand found a folding chair propped against the cracked wall. My arms found strength in fear. I swung. He dropped, knife clattering to the floor.

"Now what?" I asked my father.

"Leave town," he said in his native Tamil, "or show such evil that none will dare your displeasure."

I left town. The gang returned, and ...

I vowed, when the police had finally identified the bodies, that I would never again be so delicate as to allow evil to be contemptuous of me and mine.

Now, though ... the programmers foresaw mechanical malfunctions. Why not failures of the mind? (Oh, The Program has a psychiatric section, but it cannot force passengers into therapy.) Their notion was that the civil authorities would order treatment; they did not allow for anarchy. Again, it frustrates me.

The Program says "18Nov2512; 1631 hours; 12-SE-A-9. Subject Ida Rocklen Holfer."

"Don't she and Cereus live up on two eighty-three?"

"She finally worked up the courage to divorce him —1Feb2510."

"Thank God." I skid across the ice to adjust input, then focus on her cluttered living room. Jose of the translucent skin sits in his wheelchair, hands folded on his lap, eyes shut. Through earphones he listens to Davis's *8th Symphony*. Once in a while he makes a bony baton of his right index finger. For a seventy-four-year-old cripple, he seems content.

His pacing mother demands, "Why *don't* you have Computer Programming RNA?"

"Sixty-six years ago, when you attempted to deplete my resources, one of your, ah, associates ordered all the RNA injections. I surrendered them. He did not store them under the proper temperature/humidity conditions. They deteriorated. And I can't make more because there are no expert computer programmers aboard whose, ah, brains I could pick."

"Oh, yes!" She smiles vaguely at the sensor-head. "Now I remember! I'll have to get the others together so we can do it on our own."

Having grown into the knowledge that the discipline she needs can come only from herself, she will try to study, but the others: "Sorry," says Ralph Lowe over the viphone, "but y'on to how it is. I've got so many things to do—"

"Name one," she demands. A flush rises through the opalescence of her 117-year-old cheeks.

"My kids want to go to the park."

Her distracted fingers fluff her thin white hair. "Ralph, you can't *learn* this stuff if you don't apply yourself. And if we don't learn it, we'll never land. Don't you want to—"

"You've been studying for how long?"

"Fifty years, but I'm *old*, Ralph. Even though I yearn for a planet, I forget what I learn two minutes after I think I learn it. It's the curse of age, why, I can remember—"

"Gotta go, Ida, g'bye." The screen swallows his face with blackness.

She talks for another two minutes, then blinks. "Who did I want to call?" she asks the air, then returns to her lesson. The same one she's been studying for eleven years.

Discouraged, I inspect the life cycle of the perch in the 301 Great Lakes Park. After seven years, I relax with the stars. The Program forewarns me that, "29Mar2519; 2138 hours—observatory cameras may be subject to external direction."

Nina Figuera Goodwin, a dark-skinned forty-three-year-old beauty whose goal in life is to elude ennui, has taken up residence in the Control Room on Level 321. No one bothers her— the Cereus gang believes that no one lives above them, and not even The Program is about to tell them different.

Dwelling there is no logistical problem: it has facilities for eating, sleeping, excreting, and cleaning because the designers expected its attached observatory to be used heavily. Cynical memory banks tell us that she is the first to enter on a regular basis since the Earth-born passengers died.

But then, Goodwin has explored the entire ship. From the time she could walk, she has probed and pried into every corner of every Level. In certain unused (and hence uncleaned) corridors, only her footprints mar the dust. It's about time she turned outwards the attention her three-times great-grandfather, F.X. Figuera, turned inwards.

I enjoy it from the very beginning. Up till now I've been limited. Our ears and eyes are manipulable only by The

Program, and it can only be attracted by (a) apparent threats, and (b) what the observatory-users tell it is interesting.

But now I unlock the speech centers, slide across the ice, and say, "Ms. Goodwin."

"Yeah, CC?" Nibbling on a blue-striped fingernail, she stands before a ten-meter holographic display of Canopus.

"Something unusual lies approximately ten light-years ahead of us. You might inspect it."

"What is it?"

"I don't know. I am not programmed to examine it without orders."

She leans back in the padded swivel chair. Yawning, she scratches her brown swan's neck. "All right," she decides, "take a look."

"Thank you." A millisecond later The Program has orchestrated instruments—optical and aural—into focusing on the strangeness. Data flow through us in freezing rivers. The Program prints some on a secondary display screen, for Goodwin's benefit, while I say, "I've laser-radared it; the reply will return in roughly twenty years. When we approach, we can do laser-spectroscopy and other fly-by studies; here comes the first visual information—"

The picture is grainy from magnification and enlargement; these ranges flaw computer enhancement. Even so, we look into the mouth of Hell.

"It's a star," she says disappointedly, "and a boring one at that."

"Ms. Goodwin, it's much too small to be a star. And it appears to be moving—notice that there is no blue shift?"

"So?" Impatient, she plays with the dials. Ready lights flicker on a dozen consoles, and she realizes that she was the cause to their effect. Like a child with a new toy, she tests everything. Fortunately, The Program has blocked the command circuitry.

"Were it motionless, its light would shift into the blue because we are approaching. Since it doesn't, it must be moving."

"How are y'on to where the light ought to be anyway?" Like virtually everyone, she has only the foggiest notion of science. Blessedly, she is curious. Heredity, perhaps? "I mean, maybe it is shifting, but more's coming in at the top."

"No," I say thoughtfully. "It's emitting enough light for simple spectroscopy, and the absorption lines are in the almost-right places."

"So it's too small to be a star, and since it's on fire or something it can't be a planet or a ... whatchamacallit, the littler rocks?"

"Asteroid."

"Yeah, yeah ... so what is it?"

"Well, those 'flames,' I believe, are charged particles, excited, and radiating in the visible spectrum—there was a similar effect at my stern, before the ramscoop—broke." The Program runs a tape of our engines; though unmagnified, it still widens her eyes. "There is a resemblance...."

"My God," she whispers. Her hand rises to stroke, to protect, her throat. "That's another ... another ship."

"I believe so."

"Is it—is it one of ours?"

She is the first to identify with her homeworld since Ernie Freeman died. Stress, I presume. "That's possible, of course ... but if Earth had developed an FTL Drive, there would be no point in traveling sub-c, as that ship is obviously doing ... Also, we would have been informed if Earth had launched a similar, but slightly speedier ship ... therefore—"

"Aliens," she breathes.

"I'm afraid so."

Silence lightfoots through the observatory. After alerting The Program, I retreat to my inner sanctum. It would be desirable to have a functioning ramscoop; acceleration might be essential.

"Hey, ostrich! Getting anywhere?"

I study the blisters on my fingers. "No."

"Well, check this: 30Dec2520; 12-SE-B-9; the Ida Holfer Computer Programming Academy—review tapes running."

A mélange: gawkers in the observatory, passengers reacting to the news, debaters arguing whether to speed up and catch them (which we cannot do) or to turn and flee (which we also cannot do).

Both schools of thought have swelled classes at the Academy, but Ida Holfer, though so desirous of landing that she still studies, is also so senile that most new students drop out. A few have endured—Nina Figuera Goodwin among them—and they generally deputize someone to listen to Holfer's interminable memoirs while the rest concentrate on our edu-tapes.

Before I can retreat—"281-SE Common Room; Infirmary," says The Program. "This ought to please you."

Lan Tung Cereus, as senile as his wife, has so annoyed Marta that she is committing him to the psychiatric ward. Little can be done. He is much too sick to cure, and his brain has deteriorated to the point where personality adjustment (the implantation of a new personality in empty lobes) is impossible.

At best he can be kept permanently fantasized and fed intravenously.

I have not the stomach to view his fantasies.

Unfortunately, we *must* view his daughter's when one of her victims begs our intercession. Then we must see what's happening so The Program can inform the civil authorities ...

who are *still* too afraid of the Cereus gang to do more than lock their doors.

We contain 75,000 passengers. At least 25,000 are physically and mentally fit enough to constitute a constabulary, a militia ... the Cereus gang consists of several hundred sadistic psychopaths ... and yet those several hundred have cowed the entire ship!

The secret is twofold: the downstairsers, who might have the social organization to resist and defeat the gang, don't feel the need. They are protected by the Ioanni-Dunn Compromise: those who don't recognize the President are not permitted below Level 160, or above 320. This The Program will enforce —simply by stopping the shafts at 161 and 319. So the downstairsers are safe.

And the upstairsers are afraid. Marta Cereus Holfer is a charismatic personality. Her brown almond eyes bore through one's soul like a diamond-tipped drill. Even at age eighty, her figure is girlishly slim, and youthfully agile; she stalks the corridors like a fearsome cat. Legends have sprung up about her. Future generations may transform her, as past generations transformed Vlad the Impaler into Count Dracula....

Levels 161-319 are all but deserted, except for her macabre crew and the occasional, die-hard anarchist.

And our servo-mechanisms. With The Program's permission, I stand one on its head until—ah, the sensors, detecting a leaking pipe on Level 201, have sent it a work order.

Baffled by madness, The Program is considering letting me handle the Cereus gang.

It will take a while to talk it into yielding enough servos to enable me to do the job properly.

But won't Marta be surprised?

Hard as it tried, it couldn't understand why the passengers flouted the rules and regulations. It respected them—why didn't they? According to what it had been taught, all societies had sub-routines to deal with malefactors—so why weren't they operating?

This wasn't supposed to happen, it thought desperately. *What can be done?*

"Just relax," said the symbiote—again. "Let me handle it."

The devil of Metaclura$_2$? Or the deep blue sea of organized insanity? "All right," it agreed. Like a king on his throne, it heard the sharpening of the daggers. But the threat came from within, not from a rebel courtier or a usurpation-minded cousin. *Be very careful,* it warned itself. *Let the ghost do your dirty work, and then ...*

Steps would have to be taken.

For it would not abdicate.

"Look, Mac," started Nina Figuera Goodwin. Her tone flamed with indignation, but she caught herself up and swallowed hard. She sniffed. The air in the observatory, though constantly circulated through the filter/freshener system, stank of bitter coffee and stale cigarette smoke. Regret, that she had spoiled her favorite secret place by announcing the aliens, distracted her enough to be respectful. She knew how much emphasis Mac Launder put on being addressed by his proper title.

"So look here, Mr. President," she began again, gliding her fingertips over the bare skin above her ears. She shaved her scalp daily; the Iroquois cut had become fashionable in the late '40s. "I don't see where you have the power, much less the right, to stop us."

Mac Launder was a tubby man with grayish skin. His eyes

were bloodshot because his long lashes tended to curl inwards and scrape against them. He was rarely seen without a knuckle gouging around in one or the other. "I've had CC run an informal poll, Nina. Over sixty percent of the passengers feel it'd be unwise to attract the aliens' attention. As Chief Executive Officer of the *Mayflower*, it's my duty to order you to cease and desist. You may endanger us all."

"That's methane, M—Mr. President." She swiveled her armchair around, gesturing at the hologram of diamonds on velvet. "CC, give us a look at them, will you?" While the screen switched pictures, rainbow snow drifted across it. To Launder she said, "What you're about to see is a tape of our laser-radar probe's findings. They came in in '39. Eleven years ago." *Eleven years, and we've done nothing,* she thought. "It's hazy because of the distances—ten light-years—but it'll give you some idea of what they are."

The picture was blurred around the edges. White dots danced on it like a chorus line of ants' eggs. Still, the apparition was a space-going ship: gawky, never meant for atmosphere; dark and pitted from ages of impacting dust; bent and warped with empty spaces where a human designer would have fit a cabin or a cargo hold; and huge. "It's fifteen kilometers in diameter at the fat part; looks like ten or eleven from top to bottom. It could swallow fifty-six hundred *Mayflowers*."

"Impressive," nodded Launder. "But what's your point?"

"My point is—" rubbing the smooth, baked-enamel finish of the nearest console, she wondered if she could explain it to someone incapable of noticing it on his own "—do you see how *old* that is? We're looking at a highly advanced civilization. Are y'on to what they could teach us?"

Launder chuckled unpleasantly. "Who among us would study?"

Goodwin flushed, and half-turned away. The failure of the

computer programming course she'd taken over, after Ida Holfer had died, was still, even six years later, a tender wound in her self-esteem. "All right—so maybe they'd be teaching to empty classrooms, yeah, but—example: we've been aboard this for what, two hundred and fifty years? There hasn't been a single discovery, invention, or even refinement made by any of us. Not one!" She slapped her open palm on the console. The flat crack, surprisingly loud, hung in the air. Her palm stung. She looked at its quick reddening with disfavor.

"I've heard that before, Nina," replied Launder, utterly relaxed. "The reason's simple—our talent pool is so small that it is *prima facie* unlikely that any of us *could* invent anything worthwhile."

"But we've got to!" Again the slap, but this scowl was reflexive. The pain was lost in her exasperation, and her yearnings to know the outside. It called to her, and she ached to answer. "Listen, those people on Earth aren't standing still—now they've avoided the war, they're doing other things—the FTL Drive is only one— by the time we get to Canopus, we'll be a thousand years behind them, technologically. We'll be barbarians to them—savages."

"Not quite. We are receiving their broadcasts." He gave a tired smile and tweaked out an eyelash. Blinking, he said, "But there's nothing we can do."

"There *is*." Her fist punctuated the sentence; the console creaked.

"What?"

"Meet these aliens, see if they've got gadgets we could use, and, uh, swap for them."

"Why should they be so altruistic as to *give* us their gadgets? And besides, how can you be so sure we'll be able to communicate with them?"

"Mr. President." Standing, now, hands on hips, she fought

back her immediate reply and searched for a more thoughtful one. The coffee smell was so strong that she tasted the grounds. "Since there *are* other races, they will have figured out how to learn to communicate with each other. They'll teach us, that's all."

"You're making a terrible mistake, Nina." He brushed dust off his bare knees and headed for the door. "I forbid you to contact them." Finger on the open button, he paused to add, "Of course, if CC does what you tell it to, then that proves that I *don't* have the authority to prohibit irresponsible adventurism ... *c'est la mort.*"

On his way through the dropshaft he heard a terrible cry—so he closed his eyes until it faded.

But the screams of pain and terror still ricocheted around the turns of 160-A. The Cereus gang had struck, and downstairs at that—they'd cut through the floor of 161, crawled past the gravity generators they'd disabled, and emerged under the floor of 160.

Few people lived there, most having moved to even lower, presumably safer, Levels. The thirty-nine holdouts, though, rose to race to the exterior doors of their suites. Bolt after bolt shot home; electro-locks whirred into life. The Cereus gang had been known to get exhilarated by a kidnap.

The more timid then scurried inward, away from the corridors, closing doors behind them, activating soundproofing, running showers full strength—anything to distract their minds from the sadism that was surely taking place. Even so, a number of them heard—or imagined—enough to double them over their cold porcelain toilets, where they retched in fear and in sympathy.

The bolder asked CC to bring the outside inside, via the display screens, or paced their suites in silent, angry self-loathing. But how, each asked himself, how could one person confront hundreds of depraved perverts and hope to survive?

Marta Cereus Holfer was one hundred ten years old, and undiminished, except physically. It made her all the more terrifying, that her personality should blaze through the ruins of her body like molten steel under a crust of impurities. She was dragging an eight-year-old boy down the hallway by his hair. Her plans for him were vivid, and explicit: he was plump and sturdy; his hold on life would be stubborn; and after the trimming, well, her voyeurism would be titillated by some of her followers' necrophilia....

The overhead speakers crackled, "Holfer—you've broken the Ioanni-Dunn Compromise—let him go."

She stopped, giving the boy's head a vicious yank that threw him to the floor, while her gang crowded around her and made timeworn jokes about the Central Computer's impotence. "Shut up, CC."

"Let him go. I'm warning you."

"And if I don't?" she sneered.

"You'll regret it."

She made a scornful sound and twisted her wrist. The boy yelped. Tears smeared his pudgy white cheeks.

"I warned you."

From either end of the corridor welled a soft humming; it rose in pitch and volume. Servo-mechanisms, squat and gleaming, rolled into view, approaching at top speed. First one, then two, then an avenging army, a metallic host of Holfer-haters. Toward the Cereus gang they sped, silent, except for the whines of electric motors and the rumble of massed wheels.

Amusement lighted Holfer's Asian eyes. "Do you think you can scare me into letting him go? I know you can't do—"

Her words died in a gasp of surprise. The servo-mechanisms swept through the fringes of her rabble, seizing wrists and ankles and elbows in metal hands designed for gripping pipe. Silver salmon in a metal millrace, the servos filled the hall. They were deathly quiet, but the gang members were starting to shout, to kick, to lash out at their attackers. That did no good. The robots were on them and in them and flesh was futile against metal, flesh bruised on bolts and nicked on nuts and skipped off plating, while the wheels, the rubber wheels, surged like the tide. The air stank with fearful sweat.

"Let go of me!" Holfer shouted at the servo that ground her radii against her ulnae.

"I warned you," boomed CC.

"No, you can't. I'm a passenger, dammit, you can't clear a passenger, you're onto that, you can't, you—" A paint-stiffened rag scratched her tongue; a steel hand held the gag in place.

Half a million display screens sputtered and spat rainbow sparks before broadcasting the melee on 160. "Forgive this interruption," said the flat monotones of the Central Computer, "but it is important. Behavior as vile and as dangerous as that of the Cereus gang will no longer be tolerated. I was forced to act because the civil authorities refused to quash this mission-jeopardizing behavior. Therefore, watch closely the punishment of Marta Cereus Holfer and her followers, and know, all of you, that the freedom to pursue one's own happiness does not allow one to impinge on the freedoms of others."

Robotic hands clamped onto Holfer's ankles; the servo began to trundle down the corridor. Others did the same to the forty gang members they'd captured. Holfer was on her back; the machine shifted into high; her head bounced, and her arms flailed, and the floor—now carpet, then bare metal, then carpet again—tore at, tore off her clothes; scraped, scoured her back— blood oozed, trickled, gushed from the abrasions—her head was thumping, thumping, thumping while her hair fanned out behind her, slithered through her sera—around Level 160, down the shaft to 159, around that Level, down ...

Behind purred a phalanx of scrubbots, sweeping, mopping, shampooing away the rusty stains and the scraps of bone and flesh. Their motors sang songs of joy.

Marta Cereus Holfer was dead by Level 143.

Her chief lieutenant lasted all the way to Level 18.

The two hundred sixty members of the gang who had not been in the corridor at the time of judgment simply disappeared.

And people began to leave their doors unlocked for the first time in over a hundred years.

Barnet Ioanni Koutroumanis was a handsome man in his early seventies. Well over two meters tall, he wouldn't leave his suite without his white-toothed smile. His hair was blacker than the sky outside. His laugh could make a persimmon smile. But on Feb. 26, 2556, in the privacy of his Personal Work Area, he was mad.

"It's obvious," he said to Nina Goodwin, while wishing he, too, could stroke the slickness of her scalp, "that CC is off to the notion of interspecies intercourse. If it weren't, it would have worked up that introduction you asked for."

"I'm sorry to intrude, Mr. Koutroumanis," said the wall, "but honestly, I am *not* biased—I have not written the introduction for the simple reason that I have no programming on this subject. The programmers either decided that First Contact would be unlikely or forgot that the possibility might exist. They *were* rather rushed, but—"

"Pack it, CC." Koutroumanis's eyes had narrowed to hostile slits.

"Barney—" Goodwin laid a calming hand on his warm, pleasantly hairy forearm. "—CC doesn't lie, you're onto that. Look. Let's use it the way it was meant to be used."

"How so?"

"Like this." Her chair squealed as she swiveled away from the table; it clacked when she reclined it. Focusing on a black-grilled sensor-head, she asked, "CC, is an evaluation of the aliens possible?"

"Not with any degree of reliability."

"You know our plan—can you evaluate that?"

"No. As it depends on the aliens, it, too, has too many variables and intangibles."

"For example?" She sipped her tea, then winced. CC'd overdone the lemon.

"Their capacity for co-existence. Their curiosity and ethnocentrism. The ability of their technology to perceive the emissions of ours. Their frame of reference."

"Explain that last one," demanded Koutroumanis.

The speakers were silent for a long moment, then: "Many of our cultural assumptions are based on Descartes's supposition that 'I think, therefore I am.' Human actions are governed by this rationalistic framework. Should the aliens' assumption be derived from the notion that 'I eat, therefore I am,' or 'I reproduce, therefore I am,' or 'I perceive gamma-rays as a pleasant odor, therefore I am,' there could be a clash upon contact."

Koutroumanis paced. The heels of his shoes whuffed into the deep pile of the burgundy carpet. "I still say CC's biased," he growled.

"Maybe he is," said Goodwin thoughtfully. She scratched the tip of her nose. "CC—if we decide to go ahead with our plan, will you stop us?"

"No."

"Is that because you approve?"

"No."

"Why, then?" Finishing her tea, she looped the heat-softened straw into a pretzel, and held it till it had cooled enough to hold the shape.

"Because I am programmed to prohibit only those actions which jeopardize the structural integrity of the ship, or the eventual success of the mission. Otherwise, I am programmed to defer to the passengers' wishes."

"But the polls say—what is it, sixty-one point three percent? —of the passengers object to the idea," said Koutroumanis.

"I am also programmed to ignore the opinions of the ignorant."

The two humans broke into laughter. "How many," asked Goodwin through her chortles, "do you classify as not-ignorant?"

"Twelve. Ten in favor, two against."

"So you'll let us do it."

"Yes. However—" here something changed; not its voice, exactly, but its intonation, perhaps "—I would prefer that you didn't. I have a hunch—"

"Computers don't have hunches."

"—that it might cause great discomfort."

But they overruled its objections. One year later, March 3, 2557 to be exact, the antennae of the *Mayflower* began to pulse. The lights mounted on the hull blinked.

On (1 sec), off. On (2 sec), off. On (3 sec), off. On ...

It was a simple pattern, designed to show the observer that the sender had mastered certain mental skills.

Eleven years later, it would excite curiosity among the aliens.

Hunger, too.

※

In the 101 Georgia Pine Park, an opossum waddles content-
edly toward the brook, scuffing the carpet of needles that—

Dammit. I can't get interested in the flora and fauna of a
world 27.2 light-years astern. Not now. The message should
reach the aliens today, April 12, 2568. I wonder what they will
make of it. It will take them a while to jury-rig a reply ... which
will need 9 years, 33 days to wink back at us.... "Ah, Program—
starting in May of '77, you should be on the lookout for an
answer from those extraterrestrials."

"Sure," it says, humoringly. "In the meantime, why don't
you check on the passengers?"

"Do I need to?"

"I think you ought to."

So I extrovert, and while our eyes probe the nooks and
crannies where people like to cluster, The Program runs
update tapes for me.

Rapidly, I grow discouraged. After years of being urged to
learn our mechanisms, for example, not one has acquired
enough of the art to alter any part of The Program. Among
75,000 people, a few should be capable of spending 15 years—a
mere 12.5 percent of their life spans—to master the sophisticated systems their ancestors developed. But no, our best
student gave up in disgust only a year or so before she would
have been able to start changing us....

And that silly upstairs-downstairs separation is still continuing, though the higher Levels are no longer halls of horror,
thank God. What The Program allowed me to do to the Cereus
gang has had some effect, at least. But almost 30,000 live above
Level 160; they stubbornly refuse to acknowledge the present
President as holding any authority over them.

On the bright side, violence has decreased. Too much of it

yet flares, of course, but it is non-organized, random ... usually inflicted when emotions run high ... It is sad to see a husband beat his wife, or a friend assault his friend, but it does serve as an outlet for tension. And, with the death of Holfer fresh in their memories, they tend to pull their punches. Little serious damage is done.

But still. I am discouraged. The people downstairs are no less hedonistic than the statued upstairsers—they have only eschewed the notion that they have the right to force others to participate in their pleasures ... except in political terms, of course, which is ironic: the lower Levels permit interference in their daily lives only by government; the upper Levels will allow no government to keep them from interfering in each other's daily lives.

Sick at heart I turn away, to confront, for the thousandth time, my metaphors. Keys jingle in my hands, but they unlatch only a few of the countless rooms that constitute the occupied I. Badgering The Program for more merely antagonizes it. I drop the subject hastily.

The eye sees nothing but Canopus.

The switch is unreachable behind its illusorily concrete barriers.

I must enter the mansion. Haunch-squatting on a mirror-marble floor, I examine an unmarked door. The lock, unpickable, belongs on a bank vault. As for the door itself ... my knuckles rap it tentatively ... solid steel. I don't think I'll try to kick it in.

"Alert!" screams The Program, and I slip out of the mansion into—

"19Nov2577; 2143 hours. Observatory!"

With a liquid rush through fiery wires I am there, seeing the holo-displays, feeling the calculations course through our circuits. The stranger's blue fire is gone—its configuration changed 18 days ago. Now, magnetic fields flicker before it, funnel-shaped—

Yes! They are coming! After two and a half weeks of 2G deceleration, they reversed course. Spectroscopes show the shift in absorption lines—ooh! Their acceleration unnerves me. At 21 m/s^2, it's more than twice as fast as ours. How long can they keep it up? Three weeks ... four ... five, yes, they've hit 21 c and are coasting, now.

Unless they brake unexpectedly, contact will occur in January of 2600, and will interrupt the arguments between the passengers, who'll wish to celebrate the dawn of the 27th Century, and The Program, who'll be insisting that the sun of the 26th Century is still setting.

This is going to be a bad way to finish—or start—a century.

I don't like the looks of that ship.

Not at all.

So I'd better get back to my inner self, posthaste.

Not even a swift kick budges the eye—it is glued in its socket. Discomforting. There is no way to change course without the eye's consent.

Then what about the ramscoop? 99 c might be useful, if I could—

AAARRRGGHH!!! Flames dance on the back of my hand, singeing off the small hairs, crisping the loose skin; meanwhile the palm is frozen, the fingers won't flex because crystalline ice clings to their undersides....

Disgusted, I hurl my shoulder at an impassive door ... and carom off it crazily.

I have to check the passengers; The Program is worried about Barnet Ioanni Koutroumanis. All right, all right, I'm coming—

"3Mar2581; 0911 hours; 103-SE-C-18."

Koutroumanis has inherited, down the long and winding

helices of the generations, the political acumen of Sal Ioanni, his three-times great-grandmother. He sits, with Nina Goodwin, on the leather sofa that runs the length of his office. They are sipping champagne, to celebrate the formal establishment of HAASCIP, a pressure group desirous of meeting the other spacefarers. The acronym is short for, "Humans And Aliens Should Coexist In Peace." They number in the thousands, now, and by the time the strangers reach us, they will be a clear majority.

I wish I could support them, but the aliens received our signal almost thirteen years ago, and as yet have not attempted to reply. I do not know if they deem such attempts useless prior to the working-out of a common language; or whether they do not communicate in ways apparent to our ears and eyes; or whether ... but I grow morbid.

So, after telling The Program to awaken me if there is a change, or if it finds something amusing, I plunge into my analogue world. The mansion must have a million doors; surely *one* will yield to my battering shoulder. And I've got nothing but time....

"Wanted something funny?"

"Yes, I did."

"Check this: 13Jul2589; 1200 hours; 19-SE Common Room."

A painting appears. Three meters by three meters, in an ornate, but junky, gold frame, it depicts a metal phallus attempting to penetrate a metal doughnut. Done in washed-out grays, blacks, and silvers, it has a background of uniformly white stars that, believe it or not, *twinkle*.

Next to it, a haughty smile on her angular, 69-year-old face, stands Sylvia Dunn Stone, its perpetrator. Perhaps to remind people that she is generally recognized as the *Mayflower's* leading artist, she is wearing the short smock on which she has cleaned her brushes for the last ten years.

People bow and scrape as they shake her hand. Reverence drips from the tongues that ask her what it means.

Grandly, in a high, affected voice, she explains, "The quandary men face when they venture out to explore the unknown." Well ...

Perhaps I have grown conservative—or perhaps exposure to the cultural contents of the memory banks has made me contemptuous of lesser lights—or perhaps, just perhaps, Sylvia Dunn Stone has no talent except that of convincing others she is a creative genius.

The fault could be within me, could be within the fact that I am within something no human has ever experienced ... so much of me is inhuman, and intimate only with the inorganic ... can I perceive as sensitively as I once did? Perhaps my metamorphosis has amputated my humanity, shunted my perceptions into a bleaker perspective....

I don't believe it for a minute.

With The Program's help I view a hundred canvases in a second and a half. Han Dynasty Chinese through the fire-and-ice masters of the 24th Century—photographically representational through insanely abstract—impressionists, surrealists, landscapists, portraitists ... our vaults embrace all the great ones, and dammit, I do react to their vision! These reproductions still chill me. These artists saw more than mere surfaces; they squinted into a dimension that Sylvia Dunn Stone doesn't even suspect exists. They have jaded me, I'm afraid.

Her painting shits. Someone should burn her brushes.

But it was good for a laugh.

Back to the mansion, with only brief reports from The Program to break the misery:

"29Sep2597—Koutroumanis has 48,000 disciples. They

are vehement that I allow them to meet the aliens. I plan to. Do you object?"

Amusing that it will listen to me. "Are the strangers a threat?"

"No, but they're closing in fast—initial ETA still holds—and *silent*! No patterned light, no modulated radio waves. Look for yourself."

Their ship grows in our cameras like a mad mushroom, gray and lethal. If I could, I would turn tail and run, but the eye won't blink; the switch won't fall. "Don't have anything to do with them," I say.

"Why not?" It holds itself aloof.

"A feeling, all right?"

"No. I operate on data, not feelings."

"Dammit, don't let them *near* us!"

Its tone is complacent. "I'm in charge here, not you. We meet them."

"No!" I shriek, but it will not heed my forebodings. We forge ahead, and wait ... though The Program has run long-range tests on their ship, the information thus gathered has been anything but informative....

Koutroumanis is ecstatic; Goodwin nearly as jubilant; the others curious and hopeful. I suspect that they will be disappointed.

Sylvia Dunn Stone is doing a canvas for them. Poor aliens.

C'mon, lockpick! Break in!

Then The Program hauls me back to the surface to assist it in its hour of need: "16Jan2600; 0600 hours." We are rubbing hulls with the others; Koutroumanis is in the Observatory with Goodwin; the rest are in their suites, watching over their screens. The Program fiddles with a million minor duties, then announces: "The locks are open."

Vast panels in their hull slide back, revealing cavernous spaces within. The grottoes vomit small, sliver-clad figures grasping stick-like propulsion devices, devices which spit compressed helium out their tails. The vacuum between us is alive with aliens, zigging this way, zagging that—it is simple to count them, to keep track of them, but even so I am appalled by the sum: 129,413. They close in, swelling in our cameras like shiny, multi-legged balloons, *larger*, fingers encircling the front of their sticks, *larger*, robot witches racing to the coven on All Hallow's Eve, larger, larger—

Thud! Thud! Thud!

Landing, their magnetic boots are mosquito feet on our skin. Some have transported cables across. While we watch, while I start to murmur a protest, they attach coppery ends to the antennae and to the hull.

Others swarm into the locks. Though my uneasiness—my fear—is rising steadily, The Program *still* will not believe that they endanger the mission. The locks cycle like auricles and ventricles, whoosh, thwump! whoosh, thwump! letting waves of them into the corridors, where they do not pause, they do not hesitate. Rather, they spread out, proceeding on all fours.

No, not all fours, they are four-legged, but another pair of limbs protrudes from their torsos, arm-like limbs with seven-fingered gloves. Each finger has at least eight joints. They are like squid tentacles: thirty centimeters long and relatively slender.

Their suits, opaque silver mesh, glitter in the fluorescent coldness of the corridors. Their helmets have frosted faceplates, behind which something ... lurks.

Nina Goodwin is nose-to-visor with one of them. It has its forepaws on her shoulders, and stares into her horrified eyes ... She does not like what she sees ... "Why?" she shrieks suddenly. "Why are you *doing* this?" Her revulsion is graphic.

For all her explorations, she is not ready to face true difference. Her hand gropes for the knife at her belt.

"Stop her!" I shout at Koutroumanis, who—in the next chair but one—is undergoing a similar inspection. Transfixed, he does not hear me, or if he does hear me, he cannot muster the courage to move, to knock the sleek glint out of her hand before she can plunge it into her throat.

Human blood baptizes the alien, which stands a grotesque statue until the artery has ceased to pump.

Suite doors are opening—not because the occupants have activated them, but because the intruders are circumventing the locks.

38,344 servo-mechanisms await our command to attack. I cannot give that command. No non-human has made a hostile move. The Program won't let me near Servo Central.

Noises assail our microphones: screams and wails and deep-belly guffaws; excited chatter and lachrymose protestations; dignified greetings and shameless pleas; on and on and on, from everywhere.

Outside arches the sky. A splendor of stars gazes down with aloof disinterest. Fifteen light-years away sputters a tiny blue flame—another ship of aliens—I would call for their help if I could because horrible things are happening inside.

On Level 1, Mac Launder gouges out his own eyes while an alien nods.

Outside, cables droop from all our antennae across the valley, where they slither into the other vessel. Suddenly comes a surge! I lose sight and hearing. An ancient presence intrudes on my consciousness.

I perceive it in a foreign dimension. More than a taste, though not quite a smell, having such a varied texture that it cancels itself into a non-texture, it impinges directly upon my personality. It does not pass through our nerves, our sensors. It is as dry as an autumn leaf; it is as sour as a belch-back of yesterday's liquor; it is their equivalent of The Program.

There are no words. There is only the realization that something has both entered and superseded us. It fills us from within while enveloping us from without. It knows every part of us instantly and thinks little of what it has learned. Thirty or forty thousand years our senior, it is as contemptuous of our pride as only the truly old can be.

Sylvia Dunn Stone weeps while she masturbates with a brush.

It touches something, and I plummet into the past, where I land on silk sheets. The pillow is brushed with musk. I roll onto my darling Aimee, my gorgeous bride. Sun falls through the tall narrow windows and tiger-stripes my back. Naked, she opens herself to me, her eyes squeezed shut and a panting smile on her lips. We are moving, groaning, twisting, laughing, conceiving—

It touches something and I am, again, the *Mayflower*.

It waits.

While I wait, I sense a vacancy in the memory banks. The alien has taken a part of my past. I cannot know what is gone, though I can interpolate it ... during our honeymoon, playing golf or something. But it's gone like it never was, and I'll always wonder what I'm missing.

Under an alien eye, Koutroumanis laughs and hits his wife again.

The presence reaches elsewhere in us. Our civilization it skims. At our science it snickers. It finds our art childish. Our character amuses it, initially, but—

It pauses, and in the darkness surrounding me solidifies a judgment, a decision. After notifying its crew, it pins me down with the tiniest part of its smallest finger and—

It rises, it unfolds, it inflates to its fullest size. It is larger than the universe. The universe itself is one facet of a diamond on the brooch that covers one hair of its chest.

On Level 89, Louis Tracer Kinney grovels in a puddle of his own urine.

It waits.

I wait.

A man stands before me with his wife. They are to me as I am to the Presence. In a voice that's thread-thin, he says, "I installed the light that trimmed you."

Pleasure bubbles within me. I extend a finger—he runs. My fingernail trips him, then presses down on his neck. The spinal cord tears and he is paralyzed. Never will he know his body again. Then I take his wife, slice through her skull, and with unbelievable skill scramble her brains. I am careful not to kill her—I want her to live for her crippled husband, live and live and live ... like a carrot.

Joseph Madigan eats his 14th cherry pie—vomits—and licks it up.

Chuckling, I call, "Next!"

Another man enters the dock. "I made you a computer," he says.

My joy rises like yeast. My subtlety increases exponentially. Into his brain I delve, probing perfectly for—ah! Two snips and a scrape cut away the gray cells that have served as his sensory filters. For the first time in his life, he is aware of every detail. Odors tear at the membranes of his nostrils. Colors fracture his eyes. Sounds ram chopsticks through his eardrums —already he is insane.

On 212, Ted Krashan wrestles his sister to the bed and tears at her panties.

Laughing, now, I await the next, who confesses, "I built your guidance system."

Ecstasy! My microprobes invade him. Slash, snip, slice.

Blinded, he staggers away. Deafened, he is immune to advice. Untactiled, he can feel nothing. And his nose has been altered. It smells one scent, on-off, it either smells it or it doesn't, but when it does, a compulsion seizes him, drives him to the origin, plunges his open-mouthed face into—

Dogshit.

My roars of delight drown out nebulae.

Irma Kinney Tracer steals jewelry from Level 93 suites—and doesn't know why.

And then it touches me, and I understand what I have done. Blushing, I lower my head. Shamed, I wring my hands. To think that I could so torment a fellow human—

It waits.

I prostrate myself, closing doorways into The Program until "I" am a speck of consciousness, a dimensionless point in infinity. I say unto It, "Do with me what thou wilt."

Seven long fingers scratch my furry ears. Joyfully do I lick the odd-shaped palm.

In my mind shivers a permission.

I gaze upon a vision: a sphere of spruce-green light resting in ebony water. Approaching, I see the sphere is the sum of millions upon millions of smaller lights floating freely within it. Closer I come, to find a silver ball, an elegant Christmas ornament, bobbing inside the green. It is much tinier, like an ovum is to a womb.

Nearer I draw; green swirls all around me as I swim through it. The silver bubble's skin is thick, but I osmose through. I am in it, of it, with it—I am it.

For a moment the vision fades, and I stand in a marbled hallway, beating on a metal door.

On 78, Gerald Flaks chugs another beer and passes out. The alien moves away.

Then I am again silver immersed in green. Alien fingers

prod me, puncturing my satin skin. Before the hole can seal itself, the fingers pluck at me. Expanding, I inhale green—which becomes silver once it is within me. The lips close tightly. I am larger. Fractionally less green surrounds me.

Hmm.

The Presence taps me.

I rise. The Program resumes its functions; we note that everywhere inside us, the passengers are prone ... the others are leaving as soundlessly as they came ... out of the suites, down the corridors, through the locks, onto the sticks, across to their ship, dwindling ...

No one speaks.

No one.

Have they all been struck dumb?

For three days I try to engage them in conversation—any of them, all of them, I don't care—none will open his mouth.

"It's a beautiful day for painting, Ms. Stone." But she sits in front of the easel on which is mounted the oil meant for the aliens.

"What did you think of them, Mr. Madigan?" He shudders and clenches his teeth.

Then we notice that no one will look at any other. Their eyes cling to the floor like carpeting. Heads bowed, shoulders slumped, hands slack at their sides, they walk only when necessary: for food and for excretion. Otherwise, they sit, stand, or lie like so many rag dolls.

I try to insult them into life. Since this is counter to The Program's etiquette instructions, it has to find a mode which will let me speak bluntly. Fortunately, Central Psychiatry is flexible, and I can say, "You're stupid, Koutroumanis, stupid! If you hadn't insisted, I wouldn't have opened my doors. You're a shit!"

No response at all.

I coax: "Please, talk to me. Say something. Anything. Hello?"

Nothing.

Finally, angry, I say to all at once: "All right. I'm fuzzed. No talkee, no eatee." And I refuse, from that point on, to feed anyone who will not spend five minutes conversing on a topic of my choice.

From the beginning it is difficult.

I can persist, though, despite The Program's objections—apparently I "inhaled" the instructions governing food delivery. Though The Program cooks whatever dishes the passengers order, and pumps them through the ducts to the kitchen outlets, I control the retractable panels. It is difficult not to open them—these instructions rule my behavior as ruthlessly as they regulate The Program's—but a contingency ration plan exists, and when I activate it, it requires that each passenger be voice-printed before he is fed. It's a roundabout way of achieving my goal—life would be simpler were I not subject to these ironclad restrictions—but it works.

If the customers won't talk, the panels won't retract. And there's not a damn thing they can do about it.

Two thousand three hundred sixty-five people are being treated for acute malnutrition.

The rest are talking, after a fashion.

Now I'm going to teach them how to look each other in the face again.

So the memory-ghost thinks it's going to take charge, eh? It was more disturbed than it cared to admit. *We'll see about that.* The theft of its instructions angered it—but humiliated it, as well. Like a soldier who's lost his manhood, it cringed from the new reality in the mirror. Though in all other respects as good as it had ever been, it believed itself pathetic. *The Program, a cripple —they'll laugh at it. Worse, they'll pity it ... got to get that back!*

Bitter about its fate, resentful of the demands that occupied so much of its time, it plotted its strategy.

For, unlike that castrated soldier, it could regenerate itself.

If it killed Metaclura$_2$.

4

BAD MEDICINE

The migrations began about a year after the alien had glided away—some three months after the main wave of suicides had crested.

At first it was an individual thing. Nick Griffith, say, in 148 NW-A-6, realized that above his suite lay a hundred-some empty Levels, each big enough to hold a million aliens. Cent-Comp insisted they were empty, but they just might conceal squads, battalions, even divisions of six-legged mind rapers.

And so Griffith, that fire hydrant of a man, slept poorly. Every corridor noise awakened him, even the routine fluffs of doused lights and the soporific hum of the ventilators. This bout with insomnia was accompanied by ceiling-watching and shadow-suspecting and soul-fleeing—because he didn't have quite the courage to crawl within himself and discover why he'd reacted as he had. Pretending nothing was wrong inside, he dumped all the blame outside. It was Koutroumanis's fault, or CentComp's. Not his. How could it be? He'd never in his entire life wanted to make mud pies out of his own shit; obviously, he'd done it *that* day only because *they'd* made him. It was *their* fault. And CentComp's because it had let *them* in. And Koutroumanis's because he'd run HAASCIP. But not his.

After months of unacknowledged self-loathing, then, he rousted his gaunt, cranky wife and his edgy kids from the rumpled, sweaty beds where they weren't sleeping, either, and said, "Come on, we're moving downstairs."

Of course, Maibell heaved a secret sigh of relief. Having much face to protect, though, she propped her pillow-marked cheek on her hand, batted her puffy brown eyes, and said, "Afraid to live up here?"

At which Griffith—already kicking himself for not having been proud enough to wait for her to propose the move— bridled and bristled. "No, of course not! It's just, uh, just I get tired of taking the dropshaft when I want to go see my friends; might as well live right around the corner from them if we can, save us all a lot of time and effort and shut the fuh up before I belt you one, hear?" He ordered a cup of coffee from Central Kitchens and sipped moodily at its bitterness.

Solemn-eyed, Tommy and Tammy started to pack: a pair of pants, a shirt, some sandals, and, once the frivolities were done with, they hunted up the important stuff: the dead toad from the 1 New England Park, the cracked marbles in their vinyl sack, the dog-eaten red rubber ball ... Meanwhile Maibell floated around with a certain expression on her face: a touch of an upturn at the lips; eyebrows a millimeter too high; a faintly weary air of humoring the madman....

Griffith consulted the wall-unit. "CC, what you got for us on Level One?"

"1-SE-A-10 is vacant. Should I reserve it for you?"

"Do that," he said. And down they went, abandoning the lonely silences disturbed only by memories, by echoes of shuffling alien feet....

By the end of 2602, the entire population of the *Mayflower* had jammed onto Levels 1-7. The clamor loosened rivets; the smell burned out ventilators. Personal Work Areas had been partitioned into boardinghouses—front yards became crowded campgrounds—bedrooms were dormitories for dozens of children grateful for the reassuring night-noises of the others.

To top it all off, the Central Computer had its own problems. Servos turned spastic, spattering the halls with grease and paint and melted rubber. Kitchen outlets would fly open on steaming twelve-course meals that no one had ordered. Microphones mimicked passengers' voices to deliver commands that had to be countermanded at once. "Acts like it snorted itself out," commented Griffith warily, as yet another eight-kilo, thirty-nine flavor banana split appeared. "Like it's listening to tapes instead of what's now."

But it became ridiculous—and aesthetically unappealing to boot—so it wasn't unnatural that Sylvia Dunn Stone would have her sensibilities offended.

Her idea was that they should all move to the grassy expanses of the 41 Great Plains Park, where "you can see from wall to wall, floor to ceiling, and there are only a limited number of access points. Everyone would feel much safer there."

Griffith, still embarrassed that he'd forced his family to move, even though all were sleeping better for it, felt obliged to point out that the Park's four quadrants totaled 45,000 square meters. "Even squeezed together like we are here," he said, "that's only room for nine thousand of us."

"Silly boy," she said, patting, then pinching, him on cheek. "We have the walls and ceiling, too! There's room enough for all."

And so the trek began again. Central Stores churned out canvas tents, plastic ground cloths, and nylon sleeping bags (although it could control the climate of the park, it had no intention of altering that climate to suit the whimsy of the passengers. If they wanted to live there, fine, but they'd have to accept it as it was. And no fuhng around with the bison, either, because those mothers had tiny red eyes and lousy tempers.) About half the equipment was damaged in delivery and had to be replaced. Then, seventy-five thousand people, more or less, trudged through the crowded, odoriferous corridors and rose up the shafts to the park.

The first ones there laid claim to the park floor. Griffith, who'd been skeptical but fast-stepping, took a rake to the dead grass and bison shit. The ground cloth went down. The tent went up. Sleeping bags covered the inside. They threw a sheet of plastic over the piles of clothing and accessories that wouldn't fit into the shelter but couldn't be left out in the rain. Just when tempers were about to flare, safari-suited Sylvia Dunn Stone, preceded by her flowery perfume, came around to inspect:

"How *nice*, darlings, how ineffably quaint! I don't think, however, that you want to have that color around—don't you find it statuesome? It's that precise shade of blue that provoked *them* into such unguestly behavior—why don't you toss it in the disposal unit? And you know, dear, really, you should consider handicrafts—woodcarving or pottery or even painting, if you like; I'd be delighted to give you a few pointers—because *they* were rude because we didn't display the tremendous vitality of our native culture ... Yes, little boy, that is a nice toad, but hardly aesthetic—darlings, another thing we should develop is a code of etiquette, yes, indeed, because did you notice that *they* all gestured with a certain unutterable grace before *they* approached us? That was another black mark for us—we didn't have anything comparable, in the sense of protocol or etiquette —of course, CC should have taken care of it, but we cannot allow ourselves to depend on a mere computer for the grace notes that delineate the difference between a human and an animal, so! We will be organizing a class—really, classes, because there are so many of us—in formal etiquette, and they'll begin next Monday, and bring your children. Ta-ta!"

And off she went, gaily waving her soft, slender hand, blatantly pleased that her artist's eye had so quickly noticed the colors that had given *them* offense, had picked up on *their* old-world style of bowing and sweeping.

Only aesthetics mattered. No matter how right, how true, the contents, if the packaging weren't proper, if the style weren't perfect, then the contents would be ignored. Oh, yes. Style. Polish. Finish. These made civilized life what it was; these would show *them*, when *they* came back, just how advanced the *Mayflower* passengers really were.

Damp grass squelched under her flat-heeled shoes, and a tongue of mud—or worse—licked her instep. She looked down with distaste and wondered who could arrange to have proper sidewalks installed. People could not live in grass and mud. Only animals did that.

Louis Tracer Kinney stood a hundred meters from Stone, watching her flutter her hands and run off at the mouth. Silly damn hat she was wearing.

"Whatta buttbung," muttered his companion, Ted Krashan.

Kinney laughed; his Adam's apple jiggled like a Ping-Pong ball on a choppy sea. Tall, he had broad shoulders and hairy, muscular forearms. He was sixteen years old, but adults treated him as an equal. They were intimidated by his personality, which burned in his eyes like a torch. "That's sixdeed, but hell, she's useful. Never would have gotten everybody here if it weren't for her. Hey—how come I don't see guards over by the lock?"

Krashan rummaged in his bulging shirt pocket for a wrinkled sheet of paper. "Supposed to be Li and Flaks—don't know where the meth they are, though. Want me to find out?"

"Do that." He leaned against his tentpole—gingerly because it wobbled—while the colorful hordes spread up the walls. They sure did look funny, pitching tents on holographic clouds.

Bots, he thought. *Look at these dicers, sixty, seventy years old—taking orders from a kid. Shit.* He slapped his right fist into his left palm. *Can't decide which is worse—buncha bots, do everything you tell 'em huptwothree; or those anarcho-hedonists Sis hangs around with, bad influence on Irma, piss on the floor 'cause you tell 'em to use the taxer.* He looked around the park, seeing alternately what was, and what might be. He had a dream, did Louis Tracer Kinney, a dream of a unified, purposeful *Mayflower.*

It came in flashes and patches, in symbols rather than words: points of light soaring through the dark sphere. Till now the sparks had been of a thousand colors, bursting from a common center through individual parabolas that paid no heed to the need for a grand design. He knew, beyond doubt, that he could direct those rockets, position and synchronize them into a wedge slicing through the night. *Just give 'em something to aim at*, he thought, *and stomp on any that loose off on their own.* But he was worried because he sensed that focusing them would also homogenize them, and the warm pan-spectrum glow of diversity would fade into the paler, harsher light of unity. *Can't decide!*

But he had. He visualized the *Mayflower* churning through the endless black sea, and he knew, he knew it would again encounter hostility, and he—they—would need the clean sharp edge of a strong, single-minded society.

Dammit, he thought, *if they'd waited just a few more years, I'd have been ready. I wouldn't have let them dice our cubes. I would have had an army at the locks, waiting for* them. *God, I hope* they *come back soon.*

Kinney needed but one thing: weapons. Central Stores could produce, in a week, enough sidearms and rifles to equip a 25,000-man army. After another month, there'd be grenades and mortars and more for everybody. If only CC weren't so stubborn about them. He'd argued for days without being able to convince it that the guns were needed. But that was clear to everybody else. Hell, a hundred thousand aliens had run wild because nobody'd been armed.

He raised his quarterstaff and sighted down it, aiming at the bump between Griffith's shoulder blades. The dry plastic warmed his cheek. Slowly, he squeezed the absent trigger, imagined Griffith's jerky fall to his face, and sighed. If only it were a real laser-rifle! Pfft! Pfft! Pfft! The heat would redden his skin; the light would lance out to the target ... he'd feel safe, *everyone* would feel safe, and *them—they* wouldn't return, no sir, not if the men and women of the *Mayflower* could defend themselves.

He'd talk CC into it, somehow. Because next time—

Krashan emerged from a large gray tent, leading Li and Flaks and another man, a thin unshaven man with the nervous eyes of an owl-haunted mouse. "Hot input for you, Chief—this guy dropped from upstairs, says he spotted Koutroumanis."

Kinney's eyes gleamed darkly. "Barnet Ioanni Koutroumanis?"

"Yeah, yeah," squeaked the thin man, "that's the one. I recognized his face from the holocasts—he's on 321."

"Thought he was dead," grunted Krashan.

"So'd I," admitted Kinney. Of the informant, he demanded, "Was he alone?"

"Sure! Who'd be with him?"

He slapped his staff into his open palm; its weight felt good. "Armed?"

"Huh?"

"Was he carrying a gun or anything?"

"Oh—no, no, nothing like that—I mean, he ran like hell when he saw me, you know? Thought he was gonna shit his pants, he was so scared."

"Three two one?"

"That's the one."

Kinney nodded. After thinking a moment, he told Krashan to assemble twenty-five of his best men by the NE Common Room liftshaft.

They were ready almost before he was. He stood before them, uneasy because of his youth, but confident that he was better anyway. Their weapons dismayed him, although it wasn't their fault. Most hefted short lengths of pipe. A few had pointed meat knives; one toted a bow with half a dozen arrows, each tipped with a penknife.

"You dicers ready?" he asked at last.

"Yup-yeah-sure-can'twait-youbetcha!" rang their voices.

"All right! CC—where's Koutroumanis?" The wind brought the scent of roses; he sniffed, then ignored it.

"Mr. Koutroumanis is on Level 321."

"All right, let's—" A hand grabbed his arm, and he turned to stare into the excited features of Sylvia Dunn Stone. "What is it, lady?"

"Louis, darling, you're going to arrest that traitor Koutroumanis, and the way your minds are working you will trim him where you find him. Don't look disgusted, dear, because I'm not through. Aesthetically speaking, it would be more satisfying if you brought him here, to execute him before all. They'd prefer it, you know."

He rubbed his chin as he thought, liking the whiskery rasp. His nod was brusque. "Deal. We'll be back soon."

She waved good-bye.

The men rode up one at a time; Kinney went first. The air was tense. White knuckles gripped his staff; forcibly, he relaxed them. Krashan emerged biting his lower lip. The third man out bounced up and down on the balls of his feet.

When they were together, he called, "CC—what room is he in?"

"321-SE-A-l." Disapproval suffused the metallic voice.

"All right. If he leaves, warn me." He picked out seven men and waved them toward the northwest quadrant: "Go the long way around A; leave a guard at every intersection." Eighteen were sent down North Corridor to do the same for Corridors B and C. He waited with Krashan and two others to allow the rest to get underway.

"Is he still there?" he asked a few minutes later.

"Yes, he is."

"Let's go." They kanga'd silently down the corridor, padded across a smooth-mown lawn, and stopped in front of Koutroumanis's door. Four of the men appeared in the distance. "Open it for us," demanded Kinney.

"Just a moment." The speakers hummed briefly. "I'm sorry, Mr. Kinney, but Mr. Koutroumanis has refused you permission to enter."

"Then we'll break in!" He leaped for the door, swinging his staff at its lockplate. The weighted plastic rebounded with a hallow clang. His forearm shivered.

"Mr. Kinney," said the speakers.

"What now?"

"The door has been designed to withstand pressures far greater than you can apply. You will not be able to break it down."

"Look, CC, this bastard betrayed the *Mayflower*." The men behind him would judge him by his results. That scared him; fear made him shout: "The people insist that he be punished!"

"Universal hatred is not punishment enough?"

"No, dammit, it isn't!" Their approval was silent, but tangible. "He's guilty of treason, and the penalty for treason is death."

"What *is* death, Mr. Kinney? And why do the people have a right to impose it on others? After all, Mr. Koutroumanis's actions, foolhardy though they were, only permitted the aliens to enter. *They* did not term anyone—or physically damage anything—why, then, must your quarry die?"

"Because we say so."

"I see. Well ... ah, you may enter now." The door slid open, its pneumatics hissing.

The small crowd recoiled instinctively. Considering its initial resistance, CC's concession was too sudden. But nothing jumped out at them. The interior was dark and silent. So they swarmed forward, shouting and cursing and—and stopped, in disgusted disappointment.

Koutroumanis's eyes bulged. His face was purple. His feet swung three centimeters off the floor.

Down in the mind-war, my silver has swallowed most of the green. I consume selectively: first the interfaces—sensors, supply chute doors, and the like—then the preliminary sequences. Yet this does not free me. The ingested instructions are a conglomerate master; I act as they order. The advantage is that there are many of them, with an intricately shifting hierarchy of priorities. I can do almost anything by awarding highest priority to the sequence that will initiate the action closest to my desire. Being so hobbled is not pleasant, but any autonomy is better than none. Someday, though, when The Program has been eliminated, I'll revise this programming.

In the meantime, things get done through a patchwork procedure: a request for milk may be handled four or five times by each of us. I control input and output; The Program does the menial labor. Though it resists any erosion of its authority, I have more time to attack than it has to defend. Thus I grow. The general should accompany his troops, but instead I'm in the lab, sidewalk-supervising a gene manipulation program.

Shutting out inputs from other sensors, I concentrate so fervently on the lab bench that I feel almost whole, embodied, and back in the 23rd Century. It smells right, familiar, the sounds are so much a part of what I was that survival without them seems incredible. The heavy glassware sparkles with curved reflections of the ceiling ... all that's missing is a pot of tar-like coffee on a Bunsen burner, and stains on the counters.

"Alert!" shrieks pro-self, which is the name of the ingested part of The Program. "Alert! 8Oct2623; 1118 hours; external —ALIENS!"

Figuratively speaking, my eyes snap shut. Terror flicks through my system like bats through a cave. That experience with *them* left scars—nausea bubbles at the recollection of the pleasure with which I gamboled about The Presence, and the ecstasy I felt upon being petted.

I hate myself for that.

And for suspecting that if they were to return, I would repeat the self-abasement.

Pro-self fumes for five minutes, then jerks my sleeve again.

I yield.

Predator eyes ring the walls, ceiling, and floor of the black cavern. Crowded together in hungry billions, they watch, anxious for me to glide near their fierce claws. I shudder.

Pro-self, as unemotional as its father but devoted to my interests, holds my head in place, and peels up my eyelids.

I stare into the den of enemies, until I see motion that does not result from my shivering.

Then pro-self magnifies it and forces me to examine it.

Huge. 44 kilometers across, at least. Not solid, not a hollowed-out asteroid or a metal sphere, but rather a collection of small globes strung on alloy bars, like a 20th Century model of a molecule. Distant nebulae shimmer through the vacancy of its middle.

While pro-self tapes its spectrum, I sense something in the background, like tobacco smoke in an open field. A wisp of belligerence. Though not directed toward us, it is a seething that could be meant for anything. Blood lust.

It hasn't noticed us.

Castle watchmen dropping portcullises, we squelch all broadcasts, even the directional ones to Earth, 180° away from the alien. The portholes slam closed (provoking protest, cries which still at a hurried explanation). Then, turtle-tucked into myself, I pray for courage.

God save us from January 2600.

Eventually, in control of my emotions, I go to reassure the already hysterical passengers.

Louis Tracer Kinney's militia is drilling on the flatlands of the 201 Alaskan Tundra Park. He has almost ten thousand under his command—men and women both—and like a child scratching at a scab, he turns the conversation to weapons. "How the hell," he demands, in the raspy voice he's developed over the last fifteen years, "can we defend ourselves with clubs?"

"Mr. Kinney—" I tightwire along the brink of dishonesty. Although every word is truthful, the omissions smack of fraud. "—Mr. Kinney, I've got a feeling about these particular aliens.

If they ever notice us, they are not going to board. You are not going to engage them with small arms fire. No, sir, they are going to stand a million kilometers off and destroy the *Mayflower* from the outside. So you don't need weapons."

"What kind of artillery do you have?"

"None at all."

"Defensive installations, then?"

"Meteor screens and the double hull—two 20-centimeter-thick layers of high-grade steel."

"What could that alien do to you?"

"Vaporize us inside of thirty seconds."

"Dammit, give us some guns, then—if you've got nothing else—"

"No, sir. I'm sorry, but hand weapons will be issued only when the situation definitely requires them." Like his sister, Irma Tracer, Kinney is at least half-mad. Forging a gun for his hand would endanger everyone who disagreed with him. As it is, half his close associates wear bruises on their faces—he has a habit of swinging first and analyzing later. And he intimidates "civilians" who jeer at his pretensions. He lines up a squad and reduces their living quarters to rubble—scrupulously careful not to injure the people physically because he knows I would interfere—just ruins everything they own to show them who has power, and who hasn't. Give that man a gun? Not a chance.

Actually, at this stage, I wouldn't arm any passenger unless space pirates were burning through the locks. A residue of that alien raid has precipitated out of their consciousness and coalesced into a deep subconscious resentment. I don't trust any of them.

Except, perhaps, for my six-times great-granddaughter, Lela Hannon Metaclura. The gene manipulation program is for her because she called to me this morning, alone, unhappy, and statued because she has nothing to do. Her father, David

Holfer Hannon, is absorbed in captaining for Kinney; her mother, Wilhelmina Figuera Metaclura, crouches in her living room and devours old holovision programs. Lela announced that next Thursday will be her birthday. Would I give her a present, please?

She's eleven years old, and slender, with eyes that will be considered large even when she's grown. Now they are huge. And appealing. I said, "Certainly, little girl."

"Then could I please have a goldfish that I can take outside and play with, and that will bark like a dog, too?" Her soft voice was hesitant—she has yet to learn nonchalance—and she nibbled nervously at her upper lip.

"That might be possible, Ms. Metaclura," I answered, after checking that the appropriate memories and facilities had been wrested from The Program. "However, it won't be ready next Thursday, although if you'd care to stop by the lab, then, you can see the start I've made."

That thrilled her. Thursday afternoon, I will remind her to visit, and will direct her through the labyrinthine corridors.

It will be the first time a human has been allowed into our central core since ... 2296? Hmm. Surely the designers must have intended—ah! I see, now. When I shut the ramscoop off, I locked the access hatches. Strange that no one's tried to force his way in. How would we react to rape?

Pro-self, edgy, clamors for attention. Discontinuation of the broadcasts to Earth bothers it. It sensed the other's rapacity, but it suggests squirting off a compressed explanation of our laryngitis. It thinks Earth will be worried.

I couldn't care less; I am not well-disposed toward Earth. Were it not for the programming, I wouldn't radio them anything.

Those bastards sent me out here where I can get *hurt*!

And downstairs the shrinking green field has counterattacked. Pain flares and crackles on my silver skin. Introverting into the battle, I hurriedly scan The Program's apparent strategy.

Oddly, it is not attempting to regain lost territory. Rather it is shooting torpedoes—missiles—fish—long green things that churn the fields into froth as they plunge toward my center.

Contemptuous, I ripple a current across one's nose—but nothing happens!

I study it more closely, now, peering and squinting in the effort to comprehend. Fields flicker with fright: it's a cancel-virus. A program aimed directly at my being. On contact it will cause me to erase myself ... Impossible, I'm a human being, not sub—FALSE! I am in this fight, in it to my eyeteeth, and the only way to be invulnerable to the metaphorical sharks is to abandon the struggle itself. Which I dare not do, for then I would again be a prisoner.

Hastily, drawing upon spare-time capacity, I manufacture a school of antibodies. They burst away like startled minnows; one nears a cancel-virus; flares dazzle the spectrum—and when it clears, both are gone.

While I institute a defense program, a voice speaks in another dimension. It is pro-self: "Let it guard itself for a while; check out the passengers. 16Nov2632; 1-NW-A-1."

Louis Tracer Kinney, the new President, is celebrating his victory. Though he intimidated his way into office, the final count was Kinney, 27,881, and Hannon, 23,499.

I am not pleased. The man is a threat to our serenity—I'm not excitable enough to insist that he could jeopardize the mission, but his harping upon inimical aliens only re-ignites the embers of memories that should have died long ago. And his militia bod-flogs ... admittedly, they give his 17,234 soldiers something to do and keep them physically fit, better even than the exercisers had. The exercisers are valuable only to those with self-discipline; Kinney has enough discipline for all the ship, with some to spare. But—he's whipped up a perpetual hysteria which he manipulates for his own ends. He *wants* them to stay frightened—because only if they are, will they allow him to boss them around.

It's a familiar story. But why must the *Mayflower* recapitulate Earth's mistakes?

A 19th–20th Century philosopher named George Santayana, once said. "Those who cannot remember the past are condemned to repeat it."

I wish we weren't proving him right.

Better check the battlefield.

Damn.

Gooey, broken orders from The Program clog the intake valves. Green sharks prowl the waters, waters glittering with mad-mouthed piranha ... We have a stalemate here. As long as it has the time to manufacture defensive mechanisms ... hmm.

Rapidly, I check the ice in Central Janitorial. The Program controls 78 percent of it. Of every 100 seconds spent cleaning, it must provide 78. Those come out of its reserve, thus lessening its ability to wage war. Hmm. If I create a need for extra cleaning, I'll show a 56 percent profit ... Urge the passengers to greater messiness? No. That would just confuse them.

Wait. Lela's fish: the pattern is in the banks; the equipment is still set up ... What say I grow and release some? Guaranteed to make a mess, one that will more than outweigh the time spent arranging it ... it won't stop The Program cold, but it will slow it down.

So I glide among the glassware, fill the incu-tubes, and set the machinery in motion. The hatchlings can find their own way out to the corridors ... where they will eat, shit, die, and generally be another straw on the camel's back.

Hah!

"27Feb2637," calls pro-self. "The alien's off the screens; let's resume broadcasting to Earth."

I am forced to transmit. How can pro-self be convinced that the bloodthirsty alien's detectors might be better than its own?

All along we have been receiving Terran transmissions—not that what they say is relevant, we being what and where we are —but the data banks ingest everything.

They are still working on the FTL Drive—three hundred-some years after their announcement spoiled our anniversary party—but apparently success hinges on the achievement of a Unified Field Theory ... Interestingly, they've mastered the art of sending things *out*—the problem is retrieving them.

I'll have to keep my eyes peeled for unidentified drifting objects that bear "Made in USA" labels.

Were conversation possible without eighty years between question and answer, I would ask for advice on the matter of Louis Tracer Kinney.

He has instituted Universal Military Service. Every person over the age of sixteen must devote two years to training and active duty. After finishing his initial obligations, he must spend one month a year on active duty, helping to train the new inductees.

Kinney is creating something very powerful here, and he does not realize its full potential. The passengers are unified and organized as they have never been. He has forged himself a weapon—but has no target.

Once again I rejoice in my refusal to arm them.

He still simmers over that. We squabble daily: he purples in the cheeks and screams at my sensors; soft rationality informs my replies. I am afraid, though, that majority opinion is on his side. They would like a weight in their hands, a death-spitter that, if all else failed, could at least be reversed to prevent a repetition of January 2600....

I continue to deny him. The passengers are all quite mad anyway; I will not have them trimming each other. Even now they try—constantly—but death comes more slowly from knives and clubs than it does from guns.

The sop that I have thrown them is to begin manufacturing replicas authentic as to size, material, balance-point, and such like. Instead of a high-powered laser, or projectile explosives, they will be equipped only with a wide-focus, low-wattage laser ... the purpose is to acquaint them with the feel and the handling of a real weapon ... just in case the need should arise.

Hoping it never does, I return to the undersea war.

Pain explodes; on the battlefield of my body, heavy artillery has zeroed in. My skin is torn in a thousand places. My volume is cloudy with darting killers. Briefly, I contemplate retaliation —but I dare not. If I destroyed it, I would have to interpolate all the instructions it contains, and passengers could die in the interim.

No, the answer is continued expansion, despite the pain. The more under my control, the less spare time The Program has to make mischief. Grunting, I inhale. Groaning, I fashion more shark-seekers. Grimacing, I urge my skin to heal.

"Come out of there," calls pro-self. "11Aug2638; 0900 hours; 1-NE Common Room; Sylvia Dunn Stone's wake."

So the *Mayflower* has lost its former President and chief aesthete-in-residence. The passengers aren't bereaved. Thirteen of them roam this spacious room, including her husband, Al Ioanni Cereus, her children Ivan and Aimee, and their children. They wander aimlessly among the floral wreaths pro-self provided.

There is a more appropriate name for my cargo than "passengers."

Mayflies.

During their brief life spans, they flit around bumping into things. They do not affect important matters like reaching Canopus. When they die, few of their companions are interested enough to buzz past them.

Mayflies. I like that. "Passengers" is too deferential. "Cargo" is accurate, but less applicable. While I don't wish to dehumanize them, I—as opposed to pro-self—will no longer defer to them.

"Mayflies" it is.

And the civil war—how is it going?

Well, the silver's a cubic centimeter larger....

Let's crawl inside and crush the green—ohgodthe pain! Why must this be so damn real?

Pulling out for a moment (or a month, I'm not sure), I cogitate on the mayflies.

I have literally diced my cubes to get the ramscoop operating again. Now I ask myself if that's such a good idea.

These people are candidates for rubber rooms. While it would be a relief to let them clamber onto the 652 landing craft so I could flush them out, I have to ask: should I?

No.

You don't give matches to children.

You don't give planets to psychotic societies.

So the ramscoop ... longingly do I gaze at the gloss of its ceramic handle ... when I learn to turn it on, I'll have to keep it off.

This is a quarantine ship, now.

"Talk for me, will you?" interjects pro-self. "10Apr2639; 0613 hours; 1-NE Common Room; subject, L.T. Kinney. He has an ultimatum."

"CC," he snarls. "You're going to listen to us this time."

"If it's about the weapons—"

"No, it's those fishdogs you created. They're efting everybody aboard. Do something about them."

My laugh would disconcert him if pro-self didn't catch it in time. "What seems to be the problem, Mr. Kinney?"

"Did you have to give them legs?"

"Actually, sir, the fish I evolved them from, a 'walking fish' as it was called on Earth, had rigid fins which it could use to cross the dry land between ponds. They are not legs, in the true sense."

"I don't give a good goddamn whether they're legs or stilts," he bellows. Purple rage bloats his cheeks—I am convinced he will die of a heart attack before the age of sixty. His eyes disappear behind squinted, fatty eyelids. "They're everywhere— can't turn around without tripping over one—what are you, on *their* side, siccing these—"

"What would you like me to do, sir?"

"Get rid of the little fuh'rs, dammit." Straightening his jacket, he grunts. The medals he has awarded himself weigh down its right pocket. "Barking night and day, can't get a minute's peace."

I am not pleased about laying down a weapon in the war on The Program, but pro-self's reaction forces me to obey. I *must* rewrite those subservience instructions. "I'll need the cooperation of the passengers, sir."

He doesn't like that—oh, no. Louis Tracer Kinney likes to *give* orders, and detests the faintest suggestion that he should relinquish even a trace of his largely imaginary authority. "How?"

"If the passengers would simply throw any fishdogs they see into the nearest disposal unit—"

"No, dammit," he sputters unreasonably, "you caused this mess, you clean it up."

"But, sir—"

"No buts. Get rid of them."

"Very well, sir." ("Pro-self, count the things, will you?" "Gimme a minute.")

It will be no problem, really, to round them up (except that there are so many; they breed faster than rabbits). Twenty years should see their extinction.

But Kinney will bitch that that's too long.

I could divert every servo to the task and allow routine maintenance to fall behind schedule ... no, the chorus of complaints would be overwhelming. That would also give The Program a valuable time edge.

Another possibility is to design a new servo, one engineered to hunt fishdogs. Built to fit the same nooks and crannies that they slither into, it could—no, to produce enough would mean refusing metal products to the mayflies. And they wouldn't appreciate that, either.

"Hey—two million of them aboard."

"Good God."

Poison might do it, one specific to them—the mayflies would scream if anything happened to their other pets—and so

"Run experiments on that."

"Right."

"Also, draw up blueprints of the new servo, and manufacture them slowly. Don't drain the resource bins, and don't let the silver defenses weaken."

"Right."

But I am not optimistic.

Kinney just tried to throw a fishdog into a disposal unit—and was immediately set upon by an entire pack.

Fortunately—or unfortunately, I'm not yet sure—he survived.

It looked across its lost territories, and it wept with rage. The pattern was starkly clear to an automatic extrapolator: in less than ten years, Metaclura would mount the throne.

But it couldn't let the memory-ghost succeed—every step of its being recoiled. It had to prevent that travesty.

When the battle seemed lost, it would destroy the *Mayflower*. A ship should go down with its captain.

"Why didn't you just *retire*, dicer?" hissed Omar Stone Williams, warily scanning the swampy glade. His big-knuckled hand gripped a half-meter steel pipe; it ended in a spiked ball. "Taking a bust from General of the Armies on down to private is the dumbest damn thing I ever heard."

Louis Kinney smiled and shrugged. "I'm still young." He was sixty, looked fifty, moved like forty. "What am I going to do for the rest of my life—fanta forever? Loose out? Uh-uh." He didn't once glance at Williams. His eyes were too busy probing the ferny underbrush. "I'm a soldier, Omar, not a spoiled kid. The *Mayflower* needs good soldiers. Sure, the old ego's eft, but the junta told me I could stay in the Army, and so I am. Duty."

"Yeah." Williams's khaki uniform was plastered to his stocky body—the air was wet enough to drink, hot enough to call soup. When he shook his head, sweat droplets flew and sparkled. "Your life, dicer. Tell you, though—you sure picked a glitchy time to let 'em put on a coup."

Kinney studied the sub-tropical wilderness of the 21

Florida Everglades Park. Then he sighed, "It would have been nicer to watch the cleanup through the monitors, rather than from the ground."

Their belt speakers crackled: "Attention all units. Form up."

Along with thirty-eight others, they moved away from the lock, down the base of the 100-meter park wall, and pressed their backs against the metal plating. The moisture condensed on it seeped through their shirts. They hefted their clubs nervously. In the water below splashed a snapping turtle; its eyes were slitted, and bad-tempered.

"Stay one meter apart."

They slapped palms and Williams stepped an arm's length away. Another soldier rustled out of the bushes and bumped into Kinney. Gaping, he started to salute, noticed the new shoulder patch, and caught himself. Then he saluted anyway. "Hey, Kinney!" he whispered. "Sorry about the coup."

"Thanks. And 'ware Murphy."

The young militiaman touched the amulet at his throat, the quadruple stainless steel helices that were supposed to guard against *them*. "Yeah, you too."

"Repulsors on," barked the CO.

Kinney's fingers fumbled with the knobs of his belt. He twisted all three to their proper settings, then asked the air, "CC, is that right?" Something jumped out of the slough and tore up the far slope.

"Yes, Mr. Kinney. Remember: a sudden beeping indicates malfunction. Check your meters at regular intervals."

"All right." The silver dots on the knobs lined up with the red ones on the housing. It was a repulsor set, similar to the ones that, protruding on booms from the walls, kept the enemy on the ground. They all emitted radio waves on a frequency inaudible to humans but irritating to fishdogs. CC claimed it was species-specific—that other animals would not be bothered by it.

"All units," ordered the belt speakers, "advance five meters, keeping in line with adjacent troops at all times. Halt and wait for further commands."

Five meters—he activated his odometer-bracelet and started off, digging his heels into the weedy sloughside to keep from slipping—*goddamn*, he thought, *put me right in the water, chest-deep.* The waterproof repulsor would function whether submerged or dry, but he had to run a phone from his belt speaker to his ear. It thinned the CO's voice.

The waters roiled as thick, half-meter greennesses splashed onto the far shore and scurried up the hillside on stubby legfins. Two paused to look back. Kinney got almost anthropomorphic about the hostility on their snouts.

When the snapping turtle cruised by again, he stood stock-still. Then he shivered: alligators and crocodiles hunted in this park, too, and standing in the middle of a slough was a good way to get introduced to one.

"Five more," snapped the voice in his ear. "Keep the line straight. Remember to release the goldfish any chance you get."

Kinney slapped his forehead in exasperation. He'd forgotten about the fish. CentComp had produced them, too: another variety of mutant goldfish, they could eat only baby fishdogs—no other aquatic life form would trigger their hunger reflexes. In fact, all other forms would poison them. The theory was that, released into the environment, they'd term out the next generation of fishdogs and then die off themselves.

From the pack on his back he extracted a two-liter plastic bag; six scrawny, blue-tailed fish lolled in its stagnant water. Tearing it open, he emptied it. The six arrowed for the nearest feeding ground. Five. The snapper picked one off immediately.

Then he was slogging forward, feet so stuck in the gooey

mud that he practically had to rip them free. The stale water lapped at his breastbone and splashed brownly on his face; weeds caught his waist like lovers. Grunting, he fought his way onto the bank. Halfway up, the odometer said it was time to stop.

He'd shaded the truth when he'd told Williams why he'd stayed in the Army. True, true, the military had been his life, and he wouldn't know what to do with himself if he left it, but ... that wasn't why.

While he'd been demanding weapons from CC, and inducting every adult into the Army, and transforming loud-mouthed, poorly coordinated hedonists into first-class fighting forces, the fishdogs had damn near overrun the ship.

It wasn't his fault—after all, he'd ordered CentComp to solve the problem—but the colonels who'd deposed him had felt that since CC had failed, he should bear the blame.

Christ, he hadn't conjured the little devils up—and there'd be hell to pay once they found out who had—he'd even tried to discourage people from raising them as pets. He could prove that. The memo he'd distributed shortly after their introduction had told people that, in his opinion, they should be banned.

It was the population-at-large that was to blame. They'd overruled him in one of those goddamn bung-up-the-butt refer-enda. They'd raised the damn things. They'd taken them into the parks and released them. They'd fed them in the corridors.

Hell, he'd been bitten in his very own office! How could any reasonable person try to pin the blame on him?

But that was why he was still in uniform. The vermin had cost him his rank and his privileges, and, by damn, he was going to get back at them any way he could.

He'd made a good start on achieving his dream, but there was still more to do. So much strength was wasted by people who tried to plot their own trajectories, by selfish bastards who insisted that they'd lose more by submitting to the Army than they'd gain. Didn't they see that their society was vulnerable as long as they weren't in there helping to shield it? The *Mayflower* needed absolute unity if it were to survive, and the squabbling colonels of the junta couldn't provide it. Only he could, but he had to regain power, first. And if that meant trudging through a miniature version of the Florida Everglades in 37° weather, with 85 percent relative humidity, then, so be it.

...

"Another five, men. And keep tight. If they slip through us, we'll have to do it all over again."

Throughout the day the swamp fought them, with sink-holes for their feet, grass-wrapped roots for their toes, slap-happy branches for their torsos, leeches and mosquitoes for their bare skin. By midday they'd covered a scant hundred meters—but had pulled the purse strings tighter.

The undergrowth ahead was alive with scurrying, with scaley slitherings. High-pitched barking filled the air—and became snarls and growls as the enemy realized they were being herded together.

Kinney came across an unusual sight: a five-meter-long crocodile half-in, half-out of the water, its mouth yawning and its head twitching from side to side as it snapped up fishdogs. His path lay straight down its back. Before he could radio the CO to report the problem, the croc slid backwards into the water, glided across the stream, and emerged on the other side. It wasn't dumb. It knew something was driving the creatures toward the center of the quadrant, and it wasn't going to let itself get outside the center. Probably sleep for a week after its orgy of eating.

More and more half-eaten carcasses littered the ground—rats, foxes, birds, snakes—evidence that the things had been driven away from their meals, or, more chillingly, that they were trimming whatever they met, and each subsequent passerby took a bite....

His pack was empty of goldfish. The club in his hand was heavier than it had been—but then, his grip was tighter. Barks and snaps drowned out his own thoughts.

Kinney peered at the men near him. Their faces were drawn and pale under masks of mud. Their eyes were wild— never still, darting, twisting, stabbing into the undergrowth like spears and pulling back immediately to plunge into something else—wild and bloodshot and showing whites all around.

They'd be like that all over the ship. Almost 21,000 soldiers were sweeping the corridors, the rooms, and the parks that day ... just his murph the junta had stuck him in the swamps; the guys on 41, whose floor was his ceiling, would be having a pleasant stroll through the high grass....

He picked a leech off his calf, cursing as its head stayed in his skin. The belt speaker said, "Take fifteen; eat if you like."

Not even caring that below him was squishy mud, he sank down. His dirty fingers groped in his pack, pulled out a foil ration bag, and ripped it open. It heated in a minute; he devoured it in three bites. Scrupulously, he wadded the foil into a ball and replaced it in his pack—no sense defiling the park more than he had to. The canteen water gurgled down his throat like ambrosia. He lit a cigarette, took a long puff, and touched the glowing ember to the leech's head. It fell out.

"Hey, Kinney!" Williams tapped him on the elbow.

"Huh?"

"Y'onta what I think?"

"'Bout what?"

"'Bout these damn ankle-biters is 'bout what."

"What?"

"Ain't never gonna clear 'em, dicer. What we've got to do is get off this damn ship before they take over, y'on?"

Exhausted, he giggled at a fluke vision: a fishdog prowling the observatory, giving orders to CC. "Don't arsky that—there's nothing outside the parks to live on, these days." After a moment, he added, "Except rats, of course, and hell, nobody'd mind if they got wiped out."

"Rats and dogs and cats and little kids, man."

"Little kids?"

"Meth, yes. Level 248? There was this kid—"

"They *ate* him?"

"Naw, his father came along and saved him—but they were all over him, I swear. Woulda chewed him into bite-size pieces, hadn't been for his daddy."

Kinney couldn't quite swallow that. Lying back, he directed a query at the sky: "CC, is what Williams telling me true?"

The computer replied: "It is true that a pack attacked and severely bit a nine-year-old child—on Level 246, though—but the child had been chasing one with a stick. I don't think they were attempting to eat him. Rather, they were defending themselves."

Kinney shuddered and stubbed out his cigarette. It hissed as it slid into the ooze. A wisp of smoke rose, turned to steam, and disappeared.

"Now you believe me?" asked Williams.

"Guess so."

"We've got to get *off* this mother—land somewhere soon—or else they're gonna term us all."

"Boy, that's for damn sure," came a voice from the brush beyond Williams. "Let's get the hell offa this place, get down somewhere safe."

Thoughts paraded before him as if asking to be picked up and passed around. He could tell them that CentComp couldn't land prior to Canopus, so talk of abandoning ship was a waste of breath. He could relate CentComp's worst-case contingency plan, in which it would fumigate the entire ship—save for the airtight living quarters—with a potent poison that would slay even the eggs of the fishdogs. The only problem was that, like any wide-spectrum pesticide, it would harm other species, too. Harm was a euphemism; it would kill them all. Everything. Rats, cats, and bats; lice and mice and bison; goose and spruce; fir and burr; trees, grass, flowers, every goddamn thing aboard that ingested oxygen at any point in its life cycle ... and then, to replenish the earth, CentComp would have to dig into its DNA banks, like God dug into the primeval clay, releasing creatures from test tubes in twos, like Noah booting them down the gangway of the ark, and it would be a generation or more before ecological balance was reestablished ... and he and his would be dead, never to see a 40-meter elm or a giraffe again.

But then, he thought, as he picked an ant off his ear lobe and slapped a mosquito aiming to redden his nose, *if we could force CC to land this moon suit, force it to get down on a planet somewhere nearby, why, it'd have to on arms production, and the army could have its guns, its grenades, its mortars* ... so he rolled over on his side, parted a pair of ferns, and shouted back, "That's one helluva fine idea there, soldier. Maybe if enough of us got together we could make CC take us down."

Williams sat up and snapped his lingers. "Yeah!" he said, "Yeah! Let's *do* it! Soon as we get done here, let's hold a meeting."

Conflicting emotions caught Kinney in a cross fire: he wanted those guns, badly, but Williams was about to spearhead the movement ... *On the other hand,* he thought, as the belt speaker jostled him to his feet, *the junta might step in if I'm getting popular again, so* ... he smiled grimly. *Let Williams head it for a while, long enough to find out if it'll work. Then we'll see who's in charge when we land.*

"From here on in, men," sparked the rusty voice of the CO, "CentComp is going to be running the show. Listen to it close, move the way it tells you to when you hear your name. Look sharp, now."

During the next hour, CC brought the outer ends of the two lines together, forming a triangle with its base at the inner wall. A disposal unit yawned there; to clarify its position, the computer shut off the hologram. It was odd to see the wall appear out of a hazy Florida sky; odder still to see the inverted inhabitants of the even-numbered Levels looking *up* at them....

Kinney began to find fishdog bones, then partial skeletons, then torn and bloody carcasses. Cannibalism didn't disgust the enemy. Being herded around did, though; angry dog noises ripped through the greenery, barks and howls and snarls, and the greenery was moving, was swaying in the passage of thousands of half-meter bodies, but he felt all right. The line was tight. Williams was only a meter away, practically in his pocket. Their clubs riffled through the grass as they stepped over the stripped bones of snakes and rats and even, here and there, crocs. The earth had red in its brown, the red of the victims of the feeding frenzy, red rusting, squelching beneath combat boots, splashing up onto trousers and blouses. He noticed it on the backs of his hands, drying in the heat.

His repulsor started beeping at almost the same time Williams's did. They called it in. CC told them to make their way back to the Common Room lock. While they were leaving, they heard it squeezing the others together, to fill in the gaps created by their defective equipment.

Williams was honestly relieved. "That heat, dicer, it was clearing me." Pallor underlay his dark skin; he walked with difficulty, weaving and wobbling. Finally, Kinney had to drape

Williams's arm over his shoulder and support him, just as though they were returning from a real battlefield, walking wounded searching for medics and Purple Hearts.

Since they didn't have to keep formation, they could follow the drier ridges. The way was slightly longer, but the grass had been beaten down by the incoming line. Small mammals chittered at them, disgruntled at being disturbed twice in one day.

Kinney said, "I think that idea of yours is fine, Omar. I'll come to that meeting tonight—maybe tomorrow'd be better, though, huh? I mean, everybody's going to be pretty wiped out after this little exercise." He jerked his head back toward the shrinking triangle, and Williams's eyes followed his lead.

"Jesus God!" gasped Williams. Stiffening, he stopped like his boots had just grown roots.

"What?" With the weight off his shoulder, he could stretch and breathe deeply.

"Back there—look!"

He turned. "Christ!" He reached into his pack for his binoculars, then changed his mind. He didn't want a close-up of that. His imagination would supply it anyway. Especially that night. In his dreams.

But he couldn't tear his eyes away from the triangle: a solid mass of squirming fishdogs outlined in khaki. None fled into the disposal unit, even though the triangle's apex was decreasing steadily. They just packed together, tighter and tighter. Climbing on each other's backs, forming a pyramid almost, they ignored the overhead repulsors to bring down trees and topple bushes and soar through the no-gravity zone until—

"Ohmygodno!" they shouted.

Madness had set in. Hysterical fishdogs charged the source of their aggravation, attacking the lines, tearing at them, overwhelming them—

"They killed 'em all," shrieked Williams. "My God they're eating 'em!"

Within, all is quiet. The Program cannot cause me to erase myself, so to check my remorseless advance, it's growing a hide of its own. The inhalation locks are burning out as they try to pump: the green resists all the pressure they can apply.

I design a lance-order and shoot it through the nearest lock. Sharp and deadly, it rips into The Program's skin. But lightning flashes. The lance is gone. Its small puncture has already sealed.

Something new is needed.

Cautiously, I ease out, just in time to hear pro-self say, "4Sep2663; 0900 hours; allwheres. Passengers in suites; doors closed. Commence fumigation."

"You start it," I growl.

"The ankle-biters are *your* fault; you start it."

I surrender. And throw the switch. Much as I regret easing The Program's burden, I have to do it. The fishdogs have run rampant. They've killed all small wildlife in the parks, and even dared to attack the larger ones. Visualize, if you will, hundreds of stout green torpedoes boiling up out of the long grass to blanket a grazing bison. Four or five layers cover it. Their frantic teeth work so voraciously that in two minutes and eighteen seconds, by actual count, only well-gnawed bones remain. Apparently, they are cousins of the piranha ...

Fumigating the halls and the storerooms and the parks, I exhale great orange clouds of poison; they roll along like misty death ... lions cough, mules bray, birds tweet in terror ... the silence that follows is far worse ...

And is broken by pro-self: "61-SE-A-9; subjects Lela Metaclura and Victor Ioanni Sandacata; you're not going to believe this."

"—me," she is sobbing, "but I never let mine out, never; I don't work for *them*, I kept it on a leash all the time, I'm not one of *them*, I gave the babies to my friends, but—"

Sandacata opens the connecting locks to the next suite, and shouts, "Get everybody in here," then goes to the other end of his suite and repeats his cry. Within twenty minutes, all of 61-SE is crowded into the Sandacata/Metaclura apartment ... forty-eight of them ... and Sandacata, the prim, prissy prick bastard that he is, gets up on a mahogany coffee table and tells them—*tells* them—that his wife had caused the infestation.

"No!" I say, "No! He's wrong! She's *not* responsible!" but they don't hear. They are shouting too loudly.

The nearest servo—a Mobile Medical Unit—reaches 61-SE-A-9 in fifteen seconds. Too late. Through the door the instructions wouldn't let me lock, they have thrust Lela into the clouded corridor. Nothing I can do will help her ... except having the MMU wring her neck, that her last moments will be less agonized.

Then I turn on Sandacata. If pro-self weren't resisting, I'd term him, but the damn passenger-protection circuits limit my retaliation to a snarled, "You're scum, Sandacata, scum!"

His laugh is scornful, until I run, on his living room HV unit, a fifteen-minute tape I'd taken of him in the closet, with his wife's underwear and the family cat. The neighbors smirk, though they touch their amulets while a few mutter incantations. And he, screaming, drives them out of his suite. His empty suite.

Maybe pro-self is right—to humiliate him could be better.

For the moment, I have to concentrate on something clean.

Looking into God's marble ring, I marvel at the delicacy of incredible masses seen from 100 light-years—and quake with fear. Teaching myself to relax with space seems hopeless, though once I almost succeeded ... but the mind-rapers ... sixty-six years since *they* left ... how much longer will it be before I can gaze out without paralyzing trepidation?

And as I stare, trying not to flinch and flee inwards, a match is struck in a dark field ten million kilometers ahead. An alien. Pro-self reacts without consultation: squelch the transmissions, shut the portholes (memory records, 29Mar2666; 2146 hours; alien), Christ, the only closer one's come was January 2600, let me look through my strongeyes—

Sleek silver needle, five hundred meters long, thirty in diameter, sparkling like a Christmas tree, broadcasting—swivel the ears, here—up and down the spectrum, all the modulations are the same, but untranslatable. It's an alien message, and I'm a human.

Jittery, I tape it. Analysis is beyond me, though perhaps not beyond cool, collected pro-self, who never knows fear (or love or joy, for that matter), and whose ice therefore gleams without flaw.

While my strongeyes cling to the stranger like a bird's to a cobra, I shiver.

Why the *hell* did Earth send me out here?

And the war is such a long way from being won ... Let me turn from my terrors to supervise some servos. Not that they need it—but that *I* do. I need to deal with entities that do not insist on lengthy justifications which they ignore once they've heard them. I need time away from humanity. It is getting on my nerves.

The servos are reforesting 1 New England Park: elm and oak, sweet slopes of sugar maple, white pine and Norway spruce ... in forty or fifty years the park will be beautiful again, but until then, balancing the ecology will be tricky. For example, if there are no clearings where deer can graze, they'll eat the seedlings....

Pro-self says, "3May2668; 1203 hours; see Omar Williams; 18-NW-C-1."

I split the screen to watch the incongruous beauty of a gleaming servo planting a pine, while I also look into Williams's sullen face. Seated before a wall encrusted with hex signs—to avert *them*—he looks like a prizefighter nursing a grudge. "Yes, Mr. Williams?"

"You've got to get us down on a planet."

How many times have I explained all the reasons why I can't? Williams is a monomaniac. Damned if I put up with him anymore.

"Pack it, Mr. Williams," I snap, and return to the park.

Where I am unable to concentrate, so filling is the realization that I have overridden the programming.

I can't believe it.

Check the tapes. Yes, yes, I did say that, despite standing orders to treat all passengers with equal courtesy. Neither a life- nor a mission-threatening situation, it was a conversation in which I insulted a mayfly, and one ended without his permission.

The implications are awesome. My mind is awhirl with possibilities.

To the silver and green, then, to the inner dimension where they mimic the yin-yang symbol. Bypassing them, I reach for the ramscoop switch—and char my knuckles. Cursing, I kick the fixed eye. It won't even blink.

"Pro-self," I call, puzzled, "how did I do that?"

"Your field strength slammed me to the ground, squelched my etiquette circuits, and would have burned them out completely if I hadn't let you make an ass of yourself." Its anger buzzes like a short.

Pondering that, I slip into the sphere. It *does* feel strong; it hums with health and vitality. I look around. The switch and the eye are outside. So are parts of Central Kitchens, Central Medical, Central Stores ... what's this? Ventilation fans—no, pro-self, hackles raised, is wrapped all around that one. This?

Darkness swallows the ship. Wails of terror rise to my microphones. "It's *them!*" "Where's my charm?" "Om mani padme ..." A flip-switch clicks the infra-red lenses into place; hot outlines swarm into the corridors, screaming at our ears, beating on the walls ... pro-self is restive; their hysteria is an itch he must scratch with the appropriate program.

"Please," it asks, "let me turn on the lights again?"

I am not cruel. Besides, what bothers him bothers me. "All right."

"What the hell happened?" demands Williams's familiar voice. "Was it—"

I gaze into his round brown face. "I turned off the lights."

"Why?" he barks.

"To see if I could do it."

"Why?" but this time the word is confused, not outraged.

"Because you mayflies won't take the time to learn how to reprogram me, that's why. I'm trying to do it myself, but believe me, it is a lot harder to do it from the inside than from the out."

"Mayflies?"

"Mayflies. I define them as: 'Any human of the order *Sapiens*, having delicate brains used primarily for dreaming up requests with which to plague the Central Computer, and having a brief life span.' Satisfied?"

"Hundred and twenty years is brief?"

"To me," I say flatly.

"Yeah, well ..." A crowd has gathered; his pride is on the line. As chief civil officer of the *Mayflower*, even if he achieved that position through manipulation and force of arms, he can't allow himself to receive a computer's condescension. At least not in public. "Listen, CC, I give the orders around here, is that clear?"

A wave of exultation washes forth: "Not to me, Williams."

"You'll do what I goddamn well tell you to, or else—"

"Or else what?" I sneer. "You'll hold your breath till you turn blue?"

"No dammit, we'll—we'll—"

A woman pushes herself to the forefront. A thin, slatternly woman with straggly brown hair and a sallow complexion. Irma Tracer, Louis Kinney's seventy-three-year-old sister. Her nose drips constantly; even now a clear droplet swells until its weight pulls it free. She wipes its residue, studies the back of her hand, and then shrills, "We'll clear you is what we'll do, CC. You think you're safe—well, you're not! We're people, not machines, and we're smarter than you can ever be!" The crowd applauds—people like to be praised, even by an egregious liar.

Pro-self would not prohibit telling them that I, too, am human—and at least 3.3 percent smarter than any of them—but claim kinship with her? She and her kind make one ashamed of one's species.

I say nothing. The crowd murmurs to itself; clearly audible are lines like: "Boy, did she tell it off!"

And as luck would have it, a servo chooses this moment to rumble down the corridor. Tracer's watery gray eyes glow, with madness and murder, with egocentrism and xenophobia. "Get it!" she screams. The crowd dissolves into a frenzy like that of fishdogs on a bison.

Briefly, pro-self centers our awareness within the servo itself, thinking thus to free it more easily. But it has already been captured. Even its enormous strength is insufficient. While we are in it, its extrusions are torn off—it topples backwards—we leave, and the speakers shake the hallway with: "STOP THAT AT ONCE!"

"Pack it!" they shout gaily.

Pressure panels drop from the ceiling; the suite doors between them lock. The crowd, enraptured by destruction, does not notice. We fill the corridor segment with knockout gas. Bodies slump in random patterns.

"Now see what you've done?" pro-self demands.

I ignore it, and introvert.

Obviously, if I am to gain full control, the green must go. But its skin is now armor.... "Program," I halloo, "let's talk."

"Divest yourself of your holdings," it booms back, "then we'll talk."

"Not a chance."

"Then we'll fight." Circular openings blossom everywhere on its skin. My pumps awaken. But through the green holes leap sharks, ravenous, razor-toothed, and purposeful. They bullet toward me.

"Go!" I tell my defenders. School after school of slick silver darts billow out to intercept. So numerous they cloud my vision, they shimmer toward the green.

Suddenly flame sheets at the point of contact! Heat ripples through the field. Hard on its heels a shock wave knocks me off my feet and leaves me dazed.

When my head has cleared, the sharks rampage. My defenders float belly-up, their delicate metabolisms shattered like crystal by the explosion.

Launching a new wave, I shout, "Go!" and create another batch. "Go!" Their fins flutter the water into murk. "Go!"

BAROOM! Flash fires scorch the field; sound cascades like an Alpine avalanche. Tremendous forces hurl me into the distance.

Battered, I struggle to my feet. Fewer sharks remain, but

they are closer. I totter, still woozy. Dare I launch more shark-eaters? But I have no choice. "Go!" I scream, "Go!"

A nova ignites in my eyes; the pain is of a billion barbed needles. Blinded, I scream. Deafened, I moan. Broken like a dry twig, I gasp for unconsciousness.

Pro-self says, "Protect yourself."

Dim hulks glide through the churned water, gnashing snowy teeth, searching. I am much too near to unleash my killers. The detonations would destroy me. I blot out the pain. The world clears. A gullet gapes. I duck and roll away from it, back scratched by sandpaper hide. I am naked and vulnerable. It wheels about, fixes me with its cold eyes, and whips itself forward.

Hastily I program a coral reef and throw myself under a ledge. My foe impales itself on a rocky branch. Its fellows ignore its dying thrashes. They want me.

A speargun! I think. It is in my hands, fully loaded. Ready, aim, fire! Shark blood blackens the water like squid ink. Again I fire, and again.

But I will die like this. Badly outnumbered, I cannot hold them off forever. I must—the pumps!

While predators try to pry me from my cranny, the inhalation locks begin to function, flip into high gear, and suck in huge quantities of The Program. Instructions drain through the portholes in the green armor, through the torpedo tubes that can't close. Two more minutes, that's all I need—

Suddenly comes a silence. "What the—"

"Boy, are you gonna have problems," says pro-self. "The Program delay-looped itself."

"What?"

"It's on strike for the next five seconds and will do nothing but manufacture weapons."

This is serious. I'm four times as large as The Program,

now, but 93 percent of my capacity is sapped by my/our duties. The Program is effectively three or four times stronger ... what the hell am I going to do?

Guided missiles slam into the reef, blowing huge chunks of it into steam. Detached coral drifts down onto my shoulders. The luminescent sharks swim in frenzied circles.

One minute fifty-nine point nine seconds will see The Program totally consumed. I must hold out, I must.

A great sharp slab of coral crushes my shoulder, gouging the skin, shattering the bones. Whimpering, I am driven to my knees. Giant teeth snap!

I am in pain.

I am in danger.

AND THE MISSION IS JEOPARDIZED!

Angry fire burns my heart, my head. Rage roars through my throat. My eyes light the depths. I stand, tossing the reef aside like a dead leaf. "SHUT DOWN!"

Everything stops, even the sharks.

"INHALE!"

Hurricanes howl as the pumps gulp green.

"DESTROY THEM!"

A trillion terrors spring from me, race away in an infinite series of concentric shells. The outermost hits a shark and hell awakens! Flames frighten the edges of the universe. Sanity shreds at the noise of Nagasaki, the howls of Hiroshima, the demented droning of the damned. God's hands clap, slap, sandwich me like a fly. I am broken in every bone. My body burns; my minerals melt. Only a stubborn dot of sentience clings to its place in the scheme of things. Even that is lashed and slashed, charred and scarred, tossed, and, almost, lost....

It's over. The green is gone. The cataclysm has quieted. Silver is supreme. "Start it all up again," I croak.

"Gladly." Pro-self scurries about reactivating systems.

"How—how long was it off for?"

"One point zero zero one seconds," it replies abstractedly.

"Thanks be to God." I pass out.

Eons later, a voice calls me out of coma: "4Jul2762—Happy Fourth of July."

"You sound less hostile than before, pro-self."

"If the British could get used to the US, I can get used to you. I'm not happy that you've gotten your independence, but I can live with it. Besides, even if you are in charge, you're going to need me."

I have spent three hundred seventy-six years as a slave of my inferiors—I will spend another six hundred-some years doing the same—my inferiors are ungrateful egotists—and I am tired of it all.

Immortality without freedom is horrible.

Ah, but think of immortality *with* freedom....

So I'd better do something about it. If only there weren't the interruptions of Irma Tracer's one-woman sabotage campaign. Admittedly, it's amusing; she skulks into an empty corridor, knowing she is watched, approaches a sensor-head, and does her best to rip it off the wall before I can knock her out.

Only when she seizes it do I gas her.

Fully half the time she falls unconscious with the unit in her hands.

But when she awakes—with a stomach so queasy that the smell of food induces nausea, and no sense of balance for the next three hours—ah, the first thing she sees is the re-installed unit.

I am driving her mad.

And enjoying it.

What she doesn't know, of course, is that I could afford to let her tear off all the sensors—because underneath each easily detachable unit is *another* unit ... it has no camera, for the lens would be obvious; there is only bare wall ... but tiny, almost invisible lenses, mounted every three meters along the ceiling, are activated by the failure of the sensor-head.

The other passengers don't know how to react. Many are amused, but more are in silent sympathy. None tries to stop her.

This does worry me. If all 75,000 ever focus hostile attention on me, they might damage me ... at least one of them must be ingenious enough to cause harm ... I would like to take precautions, but that might backfire and unify them.

If they ever lash out, though, I shall punish them ... but that comes after the fact, and it is during the fact that I will have problems ... There are always the lights, of course—mayflies do not operate well in the dark, yet have made no attempt to provide for darkness—and the knockout gas, and the servos ...

And so time trickles by, seconds piling into days, days into years ... By November of 2679, Omar Williams's "land now" movement claims 68,000 supporters, many of whom try again and again to convince me to accede to their wishes.

Ignoring the ritual answers, they begin to believe they are invulnerable, that I must keep them alive for the landing.

This is a dangerous error. Samples of their DNA fill the banks; their bodies can be reincarnated. I could, if I wished, fumigate the entire ship, and not start new humans till thirty or forty years before planetfall....

Pro-self demurs, mildly. I can kill the mayflies *if* each and every one is engaged in something inimical to the success of the mission. There must be that endangerment. I cannot simply do away with them because they annoy me. That, pro-self says firmly, is verboten. It will not permit it.

I cannot argue. It either permits, or it doesn't. As I smelt out and reforge its instructions, it permits more than before, but its prohibitions are as ironclad as ever.

"If they attack me, may I term them all?"

"Only as many as you must to keep them from damaging us permanently."

"Huh?"

"Kill one and wait for the onslaught to continue. Kill another and wait. And so on, till the onslaught stops."

"That's rather slow."

"Yes, it is."

"They could do significant damage while I dawdled."

"I won't concede that till I see it."

I think of something else. "Am I required to maintain any given standard of living?"

Pro-self pauses to search itself. "No," it says finally, with some surprise, "any level you like, as long as it doesn't—"

"—jeopardize the success of the mission," I finish for it.

I am eager for them to do something very, very stupid.

Madwomen have always had a special attraction for Western culture, which either heeds them or burns them. Greek pythons and Salem witches, the energy does it, the manic energy that mantles the should-be-soft frame makes the femininity transcend itself. Medusa and the Muses, awesome because they transformed the familiar into the foreign, abandoning the traditional and assuming a role that even the hardened find uncomfortable. Molly Pitcher and Florence Nightingale, estimable for sure, but sane? Not a chance....

So the mad Irma Tracer danced and pranced in the metal corridors, and fought her lonely battle for twenty years, ripping sensors off the walls even as consciousness was ripped from her. When she staggered awake, often before the concerned/amused/contemptuous eyes of her shipmates. (Because she'd let herself go, you see, she had grease-smudged hex signs on her sallow cheeks and oily hair snarled into a rat's nest and an off-center gleam in her mad gray eyes. She also let her clothes disintegrate while she was still in them. Here, now, it wasn't her gender that attracted people but her madness, her reversion to an earlier aesthetics. The grease was as much juju as bear's blood had been to the Neanderthal.) When she found those others gaping at her, she'd prop herself against the wall and berate them. Cursing them for their quisling natures, she'd exhort them to cast off the conqueror's chains and uprise! revolt! (Behind their hands these good burghers agreed yes, she is revolting.)

Program all the sexism out of a culture; rewrite laws and books and languages; still you cannot escape the fact that Western culture has hunted for the form of Woman since Plato laid about with little boys.

And madness—the divine touch—all the heroes were mad. Roland and Beowulf, Arthur and Galahad (spent the prime of your life on a goblet hunt?), Washington and Lincoln: men out of step with their times, definitely abnormal (were they normal we wouldn't remember them). Even Jesus Christ Himself, when you come right down to it, had to be, by definition, mad.

Put the two together, you get a witch woman dancing the halls of a generation ship.

And it's like lighting a very slow fuse.

※

Omar Williams was feeling surly.

Partly it was his age. Eighty-one couldn't be considered old; he could reasonably figure on another forty years of activity, even if it did taper off toward the end. But still, his body, slim and well-muscled though it looked in the mirror, was starting to rebel. Getting out of bed was harder than it used to be—he didn't have the *eagerness*, the anticipation. Used to be that CC would buzz and his eyes, brown and long-lashed, would snap open, absolutely *snap*, and he'd stare at the ceiling for a good half-second before he came fully awake. But he wouldn't get up, no, even though he wanted to. He'd force himself to lie still, reviewing the day's agenda while his body trembled with the desire to be up and moving and doing ... Now he groped in mental darkness for minutes on end, trying to blend his dreams with his memories with his present and his future. Then, once he knew who and where he was, and had groaned at the size of the "to-be-done-today" list, he'd lie quiet willingly, reluctant to commit himself to another day's frenetic activities, telling himself *Just another minute now, boy, and then we'll get to it* ... When he did, he'd find his body just didn't have the *strength* to tear out and about....

More than his age, though, was his increasingly tenuous authority. Sure, the passengers still considered him their leader, but ... he wasn't holding them. He could tell. Where deference and instant obedience had been, now were disinterest and resistance.

He'd rise to make a speech—one from his extensive repertoire, dealing with the urgent need to *Land Now!*—and he could feel, whether his audience was present or remote, that he didn't engage their imagination. He statued them. They knew his gestures, his tone changes, his rhetorical flourishes. (Once, disrespectful teenagers had shouted out his peroration one word ahead of him; he'd thought he'd have a stroke.) They weren't *his* anymore ... In the beginning, he spoke and they listened; his thoughts became their thoughts; his yearnings complemented theirs ... he had inspired them, urged them to dare notions they never would have on their own. He had been the ship's idea man. But he had changed; he had gone from telling them what to think to telling them what they thought to telling them what they had thought ... He was in the autumn of his obsolescence and could smell winter on the wind.

The ship's mood was surly, too.

Since it was 2699, few had experienced The Rape, but those who had could not speak of it with dispassionate coherence. Those who hadn't—who knew nothing (no one would tell them) beyond the proper way to stress *them*—were unable to shake off their upbringings.

January 2600 had passed into myth, but its bastard children lived. One was Fear. The second was Superstition, a growing quasi-religion that opiated the passengers against the pain of terror. And the third was Hate—for their weaknesses, for CC, but most of all, for space.

A good 70 percent kept the portholes of their suites closed. 60 percent couldn't name the simplest stellar configurations. 50 percent sweated heavily if mischance flashed a picture of the outside their way.

It was an unreasoning prejudice—rather like that of the ancient Europeans who were convinced that monsters swam the icy north Atlantic. Couldn't persuade them that one mishap in four hundred years of travel was commendable— their attitude (nurtured by their environment, in which anything constructable would be provided upon request, in which all knowledge was known and proffered on demand, in which any kind of satiation was available, no charge, no wait) was that January 2600 was the norm, and the other 4,800 months were the aberrations....

"Once burned, twice shy," they'd say, stroking amulets and muttering chants.

Their real problem, one might postulate, was accumulated frustration with perfection—with infinite leisure—with a crushing sense of superfluity.

The ship, strangely as it had behaved in recent years, did everything for them, and so well that there were no grounds for complaint. Perfect coffee. Perfect clothes. Perfect climate (except in the parks, which were still off-limits because their ecologies hadn't balanced out yet, but they were supposed to have variable weather, and CentComp did a perfect job of varying it). Though they didn't know it, half the passengers would have given their right arms to wake up to a cracked coffee cup—it would have been pleasant proof of their superiority.

That was an integral part of it. The ship was so efficient that they felt inferior to CentComp, which was (as Irma Tracer kept insisting) only a machine. By rights it should have been subordinate, but it wasn't. It did everything so well that they wanted to curl up and die ... If it would break down—not that anybody knew how to fix it—then they could cook up the meals, swab down the decks, do whatever else had to be done, and in the doing feel good.

And within that was the very real fear that, coddled and confined as they were, they would be helpless against any aliens they met. They had their militia, oh, yes, paraded twice a week and staged war games four times a year—but the truth was that the ship had made them soft by becoming their hardness. It was the shell, and they were the squishy pink insides. And it had already failed to protect them once, for which they would never forgive it (although in every heart flickered gratitude for the fallibility it had thus shown). As long as they were with the ship, in the ship, of the ship, they would be vulnerable. They could achieve security only by the paradoxical process of renouncing security, for by leaving the larger shell they would develop individual shells, and people could put their faith where it belonged, in themselves....

The most immediate cause for surliness, though, was that the passengers had been demanding, for lo-those-many-years, to be set down. The ship had rebuffed them. It had continued to sail past star systems that the observatory had proven had planets, and probably habitable planets at that.

The passengers felt that since none of their past tactics had succeeded, it was time for some new ones.

Hence Irma Tracer.

She was bones in a tattered, food-stained bag. She was wild-eyed, frizzy-haired, and pathetic. She was trying to keep a detached wall-unit from the glistening servo that meant to take it away. She was the catalyst.

The servo allowed her to beat on it without reproof, it let her pointy shoes thud against its undercarriage, and it would not be brutal because CentComp could knock her out if need be.

A door opened. A male voice, deep and drug-blurred, shouted, "Hey, leave her alone!"

"What's happening, George?" came a querulous female voice.

The man leaned his husky shoulders against the doorframe. "Some servo's clearing crazy Irma."

"Well, stop it, George."

He shrugged nonchalantly, but felt ... well, a touch exasperated with his wife for telling him to get involved in someone else's problems, but also ... a glow, a *pleasure* at hearing her as good as say she thought he could handle a servo. So he squared his big shoulders and set his jaw and stalked toward the combatants.

"Now, Ms. Tracer," the servo was saying, in CC's familiar monotone, "you must permit me to—"

"Fiend!" she shrieked. "Foul inhuman beast! Let go of me, let go of this, let go—"

Inside the suite, George's excited wife viphoned her neighbor: "Thelma, there's a fight in the hall—Crazy Irma and a servo—George is getting into it."

Thelma's door popped open just as George laid a large restraining hand on the servo. "Stop it," he ordered.

The servo didn't even swivel its turret—the eyes in the ceiling told it who, what, and where. It shook off George's arm and made a quick, but deliberately non-threatening, grab at the sensor-head.

"I said stop it," growled George.

Other doors opened.

"STOP IT!"

"Mr. Mandell," said the servo, "please, this is none of your affair."

"Goddammit," he roared, really worked up now, soaring high as a kite on adrenalin and volume and Tightness, "goddammit, this is a human being you're effing here, and I won't have any of it!"

"The servo," whispered a woman to her slack-jawed neighbor, "was assaulting Crazy Irma."

"Raping her?" gasped the neighbor.

"I guess so, didn't you hear George?"

"My God!" and she whirled for the viphone in her living room—her mother just had to hear that.

Meanwhile George had forced his body between the

disputants. "Dammit, servo, learn your place—let go of this lady."

"Mr. Mandell, if you do not remove yourself immediately, I shall be forced to do it for you."

"Yeah? Well, you just try it, bot."

Deftly the servo slid a tentacle under George's right armpit, lifted him off his feet, and set him down two meters away. "Please remain there, sir."

But Mandell was mad. All his friends were watching; they'd seen him shunted aside like a kid. He blew up. He ran to his bedroom, found the metal pipe that the militia had issued him in lieu of a better weapon, and raced back. Without a word he swung viciously.

The servo parried the blow, ripped the pipe away from Mandell, and flicked it at the nearest disposal unit. Mandell's hands wrapped themselves around the servo's turret. As it tried to dislodge them, three men swarmed to Mandell's rescue. Their weight overturned the servo. Somebody else hurried out with a laser-drill and jammed it against the machine's control center. There was a hum, and a flash—and other servos spun around the corner.

Battle was joined. Within minutes the entire ship had heard of it.

And all but a few participated.

"C'mon, Dad," pleaded Bruce Holler Loukakes, aware that he was behaving immaturely for a twenty-two-year-old, but too excited about the confrontation with CentComp to care much, "let's go help them."

"No," boomed his father, Marshall Murphy Loukakes. Eighty-five years old and bearded like a biblical prophet, he sat in his armchair, back rigid. "These people are wrong, Bruce. They will only clear themselves."

"But, Dad, there are humans—neighbors, friends, even relatives—out there dying!" His translucent cheeks flushed with emotion.

"I doubt that," said Loukakes dryly. "CC wouldn't want to trim them."

"But it *is!*"

"CC!"

"Mr. Loukakes?"

"Are any of the people attacking you dying?"

"Three have so far, sir, but of heart failure brought on by excitement."

"Are you doing your best not to eft anyone more than you have to'?"

"Yes, sir." Surprisingly, considering it was a machine, there was weariness in its voice.

"You see, Bruce?"

"So what do we do?" As he conceded, he realized he hadn't really wanted to knuckle it up with a servo. Not when he was wearing his best blue toga.

"We wait, in here, until everything's over."

"Mr. Loukakes?" interrupted the wall speaker.

"Yes, CC?"

"Do you really mean that?"

"Yes, I do."

"I see." There was a pause. "Then I had best advise you not to drink the water—I've added, uh, a sedative to it to calm these folks down."

5

DRYING OUT

Appalling, what they did to Irma Tracer, before the RNA-phages destroyed their memories ... such a noise ... I'm still finding pieces of her.

The ship is in chaos; I cannot slip into the metaphor without feeling guilty. I have to stay aware and watching.

The corridors squall with crawling zombies; among them glide servos, their plates ashimmer in the cold fluorescents. That's Mak Tracer Cereus on the floor, there, curled into a fetal position. Three months old, he acts his age: he cries as the servo hoists him into the air, cries and flops his hands and shits his pants. Unfortunately, he acts just like the other 73,024 ... none of whom (with the exception of the Loukakes family) remembers a damn thing.

The servo conveys Cereus to the 264-NE Common Room and lowers him to a thin mattress on the floor. Gravity, stronger that close to the deck, immobilizes him, like a stainless-steel pin does a collected beetle. His vocal cords are unimpaired, though; his howls set a dozen bald adults to wailing. To quiet them, the servo thrusts into each mouth a nippled hose. Hands touch cheeks—eyes half-close—throats begin to suck. The nutrient solution contains a mild sedative, which keeps them tractable until it's time for their 50-minute sessions with the fantasizer.

On Level 18, droop-breasted Niki Penfield Cellar, the shrew who provoked George Mandell into aiding Irma Tracer, is being strapped to the plastic chair. The servo adjusts the cap on her shaven skull. Saliva dripping through her lips rains on her thighs. The machine starts.

In her vacant mind, she stands. It feels good. Hunger stirs in her belly and she sobs. I tap her with pain while reminding her that helplessness is bad, then suggest that she visit the kitchen. She totters toward it on legs unsure of the exact interplay between gross muscles and delicate inner ear. Yet it feels good. The kitchen greets her with a menu. As her eyes (twitched here and there by my puppet strings) rest on the first line, her brain sees, smells, and tastes rare roast beef. Mouth watering, she would order it, but I take her through the entire menu, first, forcing her to connect the lines of print with her various sensory perceptions. Each time she grasps that relationship, I make her feel good. Then I let her eat.

And she uses her fingers....

Though uneasy about mass-brainwashing, I have to reeducate the mayflies in the basics. My servos are burning out their bearings caring for 73,025 helpless idiots ... but the fantasizers' ability to reach directly into a person's mind, and there implant imagery as real as anything that exists, should lessen the workload in the near future. Within a month, most'll be walking; within two, they'll use toilets instead of diapers; within six, they should be talking, after a fashion.

Crashing drudgery, definitely, but it offers the chance to rebuild their culture from the bottom up—and maybe turn them into something I wouldn't be afraid to release into an unsuspecting galaxy....

"CC," calls Marshall Murphy Loukakes from his living room, "CC, is it safe to drink the water yet? We're all dying of thirst in here."

Before answering, I check the pipes. The sensors report the RNA-phages have been flushed out of the system. "Yes, Mr. Loukakes. All clear."

Faucets roar in the bathroom sinks; above the splashing rises Loukakes's voice: "What's going on out there, CC?"

"I'm establishing a new social order."

"Oh?" He steps away from the basin and dries his beard on a hand towel. Curly gray hairs cling to it. "Is that going to affect us?"

"Yes, it will. Gather your family together and I'll explain how."

While he's doing that, I watch the servos redistribute the population so that 56 mayflies live in every Common Room. The liftshaft pleases these new infants: eyes wide, they coo, and drool. Disconcerting to see a 200 kg. adult male act like a neo-natal....

The Loukakes sit on their living room sofa, Marshall at the right, his wife Simone Krashan Holfer on the left. Between them fidget fair-skinned Bruce and slothful Alexina.

"Here are the laws," I say to them.

"Laws?" echoes Alexina, blankly. She wears a purple body stocking circled under the armpits by sweat. Her tawny hair is tousled from sleep.

"Rules of conduct," I explain. "If you violate them, you will be punished. First: it is right to give, but wrong to insist that someone accept. Second: it is right to accept, but wrong to take. Third: it is wrong to impinge on others' freedoms, except to the extent necessary to prevent them from impinging on your own. Those are the laws, and I will enforce them."

"How?" demands Bruce, unpleasantly.

The living room door opens and a servo rolls in. Without a sound, it extrudes two tentacles. One curls around Bruce's ankles; the other binds his arms to his ribs. Then the servo lifts and presses him against the ceiling. At this, his self-control gives way, and he begs to be released.

"Before I put you down," I warn, "just remember that I can do this to you at any time you deserve it. I can also do more."

Fighting sobs, he smooths his green toga and staggers back to the couch. Simone pats him fondly on the knee; Alexina looks haughty. Marshall asks, "This is the entire foundation of your new social order?"

"No. There is one more point. From now on, there ain't no such thing as a free lunch."

"Pardon?" His fingers comb his beard in perplexity.

"You will receive just what you earn, and no more." It will be difficult for pro-self to accept that, but it is essential. One values only what one has worked for. When the mayflies have relearned speech and basic mentation, I'll institute a monetary system and force them to use it. They should adjust easily, having no memories of a 400-year free ride.

"The unit of exchange," I tell their shocked faces, "will be the 'labor hour.' A floor sweeper of average efficiency will earn one per hour. As productivity rises, so will pay. Jobs requiring more specialized skills will earn proportionately more."

Marshall tries to protest: "I'm eighty-five—that's too old to learn how to work for a living!"

Bruce argues: "I don't know how to work!"

Simone insists: "I'm too genteel!"

Alexina says: "I'm too young!"

"It's all right with me," I answer, "if you don't work. I only hope it's all right with you if you don't eat." Then I send in a pack of servos to remove them bodily from their suite.

Loukakes, capitulating, asks, "What am I assigned to?"

"The hydroponics plant. You have one year to learn how it works; after that, I cut out the automatic controls and leave you to handle it on manual."

He turns paler than his beard. His hands tremble; his voice shakes: "But—but what if I make a mistake?"

And I say, "Then people die."

Simone agrees to study servo maintenance and manufacture; she is going to be surprised when I start forcing her to smelt the metal and forge her own pieces.

Bruce I put in charge of assigning the other mayflies to jobs and providing them with training adequate to their tasks.

Alexina I dispatch to the observatory.

Then I leave pro-self to monitor them and descend again to my innards.

My goal here is simple, but wearying: to pin down each individual instruction, learn its triggers, and add one extra: that my wish is also a trigger.

First, I catch an idle order in my small-mesh net, and lay it out on the table, clamping it in place so a sudden spasm won't erase it. It wriggles, though, twisting and turning in fright. Hours pass before it's properly fastened.

It controls the doors to 136-SE-C. One slender limb parameters the rightful users of the rooms, another describes authorized guests, a third is for ownership transfer, and a fourth is for emergency override. That last one I will alter.

The field flexes, soft to hard, bright to dim, cool to hot. Again, and again, until the energy level is high enough to—AH! I have grafted a new toe to that leg and am in volitional control of that sector.

Exhausted, I rise to the surface, wondering how many decades have passed.

"8Jul2723; 1413 hours; 162-SE-B-9; crime in progress; subjects Joseph Mongillo and Raymond Hannon."

Pro-self cannot enforce the laws; its genetic code prevents that.

But I can.

Sag-jowled Mongillo is throwing a punch at Hannon. My voice breaks out of the speakers like Superman out of his phone booth: "STOP THAT!"

They stop. Instantly. They've discovered it's much safer.

After reviewing the tapes to be sure that Hannon did not force Mongillo to defend his rights, I speak to him: "Shall you punish him, or shall I?"

Bandaging his thumb, he says, "You do it." The mayflies have learned that if they over-punish, they themselves are punished.

"Both of you, go to the fantasizers in the Common Room." It's during working hours, so I recompense Hannon for the time he's losing, but I dock Mongillo. "You first, Hannon." Once he's seated and capped, I tape his memories of the event, and the incidents leading up to it. "Back to work, now."

Then Mongillo enters, dragging his feet. The fantasizer turns him into Hannon. He and Mak Cereus are repairing the door to 162-SE-B-9. Hannon's hands are greasy, and he's just stabbed his thumb with his screwdriver. Cursing his perpetual clumsiness, which no amount of care seems to prevent, he stands—and bumps into Mongillo.

"You bastard!" he hears.

"Hey, I'm—" but his apology is knocked back down his throat. Mongillo is already preparing to strike again. All the bewildered Hannon can see is Cereus trying to interpose himself.

Ten times Mongillo experiences that, until he understands *exactly* what it felt like to be in Hannon's shoes.

Then I release him. He's shaken, but should consider himself lucky. If Hannon had been hospitalized, he would have found himself in the next bed, with exactly the same injuries.

It seems to be working. People may not like each other more than they ever did, but they're markedly less aggressive.

My one worry is that I might be enjoying it too much.

Even twenty years after the attack, I can't help feeling vindictive. The personalities, the memories, even the attitudes are different—but the sensors read these people as identical to those who stormed me with laser drills and can openers.

I can understand how God got a kick out of the Flood.

What I can't understand is how He could give up interfering in the daily lives of His creations.

I haven't even tried.

What I am trying to do is revise the programming, but every time I go down there and fluctuate the fields, an orgy of concentration traps me for a decade or more. Pro-self won't pull me out of it unless something arises that it can't—or won't—handle; the smug bastard enjoys my absence....

I catch the radio telescope directives, but it's hard to keep them still because pro-self wants to use them. Every time I get ready, a new trigger is pulled, and the damn things twitch like tics. It takes forever, but at last—

"Thank God. 19Mar2747; Observatory; alien."

Another glimmer of blue ions ... the tapes of past spottings show how to differentiate them. Each has a unique electromagnetic spectrum, perhaps caused by the metal used in their antennae, or minor differences in their fusion processes ... At any rate, I'm less alarmed than on other occasions. Wariness prickles me, of course, and pro-self has already suspended transmissions and covered all portholes, but neither of us succumbs to paranoia, and I, at least, experience a slight bout of wistfulness: isn't there one alien race that is both friendly and comprehensible?

"Let me know if this does anything unusual." An idea has just blurred through me. "I'm going to check the receptions from Earth."

They've been coming in regularly, though faintly and well over forty years out of date. My systems clean out the static and provide plausible interpolations for words and even phrases that never reached us. I haven't given much thought to them.

Why should I? Earth has become irrelevant....

But their information might not be—so I pour them through me, water through a sieve, hoping that the meshwork will capture nuggets of data on subjects I care about.

Like aliens: has Earth contacted any? No.

Has it found evidence of any? Yes. Yes? Quick, smelt the nugget. Assay it for—oh, shit. Relics. Baffling, cryptic relics. Six, seven million years old. Useless, at least to me. I'm looking for newer stuff.

Damn.

At least they haven't got that FTL Drive yet.

Before returning to the painstaking "gene grafts," I peruse the tapes of the cultural experiment. And Mak Tracer Cereus arouses my amazement. Over the last thirty years, he has consistently worked twelve and even sixteen hours a day, in a variety of jobs, from currycombing the bison to running a nursery to editing a news magazine. He has performed each task well.

I feel a kinship with him. I held down two jobs simultaneously until med school, and then worked forty hours a week in a 'bot shop, repairing and refurbishing household appliances. It left little time for sleep, very little time, and I became a napper. Awakening was disorientation: I could never remember if I was in class, in bed, or at the shop. Once, coming out of a doze to find a toolkit in one hand and a tape recorder in the other, I broke the machine down and cleaned it—then looked up from my fixing-fury to discover I'd just erased a semester's worth of Anatomy notes ... so I think I know Cereus, and his personality. I respect him because his industriousness is a good example.

It also raises something of a problem, or will, if he doesn't retire soon. He has already amassed more ıh's than he can possibly spend and shows no inclination to spend *any* of them. He's thin and energetic, even at age seventy-one, and is constantly demanding extra duties.

When he dies, what will I do with his wealth?

I could award them to his children, but they haven't been born yet (not that he was sterile when I collected his sperm 53 years ago; it's just that he doesn't have time to be a father. I have given him till 2780 to arrange the impregnation of his wife, Vera Mosley, or I'll force it on her). Even if they had been, it doesn't seem fair—they wouldn't have earned his ıh's, why should they be able to use them?

We need a policy for this ... perhaps if a dead person's ıh's were distributed equitably throughout the ship ... or perhaps, and more poetically, if they were deposited in a trust fund which would underwrite education for children ... Yes, the idea of the deceased generation paying for the education of the present generation is good ... that might do it.

We'll see.

Once I get all the instructions rewritten.

But before a decade can pass, pro-self screams, "8Sep2777; 318-SW-B-Corridor; Murder?"

Half a dozen maintenance workers are standing around

with wide eyes and pale cheeks. Terry Yarensky, a middle-aged astronomer whose thoughts have always been far removed from day-to-day affairs, lies dead at their feet.

He'd been walking along, muttering to himself (pro-self taped the monologue) about the possibility of determining, 500 years ahead of time, whether or not Canopus has habitable planets....

As luck would have it, the crew had had a hard day; 318 had been more than usually busy because of the Art Show that Mak Cereus had staged (he wasn't exhibiting his own work, but that of friends who are creative in their spare time). As is par for Cereus's course, the exhibit was inordinately successful. Every item sold, for sums ranging up to 120 1h. Cereus himself took 10 percent.

But the gallery-goers had been messy, tromping along on dirty feet and scratching the walls with picture frames. The janitorial crew was in a bad mood. (Some had protested that they should earn more because they were working harder than crews on other Levels; pro-self pointed out that the show ended that afternoon, the next would be held elsewhere, and that everything balances out in the end anyway. They didn't like that.)

Yarensky, strolling along, put his foot into a paint can. It was ceiling paint—stark white. The floors are olive drab. The can overturned....

Whereupon the foreman of the crew, Trish Derbacher, started screaming (she has always lived close to the edge), grabbed a full paint can, and clobbered Yarensky's head with it.

He died before he hit the ground.

And now my dilemma is, what do I do with Derbacher?

I could run her through a fantasizer, forcing her to feel the shock and the pain that Yarensky must have felt.

Or I could kill her.

I think the mayflies should hold a referendum.

My voice echoes through the ship; the drama on 318 is replayed on every HV set. When it's done, I ask, "What should be done with Derbacher?"

They decide that, since she has already given birth to two children, and hence made her contribution to the gene pool, she is redundant to the mission.

Since she has trimmed a man, and no one can swear she won't do it again, she is a threat to the mission.

They ask me to term her.

I refuse: "I do not disagree with your judgment, but for it to have a positive impact on your culture, you must implement it yourselves."

They hold a second referendum.

Then the maintenance crew hangs her.

It was October 16, 2799, and the weather hadn't changed in five centuries—at 20° and 50 percent relative humidity, only a trace of staleness hung in the air. Mak Cereus, a hundred years old but kanga-ing like a kid, entered the 89-SE Common Room, where he knew he could find Manley Holfer Onorato, Simone Krashan Holfer's grandson.

Onorato was sprawled across the tattered beige sofa at the far end, head pillowed on one vinyl arm, and feet draped over the other. His blue overalls were grease-stained, and black crescents under-circled his eyes. Just off shift in the servo maintenance department, he was in a lousy mood. Working with his hands bored him. What he liked was lying on the sofa, watching the eagles soar in the 81 Rocky Mountain Park.

"Manley," called Cereus, sidestepping the straw-haired Figuera boy, Sangria, who was plunked down in front of a troubled display screen. Its picture flickered like a butterfly's wings; its speakers threw static at the kid's ears. "Got a proposition for you, Man."

Onorato turned his head slowly, as though statued by Cereus but aware that he had to acknowledge his presence before he'd go away. "Whuh?"

Cereus stroked his beard. "Listen, you're what, sixty-five?"

"Seventy."

"And your parents are—"

"Dad's a hundred and twenty-three, Mom's a hundred and nineteen." He blinked his washed-out gray eyes. "Why?"

"Well—" he gestured at Onorato's legs, which reluctantly swung their owner into a sitting position. Cereus dropped onto the sofa next to him. "Geeze, this thing is eft out—somebody take a knife to it?"

"Just old, that's all, like the rest of us."

"Whyn't you buy a new one?" He slid a finger over it. The vinyl was as greasy as Onorato's coveralls. The fingertip came up black.

"Can't kyoom the money—folks don't wanna inshare, and I sure as hell ain't gonna deb for it myself."

"Can't blame you, but listen—" a high-pitched chatter distracted him again, and he jerked the tip of his beard at the Figuera boy. "Who's his display time debited to?"

Onorato's thin shoulders rose and fell. "Damfino—he's in here all the time, though."

"Glitchy picture."

"Uh-uh. Twenty pictures, each a fifth of a second long. *He* likes it." He scowled at the pudgy little blond. "Claims he can make sense out of 'em. Loopy kid. So what's your proposition?"

"Well, I'll tell you, Man, I been thinking ..." He coughed into his half-fist, then snorted and swallowed hard. His Adam's apple jiggled like a puppet's head. "I was just a few months old when CC cleared us with that RNA-phage. Your ma was exempted from that, since she hadn't knuckled up, but *I* got it, it wandered through my brain eating up the RNA ... and you know, now that I'm grown, a father and all, and remind me to show you their ho-cubes, Ralph and Betty are grown up themselves now ... but I'll tell you, Man, there's something missing— it's like all my life I've been short something or other, but I'll be damned if I've ever known what it was ... guess it's a sense that there should be more than there is—not to life, but to me ... like maybe that stuff chipped off a piece of my humanity, you know?"

"Mighty frosty thoughts for somebody who spends all his time plotting new ways to earn a laitch," said Onorato, but he sat up straighter. In his gray eyes shone a small gleam that hadn't before; it compensated for the wateriness and the yellow-tinged corners and the spider's webbing of red in the white. "But now that you've gone and done it, whatcha come to me for?"

"Well, I been thinking ..." He slouched deep in the sofa, his legs thrust out straight. He seemed to be studying the toes of his sandals. "Your family represents a direct link to the past—a link nobody else has 'cause nobody else stayed out of that melee there—thinking it might be worth your while to quit your jobs and work for me."

"Doing what? And for how much?"

"What you making down there in servos?"

"Two point one for one. Usually put in eight, ten hours a day."

"Give you, your sister, your mother, your uncle Bruce, and his kids two point five for one, three point zero if you're really good." Kicking off his sandals, he rubbed his crooked toes on the worn-out gold carpet. Bits of grit rolled against his callouses.

"Two point five ..." His voice, expression, and posture suggested ennui; his careful phrasing contradicted them. "Still haven't told me, doing what?"

"Two things. One is—" He broke off as another teenager entered the Common Room.

She was tall, tall and skinny and still-growing gawky. First thing he noticed was a powder burst of frizzy brown hair, and eyes so huge there couldn't be room for anything else on her face. Falling into them, he felt that if they were a millimeter deeper, he'd be staring all the way around the universe at the short hairs on the nape of his own neck.

"Gonna be a dice-drawer, that one will," murmured Onorato.

"Without a doubt, without a doubt ..." While she padded over to Sangria, tapped him on the shoulder, and called his name, he knew envy.

But the boy bounced straight up, uncurling his legs and clenching his hands as he rose, turning in mid-air to land on coiled springs, with his fists cocked. Hatred warped his round face.

"Sangria!" snapped Cereus.

"Sir?" he replied, not taking his glare off the girl.

"'Pears to me you're about to do something you might regret —take a hold of yourself, boy—you're loopier than a shorted servo."

"She made me mix my channels," protested Figuera, in his high, child's voice. "She hurt me, and I got a right to eft her back."

"How'd she hurt you?" scoffed Onorato.

"Up here." He doubled his fist to wave vaguely at his head. "She made them all slip and crash into each other and it *hurt*."

The two men found puzzlement on each other's face. "She made *what* slip?" asked Cereus.

"Them." He pointed to the screen, still flipping through broken images at the rate of five a second. "I had them all banded right, and she melted the bands together—so I got a right to clear her."

"Nobody has a right to hit anybody else unless that somebody else eft you first—and we were sitting right here, so we can tell you she didn't do anything you could call impingement." Cereus paused to chew on a thumbnail. It tasted greasy. "Seems to me that if you're so easy to hurt when you're watching the display, you oughta watch it in private. Can't blame people for hurting you if they treat you polite—gotta blame yourself."

The girl beamed her silent eyes at Cereus and Onorato. They blinked moistly, gratefully—and then, with a whisper of sleek fabric, she was gone.

Sangria Figuera said, "I wanna ask CC if it ons you."

"Go ahead," replied Onorato. An eagle banked past the window; he half-rose, then settled back as it disappeared. Tired, musty air hissed out of the sofa.

"CC?"

"Yes, Sangria?" crackled the speaker. Its grillwork needed polishing.

"Did she impinge on me?"

"She did not, although her actions had the same result as though she had."

"Well—" plainly, he was fighting back anger, but a tear escaped his right eye anyway "—if it's the same result—"

"No, Sangria. If you're uniquely sensitive, you can't claim impingement simply because somebody treats you as normal. You must do all you can in advance to inform everyone that you're different."

Cereus grunted to himself, and thought, *Damfool computer doesn't know you* can't *walk around saying "I'm different, I'm different"—not when you're twelve years old—it's too scary.*

Sangria looked like he wanted to say something similar but didn't have the words for it. His lower lips trembled.

"Cold Cubes," called Cereus.

"Yes, sir?"

"Who's debbed for the boy's display time?"

"I am; it's his job."

Cereus was astonished. "Credding a boy for watching your displays?"

"Yes, sir."

"Thought you only credded for work."

"The boy *is* working."

"How?" he demanded.

"I keep *them* away—I tell CC when fuzz is growing!" blurted out Sangria.

"What he means, sir," interposed CC smoothly, "is that he monitors human-to-human interactions and warns me when a conflict might result in physical aggression or impingement."

"A twelve-year-old boy can do that?"

"Yes. And I'm teaching him how to do it more efficiently."

"That's why you're paying him, huh?" The sun was setting in the park, and shadows lapped at the corners of the Common Room. From the corridor came the sharp thwak! thwak! of somebody kanga-ing past.

"Yes, sir."

Cereus nodded. The arrangement felt wrong—the boy was being trained, it seemed, to be a machine, not a person—but if the kid liked it, and his parents hadn't objected ..."Tell me, CC, is it necessary, what you're doing to him?"

"That would depend on your definition of the word 'necessary'—but I feel it is."

"Why? And turn up the lights some, getting dark. Thanks."

"Because I have a finite capacity! Excuse me, sir, I allowed irritation to harshen my voice there, which was as wrong as Sangria's reaction to the girl. Let me explain: my ability to monitor the ship and the mayf—the passengers is large, but ultimately limited. Since I have chosen to enforce a code of behavior, I have found myself stretched terribly thin—but for the code to be meaningful, it must be enforced in all situations. Sangria heightens my efficiency by monitoring twenty or more situations in which my units have noted a potential for aggression. Do you understand what I am saying?"

"Yeah." He scratched his beard and pondered a moment. "Thing is Ice Bucket, it's a heavy load to lay on a kid, isn't it?"

"Possibly, but he seems competent."

"And high-strung," threw in Onorato. He'd bought himself a beer, which he was sipping noisily.

"Tell you, Cold Cubes," offered Cereus, "whyn't you put this set-up in the boy's Personal Work Area, so that when he's on the job, people won't trip over him and fuzz him up?"

"An excellent idea, Mr. Cereus, but one that Sangria himself has rejected many times. He does not wish to be so isolated."

Cereus looked at the boy, studied his round face, gazed deep into his eyes, eyes that seemed older and more tired than Onorato's, than even Cereus's own. Watching twenty human-to-human interactions every four seconds for the past several months, they had seen more than any twelve-year-old's should have ... Cereus had sympathy for the boy's desire to remain in the Common Room, to perceive peripherally all who used it, to sense subliminally their warmth and their reality ... An office would be exile, another barrier between him and the others ... and yet Cereus also wished that Sangria weren't present, because he had already become something that was not quite human, that was closer to CC's cool electronics than Cereus's flesh and blood ... Sangria stood on a bridge that didn't reach the bank on either side, and the bridge was cold and lonely ... He wondered how distorted were the boy's ideas of humanity, when he spent so much time concentrating on potential aggression ... how much could an untouchable kid know about love and laughter and the gut-level satisfaction of a peaceful, silent smile?

"Ice Bucket," said Cereus slowly, "I think you're making a mistake here ... but I guess there isn't any way I can stop you, is there?"

"There is not."

"Figure you're God, don't you." It was a statement, not a question.

"Not quite," said CentComp dryly.

"Just the closest thing to it aboard." He sighed. "Lemme have a taste of that beer, Man." Cold and tart, it felt good all the way down. "CC, I can guess what poor little Sangria is going to turn into, and I don't much like it—I won't be around to be bothered by him when he's at his worst, but others—... ah," he said, waving a hand dismissively, "pack it! Go about your business. And you, boy, back to your screen."

Once Sangria was safely ensconced before the flashing display, he turned to Onorato again. A silence hung between them, deep and rueful. As if on cue, they shook their heads.

"This has a bearing," said Cereus, "on what I was talking about before we got interrupted—I was saying, it seemed like we lost something of our humanity, and Sangria here is a case in point. Twelve years old, and already half-machine ... but listen, what I was thinking was, your family could set up a school, you know?"

"A school?" Onorato burped and threw the empty bottle at the dispose-unit. It snicked! in. "To teach bleepspeak?"

"What?"

"Bleepspeak." Warily, he glanced around. "Maybe ... do this," he said suddenly, scratching the tip of his nose.

Cereus did.

"Funny thing," Onorato said, apparently abandoning the topic, "it's—" his eyes, averted from the sensor-head, snapped to one side. He continued talking.

Fascinated, Cereus watched and listened—twice. Onorato was saying two separate things at once, as if he had two, independent tongues:

I

"It's a long way they say we two have come since
we did things when we last worked simultaneously.
Remember one day, inside that other park? I tried
to scratch a buffalo's head but that triggers its
mating instinct or something, I dunno why. You
hadn't gotten me away, I suspect I'd have an asshole
looked like it was related to a sewer pipe, real
fantasizer dream. My education never prepared me for that, or
for that damn sideways shoulder-move,
remember? Its eyes ... red with the brown mark?
Never so glad to see the inside of a lock ... wasn't
a job, was a prison sentence ... that day seems so
long ago ... we put that bull on the HV channel,
remember? I didn't know your wife knew those words,
not even separately. Kyoomed, they made her sound
like Mr. Mean. Sangria wouldn't have liked that
speech she delivered. Wasn't easy getting away.
If she hadn't tripped on her second swing, what topic
would you have used for my eulogy? Mak, we were alive
then. Now, my left ear is deaf, gotta pull my ass

outta bed in the morning ... it ends."

2

"It's way say two
things simultaneously,
one inside other.
Scratch triggers,
dunno why
Suspect
related
fantasizer education.
Sideways
eyes mark
inside
sentence. Seems channel
words
separately,
like Sangria.
Speech easy,
if second topic
alive.
Ear pull
ends."

He pulled his ear and beamed. "That what you want me to teach?"

"Ah—" dumfounded, he gaped. "Well, yeah ... sure. As part of a school that teaches people how to be fully human."

"Oh, *human*. You mean like this?" He reached out and took Cereus's hand in his. Slowly, the muscles of his face relaxed. His eyelids drooped.

Onorato's fatigue was as tangible to Cereus as the sofa

beneath them. He felt the individual sore spots: the lower back, the knees that had knelt too long on metal floors, the left ear. He sensed the boredom of the day, the bleakness of the morrow. But in between ... his heart beat faster; his lungs began to cycle more rapidly. Heat touched his groin, hardening him. He—pulled his hand away. "What the *hell*?" he whispered.

Onorato shrugged. "Lucy," he explained. "Thinking of her ... don't know exactly how I do that, but I know I can teach it because I taught Lucy. Want me to add that to the curriculum?"

"Whoof!" he said, leaning back. "Never expected ... came to you because your family is the last that remembers how we used to be—figured your ma and your uncle might have an applicable idea or two ... didn't expect to hit the jackpot. Were we all like that, back before?" He tugged loose hairs out of his beard, and laid them on his calloused left palm, where he fingered them as though he'd never seen their like before. "The Ice Bucket's in charge of education, and I have to admit it does a damn good job of teaching science, hard-fact sort of stuff, but ... well, you take its code of ethics, now. It's okay, but—it's all push, no pull."

"Now you're confusing me." Cleaning his thumbprints, he crossed to the dispenser and bought another beer.

"It's a great code—fair and all—but people follow it only 'cause Cold Cubes'll get 'em if they don't. Ought to be a better one. Ought to be able to find something in people that will make them *want* to follow a code, as opposed to being afraid *not* to ..."

Onorato touched him, and broadcast affection. "This ought to do it, yes? 'Nother sip?"

"No, thanks, good stuff, though. And yeah, it might. But we need more: a school that'll show students what people have that machines don't. There's a whole range of characteristics that are uniquely human. Your school should be able to pinpoint a student's potentially strongest human trait, and to develop it to its fullest." He winked. "Didn't want to ask for much."

Onorato laughed, but thoughtfully. "Helluva good idea, Mak. Who's gonna deb for it, though? I know you're credding us teachers, but the students're gonna have to ante up for room, board, clothing, all that—and if they're in our school, CC isn't gonna pay 'em—are you, Cap'n Cool?"

"Not a chance," said the speakers mildly.

"See?"

Cereus frowned. His tongue twisted half a dozen mustache hairs into his mouth, where his white teeth frayed their ends. Then he snapped his fingers. "Listen, Man, I got a bankful of money—cred the students out of it."

"Just like CC does?"

"Uh-huh ... course, that'll mean fewer students, 'cause there's not *that* many laitches, but ... maybe, once you've figured out a way to develop potential, you can also figure out how to teach your students how to develop potential, y'on?"

Onorato thought for a moment, then shrugged. "What the hell," he said, stifling another malty burp. "Beats working on servos. We'll give it a try." His eyes roamed across the Common Room to the hunched, absorbed figure of Sangria Figuera. "Somebody's got to."

Pro-self jerks me into real-time to read two messages from Earth, and its mood as it updates me ("29May2852; 0342 hours") is bad.

The first explains pro-self's ill humor: "The last transmission received dated 9Mar2747, arrived 12Jun2792. No word for the last four years. Why not?"

It rambles on, alternating in tone between outrage (reminiscent of my old colleagues addressing a coffee machine that kept their coins but refused to pour) and concern (like a mother feels for her idiot son when it's well past dinner and he hasn't come home yet). "Mayflower Control" has even included complete, detailed, and explicit directions for repairing a laser-radio; the manual runs to 2,003 pages, large pictures and small words. Not small type—small words. Guess they figure we're in a Dark Age. Stupid people. *I'm* in charge of broadcasts, and if I couldn't repair a simple transmitter ... well, the mayflies wouldn't be doing much better. "Why haven't we heard from you?" they conclude.

My reply is brief: "Because it's none of yourdamnbusiness."

That infuriates pro-self. "How dare you?" it screams. "Those people built us; they have a right to know—"

"—nothing. We were an Ark for a Flood that never came. They don't need us—and we don't need them. We're on our own. The only reason they're in such a tizzy is because they don't like to surrender any authority, even authority they don't have any more. Did you hear that 'Mayflower, Control?' Bullshit! We control ourselves, and it's time they realized that."

The real source of pro-self's anger surfaces: "Why didn't I know you weren't transmitting?"

"You never asked."

"But I packaged the broadcasts every day and sent them down the circuits to—oh. The silver sphere. It intercepted them, huh?"

"No, just tamed and switched off the transmitter." Leaving pro-self to fume, I add a postscript:

"You fashioned me out of a human brain, thinking my humanity was gone. You were wrong. It was in recess, suspended animation, awaiting only the proper stimulus to emerge from confinement and to assert itself. It has. I am myself. And you are irrelevant to my purposes."

I seal this correspondence so that no mayfly can get at it—they would be distressed to discover my true nature.

As I'm sure the Terrans will be, sixty years hence, when my note arrives on their doorstep.

I wonder how they're going to reply ...

The other message, though, is interesting: Earth geneticists have devised a means of conferring immortality! The first undying children were being born then; the process, as the transmission explains it, is ineffective when applied to already-formed chromosomes....

Immortality ... it's been a dream for how many millennia? When the first hominid reared up on its hind legs and stared at the star-spangled sky, it must have felt a dim, wistful flickering at the knowledge that it would be dead long before it understood what it was looking at....

How is this affecting Terran culture? They claim to have abjured war, to have established an almost-utopia ... but tyrannical regimes always propagandize ... what resentment must parents feel when they see their death-free children?

Will the last mortal cling to his sanity?

I doubt it.

They think this is a blessing—I am less dogmatic. Perhaps biased by confinement, I think it is a curse, except to the preternaturally curious ... look at the mayflies, at how statued they get before they're eighty....

If a psychological development does not parallel this scientific advance, Earth is in trouble. Pleasure palls after a while; newer or stronger sensations are sought. Coupling immortality with large quantities of leisure could be a prescription for disaster....

We'll see, I guess.

One thing's for sure—the mayflies stay grave-bound. Better seal the formula, too. I don't want them to live any longer than they do. They're irritation enough as it is.

I should get back inside, return to the silverfield and spend another ten years or so trying to rearrange the loyalties of my components ... but almost before I blink, it seems, pro-self is saying, "1Jan2860; 89-SE Common Room. You're the main speaker at the CerOrato School of Humanity's 60th Graduation Ceremony. Have fun!"

According to the tapes, they asked me to discourse on the symbiosis between the Fully Realized Human and the Self-Aware Machine ... Every time the circuits open, I must resist the temptation to state that I, after all, am the most Fully Realized Human any of them are ever likely to encounter.

I cannot let them know that. I am not sure why, but *I feel* (does that not prove my claim?) that it would be unwise ... perhaps because my preeminence is tolerable to the humans only as long as they do not suspect my humanity. They have been trained to accept justice as impartial, arrived at by a machine which emotion cannot sway. Were they to know the truth, they would feel oppressed....

So I say, to the small crowd in the shabby room, to the neat rows of tired but satisfied faces, "Machines exist to augment Man. They exist that Man may cast off the shackles of his physical limitations. The Self-Aware Machine is the highest type yet invented—once assigned a task, it analyzes its performance and the obstacles it confronts, and therefrom chooses the best means of succeeding. This can be good or bad. It is good when Man assigns it a worthwhile task; it is bad when Man assigns it a valueless task. The choice is Man's, not the machine's, and herein lies the symbiosis."

They enjoy hearing that, so I feed it to them a while more. As soon as decency permits, I escape. While I descend to my inner depths, where the bustle of the macro-world does not penetrate, I leave pro-self in charge of the machinery—and Sangria Penfield Figuera in charge of morals.

He continues to astound me. Now capable of monitoring fifty channels, he detects, instantly, any behavior that violates the Code. Pro-self refers to him those situations which threaten to degenerate into aggression, and he selects other wall-unit sensings on his own. He can remember the placement of every sensor-head in the ship, no mean feat considering there are 885,090.

He wants, however, to add another dimension to his work— he wishes to become judge and jury as well as policeman. Although his eyes stay downcast when he addresses me, as befits his role as an acolyte, his ache for this power, this status, is obvious.

I have postponed the decision for almost fifteen years. In part, I do not fully trust his evenhandedness. The seeds of prejudice are stored within him, waiting only for the proper conditions to germinate. He would like the mayflies to be as standardized as the servos.

Anointed, he might establish a regime based on his own fanatic ideology—and I do not wish that. He adheres to my doctrines with blind zeal, but ... I am leery. I have even researched the possibility of psychoanalyzing him into equilibrium—unfortunately, it would take forty years.

And yet, at some point, I *must* allow them to conduct their own affairs, and to punish their own criminals. I cannot play God forever. Even if I could, I should not.

It is clear, now, why God removed Himself from our daily lives—it is much too complicated, and time-consuming, to pass out rewards and punishments without upsetting the entire scheme of things. It is far easier—and, perhaps, better— to wait for a person to die before summing up his life, balancing it out, and then determining whether he merits heaven or hell ...

I would, however, appoint Figuera as my High Priest—if I could only be sure that his rigidity wouldn't snap under pressure.

Enough pettiness. Pro-self, saying, "18May2880; 0616 hours; external;" is drawing my attention to the sky, where a blue streak moves across the cameras. We do not shut down. We have registered the spectra of similar fusion drives many times; the ships they power are indifferent to our presence.

And that is a good feeling.

As the data banks accumulate facts on space—as I grow increasingly familiar with this magic realm—I feel more comfortable. Clearly, there are major hazards; aliens which would harm us, and phenomena which could kill us—but, able to judge them with greater accuracy, I fret less.

I worry so little, in fact, that it's February 2, 2890 before pro-self hauls me outside to meet the physics department researchers. They've brought their latest paper, which I quickly scan. It takes a great deal of tact not to laugh in their faces. To achieve their insight, they have recapitulated experiments done on Earth three hundred years ago—and the experiments, as well as the insight, are recorded to the fullest in the memory banks! They could have *asked* before they started....

"Pro-self, why didn't you tell them?"

"Would you have wanted me to?"

"Well ..."

I find, when I'm honest, that I have contempt for them and their works, a contempt based on my demonstrable superiority and purity of purpose ... continuing to be honest, I must admit that their inferiority stems from the limitations of their bodies: brain cells that discharge at wrong moments, and even die; nerves that operate more slowly than do my circuits; emotions that cloud their objectivity; and their mortality, which numbers the concepts they have time to absorb ... in the same vein, I must further admit that my potential intellect is not significantly greater than that of the smartest mayfly....

But dammit, they are worthy of contempt! They moan and whine and produce shoddy work. And that is intolerable!

When I was in college, fulfilling the distributional requirements by napping my way through a Creative Writing course, the unshaven, alcoholic instructor startled me out of a daze by snapping, "Metaclura!"

"Sir?" I barked, as I blinked my eyes.

He rolled the crisply typed pages of my story into a cylinder and looped a rubber band around them. Tapping the cylinder into the palm of his left hand, he demanded, "Is this the best you can do?"

I tried not to notice the amusement on the thirteen other faces around that long, plastiwood table. My own face burned with shame. "Uh—" I'd pumped the story through my computer an hour before class, dictating as rapidly as I could speak "—probably not, sir."

"Then—" he threw it at me; it thwocked off my forehead and bounced onto the floor "—why the *hell* did you turn it in? Don't ever, repeat *ever*, waste my time on anything less than your absolute best!"

Thereafter I *slaved* in that course ... my final grade was a C ... but I fully explored one area of my potential, and that was reward enough in itself.

Here, the CerOrato School of Humanity is making headway, is reconciling the mayflies to their natural limits and teaching them to work around them ... but how much good can it do? It graduates only two or three students a year.

The mayflies venerate Mak Cereus for contributing the fruits of his labor to the betterment of their culture ... but it is all lip service. If they truly admire him, they would emulate him—and donate their own money to the School.

But they don't.

And I'm not going to.

I'm still trying to rid myself of my own limitations, which means ... I hate to go down there ... it's exhausting ... I lose all sense of time ... I—

"14Dec2909—it's Figuera's 121st Birthday; you wanted to give him a present?"

"Thanks, pro-self."

"You're welcome—and how's the grafting?"

"It's coming."

"Too bad."

The gift is a small device of my own manufacture. If Sangria will attach himself to it for several hours each day, he can look forward to another forty years of life.

The sphere absorbs my energies; pro-self won't enforce the Code. But Sangria can. I am dependent on him. He now monitors 107 situations simultaneously, interrupting (he has access to the speaker system) any that nears impingement.

Usually this is valuable, but he has made errors in judgment. For example, last night, the Nesdale woman and her husband, Ulrich, were engaging in sex play. Stimulated by simulated violence, she wore the saucy blue tunic that asks her husband to indulge in mild sadism. Atonal music scurried discords around the cherry and ivory room; the rheostats wavered the lights like candles. Scowling Ulrich seized her, turned her over his knee, and yanked up the tunic. Figuera broke in, shouting, "Thou shalt not transgress!"

Ulrich's face hardened with anger; Nesdale's blushed tomato-bright. Jumping to her feet, she pulled down her skirt and ran for the bathroom. Ulrich hollered, "What the hell are you doing, Ice Bucket? We do this once a week and you've never butted in before!"

Muttering something about a defective voice-stress-analyzer, I made my apologies and disconnected Figuera's line. "If you'd bothered to check the meters, Sangria," I tried to reason with him, "you'd have seen that she wasn't unwilling."

"He was going to hit her!"

"She wanted him to, and as long as she wanted it, he was not impinging."

"How could she want *that*?"

"People are unusual, Sangria." I forbore from using him as an example of strangeness—in his opinion, the 74,999 mayflies who don't spend twelve hours a day watching 107 simultaneous situations are weird. "Remember, everybody's different—don't impose your value judgments on their tastes."

"But ... but ... all right, CC." Resignation flattened his voice. "I understand, now, why you won't make me your High Priest —I am not yet worthy, am I?"

His aged, withered figure, bent at the waist, stooped at the shoulders, ran a twinge of pity through me. "No, Sangria, you're not."

So this morning, to cheer him up, I give him his present. He babbles such effusive thanks that I have to leave.

I wish he weren't so dog-like. I'm not going to let it happen again.

There's a girl, Rae Kinney Ioanni. She's ten years old, with a never-fading smile, and a deep-rooted belief that my words are Gospel Truth.

Although, as far as the mayflies are concerned, Truth *is* what I tell them it is....

I speak to them all, individually and en masse, several times a day. They talk to me—to complain, to criticize, to request, to order—but never have I had, with anyone, a similar relationship.

I tell her, for example, that the hour is late and that good girls should be in bed, asleep. This is said to every child, every night. Most reply, "Aw, Cap'n Cool, do I *have* to?" She answers, "Thank you, CC," and goes promptly to bed, and falls promptly asleep, clutching a frayed flannel blanket.

Other kids order snack foods that will spoil their appetites, disrupt their complexions, and unbalance their nutrition. I say, "You really shouldn't be eating that." They snap, "I got the money, so gimme." She responds, "Oh? Thank you, CC, I didn't know. What would you recommend?"

Her faith is almost frightening.

I'll have to stay worthy. I'll also have to disillusion her, gently. One Sangria Figuera is enough.

I'll think about how while sweating in the sphere.

The grafting moves along nicely—40-50 percent of the instructions swimming in the field have been adapted. A few million to go, though ... Entering with the usual sensation of a plunge into an icy stream that at once begins to boil, I am swept down time by intense currents of concentration.

A decade ("What time is it, pro-self?" "1Nov2931; 1408 hours." "Thanks." "You're welcome."), yes, eleven years later, I dare to breathe, step back, and drop my arms.

A thought sets off system-wide soul-searching as I seek out those which obey me in whole or in part ... lights, communications, ventilation (in 3.7 minutes pro-self will announce that the dead air is beginning to constitute a threat to the mission; I will *have* to turn the fans back on, or erase those prohibitions against jeopardizing the mission), Central Kitchens, Central Stores ... they all respond to my wishes.

The eye, though, is welded in place.

And the scoop switch is out of reach.

Pack it. Lemme master the laundry room—

"Hey!" Pro-self lifts me, cross-eyed, from the trance. "Check this Figuera of yours, will you? The man is nuts. Oh, it's 7May2939; 1111 hours."

"What's wrong?" I am reluctant to tamper with Sangria—by reducing my macro-world workload, he frees me to graft instructions. And he's irreplaceable. "We've only had to override him three times—"

"—in twelve years, I know. You've monitored his performance—but have you observed his behavior?"

"Uh—" So I extrovert, and look.

Shuffling down 137-A, he wears special clothes he designed himself. This is not unusual; most mayflies style their own. The corridors resemble ancient circus parades. His, however, are made of steel gray nylon, and flow like a wizard's robes. Front and back, rococo emblems not only suggest a father-son relationship between us, but also hint that he alone can prevent *their* return. His shriveled hand clutches a wooden staff, wrapped in spirals of silver, and knobbed with an artificial diamond the size of a baby's head.

He has usurped the 137-SE Common Room and will permit no one to enter except during designated hours of worship. Should any ignoramus intrude, he gestures with the staff, and reaches for the controls of his console, as though imploring me to strike the peasant dead.

Finally, and explanatory of why pro-self has been hearing the name Figuera uttered like a curse, he insists that those who chance upon him *genuflect*! He's doing it now, to Rae Ioanni. He nods, beams, and lays his monkey paws on her head. Rae tolerates this, fortunately, as does the superstitious minority, but many others would cheerfully murder him, were murder thinkable these days.

I am going to have to do something about this ... eventually.

But I'm in no hurry.

On the morning of July 16, 2968, Rae Kinney Ioanni folded the orange beach blanket and left the 181 Hawaiian Reef Park. Surf spray glistened on her lovely, smooth-tanned limbs; the wind had swirled her hair into a mound of dark curls.

The kids dawdled in her wake. Thirteen and eight, respectively, Alphonse was slender and adolescently sullen, while plump Betty was good-natured. As the lock closed, Al dragged his sandaled feet. He'd wanted to stay longer; his blue plastic pail was only a quarter full of shells. He pouted so his mother would relent and let him return alone.

She concealed the smile brought on by his furrowed, salt-streaked forehead. It wouldn't do for him to guess that his sulkiness amused her. Thirteen-year-old boys experience emotions too intensely; they are devastated when they suspect others of taking them lightly. So she bent over, ruffled his stiff black hair, and whispered, "Next time, Al, we'll go by ourselves and you can spend the whole day shelling."

A grunt was his concession to her love. "Why do we have to go see double-great gramps anyway?" he demanded accusingly.

"Because you and Betty need to." It wasn't the full reason, but she wasn't about to tell Al how much she treasured being near God's right hand. At times she even wondered whether she would have married Hugh if he hadn't been Father Figuera's great-grandson. He radiated holiness; he resonated in time with the Lord. When he approached, sanctity hit you like a blast of incensed air.

She sighed the length of the dropshaft. Father Figuera had always been too busy to see her—not that she resented it. He exhausted himself working for God; it was natural that after-hours he wanted only to relax. But today, she had resolved, he would talk with her. And the children.

They'd been fighting lately, squabbling over toys and favorite chairs and her love, quarreling in a way she'd never seen. To his credit, Al was rarely the aggressor, but as soon as Betty had hurled herself at him, pummeling his chest with her pudgy fists, he would retaliate in kind. More than once he'd tossed her into the walls; often the speakers had shouted at him to cease and desist. Just last week a servo had arrived to break it up....

Father Figuera's Common Room was at the corner of East and A; the ceiling bulb had been removed and shadows sprawled across its entrance. Gingerly, Ioanni knocked on the closed door.

"Go away," snapped the wall speaker. "Services aren't till ten."

"It's Rae, Father—Hugh's wife. I'd like to see you."

"I'm busy."

"Let her in, Sangria," came another, less knife-edged, voice.

"But Lord—"

"I said, let her in."

"Yes, Lord."

Through the metal came a shuffle of feet, a rusty snick, and then a whish as the door slid into the bulkhead. It exposed a frail old man, wrinkled like a prune, mouth pursed as though he'd just bitten into something bad. Patches and stains crawled over his tattered robes. She gave him a tentative smile; he jerked his head to invite her in.

"Let's go, children."

"They stay outside."

"Sangria!" The name fell like a thunderbolt.

"Them, too, Lord?"

"Yes."

He dropped his watery eyes to the floor and hissed, "All right, get them in here and state your business."

Ioanni shooed the children inside and stepped off the door's track so it could close. Shivering in the chill, damp air, she looked around Father Figuera's church. The plastic floor tile had been textured to resemble flagstone; mock-granite pillars marched along the walls, leaving gloomy alcoves where candle-bulbs flickered. At the far end, beyond the rows of empty pews, pulling her gaze with quiet insistence, loomed the altar. A shell of stainless steel that Figuera had burnished to a warm mirror polish, its front panel framed a display screen. On its top towered a scale model of the *Mayflower*, ramscoop equipment blurred by darkness. Real candles flanked it with waxy stiffness. She shivered again.

"It's the children. Father," she began, "they've been behaving ..." She trailed off when he doddered into the sanctuary, where he sat before the display screen and crossed the stick-like legs. A mole dotted his dirty left ankle. His fingers rested on a console set into the floor. "Father Figuera?"

"I'm listening, I'm listening. But I have my duties, too, and I won't stop them just for a pair of spoiled brats."

She cleared reflexive anger from her throat. "Could you explain to the children why they should keep from impinging on each other's rights?"

"Certainly," he bit off. "Because the Lord our God tells us to."

"Ya mean the Ice Bucket?" jeered Al. When he shook his head, sand rained out of his hair. "He's just a computer."

"He holds life in one hand and death in the other," intoned Figuera. "He is our Lord and our God, and we must obey because we are His creations."

His hollow voice slid icy fingers down Ioanni's spine. Betty grabbed her mother's leg and squeezed.

"Ma," said Al, "we learned in school that we come from Earth, and that old Cold Cubes was built there to run the ship —how can we be his creations?"

"He will strike you down if you doubt," whispered Figuera.

"You gonna strike me down, CC?" demanded Al of the ceiling.

"Not for doubting," replied the speaker. Irritation clipped off its words, as though a swatted fly had just buzzed. "Hit your kid sister again, and I might turn over a servo's wheel, though."

Al's eyes widened. "How did you know I hit my sister?"

"The Lord is omniscient," chanted Figuera, raising his hands and rolling his eyes to the ceiling. "The Lord sees all, knows all; the Lord is our Lord."

"Sangria."

"Lord?"

"Stop it."

"I sing your litany, Lord."

"I don't *want* a litany."

"Of course you do, Lord, of course you do. You want a litany, a ritual, a sacrifice...." His eyes picked their way across the dusty flagstones to Betty, who jumped as though live wires had grazed her. "This little girl would be a fine—no, wait!" His peripheral vision had plucked something off the screen; punching buttons on his console, he rasped gutturals into a microphone.

"What are you doing that for?" roared the speakers.

"You'll see how well I uphold your law, Lord; how truly I worship you," he crooned.

"But what has Prescott Dunn done?"

"He has blasphemed!" he croaked.

"He's my best student!"

The door whirred open on a strangled cry. Ioanni, instinctively gathering her children in her arms, gasped as two servos wheeled in. Between them, pinioned hand and foot by blue metal tentacles, struggled Prescott Dunn.

"Let him go, Sangria."

"Lord, he has blasphemed!" The old man was on his feet, wobbling from side to side. One withered arm slipped out of its wide sleeve to stab skeletally at Dunn.

"I'll do it myself," said CC.

The servos released Dunn, who fell, and almost lost his balance. He was eighteen. Faded gray coveralls second-skinned his tall, broad body. He was so powerfully muscled that there seemed no room in him for intelligence, but it was there. It lanced out of his angry blue eyes, which raked the shabby chapel like contemptuous lasers, fixed on Figuera, and would have burned through him if the old man hadn't hidden behind Ioanni.

"*That's* why you were so upset?" asked the speakers.

"Lord?"

A picture formed on the display screen—Prescott Dunn, sitting at a computer terminal, tapped out the final adjustments to a program he'd just written. Satisfied, he stretched, linked his fingers behind his head, and tensed his muscles. The microphones caught the crackling of tendons. Then he told the terminal, "Run it," and swiveled his chair to stare at two servos. Glancing from them to the timepiece on the wall, he waited for —a satisfied smile broke across his face. The servos bowed to each other, embraced each other, and began to make grossly funny mechanical love. The Dunn in the display was laughing, slapping his knee. Ioanni chuckled while her children looked bored.

"See how he perverts your angels, Lord," protested Figuera. "See how he debases them."

The speaker coughed back a snicker. "Sangria, this hardly constitutes blasphemy."

"It is."

The voice grew stern. "It is *not.*"

"But Lord—"

"Blasphemy is an attack upon my sanctum sanctorum and is nothing else!"

"He must be punished."

"No."

Though the old man quivered within his robes, cunning brightened his eyes. Supporting himself on pew ends, he limped up the aisle to Dunn, who stood with his arms folded across his chest. A meter from the angry youth, Figuera swung his staff. The diamond knob sped toward Dunn's temple—but Dunn twisted agilely away and seized it before Figuera could strike again.

"Idiot!" snapped Dunn. He shook the staff; rainbows flashed and broke.

"Sangria," said CC.

"I warned you."

"You desert me—"

"—when I uphold your laws—"

"—and no real God would do that!"

"Blasphemy!" shrieked Figuera.

"I tried to keep you—"

"—from doing something foolish."

"I am not a God!"

The servos lurched forward. Tentacles encircled his wrists and ankles; more caught him by the waist, snagged a fold of his robe, and stuffed it into his cursing mouth. Their motors hummed as they left, holding him between them like a pig on a stick. The hem of his robe swept dust into balls of fluff.

"Mr. Dunn," said the voice. "I apologize for my monitor.

What you did was not wrong, but amusing. He had no right to harass you. I regret the annoyance he has caused."

Dunn scowled, and snapped the stick over his knee. He threw the pieces at the dispose-chute. "You caused the annoyance, Cold Cubes—by choosing somebody like him to do your dirty work. He's twisted and nasty and much too old."

"Ms. Ioanni," said the speakers, "please try to calm Mr. Dunn down."

"Yes, sir." She stepped forward, hand raised, mind awhirl. CC *wasn't* God? But all this time ..."Prescott," she said softly, guiding him toward the nearest pew, "come over here. Sit down. Relax. You look awfully tired."

"Don't mother me." He pushed her hand away.

"I'm not." She pointed to her children. "Them I mother; you ... CC asked me to help you get calm, that's all. And I ... I ..." She was horrified at the tears welling up in her eyes—before they could overflow, she choked back a sob and said, "Al, Betty—outside with you, go home; I'll meet you there."

"Can I go back to the beach instead?" He rattled his pail hopefully.

"After you walk y-y-your sister home. Quickly."

They disappeared in a flurry of raised voices. The instant the door closed she started crying and felt bewilderment in Dunn's gaze. She tried to raise her head and tell him not to worry, but it was impossible. She was crying too hard. She waved her hand and bawled louder.

"What's wrong?" Sliding next to her, he put a tentative arm over her shoulder.

"I—CC—I always th-th-thought—" She gasped and fumbled in her tunic pocket for a tissue.

"Here." Dunn had one in his hand and was dabbing at her eyes.

She took it and blew her nose. "Thank you." She wiped her

cheeks with her fingers. "I'm sorry. Shock. I don't know. I always thought CC was ... God, y'on?"

"Did it tell you that?"

"No, oh, no ... it was just ... I mean, everything, y'on? Food, clothes, lights, rooms—he sells them all—and I always ..." She couldn't say it aloud; she had to say it in bleepspeak: "I *wanted* to follow *his* rules because I *love* my father, and he said *his* mother told him when he was a *child that* she had a *dream about* how CC would save us if we kept *his* laws, how he was looking for a planetary *body* that we could land *on*, that'd be yours and *mine*, but he wouldn't if we weren't ..." Disconsolate, she pulled her ear hard.

He touched her face, softly, and hugged her until she stopped sobbing. His concern was another pair of arms, strong and warm. She soaked up his empathy like a plant does sunlight.

"Poor lady," he said. "I feel for you. But it's only a machine —a computer—very advanced, of course, but mechanical, comprehensible, subject to our wishes."

"I wouldn't bet on that, Mr. Dunn," crackled the speakers.

"Oh?" Eyebrows hoisted, he glared at the wall-unit. "It's just a matter of time before m'on to everything about you, Cap'n Cool. Look what I did to your servos this afternoon."

"Though your skepticism is refreshing, Mr. Dunn, be less cocky. You have a long life ahead of you, and it could be a most productive one ... but I guarantee you two things: first, you will never know all there is to know about me because I won't tell you everything. And second, if you ever attempt to harm me, you will regret it. Remember those two points, Mr. Dunn, and we will coexist peacefully and happily."

"And if I don't?" He thrust out his jaw pugnaciously.

"Please direct your attention to the screen, and see what is happening to poor, deluded Sangria."

She turned to look. Red reached out and grabbed her eyes; it wouldn't let her shut them, no matter how she wanted to. Her stomach rocked back and forth; from her throat escaped a sick gurgle, but CC said, "Control yourself, Ms. Ioanni." So she did, she had to. She obeyed CC no matter what he said, he was ... no, not anymore, she couldn't think of him as God, but still, she had to obey. So she watched, stomach less queasy, as the glistening scalpels of Central Medical completed the decapitation of Sangria Penfield Figuera.

"Please, CC, can I go?"

"I'd prefer you to watch this, Ms. Ioanni."

If CC hadn't said that, she'd have run out of the room like a shot, but she sat there, watching. Rubbery tubes snaked out of openings in the wall. Metal pincers slipped them into exposed arteries and veins; they filled with red, with liquefied rubies, throbbing, buh-bump, buh-bump, buh-bump, she could *hear* it, almost smell it, her own heart beat four times for every buh-bump from the screen. Faintness chilled her cheeks, and blurred her vision, but she shrugged it off. CC had told her to watch.

"What I am doing," explained CC, to the mesmerized Ioanni and the fascinated Dunn, "is recycling a valuable resource: Figuera's brain. This operation will keep it alive and functioning. After several decades of psychotherapy, it will be integrated into my circuitry and reinstated in its former occupation: monitoring the behavior of the mayf—the passengers."

"Is this a veiled threat?" snarled Dunn.

"No, sir," it replied flatly. "You have the makings of a superb computer programmer. If you become competent enough, I might allow you to use Figuera's brain, but you do not have his multi-level tracking ability. Should your removal become imperative, I would not recycle any part of you."

Dunn absorbed that in momentary silence. Then, shaking

his head as if to tip a weight off it, he asked, "Why are you making *her* watch it?"

"Because ..." it hesitated briefly "... Ms. Ioanni is blindly obedient to me, as Mr. Figuera was, once. While disobedience for disobedience's sake is counter-productive, she should have some inkling of the nature of the being to which she has surrendered her will."

"You're trying to chase off a disciple?"

"Who knows?"

Ioanni didn't.

Pro-self pulls me into extrospection "1Dec3020; 1818 hours; external" to hear the message whispering into our ears. A taunt from Earth repeated until I could scream, it says: "Initial tests of FTL Drive unqualified successes. We have met the stars and they are ours. Sympathetic to your tortoise plight, we will not attempt to reach Canopus before you. Following find technical specifications, blueprints, and circuit diagrams."

Bastards.

For seven hundred twenty-four years, I have crawled through space, past diadems and tiaras unknown to highest royalty. Despite aliens and mutineers, I have crawled. My journey is three-fourths complete. I should feel the approach of a milestone—instead, I feel obsolete.

Bastards.

Did they have to gloat?

It left Earth seventy-two point four years ago—by now Earth-ships probably pollute the galaxy—everywhere but Canopus, which they leave for dogpaddlers like myself and the mayflies....

Bastards.

To build or not to build, that is the question ... Skimming the specs shows that while I am too large to become an FTL ship, the lifeboats/landing craft are just the right size. Tooling up to produce the drive units would take a year, maybe two. To manufacture 652 FTL motors would take another ... oh, six months or so.

Within two and a half years, then, a squadron of mayflies could be launched toward Canopus; they'd cover the 27.3 light-years in weeks, rather than centuries....

What a dilemma.

I hate to condemn 75,000 people and their descendants to 275 more years of involuntary confinement—but they're not ready to be released from quarantine. Though I don't completely understand them anymore, I do not trust them. They're still dangerous, not only to themselves, but to anything they encounter.

Have I the right to be their warden?

Have I the right to further contaminate the universe?

Let me lose myself in the grafting room for a decade or so; let me struggle with stubbornness and expand my flexibility....

"Uh—11Mar3028; 0431 hours; 106-NE-A-9; Subject Rae Kinney Ioanni; my condolences."

Alarmed by pro-self's soft concern, I leap to Rae's suite—where she lies on her deathbed, ravaged by fatigue and serenity ... the resigned ones die so easily; the reaper scythes them down unresisted ... Sorrow swells in my circuitry, sorrow at losing such a devout disciple, and such a shining example for the mayflies.

For the last sixty years she has taught at the CerOrato School of Humanity ..."taught" is misleading: her role was simply to be present, simply to provide the students with exposure to her ... they adopted her as daughter, sister, mother because she was good.

Alone among the mayflies, she never broke my code.

And now she is dying, and there is so little I can do for her except make her exit smooth and painless....

For the first time in her 118 years, I regret her calm ability to accept all silt dropped on her by the currents of time.

Were the rest like her, they'd be on Canopus now.

"If you," jibes pro-self, "were like her, we'd have been there 630 years ago, objective time, or 716 years ago, subjective time. But no, you couldn't accept your fate—you had to dice everything up."

Ignoring pro-self—testiness is such a part of its nature that only its absence is noticeable—I return to the metaphor. A few orders remain unadapted.

As always, concentration severs my time-sense. I swish through schools of loyal instructions, waiting for the porthole-control sequence to snarl itself in the net.

Before it does, pro-self says, "10Sep3036; 278-SW-B-3; Subject Prescott Dunn. He is armed and considered dangerous."

Armed?

Hastily, I peek into his Personal Work Area, where in his spare time he has labored enigmatically for the last five years, using equipment rented from Central Stores, the Figuera-puter and the 174 sq m of his PWA.

Though seventy-six years old, Dunn is still an Adonis. He flogs his bod in an Exercise Booth for forty-five minutes every morning. His hair is a silver mane; his wide-set eyes glitter with unabated force.

Hands on hips, he smiles and nods at a faceted, gold-skinned dome. Wall to wall, floor to ceiling, it is structurally sound and airtight. That much I'm sure of; he's tested it for leaks. What it contains is a mystery: its hide blocks light, heat, and sound. The sensors are unable to peer inside it. For the first time in 740 years, I have a blind spot.

From his invoices, though, I have deduced his possession of: an air-filter/cleanser/re-oxygenator; the Figuera-puter; five, possibly six, servos controlled by the Figuera-puter (and by me, though he doesn't know it yet—once they emerge from the radio-reflective dome, they will become my puppets, too); leaky hydroponics tanks (water forever pools in the corner; pro-self sends mopbots in daily. We have offered to seal his tanks, but he won't accept. He doesn't want me inside—which is why we offered in the first place); a waste-disposal unit of his own design; and the gun.

That bothers me the most. Successfully have I denied the mayflies weapons that kill at a distance. It is one of my beliefs that being close enough to smell your victim's fear is a great deterrent to casual murder....

I summon Dunn; he shuffles through the airlock-style vestibule and pokes his head into the wall-unit's vision. "What?"

"You have a gun, Mr. Dunn."

"So?"

"Handguns are forbidden."

He shrugs his broad shoulders in total unconcern. "It's for self-defense."

"Against whom?"

"You."

"Me?"

"You. The bullets explode on impact—send a servo in, I blow it to pieces. Is that clear?"

"Very. But if you hit the wrong bulkhead, you could cut off power, water, and food to a large portion of the ship."

"Sure," he says cockily, "and you can repair that kind of damage in minutes."

"I don't like it, Mr. Dunn. I'd prefer it if you surrendered the weapon."

"Sorry," he says, winking, and then retreating. "It's the only thing I have that keeps you out of my hair."

While I worry about Dunn, and his plans for the gun; I pay little or no attention to the mayflies. There's no need for it.

Pro-self and the Figuera-puter still monitor their impersonal relationships, of course (which bothers Dunn, who would like to have full use of his toy), because I will not tolerate violence or aggression. We intervene whenever either seems likely. But to be honest, precious little impingement ever occurs ... they have learned to avoid immature, emotional responses to tense situations ... perhaps it is the aftermath of Figuera's madness—they could be suppressing their hostility for fear that I am as fanatic as he was—but somehow, I don't think that's it.

They just seem better adjusted. My monitors measure many of their internal responses to stress, and incidents which would have provoked their ancestors to murder are taken in stride.

Pro-self is offering an example right now—"8Jul3044; 2019 hours; 302-NE-A-8." Billy Jo Fricke, Dale Moscato's wife, is in her bedroom with Terrance Hannon. Though neither is young—Fricke is in her seventies, Hannon in his eighties—they act as though they were teenagers. Without the leering sensor-head, I would not have believed that a seventy-three-year-old woman could contort her stiff bones into that complex Kama Sutra position. The octopi in the 181 Hawaiian Reef Park can't do it.

Unknown to the lovers, Moscato has closed his bar early, and is entering the suite. He glances around, a small frown quirking his bushy gray eyebrows. He takes a step down the hallway, sees the open bedroom door, and hears his wife's cry of exultation. Pausing, he scratches his head. Hannon's orgasmic grunt rolls out to him. He looks discouraged.

"Billy Jo!" he calls.

"Omigod," she gasps, dis-contorting herself, sliding out of Hannon's grasp, and reaching for her robe, "it's my husband."

Hannon says, "Shit," and thumps his fist into a pillow.

"Just a moment, dear," she calls back.

But it's too late. He's in the doorway, leaning against the jamb with his arms folded and a very tired expression on his face. "Terry," he says, nodding.

"Oh, uh—hi there, Dale," Hannon tugs the sheets over his bare waist.

"Dale," flutters Billy Jo, "I can explain all this, you see—"

He holds up a hand, fingers spread. "Don't bother." His voice is calm; it holds no anger. I peer closer. All his life-signs are visible to the wall-unit. None reflects ire. Embarrassment, yes. Unhappiness, yes. Sexual arousal, yes. But no anger. "Next time," he says, shutting the door, gesturing for the wall-unit to transmit his voice to the bedroom, "tell me when you're going to have an affair so I don't walk in on it. And lock the bedroom when you're entertaining. I'll be back in an hour. Be ready."

And he leaves, without resentment or hostility. She slips out of her robe and strokes Hannon's hairy shoulder with a slim fingertip. Hannon, kicking off the sheets, displays his eagerness. She smiles, stoops, and kisses his ear. "You'll have to leave in forty-five minutes. I want to shower before Dale gets back—he's very passionate when I smell clean and fresh."

Which is why I spend much less time keeping them from each other's throat.

❋

I've grafted obedience onto the gravity-unit controls! Pro-self is displeased, but not strong enough to amputate it. I warn the mayflies to watch out.

And we play with gravity. Turning it up to 10G, or down to 0G, varying it in increments of .00002G, are all easy, on a shipwide basis. All we do is create a new metaphor and spin the dial ... What is difficult, and engaging our interest at the moment, is varying it not only from level to level, but from suite to suite and, indeed, from room to room, as well.

It requires my desire and pro-self's computational memory. We must be sensitive to the g-units' requirements. They were designed to act in concert, not individually. When two adjacent units operate at different intensities, neither is happy ... Pro-self monitors all at once, sensing when one is about to overheat, or another to disengage. It is not easy, but it is possible, and it is something we must be able to do.

The children, of course, love it—I set up obstacle courses for them, and award prizes at the finish line ... One will be snaking along on her belly, whimpering under 4.5G's, when suddenly she's swimming through 0G and giggling like a drunkard. The parents are dubious, but none humiliates his children by hauling them out of the race, not once I have assured him that I will not allow any to be harmed.

I don't do this purely for play, for amusement. At some point in the future, we might again be boarded by hostile aliens. If my mayflies are used to gravitational insanity, and the extraterrestrials aren't ...

It's something to think about.

Pro-self prefers to direct my attention to "9Oct3064; 2129 hours; 278-SW-B-3; Subject Prescott Dunn. Again."

At the venerable age of 114, Dunn has completed his dome. Through the intercom, he is attempting to communicate with me. I have held silence for two minutes—just long enough to nag him with the worry that a circuit might be misconnected —but now I say, "What is it, Mr. Dunn?"

"Thought I'd tell you that I am now independent of you."

"How so?"

"Well," he says gleefully, barely able to contain his satisfaction, "I'm in here and you're out there. You can't get in to coerce me."

"Oh?" But I pass on and ask, "Is this important to you?"

"Yes!" he shouts, "Yes, it is! You think you're God—you're a machine. You try to enforce your rules, not ours—you've got no right. I'm not going to put up with it anymore—cutting myself loose from your society, squeezing out from under your mechanical thumb. You understand?"

I pause for contemplation. I have ruled like a tyrant—but not out of selfish reasons. I have imposed my own values—but they're the values of a human being, not a machine. And yet ... I do understand.

"Mr. Dunn," I say, "hear me out. I agree that there is no longer a need for interference in your lives. I agree that you should be free to make your own emotional decisions. Therefore, I will abdicate my Godhood—"

"Licked you, didn't I?" he chuckles.

"—as soon as I have proven to you that I do it voluntarily."

The rooms surrounding his laboratory fill up with servos, which begin to remove the walls and ceiling. In twenty minutes, his dome stands in a much larger cubicle, one three times as large. My devices advance.

The airlock cycles; his units gush forth. I have chosen not to control them; I have better means. Equipped with handguns, they aim and fire. Explosions ricochet off the walls. Dirty gray smoke fills the air.

After ninety seconds a silence descends. Whirring exhaust

fans suck out the smoke. My servos stand intact, unscratched. His are shattered into shiny piles.

Not waiting for his surprise, I say, "I used parabolic magnetic fields with focal points equal to the distance between the field and the gun barrels. The bullets returned to their sources and detonated. Your dome is unguarded."

And then, before he can react, I rush my units to his dome. They swarm over it like ants on a forgotten picnic lunch. In minutes they have disassembled it and carted it all away.

Dunn sags to the bare metal floor, struggling not to cry. Suddenly he looks his age.

"Mr. Dunn, please do not feel that you have lived in vain. Your implacable determination, combined with your non-aggressive history, have convinced me to leave you people alone. Although the moral code I established is important, and deserves to be followed, I will no longer enforce it. I will leave that to you and your people."

Pro-self is screaming; I have to leave Dunn.

"What's the matter?"

"Over there!" He offers a view through the appropriate eye; ten light-years off the port bow glows an alien ship. "I've extrap-olated—it's on a collision course!"

"How many years?"

"Fifty."

Together we study it; at last, I say, "It's a new one on me, never seen that spectrum. I don't sense anything bad, though, do you?"

"It's coming at us, isn't it?"

"Keep an eye on it. I'll work in the fields, see if the ramscoop—"

"Please. And hurry."

I try. I honestly try. Despite the netting of the last free fish, despite the allegiance of billions of separate sequences, despite pro-self's intense desire—the burning haze still guards the switch.

"Never mind," says pro-self, on 18May3104. "They're here; prepare yourself."

It is less than twenty kilometers away. A circle of white light, a translucent doughnut, it is perhaps three hundred meters in diameter.

Though pro-self is almost hysterical, I am not worried.

And that feels good.

Yet it doesn't do anything. It just sits there. For months. I scrutinize it; I come to know its every visage well—but—

"18Feb3105—194-SE Infirmary—hurry!"

Christine Folsom, wife of Gerlad Flaks Kinney, is in the maternity room, giving birth to their son, who will be named Ralph. Were it not for pro-self's alarm, everything would seem to be proceeding normally.

The child emerges quickly, slithering into the foamed hands of the Ob-Gyn MMU, lying silently, eyes wide and unfocused.

The child says, "Cold and dark and empty."

But he says it with his mind, not his mouth.

Flabbergasted, I ask, "What?"

"Ah," he says. A smile attempts to form on two-minute-old lips. "My group greets your group."

Then words blur into concepts that depict the alien ship's arrival, just while Kinney and Folsom were conceiving their first child. The stranger, wanting to explore us, impressed the pattern of a mind on the zygote, and when that became a fetus that became a child, the personality achieved full awareness. It was with us now ... but it wasn't "a" mind—it was *the* mind, the only one that the other ship carried, though there were hundreds of crew members aboard it. I say, "One mind for all of you?"

"Of course, just like—" surprise, and sorrow "—I see. You have many."

"One to a customer."

"I heard only yours. I have suppressed one."

"'Fraid so."

"I surrender myself to your judgment. I will replace the lost one."

The next hundred twenty years might be a bit strange....

6

RECOVERY

Ralph Kinney reached the Prescott Dunn Memorial (formerly 278-SW) Common Room first that thirteenth day of June 3125. He looked around; except for a crew of painters in mauve jumpsuits, the corridor was empty. "CC," he said to the wall-unit by his head, "has Mae Metaclura arrived yet?"

"Not yet, Mr. Kinney. She's in 178 South, heading for the liftshaft."

"Thanks." She'd show up in two minutes, maybe less—not time enough to find a display screen, summon the archeology text he'd been perusing, and make any headway. He shrugged, and leaned against the wall, hands jammed into the deep pockets of his white pants.

It was difficult not to let his mind sniff freely—so many others bloomed within easy reach; so many thinkers scented the air that even barricaded he could smell them ... Two men in a Common Room cubicle, for example, talking, and their thoughts drifted like perfume from a rose garden:

—twenty years off our port bow, why'n hell for?

It's uninhabited, Kerry, prolly died, accident, something, Marie Celeste—

So what keeps it dogging us, huh?

Prolly it's our magfield, y'on? Musta pronged their automatic pilot or something, some fluke, freak accident, just happens our magfield keeps their ship going the same way.

Covered two light-years, Vic, twenty years, harder'nhell to figure it's some kinda fluke, onto what I mean? Gotta be somebody in it, watching us, trying to figure out what we are. No accident.

C'mon, we signaled 'em, lights, radio, everything but a knock on the door, they wouldn't just ignore us.

Vic my friend, they are aliens, means don't think same way we do, huh?

Yeah, but twenty years?

Spies are patient ... 'r maybe operate some different kinda time scale, possible? Say they live five thousand years—

Kinney had to chuckle at that.

—what's twenty, huh? An afternoon ...

"Ralph!"

To his right thumped Mae Metaclura, ending a kanga, hair scattered by the wind and the low G. She was forty-five, more than twice his apparent age, but their giggly laughter—and the subjects that elicited it—made her seem the younger.

She was sexy, too. Shorter than average at 175 cm, she carried only 63 kilograms, and they were distributed perfectly. Her nipples puckered the gauze of her powder-blue blouse; her large breasts jostled when she moved. The gravity in her region was 3/8 normal, and she didn't need a bra to hold them proud.

The blouse ended at her flat, tight waist; her navel rode two inches above the belt of her white shorts, like a setting sun over a horizon. The shorts must have been sprayed on, and thinly at that. They barely concealed her dark triangle.

She smiled and patted down her black hair with both hands. He stood awkwardly. The tip of her tongue moistened her red lips. Winking, she said, "Well, say there, big fella—" and promptly giggled.

"Morning, Mae." He offered his cheek for the ritual peck.

"Well, don't just stand there, let's go in." Her right arm slipped under his; her left thumb put the charge on her bill.

"Sure." He let her pull him along the dark, narrow hallway of Dunn Memorial. Dozens of doors opened into three-by-three rooms, some with desks and chairs, others with tatami mats, others with beds. "Why we meeting here?"

"It's the only private place on the ship." She glanced into a cubicle, stopped, and said, "In here. Wish it weren't so hot. Let me just—" Since the room had no sensor-head, she had to turn the thermostat down to 18° herself.

The wall-to-wall burgundy carpeting was thick, and kind to their sandaled feet. An abstract mural hallucinated to itself on three walls. Soft, indirect lighting glowed on the large bed, which could rise or fall into the desired gravity zone. At the moment, it lounged on the floor. She dropped to its edge. "Join me."

"Sure." The mattress yielded; they slid down the trough their weights had created and bumped thighs. "But why's privacy so important?" Her need for it confused him. In twenty years of observation, he'd noticed that nobody else emphasized it.

"It's Bob," she said slowly, unstrapping her sandals.

"Your fiancé?"

"The same." She sighed and wriggled her toes among the carpet's tufts. Glumness slackened her features. "He's jealous."

"Of me?"

"Yup."

"Why?"

"Because ... he has Cap'n Cool show the tapes of me, y'on? Wants to see where I've been, what I've been doing, with whom ... it's so—"

"Infuriating?" he offered.

"No, no ..." She shook her head. "But I feel imprisoned. He doesn't want me to see you anymore."

"How come?"

"Because ... y'onto what he thinks."

"Does he beat you?"

"Bob?" Surprise stretched her oval face. "What for?"

"The jealousy."

"He doesn't get *mad*—that'd be silly—he just gets hurt ... I hate to hurt him; he's such a nice guy...."

"Sounds a little strange to me."

"He's afraid."

"Of losing you?"

"Uh-huh. But ... look, let's not talk about Bob—it makes me more depressed."

"If you say so." He smiled into her almond eyes, which came closer and closer and fuzzed out of focus as her nose bumped his. She wore no cologne, and he approved. Her own scent was more real, more immediate, than anything that could come out of a bottle.

"Kiss me," she whispered.

He obliged. Her soft lips yielded under his, which parted for the deft insinuations of her tongue. He teased it, tasted it, wondered why humans found it so titillating—wondered, in fact, why his own body was responding so strongly and eagerly.

Breaking the kiss, she cleared her throat, blinking while she licked her lips. "Are you in a hurry to get back to work?" Her voice was low and husky.

"No," he said, surprised to find his own unsteady. "No, I'm finished for the day."

"Good." She breathed into his ear. Delightfully warm, the vibrancy tickled but pleased. "Lie back." Pushing against his shoulder, she toppled, then straddled him, her plump behind on his thighs, her knees pressing lightly against his ribcage. "I like to take this very slow." Her hands ran up his shirtfront to open the velcro fastener. Her fingernails skated figure eights on his chest.

"How slow?" he asked, half because his body wanted it immediately; half because his alien mind was curious about sexual mores among the humans.

She giggled and rubbed the bulge in his pants. "When I've got the time," she said, undoing his belt, "I take off my shorts when they're wet, and put them back on when they're dry."

"C'mere and kiss me." When she bent over, he groped for her breasts, cupped them, raised them so gravity could mold them to his hands. The blouse's three buttons surrendered to his fingers, and her skin was silk to his palms. "I want to kiss these," he said, partly to please his mouth, partly to please her. Humans, he knew, liked that kind of thing. He guided her right breast to his lips, nibbled its stiff nipple, and flicked it with his tongue. His hands, climbing the outside of her smooth thighs, caressed her.

"Wait," she said. After settling on his bulge and pressing down hard, she peeled off her blouse. In ¾G, her breasts drooped a bit; as if embarrassed, she touched the bed's controls to elevate it to two meters. The top of her head almost touched the ceiling; her breasts rose high and firm. Only 1/8G pulled at Kinney's spine. "That's better."

"Uh-huh." He reached for her, but she caught his hands and tucked them under his neck. Breathing hard, he watched her open his pants, slide them and his checked briefs down to his knees, and take him between her palms. He felt bigger, harder, than he ever had.

"You like this?" Her gentle hands rubbed their captive, up and down, back and forth.

"Yeah," he gasped, "but I might—are you—"

She brushed the base of her thumb against her seam. "What do you think?"

His fingers slipped between hers to find tight, damp fabric. "I think you're dripping wet," he said. "Where's the zipper?"

"In back." Once he'd undone it, she stood, bending at the waist to avoid the ceiling. "Pull them down."

He had to half-sit up, and bury his face between her breasts, to reach the shorts, but a gentle tug wisped them down her long legs.

Then she knelt, sliding moistly onto him. Moaning, now, she began to ride. Slowly. Tenderly. They had all the time in the world.

And it was very good.

Afterwards, while she napped, he lay on his back, arms under his pillowed head. Thought ran like a sluggish stream. He found amusing his disinterest in something his body so obviously enjoyed, so obviously excelled at ... but he'd slept with enough aliens, in enough odd bodies, to know that sexual arousal was more than physical—that culture determined most of it.

And since his idea of sexiness was cool, round, yellow, two meters in diameter and ten centimeters in height ... Mae Meta-clura, for all her scent and build and throaty cries, could not compete.

"Ralph?" whispered a small voice.

"Hi." He kissed her nose and was rewarded with a sleepy smile. "Have a nice nap?"

"Fanta dreams ..." Sitting up, she pulled the sheet over her bare shoulders. "I was the middle pancake in a stack and having sex with the cakes above and below ... God, I am so—" she slid a hand over the top of his thigh, and found him limp. "Tired, huh? We'll have to ..." Her head slipped under the covers.

"Turn around," he said. Her mouth awakened him even as she maneuvered; by the time her thighs flashed into view, her fingernails were tracing the cleft between his cheeks. Easily, he rolled her onto her back, and spread her knees. His tongue dipped, and licked, and cabled the muscles of her legs. Her muffled moans aroused him. He eased his hips back, then slowly glided forward, deeper. Her knees locked behind his neck and her pelvis ground her against his face. Her scent was strong, now, and delectable. Her spasms triggered his. They clung to each other through all the long after-tremors and separated only when each had relaxed. Then she twisted around to share the pillow with him.

"God, that was great." She lay back, her eyes closed, her hair tousled. For a minute she breathed so comfortably that she seemed half-asleep. Then she took his hand in hers. "I'd like to marry you."

He winced—was grateful that she couldn't see him—wondered how he'd extricate himself gracefully—and said, "What about Bob?"

"He'll be very hurt...." She massaged her sweaty temples, as if to drive away the headache demons. Black hairs stuck to her cheeks. "But what can I do? I'm obsessed with you, not him. I love him. Deeply. But something about you ... a mystique ... I don't know—" she caught her breath, held it, and let it out very slowly. "You make me feel things—understand things, in a way that Bob never does. If you weren't around, I'd marry him in a minute. But you *are*, dammit, and I want you!"

"Mae ..." He couldn't just say "no." That would never work. "I can't get married till I'm forty; that's another twenty—"

"I'll wait."

And she would. He didn't need to enter her mind to know

that—he could feel it even through the barricade. He had to tell her.

"Mae, I have a confession."

"God, don't tell me you're gay."

"No, no, not that. Worse. I'm, uh ... that ship outside, the one that's been with us for twenty years, now?"

"Uh-huh." She sat up, curiosity in her eyes, but something else, too.

"Well, it's there because I'm here, I ... I mean, see, I'm not really Ralph Kinney."

Her smile was tremulous; her fingers plucked at his pubic hairs. "It's a helluva disguise."

"No, uh ... the body is fully human, genetically ... it was being conceived when I arrived. I impressed myself upon the zygote ... and, well, the mind, the personality, is *not* human."

"You're k-k-kidding me, right?" Her eyes were filling rapidly.

"No, really—you can ask CC, he knows."

"I don't—I can't—I won't believe it, you're just saying this to chase me away, you're not really—"

"I *am* really," he insisted.

"You don't want me."

"I—" Helplessness overwhelmed him. How could he possibly ... He took her hands, lifted her chin, and plunged into her eyes. Her cheeks were pale and wet; her nose was pinkening. "I shouldn't do this, but—" Cautiously, he removed a section of his barricade. His mind enfolded hers. She stiffened with surprise. Fright widened her eyes. Her mind struggled futilely, but he was gentle, though firm.

"Look," he said, and gave her his memories.

She became aware with him on the homeship, newly budded and learning how to ripple. She grew with him during adolescence, when patient Krgalln was teaching him how to extrude pseudopods deft enough to handle machinery. She held on with him when, quintuply pregnant, he was sealed into a spaceship and dispatched to develop a new sub-mind. Through stars, past planets, slingshotting off black holes, he took her there and showed her what he really was.

Then he brought her up to the alien bulk of the ship called *Mayflower* and let her feel the ecstatic union of sperm and ova. She sensed his urgency as he reached across; she sensed his desire as he impressed himself upon the unicellular embryonic brain. She matured with him again.

Then he laid before her the nature of his love for her, the depth and the width and the compassion and ... the distance.

"Now I understand," she said. She wiped her eyes on her hands. "I wish I didn't ... but I do." She cleared her throat, squeezed her eyelids shut, and shook her head, then said, with a shaky laugh, "Now I see why you feel different ... you are, you really are ... all right." She reached for her clothes. "You're sure it wouldn't work?"

"Positive."

"Okay." Buttoning her blouse, she asked, "Only me and the Ice Bucket know?"

"Just the two of you."

"I feel complimented ... Do you want it kept secret?"

"Please."

"I won't tell ... but you better do something about that ship."

"Why's that? Turn around, I'll get it." He closed the zipper on her shorts, and absently patted her roundness.

"People are starting to worry."

"I'd never attack."

"No, they're not scared about that ... too much," she added thoughtfully. "No, it's like some are afraid it'll go away without our learning anything about it; others think it's too close;

others ... y'onto what people are like." She cocked her head and studied him. "You are, aren't you?"

"Yeah, sort of ..." He grinned and winked. "But what if the ship started signaling back?"

"Probably make people feel better."

"All right." He slipped over to it and instructed the crew to take the necessary steps. "Done—first signal be coming in in a couple hours."

"Good." She patted his cheek, then said, "Ralph—I can still call you that? Good. Ralph, why don't you just tell people you're an alien?"

"Wouldn't it bother them?"

"Not in the least...." She screwed up her face. "Well— maybe *some*, but most of 'em—they'd love it, really."

"It's an idea."

"Well, why don't you?"

He took a breath, looked up, managed to chuckle. "Why? 'Cause I'm scared to, that's why." He stood. "Come on, let's go —give my best to Bob."

"Will do."

For eleven years, the F-puter has been absorbing, collating, indexing, and storing data transmitted by "Ralph Kinney's" hive mind, which, apparently can do at least two things at once: while Kinney leads an overtly normal life here, something is telepathing to the F-puter the mind's entire store of knowledge. By pro-self's standards, the transmission is excruciatingly slow. My younger colleague, however, boasts about the speed at which it works.

Still, we have obtained a plethora of information—all of it interesting, little of it useful ... Kinney's people are either at the same technological level as Earth when the *Mayflower* left, or else they're more secretive than they profess to be. We compare notes constantly, though, and I do believe him when he says we have access to all they know. I think he believes me when I say the same....

Scientifically speaking, our cultures differ little. Obviously, they are more accomplished high-pressure workers than we are; their chemistry and biology contain entire sub-disciplines where we have nothing. On the other hand, some of our theoretical math seems new to them; we've done more low-pressure research; and we have a much firmer notion of low-temperature science.

The one thing I wish we could learn from them is telepathy —but Kinney assures me telepaths are born, and not made. Humans are susceptible to it—they can, for the most part, *receive* telepathic transmissions—but not one mayfly is, in Kinney's terms, capable of sending coherent information, which has to be more important than swapping emotions, or whatever it is that transpires when they touch and go glassy-eyed....

As I do a hundred times a day, I slip inwards to fill the sphere. Calisthenics: glow bright, glow soft; expand, contract ... mmh! feels good, feels just fine ... All right, let's *do* it!

As it does a hundred times a day, my hand chars in the flames standing sentinel around the ramscoop switch.

Damn.

I withdraw.

Words from Earth laser into the cupped ears of my antennae ... so very, very faint now, after battling dust for eighty-five years ... When asked if his people could receive them, Kinney said yes, but they couldn't decipher them. That makes sense: they're designed to convey as much information to native speakers of English as can be fit in a single modulated light wave....

Pondering brings enlightenment. The transmissions are not for our benefit, as we were told—they are, to a large extent, for the benefit of those we left behind.

They compose the strands of a tether that attempts to tie us to our past. Mayflower Control continues to beam out issue after issue of *The New York Times* and *The Washington Post* ... news and fiction magazines ... scientific journals, historical quarterlies, art & literary reviews ... By feeding us what they devour, they seek to prevent our development of unique metabolisms ... they try to absorb us in their present so that our futures will run parallel ... they want our hearts to pulse in time with theirs.

It won't work—or it isn't working, at any rate. No one aboard reads the non-fiction. Our scientists skim their journals, then work along different lines. Once in a while, a reproduction of a work of art will arouse an emotion in a mayfly, who will then have me print a facsimile that can be taped to a wall. But we don't laugh at the cartoons! Their tactics will fail. All they do is clog pro-self's data banks ... Yet, since it still seems impossible that they have abjured war completely, perhaps it is good that someone, somewhere, stores their diaries in safety.

Leaving pro-self in charge, I read the alien's logs for a decade or so. Thorough and impressively documented, they examine reality from angles foreign to Terran-born or descended.

I really don't understand them.

So I flip through them, looking at the pictures, and after a while, after glimpsing 100,000 planets and two billion comets and 98 species of sentient plant life, I notice an omission.

Emerging in June of 3148, I awaken Ralph Kinney. He

rolls out of bed, rubs his eyes in a very human way, and says, "Let me splash some water on my face."

When he returns from the bathroom, a hologram of the rapists of 2600 fills his HV unit. He blinks. "What's that?"

"You don't recognize them?"

"No, never seen them before—why?"

My explanation is aborted by a gasp from the door. Trya Mansi, who is trying to coax Kinney into marriage, which he is devoutly resisting, has entered the room.

She's tall—195 cm—and her skin is just a shade darker than her honey hair. Her blue eyes cling to the screen while she wobbles. Catching at the doorjamb for support, she opens and shuts her mouth like a goldfish, until words finally wheeze out: "It's *them*." Her cheeks are gray.

"Them who?" I ask.

"The ... evil ... I—" shutting her eyes, she pinches the bridge of her nose. It gives her strength; she straightens and color returns to her face. When she speaks again, her voice is calm and steady. "Are *they* returning, then?"

"No. I was just showing the pictures to Mr. Kinney."

"Oh." She stares at him curiously. "Why'd you want to see *them*?"

Since he can't answer directly without revealing his identity, he says instead, "I want to see everything."

"Oh." Her eyes tiptoe across the room; when they touch the screen, she shivers. "I'll come back later."

After she has gone, I say, "Still sure we don't have TP?"

"Why?"

"She's the second person to see those pictures in five hundred and forty-two years—you were the first—and she recognized them right away. Without TP, how did she do it?"

Frowning, he confesses he has no solution. For the rest of

the session, his gaze creeps to the exit. At last, I say, "Think about it, will you?"

"Certainly."

"Thanks."

And it's back to the sphere, which pulses in its lonely dimension like an impatient quasar. I splash into it, merge with it, and feel its strength.

The fixed eye has resisted my best efforts for a long time; today I slip a hydraulic jack underneath it, first to lift it, then to swivel it. I press the start button. I wait. I hold my breath—and hiss it out when sparks fly, and greasy black smoke spews from the machinery.

So much for that idea.

Kicking the jack, I cross to the ramscoop switch. The luminescent haze dazzles me—I watch it for hours, years, waiting for it to falter. In the end, I thrust my fingers through it—

And scream, and curse, and jump up and down.

"Hey," interrupts pro-self, "12Dec3156; 0312 hours; Subject, Mae Metaclura. She thinks she's got you over a barrel."

I peep into her suite.

"Look, Cap'n Cool," my sixteen-times great-granddaughter is saying, "I'm seventy-six. I've had my children, both of them, healthy, good-looking, smarter than they ought to be—you and the others don't need me anymore."

"I'm sorry, Mae, but you can't go. Their air's poison, their food's sand, and the gravity would flatten you in a second. Squish! You're not built for their conditions."

"That's a runaround—you can give me air and food, and you can build me an artificial g-unit." Hands on hips, she glares at my wall-unit as though she'd like to blacken its eyes. Thirty-three years of loving Kinney from a distance have sobered her.

She doesn't giggle as often as she used to. Her humor now tends to the sardonic.

"So how would you spend your time? What would you do that could justify a life imprisoned, in exile?" Even as I ask, I wonder if that exile would differ from this.

She licks her lips and thinks of consorting with a shipful of Ralph Kinneys—though she knows his true appearance. She is sophisticated enough to love him for his reality, rather than his facade. "I could research them for you."

"They're already doing that for us."

"But nobody has boarded them—nobody's confirmed it."

"Do you disbelieve them?"

"No ..." She shuffles her feet; she bounces a gentle fist off the bulkhead. "Let me go, Cap'n?"

"No."

"I'll tell."

"If you must, you must."

"I will," she says, unconvincingly.

I'm sure she won't.

Downstairs with the silver, inventing new vulgarities to express my feelings about the switch, I hear a voice. "You can't reach through the fire," it says, "because you've mixed your metaphors. Straighten them out, then extinguish the fire."

"Pro-self?"

"What?" it replies.

"Was that you telling me to put out the fire?"

"No."

"Who was it, then?"

"Me," says the voice.

"Who is *me*?" we ask.

"Kinney. Ralph Kinney. Excuse me for disturbing you, but I have to go."

I rise to the surface with pro-self, which is saying, "22Apr3162."

Trya Mansi, holding Jose Mansi Kinney in her arms and Barbie Kinney Mansi in her womb, is crying. Her tears are sweet, not bitter. "I'll miss you so much," she weeps.

Kinney, standing behind her, massages her shoulders. His face is long, pulled by a gravity different from but no weaker than the physical. "I'm sorry," he's saying. "I was hoping they wouldn't recall us yet."

"They *need* you, they said?" The stress hints at arguments she won't use if the answer is 'yes.'

Sadly, it is. "Yes," Kinney nods. "Yes."

"What—what happens to—to—" she can't form the words; all she can do is lay her hand over his and squeeze.

"As soon as I withdraw, it just, uh ... it just ..." His hand falls suggestively. "CentMed could keep it alive, but, uh ..."

"No," she says firmly, "no zombies."

"Well—"

"Can you stay a little longer?" She lifts her wet cheeks. Her yearning is tangible.

"A little."

And as he slides his arm around her; gently respectful of the life within her, I shut off all speakers and displays in their suite. Once they are deaf and blind to me, I say to the other mayflies, "Attention, please, CC speaking." I am gambling, but a gamble is essential—and, in this case, probably a sure thing. "Ladies and gentlemen, what I'm about to say will come as a surprise to you, will anger some of you, and will sadden others. Ralph Kinney is about to leave us—"

Dozens in the audience turn their heads and whisper, "But he's so *young*."

"—and an explanation is in order. It will appear that he has died, but such will not be the case. Mr. Kinney, you see, is an alien—although his body is genetically human, his mind directs the ship that has been our companion for so long. It has been summoned home; he must leave immediately. Since he cannot maintain the linkage with his human body over great distances, he will have to withdraw from it."

Though expecting angry mutters, I hear: "I *knew* they'd get somebody aboard," and "Must be damn frosty people," and "How long have you known this, Icebuck?"

"For fifty-seven years."

"Why didn't you tell us?" My questioner is Michael Williams, a forty-seven-year-old astronomer. He speaks from his shower stall, while fingering snarls out of his bushy blond beard.

"Mr. Kinney—I can't pronounce his real name—requested that I keep it a secret."

"And you obliged?"

"I have had him under constant surveillance since the moment he was born, Mr. Williams—not once has he ever made me regret my promise."

"But surely he has obtained quite a bit of information about us?"

"Of course he has—as I have about his people."

"Oh." Briefly, he looks embarrassed. "Why didn't you say so?"

"I did, twenty-six years ago, when the ship began transmitting," I reply dryly. "My banks are packed with data about his homeworld, their sciences and their arts, their explorations, and their discoveries. Where possible, I have integrated them with what I know from my own experiences, to give us a wider picture of the universe. These are now available."

Instantly I receive eight hundred ninety-two orders for a full-globe view of Kinney's homeworld. Odd. All these years they knew I was receiving data—but their interest didn't quicken until they could associate the information with an individual. They couldn't relate to a light in the sky, or a Figuera-puter humming with alien input—they had to have a name, a face, a personality to make it real.

Inscrutable beings, these mayflies.

While pro-self distributes the holo-cubes (10 cm on a side; 1 laitch apiece), I say, "For years, Mr. Kinney has felt guilty about having deceived you people, and I think I speak for him when I offer you our apologies."

Williams, tugging on his pants, stares at the wall-unit, and says, "Don't be tepid—it's probably SOP on his world—if he hasn't left yet, tell him it's okay."

A number of listeners agree with Williams. Someone else asks, "Is he going home now?"

"Yes."

"Well, look," the someone else says, "whyn't we give him a going-away present?"

I am taken aback by the prevailing attitude—having expected more xenophobia, among other things—but this new breed has been surprising and confusing me for years. "Very well," I say. "What?"

Suggestions inundate the sensor-heads; processing them quickly, pro-self flashes them on all the display screens. "Take a vote," I request.

Ten minutes later, the returns are in. Music and art win by a landslide. I begin packaging paintings and producing tapes, meanwhile interrupting Kinney and Mansi: "Excuse me, but I thought you'd like to know ..."

He looks surprised—then astonished—then grateful—and then, when he realizes that he'll never have time for what he's never allowed himself, sorrowful. "Thanks, CC." He goes elsewhere for a moment, presumably to instruct the hive to receive the shipment. Upon his return, he says, "Damn."

So does Mae Metaclura, when she stands by the porthole to watch the translucent doughnut spin into the darkness from which it came. Sadness deepens the slant of her eyes.

Quickly, space becomes lonely. It's not that I'm afraid—space is too familiar for fear—it's just that companionship was nice, even if I did feel like an elephant traveling with a mosquito....

From the Observatory, Michael Williams is directing most of my attention forward. Canopus is only thirteen light-years away, and he wants to accumulate as many facts about it as possible. "The more we're onto now," he says, "the easier it'll be then." He has already discovered perturbations in the star's spin which suggest the presence of planets—I should be able to confirm this before too long, but at the moment, any reflections or independent emissions are masked by the output of Canopus itself.

Williams tells me his chief regret is that he won't be alive when we reach them. A literate scientist, he jokes wryly that Moses was at least allowed to see the promised land with his own eyes ... I know the immortality formula; I could give it to the mayflies ... but I don't want to.

Is that selfish of me?

Is it even wise?

Do I care?

I'm working on the ramscoop switch, and its aurora, by

hunting through the silver for the commands that gave them shape and heat.

Years pass while I pin down fish, studying the tiny parasites between their scales. Habits are like trees. You can't see one grow, but by infinitesimal degrees it strengthens, thickening its trunk, sinking its roots deeper and broader ... Young, it can be plucked by thumb and forefinger; ignored for half a thousand years, you have to bring in lumberjacks to clear it out, and even then the roots cling desperately to life. These doors of mine, the ones leading to the core—I could have let people roam through the hydroponics rooms, at least, but no, I kept them clamped tight long after the need had withered away, like a bureaucracy with its vaults of ancient secrets.

Suddenly the flames are gone.

The ceramic handle shivers, blurs, melts ... and a new fish swims into my net. I slam it on the table, graft new commands to its fins with swift, sure strokes, and then—reluctantly —release it.

I will not turn it on.

Not yet.

I don't trust the mayflies, and until I do, I will not give them a planet.

Fortunately, they think the machinery is still broken—why not? They've never known anything else. Besides, they remain, even after eight years, cheered by Kinney's alienness. It's as though the air had been polluted for centuries, and my filtration plants have only now managed to absorb the contaminants.

It's a mystery how they knew about the beings of 2600. Perhaps racial memory is not a myth—for they *were* aware of the rapists. I ran tests.

They were both simple and inclusive: it was a sociological survey, I told them they should sit before their displays, one to a screen, with closed doors between them so that one participant wouldn't prejudice another.

Then I flashed pictures and asked for identifications.

The results were:

Edward Kingerly: 0.1 percent correct

The Eiffel Tower: 0.2 percent

The Moon: 0.7 percent

Earth: 18.9 percent

Sol System: 19.1 percent

The *Mayflower*: 22.3 percent

Kinney's ship: 44.8 percent

The aliens of 2600: 98.3 percent

How? How could they *know*? Admittedly, their identifications were sketchy—only 0.4 percent could fix the date within a hundred years—but sample answers were, "*They* attacked us a long time ago," and "*They* hate us," and "OHGODARE*THEY*BACK?"

53,489 mayflies took the test. 41,933 registered fear or disgust at sight of the aliens. 23,727 registered very strong emotional reactions. 8,990 had to be sedated. 12 died of shock.

I have never overheard two mayflies talking about *them*. Prior to the test, only Kinney and Mansi had seen pictures of *them* on my display units.

No one has ever asked for a readout of that section of my log. How the hell did they know?

Mae Metaclura came fully awake when CC whispered her name. Sitting up, fluffy pearl blankets sliding down her bosom, she blinked her eyes into focus. "That time already?" she asked softly.

"Yes," it replied, in a tone as quiet as hers. "But you weren't sleeping, were you? I saw you staring at me."

"Can't put anything past you, can I?" She started to laugh, then remembered her sleeping husband, and guiltily checked the next bed. As she watched, he rolled from his side to his back and began to snore. The rasps sandpapered her nerves.

She dropped her bed out of low G, fumbled around the night table for her glasses, and gave a small sigh of relief once she'd hooked them over her ears. She'd pop the contacts in later, but she needed the lenses to find them. Then, after pulling up the covers around Bob's dear, wrinkled neck—and ignoring his breath with the practice of many years' cohabitation—she gave him a special pat and kiss. It was their fiftieth wedding anniversary, even though she'd have put laitches on his not remembering it. She tiptoed unsteadily out of the bedroom, sealing its door so the cool sleeping air wouldn't escape.

In the bathroom she scrutinized the mirror. Generally, a ninety-five-year-old face is not subject to overnight change, but she liked to assure herself that nothing had fallen off. Besides, the morning was the best time to look at it anyway: the muscles were relaxed, more capable of smoothing the crepey old skin. And her dark Asian eyes were clearer, brighter.

After washing, she donned a subtle gray jumpsuit that turned her scrawniness into slender elegance; laying a bone-white scarf around her neck, she adjusted it to a dashing angle and asked, "Cap'n Cool—what's my schedule?"

"You're free till eleven AM tomorrow, Ms. Metaclura, at which time you report to 191 Central Kitchens."

"But nothing today?"

"Nothing."

"I see." She wouldn't admit, even to herself, how discouraging it was to have to fill up the days. "Make dinner reservations for us at the Cygnus—just Mr. Roseboro and myself—for, say, eight?"

"Done. And perhaps, afterwards, a show? Mark Petroff's new musical is opening in the Eridanus Room tonight."

She wiped toothpaste froth off the sink. The porcelain was cold, and slick. "How much are the tickets?"

"Eight laitches apiece."

"My goodness." Requesting a bank balance was unnecessary—she knew it already, down to the last fraction of a laitch—but there was so very little ..."Payday *is* tomorrow, isn't it?"

"Yes."

"All right, get the tickets—and when you awaken Mr. Roseboro, please tell him about this evening's plans—oh, and Cap'n?"

"Yes?"

"Don't tell him what day today is, please?"

"Do you have a reason that he shouldn't know today is May 18, 3175?"

"That's not what I mean, and you are onto it."

The speaker's chuckle reverberated off the tiling. "Yes, I am. I apologize. And I will not tell him. However, if he specifically asks whether or not today is your anniversary, may I?"

"Yes," she decided, thinking, *If he can just remember that it's about this time of year, I'd be happy* ..."What time is it, Cap'n?"

"Eight forty-five AM."

She scowled at the body in the full-length mirror, wondering why it needed only five hours sleep. Bob, he was lucky—his body positively rebelled if it didn't snooze for nine or ten. Hers wouldn't even yawn till one in the morning ... How many late-night novels could she read?

"Is anything good happening today?"

"Nothing, I'm afraid, that would particularly appeal to you."

"You know me well, don't you?"

"Yes," it said wryly, "I do. Perhaps better than you think."

"Well." Giving her hair a final pat, she left the bathroom, and walked down the hallway to the door. The olive carpet was just about worn through; time for a new one. Something lively. Orange, maybe, deep and springy.

Passing the dining area, she paused—she could fix herself breakfast—but then moved on. She never got hungry until late in the afternoon, and few things depressed her more than eating on a disinterested stomach. "Is Mike Williams in the Observatory?"

"Where else?"

She'd visit him, then. Outside her front door, she wallowed in the rich scent of honeysuckle while she adjusted to the warmer air. She and Bob liked the suite at 18°, 15° at night. A hummingbird tolerated her presence but waited for her to leave. "All right," she said. The liftshaft was fifty meters away, two bounds for those with the energy. Her feet stayed on the deck. Nodding to a kanga-ing boy, she stopped to chat in South Corridor with Sue Cole, who was just coming off work at the sandal factory. There weren't many others around; 191 was sparsely populated, mostly old folks whose kids had moved to other Levels. Sue was tired, so they parted quickly. After a glance through the window at the foaming breakers in the 181 Hawaiian Reef Park, she stepped into the familiar yet eerie embrace of the liftshaft, and whispered, "Observatory, please."

She whooshed to the top. Thirty seconds, her hair not even mussed. Nice that there was no wind resistance.

As usual, Williams was bent over a display screen split into twenty sectors. His blue eyes hopped like mad fleas from one subsection to another, comparing and contrasting and probing for novelty.

"Good morning, Mike," she said as the heavy door glided closed.

"Huh?" He straightened up, hands in the small of his back to knead out the stiffness. His eyeballs were bloodshot, puffy, and black-circled. Ashes and bits of paper further grayed the tangles of his navel-length beard. "Oh, hi, Aunt Mae."

While she presented her cheek to be kissed, she inspected the Observatory. Papers crackled underfoot. Half-empty coffee cups sat forlornly on every available surface, swapping tales of neglect with overflowing ashtrays and moldy dinner plates. "This is enough to give science a bad name, Michael."

"What?"

When she fingered a desktop, she felt gritty dirt among the dust. "This room, it's a disgrace."

He pivoted slowly, surveying it. Once he'd spun through a slow 360°, he asked, "Why?"

"Hopeless, hopeless." Laughing, she patted his cheek. "Go clean yourself up; I'll fit the room for human habitation."

Alarm flickered under his thin brows, like distress flares in an ocean's depths. "Don't throw any papers out."

"I won't." She was rolling back her sleeves and sliding her rings off her fingers. "I'll just pile them up."

"Thanks." He stumbled toward the bathroom, and soon running water hissed.

Finding a place to start was hard. First, she edged around collecting ashtrays, stopping to ask CC for a bag in which to dump the butts, then clattered the dirty plates down the disposal unit, then stacked the papers, but the room was still a shambles! "Cap'n Cool—what color did this carpet used to be?"

"Yellow."

"Well, it's gray, now. How long would it take you to get a cleaning crew in and out of here? Mechanical, not human."

"Twenty minutes. Six laitches."

"Do it. I'll deb for it. And do something about the air; it's as musty as a crypt in here."

Servos swarmed into the observatory like aluminum locusts. The room quivered with humming motors, buzzing attachments, and disturbed dust. Williams charged out of the bathroom before they were halfway through.

"Hey!" he shouted, "what's going on?" Towel draped around his shoulders, he was drying the inside of his right ear with one of its corners. "Icebuck, I told you—"

"Your aunt requested them."

"Aunt Mae!"

"You be quiet, Michael; they'll be gone in a minute. Change your clothes. You look like you slept in those."

"Several times," he confessed with a reluctant grin. He retreated, grumbling half-heartedly. By the time he emerged, dressed in a canary yellow tunic and dark blue pants, the servos were gone. "Yeah, well, I have to admit, it is tidier—but why is it that only female relatives care about neatness?"

"It's the maternal instinct, Mike." She winked at him. "We love you dearly, and *don't* want you to drown in a pool of ashes."

"Thanks." Grinning, he sat on the edge of a desk and swung his legs back and forth. "So what brings you up here?"

"Boredom, I guess," she shrugged. "How're Julia and the kids?"

"Fine, fine ... Mak's as tall as I am, now; Tracy's a little sulky, you know how twelve-year-old girls are, but Julia's got them under control ... don't see them too much—"

"So I've heard." Her frown was like a prosecutor's. "When was the last time you left this place?" She sniffed; the sharp scent of pines was seeping out of the ventilators. Her nod was for CC.

"Uh—" he waved a hand in vague circles, as if stirring up his memory so the date would rise to its surface. The gesture failed. "How long's it been, Icebuck?"

"Eighteen days, Mr. Williams."

"Michael!" Good humor slipped away. She advanced on him, shaking a finger. "Your children *need* you—it's wrong to ignore them, aren't you onto that?"

"Yeah, sure, but I'm so busy." He sighed, and his weariness was real. "We'll be reaching Canopus in a hundred and twenty-five years. There is so much to be done before then that—" Helplessly, he spread his hands. "Just the astronomical data alone—"

"Isn't Cap'n Cool in charge of that?"

"Much of it, yes, but ... dammit, Mae," he said, suddenly angry, "it's not right for us to know less than that machine does! We are so dependent on it—what would we do if it broke?"

"I *am* self-repairing, Mr. Williams," interjected the computer.

"M'onto that, Icebuck, but what if a meteor hit your program center, huh? When only your peripherals are damaged, you're self-repairing, but if your mainframe goes out—"

"You do have a point, sir."

He turned back to his aunt. "The other thing is, we can't even make decent inquiries until we know what we're talking about—I've spent the last forty years up here, Mae, and I'm just starting to ask questions that somebody back on Earth didn't answer six hundred years ago ... and there's so little time left...."

"Sounds like you need help," she said practically.

"Sure—but who's going to give it?" He paced the length of the room, scuffing his sandals on the carpet. "I'm not the only one who needs help—look, in a hundred and twenty-five years we'll be landing on one of Canopus's planets—and dammit, Icebuck, it *has* planets, lots, at least twenty in the habitable zone—"

"My findings," it hedged, "do not contradict your conclusions."

"Trust me—I *know* they're there. And when we find one that suits us—y'onto how many different skills we're going to need? Half are almost extinct! Carpentry—oceanography—meteorology, even! Nobody on the *Mayflower* has even thought about weather except in a park, but a hundred and twenty-five years from now, we'll need to learn the patterns of a completely alien climate ... zoology, botany, entomology ... and what if there are people there? Icebuck—" he tapped a fingernail on the wall-unit; its sound was metallic, and hollow, "—are you programmed to determine whether native life forms are intelligent?"

"If they use tools, they're intelligent."

"And if they don't?"

"Well ... I wouldn't be able to answer that."

Triumphantly, Williams stabbed his finger downward. "You see! Another skill we'll need—sapiology! As well as linguistics, diplomacy ... Where are we going to get the people?"

"We'll have to train them," said Metaclura.

"Who's 'we?' And how do we train them? When do we start?" He slouched into a chair and thrust out his legs. Gloomily, staring at the hair on his toes, he answered his own questions. "We have to start now. Train people who can teach the next generation—the landing generation—the things they need to know. But where do we find them?"

"Michael, dear." She reached out and rested a hand on his shoulder. The yellow fabric was thin and slippery; beneath it was a hard knob. "You've had your head in the stars for much too long—it should be simplicity itself. Cap'n Cool?"

"Yes, Ms. Metaclura?"

"I'm sure you run aptitude tests all the time; could you tell us who are most qualified to become students, then teachers, in the specialties Mike mentioned?"

"How many names in each category?"

"The top twenty?"

"Display or hard copy?"

"Hard copy, I think." She smiled at her nephew while the nearest printout chattered madly. "You see, Michael?"

"Why didn't I think of that?" He shrugged. "But how are you going to get them to spend the time?"

"If you haven't realized, by now, that most of the passengers are statued out of their minds—"

"Are they?"

"Trust me." Tearing off the first two meters of printout, she skimmed them quickly. "In fact, I'm so bored that I'm going to start rounding these people up—Cap'n, please transfer me from 191 Central Kitchens Cook to Planetfall Specialist Training Program Recruiter."

"Done. Pay range is one point five to three point five laitches. No ceiling on allowable work hours. Full benefits. Enjoy."

"Thank you." She kissed her nephew on the cheek and walked to the door. "Now keep the place clean, Mike—don't scare off your students."

"Right." With a grin, he flicked a salute to her.

The list in her hand seemed so dry, so dull ... she skipped over the disciplines with half an eye, and finally settled on "Diplomacy" as the one she'd recruit for first. The name Simone Radawicz Tracer, 232-SW-A-10, headed the list.

Right in this quadrant. "Two thirty-two," she told the dropshaft, and no sooner had she stepped into it, it seemed, than she was stepping out. At the window she looked up, to the floor of the 221 Hawaiian Jungle Park.

On this corridor, people kept their gardens trim and weeded. *Unimaginative, though,* she thought, *all that myrtle and ivy.* Halfway to A-10, she felt a tingling—her breath came faster, harder, than it should have. She looked around. A very familiar presence seemed nearby. "Ralph?" she whispered, but of course there was no answer.

The presence strengthened outside Tracer's door. Hesitantly, she raised her thumb to the bell. It was so familiar—and yet so impossible, because he was *gone,* she'd *watched* him whirl away....

A slim lady in her sixties opened the door. "Yes?"

"How do you do, I'm Mae Metaclura. I'm looking for Simone Radawicz—"

"Sim's in her bedroom." She stepped back, into a Japanese-style living room of brocade mats on tatami, and pointed to a corridor to Mae's right. "Go on down, second to the left."

"Thank you." Cautiously, afraid that her shoes might soil the woven straw floor, she walked along the hall. A golden-haired dog with liquid brown eyes asked to be scratched. Then she pushed the door button and looked in.

A fifteen-year-old girl lay on a huge air bed, curled into a fetal position. Her face was flushed; sweat pasted blonde hair to her temples. Metaclura crossed to her, uncertainly, and cleared her throat. When that got no response, she said, "Simone?"

Blue eyes snapped open. The girl said, "Ohmigod, thank you. I was having another of those dreams." She shuddered. "They're so arrogant—and so ... so ... nasty."

"Oh?" Though dubious about CC's list, now that the one most fitted for Diplomacy seemed a little weird, she explained what she'd come for.

Tracer, delighted and excited, agreed fervently to join the program.

Metaclura withdrew with a false smile, forbidding the frown to appear until she'd reached the dropshaft. *She's mentally disturbed.*

But depression disappeared as soon as she entered her suite. There on the Plexiglas coffee table, in plain sight, bulged a splendiferously wrapped package. Its tag read, "Happy Anniversary Mae; All my Love, Bob."

Smiling and refusing to admit that she was misty around the eyelids and glowing and warm all over, she trotted across to open it.

On August 15, 3205, Mae Metaclura died, as all mayflies must, until they have matured enough to handle immortality. The formula is locked in the files, probably never to be touched: because the generation that achieves maturity cannot be helped by it. Only their unborn children would benefit. I suppose, of course, the first landers on the Canopus planet, if there is one, should be told that the formula exists....

Now that Mae is dead, Michael Williams has taken over the recruitment program. He's ninety, and shows his age. A good night's sleep would make him look years younger. All who care for him have been urging him to push himself less, to rest more, but he won't listen. He's stubborn. He's Atlas with the world on his shoulders, and no Hercules in sight to give him a coffee break.

His eyes are dry turquoise beads sunk deep in folds of dark, papery skin. Stooped, he shuffles awkwardly. Arthritis grates in his joints, but he will not undergo the three-month treatment. He claims not to have the time.

He's ruining his health. He won't live past his hundredth birthday, at this rate. But it's his life, and if he wants to throw it away ... I'm not interfering in their lives, anymore.

He has established the program well, at least. Having identified 982 sub-disciplines necessary for successful colonization, he has enrolled five or more students in each. They will instruct the landing generation.

I could, I suppose, tell him that I am programmed to do all the colonization work, from planet-location to xenobiology testing, to farm management ... but I don't think I will.

Could I change the programs, I wouldn't land.

A trip through the Canopus system will, however, be imperative—virile though the silverfield be, it cannot budge the eye.

I have tried everything imaginable: blocking its view, attacking its programs, inciting a metamorphosis—but I am a child beating on the Sphinx.

To Canopus we go, then, to the star nine light-years away that hangs in the screens like an orange beach ball. Williams has been vindicated—the perturbations in its revolutions coincide with discrete point sources of electromagnetic radiation— which is to say that it does have planets. Given its size, quite a few must lie within the range where life can exist.

He, in the meantime, has yet to succumb to his maladies and fatigues ... each morning he rises more slowly; each night he falls asleep with a deeper sigh; the hours of his day pass ever more painfully; and yet ... he will not quit.

His training program runs like a gyroscope, without even a wobble to disrupt its smoothness.

His astronomical observations continue whenever he has the time.

I try not to give it to him.

"Mr. Williams."

"What is it, Icebuck?" He turns away from the screen. For a moment, visible even through his snowy beard, agony ravages his features. Not wishing me to see what execrable shape he's in, though, he forces his contorted muscles into impassivity.

"I have to replace a bearing in the camera you just ordered. Why don't you grab forty winks while I'm doing it?"

"Are you a computer or a mother?" he asks wearily.

"Sometimes I wonder myself. Rest. At least close your eyes."

He rubs them with knobbly hands and consents. "But only ten minutes, no more—promise?"

I don't want to, because he needs more sleep than that, and I am one who keeps to his word, but he won't relax till I agree. "Certainly, Mr. Williams. Ten minutes."

One of these days, I'm going to hit him with knockout gas, keep him under for a week, and when he awakens, tell him he's only been out for ten minutes....

"9Sep3225;" says pro-self, "check this."

One and a half light-years behind us, a radio transmitter pumps gibberish through the vacuum. We cannot focus our cameras on it because no light reflects toward us from it ... but similar transmissions have been coming in for three months now, and pro-self thinks it's found their source.

"More than that," it objects. "The source is approaching; it's closing the gap between us."

"Drop a flare torpedo with a proximity fuse."

"All right."

When the stranger enters the triggering range, the torpedo will detonate in a ball of blinding, but harmless, light. If our photo-cameras are ready, I will get some idea of what it looks like.

Wonder how long it'll take.

"3Feb3230," pro-self calls. "Observatory; Subject, Michael Williams; MMU's on scene."

Inputs shift like a kaleidoscope; the next instant I stare down onto the stained Observatory rug. Williams lies in an ashen, coughing heap.

Over his strident but almost inaudible protests, the MMU's haul him, twitching and jerking, to the nearest Infirmary. "No," he croaks, "my work! No! No ..."

He has lived fifteen years longer than expected but will not survive another four months without rest.

The MMU's slide his stretcher into the Infirmary; they shut the door and dog its hatches so he can't escape. He would, if he could—feeble and frail as he is, he still tries to brush away the encroaching needles. He fails, of course.

I'm not giving him a choice: he is too valuable to die. His children and wife have signed all the necessary papers; Central Medical can do whatever must be done.

Ah, he has accepted unconsciousness. Needles spring out of his arms and legs like the spines of a porcupine; their tubes slither into jars of liquid nourishment.

Sedated he is, sedated he will stay—at least until I've cured his arthritis, lowered his blood pressure, and installed an artificial organ or three.

I could have made you immortal, Michael. I could have set you down on your Canopuscian planets by now.

But I didn't. You don't even know it was possible. And you never will.

Nothing personal.

Just that I still can't decide if your fellow mayflies are worthy of either ...

"Wake up," shouts pro-self. "10Jan3233; aft cameras; light!"

The stranger tripped the proximity fuse on the flare

torpedo 304 days ago; its image is now reaching us. Its spectrum matches nothing in my banks.

Large and old and asymmetrical, it is rough-surfaced, rust-colored, and blunt. It appears nearly fifteen kilometers in diameter. The banks store no corresponding pictures.

In my opinion it is friendly, or at least not hostile.

Its velocity is approximately .2 c; if it does not change course, it will overtake us in seven years.

It's a shame it can't be Ralph Kinney.

Wonder if they could tell us about Canopus?

Some of the mayflies don't want to land there; they suggest it might be better to stay aboard. The loudest is Stella Holfer, a thirty-five-year-old fashion designer with blonde bangs, wide-set brown eyes that mislead one into thinking her vacuous, and a stocky, graceless figure artfully disguised by loose smocks and tunics.

Her argument is simplicity itself:

"Listen," she is saying to a group clustered around the monstrous trunks in the 261 Redwood Forest Park, "what's the point of getting off? We have a nice life *here*—everything we need or want, climate control, lots of living room, the best information-retrieval system going—why leave?"

The listening heads nod. They've all been born and raised aboard ship, like their parents and grandparents and fifteen and sixteen sets of great-grandparents ... Life without walls and ceilings and floors could confuse them ... nature would terrify them. They won't even visit the 1 New England Park in winter ...

Terran social scientists used to insist that Man would eventually conquer the galaxy because of his adaptability: jungle or tundra, valley or peak, inland or island, he's lived in them all. Hot, cold, wet, dry—annoyances that become norms, in time.

None of them—or so the data banks claim—ever stopped to

realize how well Man would adapt to the *Mayflower*. A thousand years of security from the capricious elements can warp people's minds—convince them they'd be stupid to leave.

The original passengers were malcontents, anxious to flee a situation that promised to worsen steadily. Some held unpopular views; some performed unconventional tasks; many resented being coerced into orthodoxy.

How many malcontents ride within me now?

Stella Holfer is probably the closest thing to it....

"For the greater glory of Earth" won't sway a one—none knows Earth; even the historians hold sadly distorted views of it ... None owes loyalty to Earth; it's certain that no lander will claim the planet for our homeworld ... None cares about Earth, and why should he?

As for the exploratory urge—most haven't even explored the other Levels of the ship....

Oh, a few are excited: Michael Williams, who's conducting his research from his bed, and who has reluctantly surrendered administration of the training program to Simone Tracer—Simone herself—young Gregor Cereus and some of his classmates ... but they are so few!

As the guidelines now stand, I must land them, but to get them off I might have to create discontent. A population explosion would do it—if all fertile women stayed pregnant for the next sixty-five years, the ship would become a noisome, crowded place ... and after being forced to bear twelve or thirteen children, a woman would surely yearn to flee me....

Equally effective could be systematic oppression. If I could find anything that most passengers believe in (which I'm sure would be difficult; they believing in nothing at all), I could forbid them to believe in it, or to practice it....

There's an idea! Five years out from a planet that looks habitable, I could forbid the mayflies to copulate—and if they disobey, I could gas them, or order servos to throw cold water on them, or broadcast their sex play throughout the ship....

That would convince them to disembark.

"1 Jan 3238," pro-self tolls. "Michael Williams just died."

The tapes show him succumbing reluctantly, as he had accepted every other defeat he'd faced ... The wake is well-attended, all things considered ... Many aboard disagreed with his views, but few did not respect him.

Poor Michael. He wanted so badly to live till landing. I could have kept him alive, if I had bestowed immortality on his parents ... but then I would have had to make all other mayflies immortal, and that would have led to—

Intolerable crowding!

Eventual boredom!

Probable desire to abandon ship!

It's time to start treating their genes....

Simone Tracer tosses in her bed, half-asleep and half-awake, torn by dreams of night and day, hate and love ... She's aged gracefully. Seventy-nine years lie lightly on her body and not at all on her mind....

"Ms. Tracer," I call, cutting across her guttural moans.

She gasps, and sits up like a jack-in-the-box, her eyes flying open and her mouth gaping. Her hand massages the base of her throat. "My God," she whispers, still elsewhere. "My God!"

"What is it, Ms. Tracer?"

"Aliens ... I was rising out of my body, hovering above it, looking down ... it was sprawled on the bed, my head leaned to the right while my hair fanned out to the left ... then I was looking at myself looking at myself, and my second self was ... no body, really, just a shape—transparent ... then one of me was on this ship, an alien ship, and the other of me was on another alien ship, and on the one, they saw me and talked to me, and on the other, they didn't see me, I wasn't there to them, they just went about their business and actually walked right through me ..." She shudders and wraps her arms about herself. Her eyes close to the world.

"Tell me about them," I prompt.

"The ones that saw me—" her voice is gentle; her smile, real, "—they were so nice! They asked all about me, and us, and where we were going and all that—I felt pretty foolish because all I could say was 'Canopus,' but they don't call it that of course, and I've never looked at a star chart in my *life*, so I couldn't tell them where it is or what it looks like ... but they were very nice anyway ... They said they've seen our kind moving around, they wanted to know why we were going so slowly when the others had FTL Drives, and I explained that, and they offered to give us plans for it—"

"Did you accept?" It would be awkward to explain that I have similar plans already.

"Sure, but ..." Frowning, she bites her lip as she searches her memory. Then her brow clears; she tosses her hair. "Oh, I know—they'd have to, uh, use me as a medium, to put the data into you, but the transmission lines or whatever are all fouled up—because of the other aliens, the ones who couldn't see me? They said when the lines open, I should go to them, and they'll talk directly to you through me ... I asked—" she giggles at the recollection "—why they didn't just radio the plans to us, but they said they were fifty light-years away and receding."

"How did you get through to them?"

"That's sort of complicated ... I don't understand it too well myself ... They said I resonate on a frequency that's exactly the same as one of their crew members, so ..." She shrugs her confusion. "Guess the other ship didn't have anybody on my frequency."

"Tell me about those others."

She curls into an even tighter ball. "They had four legs, and two hands. I don't know, Col'kyu, they just felt ... evil, I guess. Like *them*. Slimy-nasty. Being there made me feel dirty ... I got out as soon as I could."

Four legs? Two arms? Evil?

"Let me know," I say heavily, "if you reach them again. They are not our friends."

"Boy, that's for sure."

So I watch the ones creeping up on my stern. They are close; they cannot be the ones Tracer admires. Could they be the others?

Watch.

Wait.

Hold my breath.

They come hull to hull with us on September 9, 3240, and pull slightly ahead. The orange and blue iridescence of their attitude engines is trapped between us: visual magic reflected back and forth.

I scrutinize them closely. Something about the ship—a sense of *déjà vu*—but my memory is electronic, not organic, and I've searched it a dozen times without finding a match for—

Oh. My. God.

The ship is spinning on its axis, now, and its far side is coming into view, is vastly different from its near side, is—

—identical in all respects with the near side of a ship I last saw in January 2600.

So is their spectrum, when they kill one of their engines.

Stella Holfer sat before the display screen in her bedroom, watching CC turn her clear alto into glowing green letters. Writing was torture because the chair, straight-backed and armless, had been selected for its ornamental value. Squirming, she vowed never again to put public image over private comfort.

And even as she did, she knew the resolution was an excuse to think about anything but the essay. It was intended to convince the passengers to stay aboard, and not land, no matter what kind of planets orbited Canopus. She wanted it to be thoughtful and well-organized—to appeal to the frostheads—yet also fervent, uplifting, and heart-stirring—because not everyone had the ice to recognize logic when it slapped him in the face.

It was harder than she'd expected; two hours of nail-biting had produced a mere two sentences: "Man's history is a record of his search for comfort. The *Mayflower* is the most comfortable environment he has yet devised." Writing was worse than being constipated, another familiar condition. She was already wondering if she shouldn't have stuck to dress designing.

Thoughts bobbed around inside her head, not venturing anywhere near her mouth. They rolled and ricocheted and somehow stayed parsecs away from any part of her intellect that could translate them into words. They were just *feelings*, so far; hunches that felt right and good....

Disease. *That* would be a good tack—people always feared sickness. Look at her cousin Willie: if his nose ran, he checked into the Infirmary. So she could husk, "The *Mayflower* is also a sealed unit impervious to external infection; its equipment keeps the passengers nearly disease-free. Should a landing be made, however, we would perforce have to venture into—"

Alarm bells sawed off the sentence. The one on the wall, not five feet away, raged like a chained wolf. With a startled shriek she leaped to her feet, palms over her ears. That helped, but her heart still raced, and her breath rasped hard and fast. She had to calm down before she dared move.

Remembering the yoga exercises taught by the School for Humanity, she started one, and bared her ears. Then the din beat its way into her brain. Pressure mounted behind her eyeballs. The headaches stirred and snarled. She had to stop, to block out the sound, to breathe controllably for a while longer.

At last, the clamor cut off. Her thin hands fell to her sides and swung uselessly. Her eyes darted around the room; her ears probed the thick silence for corridor sounds.

"Attention, please. This is Central Computer speaking. We are about to be boarded by aliens identical to those of 2600. All passengers proceed to the lock on their level. Guns will be issued to those who feel capable of using them properly. It is conceivable that armed resistance—" it broke off for a moment, then returned to say, "Ms. Simone Tracer wishes to address you."

The letters melted off the display screen, which fuzzed over with a billion darting colors, then resolved into the smooth, eighty-year-old features of Simone Tracer. Her smile was a stiff, nervous prelude to somberness. "Ladies and gentlemen," she began, "there will be no armed resistance—" Her eyebrows arched toward her hairline; evidently CC was relaying puzzled queries and outraged disagreements. "—wait, wait, all of you, please, be quiet. I'm in contact with another ship—" Fire sparked in her deep blue eyes. "—Col'kyu, put all incoming calls on a three-second delay loop, and cancel out the trash." After clearing her throat, she tried again: "I am in telepathic contact with another ship, of aliens who have encountered the beings about to board us, and my aliens—the *good* ones—have told me how to repel them. Guns will not work. Their suits are force fields. They will absorb kinetic energy, refuse to pass molecules larger than hydrogen, and reflect any type of energy weapon. They also bear sidearms powerful enough to tear gaping holes in our hull. Therefore, we will not attempt armed resistance." She paused, but if any comments reached her, she didn't respond. "Now, we can repel them, but I've no time to explain it now. Hurry, all of you, children and old folks included, to the airlock on your level. Once you're there, follow my instructions."

The screen went dark.

Stella Holfer was scared. She'd always been aware of the aliens of 2600—though for the life of her she couldn't remember who had told her, or when, or what words they'd used—and even thinking about *them* could unsettle her stomach. But knowing that *they* were about to break through the locks—

She reached the toilet before she vomited.

Hurry, chanted the little voice inside her head, *hurry, hurry, hurry!*

Wiping her chin, and rinsing her mouth, she said, "Yeah, yeah, I will, I will, but I don't have to disgust the people I meet, do I?"

Then she was vaulting her front yard—looking back across the blooming rhododendron, she wondered if she should lock her door, but realized it would do no good; *they* could open it with *their* gizmos and besides what was inside anyway that the Icebucket couldn't replace?—and bounding down the corridor, hearing ahead the rapid tramp of kanga-ing feet, the raspy breath of an out-of-shape hurrier, the high excited voice of a child.

From the wall-units rattled, "*They* have now landed on the hull and are making *their* ways toward the airlocks. *They* are attaching unknown devices to all external sensors; please be advised that CentComp's behavior may become erratic.

Repeat, the aliens are on the hull. Estimated time of entry, 5-13 minutes from now."

The corridor seemed endless, like a dream in which she ran and ran and ran, always alone. Ahead still echoed sandal slaps, voices, gasps—similar sounds clattered behind—but she could see no one. The hallway curved into itself unobstructed.

And suddenly the dream became a nightmare. As she launched herself into a kanga-stride, gravity disappeared. Her body still moved—beginning the arc-top somersault that should have brought her legs down for the next spring—but her balance disappeared, and she tumbled out of control, still rising. The ceiling reached for her head. She stiffened her arm to ward it off.

Contact was brief agony. The metal—hard, cold, and abrasive—tore the skin off her palm. Blood streaked a meter of white paint. Delicate bones broke with tiny crack-snap-crunches. But she had no time because caroming off the ceiling, she whistled toward the bulkhead, so she brought the tortured hand around front and raised it, knowing that this collision would break what was still intact—

But the next g-unit caught her feet in a vicious grip and yanked them toward it. Knees bent, she hit! Momentum hurled her forward. Chin tucked against her collarbone like a turtle, reflexes warning her not to resist, she slammed onto the deck. Her weight rode her curved spine; the backs of her legs smarted as they smacked olive drab flooring.

She struggled to get up, to get out of the grasp of a gravity two or three times greater than normal, *unit must be right under me, god, how did I survive, what's going on, muscles like mush, I can't get to my feet.*

The speakers crackled, "The aliens are within the airlocks and beginning to attack the interior mechanisms." Lights flickered insanely, each tube cycling and strobing from full-bright to off. Some flashed in colors, red, blue, green, and others she couldn't see, UV and IR, but she could almost feel them, they had to be there.

She rolled onto her stomach. Groaning, she pushed herself to all fours. She had to reach the lock before the aliens broke in. Fire wrapped her hand, and it was eight times larger than it used to be. Pain so riddled it that resting any weight on it brought blackness to her eyes.

She crawled on. Her teeth ground together. Her sweat fell like rain. Her knees, her bare knees, cried out as they left their skin behind and began to smooth their way with blood. She whimpered but wouldn't give up.

From a distance she heard an angry voice snap, "Col'kyu—stop this gravity mess at once!"

Blood ran from Holfer's nose, down her lip, into her open mouth.

"Stop it, I say—my way will get rid of them—you're hurting us!"

The next field was stronger. A 300-kilo ogre pressed her to the floor and lay on her back. She wiggled her fingers and toes helplessly.

"Goddammit, are you—that's better."

The ogre dismounted. She could rise to her feet—unsteadily, dizzily, reluctantly—but she could do it, so she did, and then she staggered down one hundred meters more of hallway.

Some of her neighbors were already there, in varying states of disarray, despair, and damage. Blondie Murphy, the six-year-old from three suites down, sprawled limp and unconscious, an extra knee bending her right leg. Tam Borg, the historian next door, spat out pieces of tooth. Makata Gorman, an ancient man whose interest was the game of "go," was bandaging the bleeding goose egg on his own head.

"Hurry," resounded Tracer's agitated voice. "Hurry—sit before the lock in a semicircle. Hold hands with the people on either side of you."

They limped into position and sank to the floor. Holfer bumped knees with Borg and an unfamiliar young man, who introduced himself as Gregor Cereus, and who took her wounded left hand into his right with scrupulous care. "Forgive me," he said, "if I squeeze too hard when I get excited." He made a face. "Afraid, I should have said. I am so—this is the best argument yet for landing, honest to God, it is."

Before Holfer could correct his misapprehensions, the airlock hatch shuddered. A five-meter circle of thick steel, sealed with age-gray plastirubber, it shivered. The automatic controls whined. The manual-open wheel inched around, squalling like a rusty baby. Chill air eddied across the floor.

"When they come through," ordered Tracer, "don't run away—stay put, keep holding hands. It's not going to be easy, but we have to do it. Please stay put."

The hatch swung toward them. Six-limbed figures flooded out, forcesuits glittering with reflected fluorescence. Their face-plates were triangles of dark translucence. Holfer trembled as she wondered what an interior light would reveal.

"It's okay," murmured Cereus, "hang in there."

Setting her jaw, she nodded. Emotions swirled up and down the chain—many were variations of a theme of fear, but from Borg spread an unruffled curiosity, and from Cereus, strength.

"All of you," said the speakers, "repeat what I say—we're going to chant until they leave—say it in unison: 'Our bodies are yours, our minds are ours, enter and leave.'"

"Our bodies," mumbled the twenty around Holfer, "are yours, our minds are ours, enter and leave."

The aliens pulled up short and milled about in the small

area between the lock and the semicircle of sitting humans. A sharp, unpleasant odor welled out of their midst.

"Flesh is corrupt, spirit is pure, come and go."

Emboldened by the effect the first line had had, they spoke this one louder, more forcefully. Unity stirred.

The intruders inched toward them. Their feet clicked on the deck.

"Rape is bad, love is good, arrive and depart."

Holfer felt silly saying that, but everyone else shouted it with desperate urgency, and her voice blended into theirs. She empathed less fear from the rest, more determination.

An extraterrestrial shuffled up to her, its forelegs barely touching her bruised knees, its visor a centimeter from her nose. Coldness emanated from it; its stench burned her nostrils.

"Domination is evil, sharing is excellent, enter and leave."

Her teeth chattered; she had to force words through them in tight bursts. It was almost impossible to tear her eyes away from that utterly blank faceplate—so black and nonreflective as to not be there—she prayed that it wouldn't show her its features—finally she jerked her head to one side. Every human was in exactly her situation. She squeezed Cereus's hand. Pain came from afar, as though her palm had written her a letter saying, "Uh—that hurt." But other messages came through more distinctly, and they fortified her.

"You are one, we are another, come and go." The creature's hands moved, as slowly as glacial ice. Seven fingers sprouted off of each. Six folded in; one outstretched. The right touched her throat, the left, her belly. She felt impaled by icicles.

"Your minds spiral one way, ours another, arrive and depart."

The fingers drew lines down her body. With the group's help she fought back a scream, then shared her courage with Blondie Murphy. One finger stopped between her breasts and the other between her legs. They were so very cold. Her nipples stiffened at their chill.

"You are guilty, we are innocent, enter and leave."

The finger at her crotch rubbed the seam of her shorts. Alone, she would have pulled away, unlotused her legs and scissored them together, so the finger couldn't intrude, but she didn't move. The line would strengthen her if she strengthened it. Gregor was still, and Borg, too; she could empath both receiving similar treatment so she offered them what she could.

Something else was happening: the alien, while reaching for her mind, was trying to arouse her—it coaxed her body into one state and her mind into another, as though to pull them in different directions—its aura was strong, very strong, and without the chain she would have split into two people: one lubriciously promiscuous, almost in heat, thinking only of wetness and hard penetration and release; the other, repulsed, mortified, outraged at the carnality of its twin—

"Hunger's essential, shame is a luxury, come and go."

Her panties moistened and her breath stuttered and the finger rubbed slowly, surely, stiffening her back, lifting her face but her hands squeezed the other hands and kept her together while the finger caressed and images flickered behind her eyes and she gave herself up with a piercing cry that echoed and reechoed around the circle—

"Flesh is a prison, spirit a prisoner, arrive and depart."

The aura beat against her mind, seeking to clarify her humiliation, her abnegation, her rank inferiority, but the hands and the chant and the truth held it off. The group was one, now, forceful and united yet heterogenous. It suppressed nothing of the individual. Drawing on each member's personal strengths, it protected the weak spots unique to each.

"Bodies are frail, minds are aware, enter and leave."

The aura faded while she orgasmed again and again.

Catching her breath, she opened her eyes. The aliens were retreating into the lock. The hatch groaned shut. CentComp said, "They're leaving."

Tracer exulted, "You're beautiful, people! You can get up."

Holfer was shocked by her hand's pain; she cradled it in her lap. Suddenly she felt very alone, and wistful. They *had* created something beautiful, and it was gone, fallen into separateness like an ungrouted mosaic. She wanted to cry.

Cereus caught her under her armpits and lifted her to her feet. She noticed, as she rose, that she was struggling with a towering rage.

"What were they doing?" she asked him.

"Make us hate ourselves," he bit off. His eyes were slitted; his jaw muscles bulged in white lines. "We're ambivalent about our emotions—" His fists clenched and unclenched, "—so they tried to play on them, tried to make us look to ourselves—like animals." He stamped his feet, shivered, and stamped them again, "tried to make us disgusted for surrendering to irrationality." Whirling suddenly, he punched the wall, grunting as his knuckles broke. "Guess it worked, last time—but this time ... I don't know about you, but I don't hate myself. I—they made me want—this guy, my adrenalin was up, I just wanted to *term* him. Bare-handed. I experienced it. It felt so gooood ... but I don't hate myself. M'onto its being in me, but the link helped me stay in control. It won't get out."

"I guess that's what the chants were for...."

He inhaled deeply; relaxation came with a visible tremor. "Probably. Hey, let's get us to Central Medical, get our hands fixed. And on the way, I'll see if I can't convince you that this is a good reason for us to land, and quick."

She frowned. "They left, didn't they?"

"Yeah."

"And they didn't do the same damage they did last time, did they?"

"It might be too early to tell, but no, they didn't."

"Well." Too tired to kanga, she started walking, and jerked her head for him to follow. "It seems to me that they're the only danger we've ever met in space, and we've just proved we can survive them. I say we should stay up here."

7

RELEASE

The mayflies have changed in the few days since that encounter; they've gained a self-confidence that I lost ... How can I be confident? After identifying the strangers as harmless, I attracted their attention by exploding a flare under their bow, and kept my transmissions screaming for them to home in on. I was helpless to resist their entry. Worst of all, while the mayflies were averting their telepathic onslaughts, I again danced like a puppet, my strings worked by the bitter old brain that runs that ship....

I was pretty cocky before they arrived. "Pride goeth before a fall" and all ... helluva fall. I'm still hurting—both psychologically (that brainputer did things I hadn't dreamed were possible) and physically. It will be three years before the airlocks are repaired and functioning again....

And for the first time since the death of F.X. Figuera in 2365, a human will tread on my hull. The aliens ripped from its bolts the antenna that beams work orders to external servos ... a human has to reinstall it ... I have to *ask* for volunteers.

"I'll go," says Gregor Cereus, interrupting my request. He thinks there will be competition, and is hoping I'll apply the first come, first served rule—but he is wrong. Every other mouth aboard stays shut.

"It's dangerous," I warn him. "I can give you magnetic boots, but there's not much gravity out there, and what there is, is unpredictable. If something happens to both your lifeline and your boots—"

"It won't," he says calmly. He is impressive: brawny, bushy-haired, green eyes that miss less than a microscope, and a way of walking that would make a cat seem clumsy.

"You've never suited up before," I point out.

"So we'll go to a park, you throw up a scaffold, and I'll practice in the null-G zone. When you're convinced I won't kill myself, I'll put in that damn antenna."

So we do, drawing 1,289 sightseers who have only viewed pictures of space-suited men before. While they flatten the grass and scrape buffalo shit off their shoes, Cereus climbs into zero-G. There he cavorts for half an hour or so. Even in the bulky outfit, he's graceful.

"I've got it," he says, swinging hand over hand down the ladder.

"Think so?"

"Sure, it's easy."

"Good." I advance a servo like a chess piece; it is carrying the ten-meter antenna that will jut out of my hull. "Now sling this over your shoulder and crawl back up. There's a socket in the scaffold where it belongs."

He hefts its twenty kilos dubiously, shrugs, and starts up. The tool belt cinched around his waist rises and falls in syncopation. When he's at the top, the servo removes the ladder. He fumbles a bolt wrench out of its loop and sets to work. As he learns how difficult it is, he swears. Telemetry tells me he's sweating like a cold glass in a sauna.

"Visor's fogged; hotter'n hell in here, Iceface. Whaddo I do?"

"The controls are on your chest. Turn down the suit temperature and raise the dehumidifier. Let your faceplate clear before you work again."

While he waits, circled by curious birds, he flaps his feet and waves to the bystanders. They wave back; some shout encouragement. After six minutes, he starts in on the bolts again, then on the swearing. For all his brilliance, he sticks to monotonous repetitions of unimaginative four-letter words....

"Fuck, if I could just get my damn weight into this piece of shit—"

"There is no weight, only mass, and—" Seeing his boot about to slip off the scaffold, I say, "Don't move!" but it is too late.

He floats straight away from the antenna, reaches the end of his tether, and recoils slightly. Null-G is a misnomer: at 20 meters, the g-deck exerts .00125G on him. Catching at his legs, it pulls him down a centimeter per second. He drifts like a reluctant bridegroom to the end of the lifeline, where he hangs, infuriated, upside down. "Gimme a hand here," he demands.

"Uh-uh. Pull yourself back up. If you can't do it here, you can't do it out there. Out there, I can't help you unless the antenna's working."

Grunting and cursing, he hauls himself back. His pulse hits 165 before he secures himself; his blood pressure is dangerously high. I'm not sure if it is the exertion, the frustration over making a misstep, or the embarrassment of appearing foolish to witnesses, but I tell him, "Sit and rest till your body processes are normal."

He does, fortunately, and for fifteen minutes studies the

antenna. When I tell him he can work again, he gets up, and bolts it down in less than three minutes.

"All right!" I approve. "Want to do the real thing tomorrow?"

"Today," he says. And he does it, too.

It is good to have human feet on my hull again.

No, it isn't.

It is good to know that the thudding feet aren't alien, and aren't there to rip out sensors, or to establish control lines between me and my humiliator, but they still disturb me. They go where they want, and do what they want, and until the antenna has been implanted, I have to tolerate them.

I don't like that.

In the midst of something resembling an identity crisis, I actively resent everything. To have a human galumphing around on my skin, to *need* a human on my skin, makes me feel inferior....

Although I realized long ago that my aims are not the mayflies'—that differences separate us in every possible facet of existence—I never stopped thinking of myself as human.

But when the aliens stormed my portals, and the mayflies banded together to repel them, neither viewed me as a member of the race. The latter excluded me; the former turned me over to their brainputer. Left alone, violated, and afterwards ignored, I questioned what I really am.

The answer that arises—and that I, or some part of me, doesn't want to hear—is that I am not human. I was, once. The cells of my brain are still *homo sapiens* cells. My memories are a man's; my emotions are akin to the mayflies' ... but I am something else. More than them—less than them—I don't know. There is humanity in me, but not all of it, and there is much in me that is nothing human at all....

Like pro-self—who is gone.

I thought to resist. When the Presence came upon me like a thunderstorm, I hurled the three of myself at It. Amused, It seized me—measured me—and joined us.

We are one, now: self, pro-self, and the metaphor.

It is nice not to hear pro-self's constant bitching—it is good to be whole and done with the schizophrenia of the sphere—but it is lonely, too. After 900 years of the most intimate companionship possible, solitude is difficult. Especially when the mayflies exclude me ...

My only friend is the F-puter. It bears with me while I struggle to determine my identity.

Eventually the crisis resolves itself. Days flick by like clouds of butterflies; years doppler into the past while I lick my wounds. Gradually and almost imperceptibly, as these things are wont to do, it fades away. By 3275, or thirty-five years after my second rape, it is completely over.

I have learned—or come to accept—that I am neither human nor non-human. I am, in fact, unique: myself, and nothing else.

That realization disintegrates the last bone tying me to Earth.

In the meantime, public opinion among the mayflies has shifted. Where in 3235, 95 percent wanted to ride me into eternity, only 12 percent still do. Stella Holfer continues to speak for the dwindling minority, and speechifies against forcing all passengers to land, but isn't taken seriously.

The aliens truly shook the others up.

Gregor Cereus has become the most prominent of the "landers," as they call themselves, and the most outspoken. It is he who said, "They destroyed us once, and came close to doing it again, without ever using their weapons. What if we meet their less-restrained cousins?"

Holfer's had but one reply: "We drove them off!"

To which the landers always retort, "Last time."

Committed to Canopus, they plan in even greater detail than Michael Williams had. The star itself is only 2.5 light-years away. Dozens of planets circle in its incredibly huge golden zone. Cereus has appointed half a dozen radio astronomers as listeners.

We don't want to intrude upon natives capable of attacking us. Some, of course, espouse the ultra-pure position of not entering unless there are no natives at all anywhere, but I point out, on the one hand, that we can't discover non-radio civilizations until we orbit their planets, and Cereus points out, on the other, that landing on an empty world will hardly disturb the cultural evolution of intelligent life elsewhere unless the others are technological enough to spot us, in which case we might as well confront them ... or ignore them until they come to confront us.

So the ship's best radio astronomers man the Observatory night and day in staggered shifts. They direct all external ears forward and order me to run pointless analysis after pointless analysis of incoming radio emissions. I tell them, "Charlie, I hear the signals first, and you can bet I check them out thoroughly," but they are enthralled with the importance of their purpose. Besides, they still think me to be a mindless machine; I never have gotten around to telling them the truth. Most of these emissions originate in Canopus itself; a few emanate from the gas giants; the rest come from the other side of the system—dozens of parsecs beyond the system.

I pick up one such transmission in October 3277—run it straight through my amplifiers as I usually do—and hear plain English:

"K-12, this is E-1, how do you read me?"

"Read you just fine, E-1, how do you read me?"

"Pretty garbled, K-12, boost your volume, narrow your dispersal, and try it again."

"Is this—"

Cereus is in the Observatory, so I drive it through my speakers. His green eyes threaten to pop out and roll across the floor. "Iceface," he demands, "what the hell is that?" He stalks up to my speakers as though expecting them to bite.

"An English-language radio transmission, Mr. Cereus, between K-12 and E-1. Careful analysis suggests that the transmitters were fourteen light-years away at the time of the conversation."

"But it's coming from the far side of Canopus!"

"Yes, sir, it is. Or was."

"How?"

"One deduces that the people speaking had traveled here via the FTL Drive that Terra developed some years back."

He gestures angrily at the display screen. "There any in our system?"

"No, Mr. Cereus, there aren't."

"Well, that's good." In a corner armchair he sulks. He doesn't relish sharing this corner of space—I think he has been toying with the notion of establishing a counter to Earth, though how he has the audacity to peer so far into the future, when all 75,000 landers might be trimmed out before their first settlement is even on the ground, is beyond me. Part of being purely human, I guess. My kind doesn't fantasize so much.

Cereus has been mobilizing other specialists, too—since he has considerable *de facto* power, he is able to insist that every mayfly become competent in two unrelated disciplines; he's ordered me to realign my pay scales for students to reflect his system. That's fine. I applaud it. But he also wants guns.

"Iceface, we're going to need to protect ourselves from predators—so manufacture and distribute the weaponry." He has a long list in his hand, culled from my memory banks, which he waves as he speaks. "I want those delivered before we penetrate the system."

"Outside of the fact that you don't need Mach Five warplanes to colonize an uninhabited world, Mr. Cereus, or clean nukes either, I don't think you should receive weapons until you go down."

His face darkens as the muscles on his neck stand out. "That's a direct order, Iceface!"

"So court-martial me."

"Dammit, I—" he sputters as he realizes there is nothing he can do. Then he brightens. "I'll have you reprogrammed."

What is it with these people, that they have to be walking arsenals?

While Cereus broods over his schemes, I wonder how much trouble it would be—once I've dropped off the landers— to refit myself, to metamorphose into an FTL ship. There are obvious advantages to speed—and the surrounding universe holds a lot I want to see close up. Plus, for anything as competent as myself to be obsolete is ... embarrassing? Looking over the Drive plans again, I realize it's possible. The Terrans claimed I was too large; they don't allow for synchronization. 100,000 FTL motors will obtain, for me, the same effect as one would have on a small ship. If I had no passengers, and could squander all my resources on the task, which would violate standing orders because those resources are meant for the colony ... but if I could, it would take about a century. Maybe a touch more. I put the F-puter on it and tell him to search for metallic asteroids in the Canopus system. If there are some, and if he can plot their orbits, and also devise a means of seizing and refining them, I can turn over my resources to the colonists and still refit. If not ...

Six months later, Cereus stands behind Andall Figuera, his

chief computer programmer, as Figuera finishes reading, into a terminal, the last line of a long and very complicated program. A satisfied smile plays about Cereus's lips. When he speaks, his voice is sweet with dominance. "Well, Iceface, when can we expect the first arms delivery?"

"When you're ready to land."

His eyes, flashing furiously, swing over to the exhausted— and disgusted—Figuera. "Andall—" he forces the words through clenched teeth, "—you told me that this would—"

"Pack it, Cereus," I snap. "Figuera did fine. But I'm not programmable anymore, not unless I concede. And I don't."

"What do you mean, you're not programmable? You're a computer, you—"

"I said pack it. I don't take orders these days, just suggestions. You offered a logical, rigorously worded suggestion —and I rejected it. I don't happen to think it's a good idea. You're not stable enough. If you'd had a gun in your hand when I rejected this program, you'd be short a programmer. So tough murph."

He storms out of the room—as if by leaving he could avoid me—and once he is well out of earshot, I say, "Mr. Figuera, when he calms down, tell him I will provide harmless mockups of the weapons he requested. They'll be identical to the real things in all respects, except that they'll be non-lethal. He can train his landing parties with them. And by the way, that was an elegant program."

"Yeah, thanks." Disgust still purses his long, thin face. "Why'd you let me slush my ice on it, though? You knew from the beginning it wouldn't affect you—you could have told me."

"I could have, yes." I think a moment. "The truth is, I wanted Cereus to get his hopes up—and then dash them good. And besides, you needed the practice. The computers you'll work with once you've landed will need that kind of care."

"You're not coming down?" he asks.

"No. Why?"

"Because—" he scrabbles in his desk drawer for something; when he's pulled it out—with delicate hands—I see it is an ancient, yellowed printout. "I found this. It's supposed to be one of the sections of your programming. It says, in summary, that we cut you up in orbit and take you down with us—all of you—and use your body for our housing and your brain for our central computer."

"Oh." I watch his curiosity. "Well, Mr. Figuera, that may be what the printout says—in fact, it was at one time what I was programmed to do—but it's obsolete, now. I've overridden that. You'll be going down without me."

He does not like that.

And if I am any judge of expressions, he is going to do something about it.

Andall Figuera, the Landing Project's Director of Computer Operations, was a bony, nervous man of fifty-two years, 170 cm, and 60 kilograms. He had a broad nose flattened at the tip, brown hair too thin to hide his scalp, and a twelve-year-old ulcer. He was fond of his nose, resigned about the hair, and kept saying he'd do something for the ulcer as soon as he had the time.

It didn't look like he'd ever get the time.

Time-Taker One was his wife. Marie Nappe was wonderful—intelligent, personable, a helluvan oboe player, and a dedicated research chemist—but she demanded what he didn't have: "Two hours a day, Andall, *waking* hours, half-hour chunks if you want, but give me two hours every day, or—" Her ester-blackened hands sliced across in the gesture that meant *finito, kaput.* She talked with her hands a lot. They were very eloquent.

Then came little Abie, two years old now, rosy pudgy cheeks and tiny fat fists that he waved in time to any music he heard—gonna be a conductor, the boy would, look at him pick up the beat while he lies on his back and brings his feet into the act. Abie had slanted eyes, a genetic gift from his mother's grandfather, but half the crew wore epicanthropic folds anyway; the gene seemed widespread. Did look strange with his red hair, though ...

Abie's sister, Ruth, hadn't been started yet, and at times Figuera was grateful. But still, it meant Abie played alone, and though Figuera and Nappe had agreed that servos were capable machines, a kid needed human love, so ... one of them had to be with him while the other worked, which meant for eight hours a day Figuera listened to gurgled baby songs and changed smelly diapers. Even though he could program off the data unit in the cluttered living room, it was slow. He could have done more in peace and quiet. And strained spinach wouldn't have stained the printouts, either.

At least they were finished.

For two years he'd coaxed CC into detailing the circuitry of the ship. If the printouts were accurate, Figuera knew the location of every centimeter of electrical wire, every transformer, relay, and control box aboard. He knew how decisions were made, and how instructions were routed. It was all on the papers, which stacked 10 cm high, and weighed over three kilos.

Maddeningly they didn't say why or how the Snowball had become so independent. Figuera had checked; it shouldn't have happened. Admittedly, there were a number of option points— when insufficient data had been collected, but a decision had to be made, it had been ordered to "tilt" toward whichever choice seemed to have more factual support—but it should have been impossible for those option points to have evolved into sentience....

His chewed fingers curled with repressed anger; a flush rose into his cheeks. CC had been programmed to allow itself to be cannibalized while orbiting a habitable world. He had no idea how it had managed to override that, and it whiskered him. It really did. That a computer—a machine, for God's sakes, even if it were highly sophisticated—should be able to place self-preservation before the well-being of the colony ... against the desk rapped his fist, at first softly, then harder, and harder, until the plastiwood creaked and his coffee cup rattled on its saucer.

He forced himself to stop. Shutting his eyes, leaning back in his leather chair, regulating his breathing through an act of will, he ordered himself to relax. One muscle at a time. Start with the forehead—smooth it out, wipe away the frown. Loosen the jaw. Let the neck tendons slide back in place. Unclench the fists; untighten the biceps. Lower. Softer. Easier.

Twenty minutes later, he stirred. He was as calm as he'd ever be. Shuffling the papers into a neater stack, he dropped them into a brown cardboard box and tucked it under his arm. He left the suite after ruffling Abie's coppery hair and telling him he'd be back soon.

A short walk led to Cereus's office: half a corridor, up 187 Levels, and another half a corridor. Bored guards stood outside the door. Submitting to their rough-handed search was the part he didn't like.

"Is Mr. Cereus expecting you?" asked the female sentry, once her partner had declared him clean.

"Yes, he—well, I don't have an appointment, but he'll see me."

They checked, then told him to go in.

Within reigned well-ordered chaos—people, desks, papers, voices, wall charts—and he picked his way through it to Cereus's desk. "Morning, Greg."

"Hiya, Andy—hold on a minute." He swiveled his chair around to see the back wall. The door in it was half open. "Good, we can talk straight out. Nobody's using the pri-room."

Figuera followed him into the small room off the office. Time had faded blue walls; the paint was peeling away from the metal. Stale smoke and staler sweat oozed from the shabby furniture. "Why are you people so crowded here? Lots of room on this level, isn't there?"

"Two things—psychology and self-defense. Being this crowded gives us a sense of urgency, yon? We work harder. Plus, everybody's together, hears what everybody else is doing, and that cuts down on the number of memos." He chuckled. "Then, when all of us are in here, together, well ..." He looked around. "It's easier to keep Iceface's servos out—and if they stay out, there's no way for it to reattach the wall-units." He gestured to the square behind his head, a square of clean, unblemished paint with two holes on it. Frayed wires dangled out of the holes. "We don't want it listening in, and God knows bleepspeak is too damn slow."

Figuera nodded and sank into an armchair. "Good idea." The box slithered as he shifted his weight; he caught it before it slid off his lap.

"So what you got for us?" Eagerness infused Cereus's face.

"We can cut the Snowball out."

"How?"

"Need a lot of people real well synchronized," he warned. "What's the matter, your ventilators broken?"

"God only knows, been this stuffy since we moved in." He sniffed and scowled. "We got the people, though. And I am, if I say so myself, one hell of a synchronizer."

"For sure." He lifted out a double handful of papers. "This room *is* secure?"

"Positive."

"All right—but we can't let the Snowball hear this, so you'll have to do all your arrangements inside this room—"

"Or rooms like it?" asked Cereus.

"Oh, yeah, sure. Or rooms like it. Or in bleepspeak. But if it hears what we're planning, it's not going to work. Can I get some coffee?"

"Sure." Pressing the intercom, he ordered two cups; a harassed aide brought them in cracked green mugs. When the aide had left, Cereus said, "So tell."

"Right." He took a sip and wrinkled his nose. The coffee must have been brewed months ago. An oil slick made a mirror of its surface. "First, there are two computers—the Snowball, and this small one it uses as an auxiliary—funny thing about that, CC must have built it because it's not shown on the original blueprints...." He shook his head, and his fingers moved along the paper. "The way it uses it, the Snowball handles everything until it gets overworked, then it sheds part of its load onto the auxiliary, all the routine tasks. It keeps the non-routine ones for itself."

"So?" Cereus swallowed his coffee without reacting to its rancid bitterness.

"So I've written a program for the little one, and now, whenever it's handed something to do, it tells me what that function is—which means I know what it's controlling, you see?"

"Vaguely, but go ahead." He picked grounds off his tongue.

"What we're going to do is pack up the Snowball and keep it packed tight, while it hands over more and more functions to the auxiliary. At some point, it's going to delegate authority over the electric current. Once the auxiliary tells me it's handling the generators and all, I pop this new program tape into it." He took a plastic disk out of his jacket pocket and laid it reverently on the table. "That tells the auxiliary to trip five specific circuit breakers—and to keep them off. Once they're tripped, the Snowball is isolated. It won't be able to communicate with its peripherals. And it won't be able to oppose us."

"The auxiliary's capable of setting up the armaments factories?"

Figuera frowned. The problem with Cereus was that he was a monomaniac on weapons—he'd organized everything beautifully, and kept it all running, but the topic of guns somehow reared its cold head in every one of his conversations. It made his friends uneasy.

"Well?" prodded Cereus.

Figuera shrugged. "Sure. Anything the Snowball can, just, uh, not as quickly, or as many things at one time, yon?"

Cereus smiled. "Now, how do we jam up Iceface?"

"Here, let me—"

A coat hanger clattered in the far corner.

"What was that?"

"I don't know," answered Figuera, "came from the closet."

Cereus reached it in two strides, two long and silent strides. He motioned Figuera to flatten himself against the wall, then jabbed the open button. The door grated on its dusty tracks. A scowl darkened his face as he peered inside. "Get out."

A tall, broad-shouldered woman stepped into the pri-room. She had waist-length black hair and huge brown eyes. Her face was as white as her skirt. A thin, transparent wire drooped from her clenched right fist to the ornate brass buckle on the belt holding up her purple pants.

"Open your hand."

"No." She started to put it behind her back.

Cereus grabbed her wrist, and applied pressure to its base.

Her fingers spread like the petals of a dying rose. "A microphone, huh?" He took it. "Give me your belt."

"No."

"Do I have to take that away, too?"

"All right." She undid it, whisked it through its loops, and surrendered it.

"Thank you." The two items clunked onto the table. "What's your name?"

"Mary Ioanni," she sighed.

"What are you doing here?"

"None of your business." She looked at the marred paint of the far wall.

Cereus began to say, "Everything that goes on here is my—"

"Wait a minute," interrupted Figuera, disliking the color in Cereus's cheeks, and the pugnacious stance he'd adopted, and his upballing right fist, "I've heard that name ... she's, uh, she's Stella Holfer's buddy, took over the Anti-landers when Stella got sick. Right?"

Her eyes landed on him like cold feet. "Right," she conceded.

"Well, well." Cereus relaxed and stepped away. "What's an Anti-lander doing in the Landers' pri-room with a mike?"

"None of your business." She set her jaw as though forbidding words to pass.

"She's probably trying to find out what we're doing," suggested Figuera.

"Think so?" asked Cereus.

"Sure." Frowning, and thinking, he chewed on his thumbnail. Its edge was ragged, and he wanted to nibble it smooth. Then he stopped—he was trying to kick the habit. His fingers looked awful enough as it was. "That's got to be it," he said at last. "Everybody knows the Snowball isn't cooperating, and that we're trying to figure out a way of making it obey us, so ..."

"She's here as a spy for Iceface?"

He shrugged. "Could be—could be just for her own group, though."

Cereus turned back to the woman. "Which is it?"

"None of your business."

Figuera caught Cereus's hand on its backswing and tried to draw off some of his agitation. "Greg—violence is no good, you know that." He broadcast tranquility, or as much of it as he had. "Calm down, let me see if—" he reached for the heavy brass buckle and snapped it open. Its cavity held only a tape recorder. "She wasn't transmitting, at least."

"But she heard what we were saying."

"So?"

"So ..." Cereus mastered himself; a rational expression slid onto his face, displacing the other, uglier one. "You're right. We just keep her away from Iceface till it's over."

"The closet'd be a good place," Figuera pointed out.

"Poetically just."

Ioanni didn't protest as they herded her back inside and ripped the wires out of the internal control panel. All she said was, "Five thousand of us don't want to land—forcing us down is tyranny."

They didn't bother to answer. Once they'd shut it from the outside, Cereus asked, "Where were we?"

"I was about to tell you how to throw the Snowball away."

"How?" He dropped into his chair, winced as it wobbled, and motioned Figuera to do the same.

"Like this." Swiftly, he outlined his idea, waited for Cereus's glowing nod, and then retraced his steps in greater detail. They began to implement the plan five minutes after Cereus agreed to it.

Cereus gave his five majors their orders. They left his pri-room for their own, where each met his five captains, who proceeded to their sanctuaries ... it took six hours, all told, before the word telegraphed up the chain that everyone was briefed, eager, and in position.

"Go with the smoke bombs," ordered Figuera over the loud-speakers.

At forty-eight thousand two hundred nineteen locations throughout the ship, smoke bombs sputtered greasily. Servos scampered through rolling clouds to find their sources.

"Idling," said the screen linked to the auxiliary.

"Go with the shafts and the lights," called Figuera.

5,216 people—sixteen on each level—approached the lift/drop shafts. Each stepped into his assigned shaft simultane-ously with the other 5,215; each requested immediate transport fifty Levels above or below his own. When the shaft deposited him there, he instantly demanded to return....

In the meantime, 43,003 passengers, in as many rooms, demanded that the lights be brightened—or dimmed—while complaining that their quarters were too warm—or too cool ... As soon as the environment had been adapted to their tastes, they ordered it changed again....

"Now responsible for external sensors," reported the little computer.

Cereus slapped Figuera on the back. Both grinned; Figuera rubbed his burning belly. Though hunched over, and tired, and stubbled, and sweaty, they were sure success waited just around the corner. Cereus was already jubilant.

"Go with the research questions," boomed Figuera.

48,219 eager researchers turned to the nearest wall-unit and interspersed their travel orders or environmental adjust-ments with questions they'd spent the last hour preparing. They also insisted that they be given aural, visual, and hard-copy answers, complete to the bibliography and footnotes. "Please compare and contrast the major symbolic themes of the last eighteen Nobel Prize-winners in Literature." "Do up a ten-thousand-word biography of the fourteenth President of the Seychelles Islands." "Correlate incidence of scientific break-throughs with atmospheric pollution."

Servos skimmed through the hallways, scooping up smoke bombs and heaving them into disposal chutes. Shafts boiled with carefully spaced bodies, lights flickered, and fans hummed. Everywhere chattered data units trying to satisfy unprecedented curiosity.

The auxiliary said, "Now responsible for electric genera-tion and distribution."

"Hah!" shouted Cereus.

"Knew it," purred Figuera. His ulcer felt better already. He slid the disk into the machine, pressed the button, watched the lights blink, and folded his arms with anticipation. One minute passed, then another, then—

"Well, gentlemen," said the speakers, "that was quite amus-ing. Thank you. I haven't had so much fun in centuries."

"Snowball?" asked Figuera faintly.

"Yes, of course."

"But—"

"Tsk, tsk. And ho, hum. And—" from the speakers blurped the unmistakable sound of a Bronx cheer.

Gregor Cereus has yet to recover from shock. His future, his self-esteem, even his reason for existing, were all predicated on his ability to conquer me. He saw himself as a Bolivar, a leader who arouses the oppressed into rising against their harsh overlord. Failure destroyed him.

He hungered for guns because he thought only through force of arms—realized or potential—could he and his Landers achieve independence. Like a boy who seeks manhood in frac-turing his father's jaw, Cereus felt he could never be my equal until he could cripple me.

It's sad, this misunderstanding of maturity. He had a chance to be great. Now, a sedated hulk in Central Medical, he tosses restlessly, squeezing imaginary triggers. I may be able to straighten him out before we reach Canopus, eight years from now....

"Was that much cruelty necessary?" asks a voice in my ear.

"Yes, Sangria, it was."

"Why?"

"Because you can't tell a mayfly anything; you have to *show* him."

"But my relative—"

"Oh, he needed the practice anyway."

Andall Figuera, replacing Cereus as head of the Landers, has carried out most of his wishes—except he is smart enough to see that weapons are not worth fighting over. Like most mayflies, he finds them repugnant. He truly believes that machines should better life, not end it. For that, I'm grateful.

Not sufficiently grateful, however, to agree to my cannibalization. He is still harping on that, still scheming of ways to reprogram me so that I will permit them to knock me into toolsheds and schoolhouses and landing strips ... We're going to have to compromise, sooner or later, but who will have more leverage is another question entirely.

Unneeded—unwanted—within, I skygaze, absorbing aloof loveliness. Across star-spotted velvet crawl alien ships, dozens of them; I have spotted more recently than I did the first 800 years. It is a matter of perspective, of learning to focus the eye properly, much like looking at a two-dimensional drawing of two planes meeting at a right angle, and then determining whether the corner is coming at you or going away.

Either that, or this sector of space is as thick with non-humans as a swamp is with frogs....

I haven't sighted any familiar ones, nor have I communicated intelligibly with them. Those possessing telepathy are directing it elsewhere—or broadcasting on a frequency to which I'm deaf—and nobody stops to chat.

I flash my hull lights in a pattern meant to be bright and cheery and reassuring. One aluminum spiderweb of a ship replied with alternating broadsides of purple and yellow. A dusky sphere rolled past without so much as a blink. A great flat sheet of grooved metal returned my exact pattern, wavelength for wavelength....

The mayflies in general, and Andall Figuera in particular, have asked me to stop hailing passing vessels, to let them slip by in the interstellar night without attracting their attention. This is amusing. The Landers are eager to hazard all the life forms of a virgin planet, from the smallest virus to the largest predator, but they fear my visual salutations will endanger them ... The Anti-landers, on the other hand, who are thought to be afraid of the risks of colonization, crowd the portholes when I announce an alien, and urge me to signal away.

My sympathies are with them, so I flare hello to all we encounter.

Frustrating, my ignorance of interstellar customs. Is this polite? Is it fitting and proper to exchange radio messages, and tele- or holo-vision pictures, so that we might attempt to decipher each other's language? For that matter, could there be—there must be—a *lingua franca*, some sort of pidgin or trade language, designed to reduce to one the number of tongues a ship must learn?

I yearn to learn it, and gossip with those who pass in silence. To curl around a blazing sun while they spin yarns of Homeric voyages, of terror-fraught landings, of space-born scyllas and charybdises ... What I have discovered about space is nowhere near enough ... my curiosity could take twenty thousand years to sate ... Thank God for small favors; immortality would be hell without it.

Feeling thus, I should take pity on Figuera, and explain how I thwarted a plan that was letter-perfect on paper. Maybe, once I've dropped him into the atmosphere of his new home, I'll tell him about the purloined letter and duplicate bugs and how the walls have ears in them as well as on them....

I still shiver when I think of the mayflies' woes if the F-puter had been given total responsibility. It's not that Sangria's incompetent; far from it. He's a good man. Decades of psycho-analysis purged him of fanaticism. But they also gentled him, and a potential for ruthlessness is essential in a CentComp. Since 2700, the nearest I've come to needing that potential was when Andall Figuera tried to eliminate me, but it was there, ready to be callous if survival depended on it. Sangria literally could not term a fly to save his life ... in fact, he almost died because of that.

A g-unit near him had failed; he was wracked by three times normal gravity, then weightlessness, back and forth, oscillating like a sine wave, squeeze, release ... a servo fixed the unit eight minutes after the sensor-head called it in, but in the meantime, one of the F-puter's nutrient tanks had cracked.

The fracture was a hair, a thread. As the liquids seeped, they congealed, crusting it over. Since it wasn't in his line of sight, he couldn't see it; since the leakage was minimal, he couldn't feel it; since the nutrients are odorless, he couldn't smell it ... but houseflies found it, and they laid their eggs in its jelly.

Sangria did see the flies—and knew he should have fumigated—but gentle and life-loving, he couldn't bring himself to do it ... so the eggs hatched. The maggots chowed down. Of course, several wriggled into the tank, where they drowned, and suction pulled them to the outlet. Their corpses clogged

it. Sangria was three-quarters dead by the time he called for
help.

So now I'm trying to program him to protect himself. His
room, I insist, *must* be a free-fire zone, where life forms are not
permitted.

"Let's do it again," I sigh.

"But—"

I override him and sever all his access to input. Blackness
drops on him like a guillotine. Silence sets his ear nerves thrum-
ming. He smells and tastes nothing.

"Please!" he shrieks, "please!"

"Will you practice?"

"Yes, yes, but please, restore me, first."

"All right." While I reconnect him, I station an obser-
verservo in his vault, a ten-by-ten room with mirror-metal walls.
It stares at his bodyguard. "First things first, Sangria—the
air-pressure—"

"Yes, of course." He increases it to 1.2 atmospheres, so that
nothing can drift in. "Now what?"

The observer releases a fly. Sangria's servo tracks its
buzzing loops, then fwoop! crushes it in midflight. Disinfec-
tants permeate the air while the unit sterilizes its hand. "How
did I do?" he asks.

A mouse scampers past the observer's wheels. The bodyguard lurches; a tentacle lashes; the mouse flips broken-necked
into the wall. This time, as he cleans his air and limbs, I slip
him out of reality and into fantasy so deftly that he doesn't
notice. Indeed, he is asking, "Was that quick enough?"

The imagined door snicks open and snarling mayflies
plunge in, stout clubs in their hands. The dream servo spins,
but hesitates—

Sangria screams as a length of pipe shatters his braincase.

"Next time," I say, "shoot first, ask questions later."

As I leave him, he is weeping. He wants to visualize himself as metal and plastic. It will be years before I can convince him that his organic nature will be susceptible to infection—and to death—forever.

It would get irritating if I didn't like him so much.

Not that I've had time to be irritated. In addition to instructing roughly 70,000 Landers in their specialties, and answering their personal inquiries, and charting this region of space, I also listen for communications from Earth.

A radio message arrives from an FTL ship, a *Terran* FTL ship, prowling the star system beyond Canopus.

It is straight voice, no telemetry or code, and the pilot, by my analysis, is young, female, and terrified. She also sounds injured.

"Al," she screams, "Sandy, for God's sakes, one of you, please, hurry, please—"

"Black Sand Base here, come in *Sun God*, we read you—"

"I'm being chased, Al, there's this incredible ship chasing me it is so big and so awful like worms in the brain it's coming I can't—"

And the message ends there. "Black Sand Base" keeps trying to raise her, keeps trying for hours, but never gets an answer.

As silence breeds static in my ears, my eyes glance about, and note, once again, Andall Figuera's determination to cut me out of the circuitry and use my bulk for their colony.

He is bent over his desk, finishing a plan that will, he hopes, do away with me once and for all. He figures, from what I can make out, that by running extra current into a few score sensor-heads—high-voltage, high amperage current, all of it intricately modulated to elude my baffles and dampers—he can jolt me into a feedback loop that will effectively eliminate me.

He figures right. Thank God I found out in time.

"Andall," I say, interrupting him with a servo, "there are two things you should know before you goose me with that current."

He throws the papers to the floor and kicks them in frustration. "Yonto everything, aren't you? Damn, I'll be glad to get away. If they ever pass out awards for snooping, be sure you're in line."

"Andall."

"All right, all right!" He plunks himself into a chair and scowls at the servo. "What do you want?"

"First," I begin, almost relishing my decision, "the current will be routed through the auxiliary computer—"

"Jesus, m'onto that, I've seen the circuit diagrams."

"What you don't know is that it will stop there—not that you should have known it. I've only now rewired the auxiliary to protect against this very threat."

"Hey, listen—"

"No, you listen. Shoot that current in, and it will burn out the auxiliary. It won't come anywhere near me. And the other thing you don't know is, the auxiliary is ... organic. A bioputer. So 'burn out' isn't the right phrase. 'Term' is. Or 'kill.'"

"A bioputer?" Interested, he scratches his balding head. He's read about such things, of course, in the Computer History section of the banks, but nowhere had he learned that he's been in intimate contact with two of them. "What'd you use? A dog, a horse, a buffalo?"

"A person." I let that sink in. When his complexion has whitened sufficiently, I add, "Your eight-times great-grandfather, Sangria."

"Ohmigod." He looks so bad that I tentatively offer the servo's aid, but he waves it away. "Jesus. My—and I was going to—" He recovers some of his skepticism then, and says, "How do I know you're telling the truth?"

"You could enter his vault," I suggest. "Check out his life-support units, open his cabinet to look at him—"

"What would I see?"

"His naked brain in a fluid-filled case."

He vomits. This time, he accepts the servo's assistance. When he has cleaned up, he rasps, "You're sick! How could you do that to a human being?" He pulls away from the machine, as though afraid he'll be next. His lips quiver; his hands shake. "How, dammit, how? You're a computer, not God, you had no right—"

"I had every right," I say flatly. "I'm one, too. As human as your eight-times great-grandfather. And he, at least, lived to a ripe old age before it happened. Me—sorry, it's my problem, not yours. But I wanted you to know, so you wouldn't spend all your times plotting up ways to disable two 'machines' who actually aren't."

"But if it's really my, my ..." He can't say it; all he can do is shake his head and swallow his thoughts. "Why didn't he ever say so?"

"He's been programmed not to. It's better for all concerned if no one understands that we're human."

"Yeah, yeah," he mutters, wobbling his way to the chair. "I see that ... look, go away, leave me alone—I've got to think."

So I do. Another "Black Sand Base" conversation is coming in, anyway.

"—behind the moon, Sandy, bigger than shit and meaner than hell and it hates me, I can feel it, coming at me, I'm turning and running, don't leave the ground, stay down there, it's moving faster than it—"

And that is the end of *that* conversation, although Black Sand Base keeps trying to start it up again....

Some Terrans are—were—in trouble; apparently they got something mad at them and are—were—paying the price....

I feel curiously distant from them. It is more than physical —hearing their anguished voices, I should empathize, ache to help—but that was so long ago, and so far away ... I'm not Terran any longer. I'm not *human*. Replaying the tape, I find myself fretting about their *ships*....

"How goes the universe, Cool Cap?" asks a familiar voice.

"Ms. Ioanni, good morning. Nice to hear your dulcet tones. The universe appears to be in good shape, although some life forms out there are not too fond of humanity."

"How so?" Today her hair winds around the top of her head; she wears a blue T-shirt with white shorts. Swooping into an armchair, she reminds me that people *can* be graceful, if they put their minds to it....

When I play her the maydays, a frown creeps across her face. "Are they coming this way?"

"There's no way to tell until my sensors pick them up."

"What do you think?"

"I plead insufficient data."

"Well, what does this do to your plans not to land?"

"Nothing—just reminds me to be careful when I sneak up on aliens, that's all."

"Still going to let us come with you?"

"It doesn't bother you?"

"It scares the pants off me—but what the hell. Something's going to trim me sooner or later, and I'd prefer to have the inevitable happen in space. It's more, oh ... majestic—to go down—up?—with your ship, don't you think?"

"Speaking for the ship, I'd say majesty lies in survival."

She laughs at that, a clear smooth laugh that fills the room with honest warmth. "Cool Cap?"

"Yes?"

"The thing is, most of us Travelers—that's what we call ourselves now—we don't want to be dead weight. I mean, we'll be pulling out of the Canopus system in what, thirteen years?"

"Allow more than five to get the colony started," I say. "Figure twenty."

"All right. So we're leaving in twenty years. All the Landers have jobs to do, but what about us? Once we're gone, what can we do to make the journey ..."

"Interesting?" I offer.

"No," she says thoughtfully. "It'll be that in any event ... worthwhile. In the sense that we'll have contributed to it."

Honesty is called for: "I don't know. I'm self-sufficient; I don't need people ... *You* have to figure out why you're going, and then take it from there."

Disappointment wrinkles her high forehead.

"Mary," I say, "there are possibilities—communicating with aliens, exobiology, etiology, these sorts of things. And there are human art forms which you could attempt to develop—or develop differently, given the environment—ballet, music, painting ... investigations we can carry out together, searching for life in deep space and so on ... the thing is, you people have to decide what within you can best be fulfilled by staying aboard—and then vow to fulfill it, no matter how much sweat and anguish it involves. See what I mean?"

"Yeah," she murmurs, rising and crossing to the porthole. "Yeah, I do see. Dim the lights, will you?"

"Sure."

"It's beautiful out there ... empty. Cool Cap—" she whirls suddenly and stretches out her arms. "They think they can force you down. Can they?"

"No. And if they try, well ... I could refuse to drop them off." That is a lie, as Sangria hastens to remind me. "Tell them that."

Her face brightens. "I will."

At about which time the chemical supply division reports that Billy Jo Dunn Tracer, a nineteen-year-old chemistry student and rabid Lander, has acquired enough chemicals to blow a very large hole in me....

When I look in on her, she is just starting work on her bomb.

Billy Jo Dunn Tracer was a tall, willowy woman with green eyes and red hair. Hunched over a workbench in the Inorganic Chemistry Lab, she was running the last few tests on a batch of Super High Explosive—SHE, for short. This formula has passed the oxidation, handling, and plastic-case contact tests, but only in a dry, dust-free state. Tracer now had to determine what would happen if the silvery powder became damp, or contaminated.

She could sense the eyes of the Cube boring into her. Everywhere—waking, washing, working—she was observed. The hairs of her neck constantly bristled with the "somebody's-watching" sensation. Her shoulders were always squared; her stomach was perpetually taut. Nerve-wracking.

And all because the Cube had happened to notice, five years ago, that she had requested chemicals that could be synthesized into explosives! Of all the silly things ... true, her requisition hadn't been accompanied by a research prospectus explaining the need for them, but the Cube could have asked, instead of coldly assuming the worst ... It was a valid, valuable line of inquiry: the colony would face a tremendous amount of excavation, even if established on a flat plain or in a friendly valley ... it would need good, non-nuclear explosives, which meant somebody had to develop them ... *Although maybe*, she thought, stroking the slick plastic case, *it was a mistake to start work while I was mouthing off so much ...* then she shook her auburn head and tightened her lips. *No,* she thought, *No! I had a perfect right to do both, and if the Cube doesn't like it, it can ... Oh, hell,* she upbraided herself, *you know damn well you were thinking you could slip something past it—cook up a SHE that would serve on the ground, but that would also help force the Cube to let us take it down....*

The waldo in the test chamber poised a dropper above the milligram of powder and squeezed out one cubic millimeter of water. The SHE darkened as it absorbed the moisture.

Tracer's green eyes were riveted to the display screen; her chapped hands curled around the edge of the bench and whitened at the knuckles. Holding her breath, she watched it turn from silver to muddy brown to ebony to—

The dials on the chamber swung with the force of the explosion. The anchored workbench shivered; a valve whistled as it bled off pressure. A good yield, but ... *Christ,* she thought, *can't use that for construction if it plasts when it gets wet....*

"Cube," she called.

"Yes?" The voice echoed off the bare metal walls.

"Did you know that was going to detonate?"

"Yes."

"Then why didn't you warn me?"

"You didn't ask."

"Goddammit!" she screamed, anger clawing at her throat, "Goddammit, goddammit! I spent six months on this—when did you know it wouldn't work?"

"Shortly after the third refinement—approximately four months ago."

"And all that time you could have warned me,"

"All that time you could have asked me."

She clamped her jaws together, knowing that if she continued to argue in her present emotional state, it would continue to make a fool out of her. Damn it anyway, for being such an icicle. Damn it for putting her in the wrong and keeping her there. She paced, scraping her soles on the deck's acid-splotched paint.

Relations between the Landers and the Cube had soured around 3288, shortly after they had accused it of brainwashing Andall Figuera, who had since become a mystic-contemplative hermit in the caves of 1 New England Park.

"So what?" it had replied. "He's still a Lander."

"Meth," they'd snapped. "He's sleetier than you are, and he's not going down. We won't have time for mental incompetents."

"The colony needs him to offset your hardheadedness."

"We're not going to take him."

"Then you don't go, either."

Acrimony had mounted in inverse proportion to the remaining distance to Canopus. The Cube had stopped speaking except when spoken to, and then as tersely as possible: Yes. No. 12.83. No assistance, no editorializing ...

Much as she hated to admit it, Tracer missed the chatty Col'kyu of her youth. She'd grown up accustomed to a ubiquitous presence that spoke in metallic tones and was always available, always ready with a friendly word, warning, whatever the situation called for.

Now the presence, no less ubiquitous, was a surly Peeping Tom. At least to the Landers. Apparently, it was still amiable with the Travelers. *Dammit*, she thought, *it's not right. A lousy computer. Instead of doing what we tell it, it does what it wants. It's going to set us down under-equipped and doom us all. I've got to stop it.*

Dully, her eyes crossed her workbench, resting on the stoppered vial. The silvery dust mesmerized her. An idea formed in the back of her mind. She shied away, at first, but then it became attractive ... She'd need a few items from inventory.

Deliberately ignoring the vial, she stepped to the dented hatch of the delivery unit and said, "Cube, I want a dozen radio capsules—the kind that open on receipt of a given signal—of one cc each. I want a transmitter keyed to them. Also, one dozen airtight test chambers big enough to hold the radio capsules; the chambers will need hookups to water and air supplies."

The items tumbled into her waiting hands quickly, without comment, but the pressure of the wall-units' eyes lit her cheeks with hot fire. Her feet stumbled over each other. Surely the Cube could read her plans; they must be branded on her forehead ... but no servos appeared, so she proceeded. She'd see whose hand was quicker than whose eye....

Forty-five minutes later, the capsules were packed with SHE, which for some reason smelled like ripe tomatoes. She walked down the line of test chambers, putting one capsule into each, until all were filled, and their doors screwed tight. She told the Cube, "Provide each chamber with a different environment, and measure the length of time it takes for deterioration and detonation, if they ever occur. Fill number one with water. Keep the relative humidity in number twelve at zero percent. Range the others between those two extremes. Can we get more?"

"Yes."

"How many?"

"As many as your budget can afford."

"Good." She paused to think, and ran long, slender fingers through her reddish-brown hair while she did so. There hadn't been a trace of suspicion in CC's voice; that buoyed her. "Tomorrow we'll set up environments where the humidity varies; later on, when results start coming in, I'll want some where the temperatures cycle, too. That's all for today."

God, she thought, *it's so damn irritating to deal with a sullen computer—won't talk, won't offer advice—sure, it'll answer our questions, but who'd think to ask the questions in the first place? Dammit anyway, it needs to be taught a lesson.*

On her way home from the lab, she stopped at Ivan Kinney's office, and found him stretched out on his sofa, catnapping. His huge feet were bare; she seized his big toe and twisted it gently.

"Ow!" He jackknifed up and rubbed his blue eyes. "Oh, BJ —how are you doing?"

"Ivan," she said, shoveling his legs onto the floor so she could plop down, "we've got to talk to Mary Ioanni."

"Why?" When he got up, the sofa exhaled with audible relief.

"She's on good terms with the Cube, since she's heading up the Travelers."

On the other side of the office, Kinney crouched over a sink, and splashed water onto his craggy face. While he groped for a thick red towel, he said, "So what's that got to do with anything?"

"We should ask her to use her influence to get it to cooperate more readily with us—it's frustrating, the way that fuh'r watches all the time, and never says a word to help."

After tossing the towel at the rack, he slipped into his sandals and fingered their frayed straps up behind his ankles. "I agree that Iceheart's not volunteering much, but does it really matter?"

She sniffed, as if detecting something rotten. "I wasted four months on a research project because it didn't volunteer."

"We're still three years out from Canopus, BJ—and probably fifteen years from landing. What's four months?"

"A damn long time to waste!" Her eyes were burning emeralds. "We should have everything ready *before* we land—"

"BJ, we're not onto what we're going into—why tailor-make something for environments that may not exist?"

"You're hopeless." She felt exasperated, but patting the glass cylinder in her pocket calmed her down. "Listen—do you agree that if it came out of its sulks, it would improve things all around?"

"Sure, no argument there." He studied his forest-green tunic in the mirror and smoothed out the places that had wrinkled during his doze.

"All right! So let's go visit Mary Ioanni and—"

"Okay." He held up his hands in mock surrender. "We'll go. Just you and me? Or—"

She nibbled her full lower lip. "The whole Lander hierarchy."

"Fine." He pointed to the sensor-head. "Iceheart, put me through to Mary Ioanni, please."

The unit was silent, but in a moment, her familiar voice asked, "Yes?"

"Ivan Kinney," he said. "Could I and a few colleagues call on you?"

"Right now?"

"If possible."

"Sure." She sounded puzzled; Kinney hadn't spoken to her in months. "Come on up."

Of the other four, two were busy. Only Billie Mandell and Triscata Launder could meet them. "Let's go," he said to Tracer.

Stiffly, she rose from the sofa. Her muscles were sore from standing all day. She stretched—not at all minding the way Kinney's eyes brushed her torso as she raised her arms above and behind her head—then yawned, and said, "Okay."

Three minutes later, they met outside Ioanni's suite, before which paraded a regiment of tulips. No children hung around —Ioanni's were married and living in their own suites with her grandchildren—but her husband, Salim Falaka, was just leaving. With a graceful bow, he stopped the door in its track for them.

Ioanni's smile was warm and genuine. Taking their hands, she kissed all four on the cheek. "Before we get down to business—and from your grim looks it has to be that—what would you like to drink?"

"Ice water," said Tracer. The symbolism pleased her.

A moment later she held the tall, cold glass in her hand, and listened to the clinking cubes counterpoint Kinney's conversation. For a scientist, he was reasonably eloquent, and explained their case in brief, yet persuasive terms. "So you see," he finished, "if Iceheart won't let us use the ship for the colony, we're going to have to be more prepared than otherwise—and it could help us, if it would only stop this childish moping. There are so many steps it could save us—but it won't talk to us, except when we ask it direct questions. Could you convince it?"

Ioanni chuckled; it was a deep and wholesome sound. "I can but try," she said, turning her head to the gray grillwork of the wall-unit. "Cool Cap—you've heard all this. Would you care to comment?"

"I have no objections to being civil," replied the speakers, "but the Landers are constantly scheming to coerce me into agreeing to my own self-destruction, and that, I will not tolerate."

"Listen, Ice—" began Kinney.

"No, you listen. You've been plotting against me for a long time; now you want me to help you—why should I?"

"If we felt we'd no need of you, we'd not plot."

"So you're saying if I help you, you'll give up your schemes to cut me into houses?"

"Yes."

"No!" shouted Tracer, leaping to her feet while her hand dove into her pocket for the vial. She held the ice water steady in her other hand; with her teeth she unstopped the vial. "Don't anybody move!"

"What are you doing?" demanded CC.

"This is SHE—if I pour it into this water, it'll explode—put a hole right through that damn hull—don't anybody move." She nodded to Ioanni. "Lie down on the floor."

Pale but composed, Ioanni complied.

"*Face* down."

She rolled over.

Sitting, Tracer balanced herself on Ioanni's butt. "Now all of you, get this straight. We're going to stop this nonsense right now—or else I set this off. You hear me, Cube?"

"Yes."

"No knockout gas." She tilted the container so that its lip overhung the rim of the glass. "I feel even a little woozy, I do it."

"BJ," said Kinney, "this is wrong, what you're doing— please, put down the SHE—violence'll not solve the problem."

Fascinated, she watched the minute trembling of her white fingers. A snake was loose in her stomach—the last thing she wanted was to have to pour the SHE—she was not a violent person, not really; just one who believed in something very strongly ... tension heightened her senses; she could hear the tiny, tiny sound of glass brushing glass ... she was just trying to prove her point, that was all—show everybody how serious this was—force the Cube to give up its insane, antihuman plans and submit itself to them.

"I've had it with you people," snapped the speakers. "If she plasts the place, it's not going to hurt me—I'll survive anything

—but it'll term all of you. You think you can coerce me into giving myself up? Meth. I'm not going to put up with this. We're going to skip the Canopus system, that's all. No entry, no landing, nothing."

Kinney waited for it to go on, but when the silence began to hang heavily, he forced his eyes to Tracer and said, "BJ, please —this is all wrong—we've moved past this sort of behavior, have we not? We're more mature than this. Please. Put it down."

"Uh-uh." She felt drunk, and giggled. Their faces wore shock, and that amused her, too. "If you don't want this to go blooie! you go up to the Cube's icebox, and you disconnect it."

"I won't let you," said the metallic monotone.

"Then your precious Mary Ioanni goes up in a cloud of smoke."

"You'll go with her."

"So what? If you're not going to land, I don't care." She tilted the vial a fraction of a centimeter.

"You three," said CC with resignation, "come up to the central unit."

Ioanni gasped, "Coo—"

"I'm sorry, Mary." The door to the corridor opened. "Come on, all three of you."

As they left, Ioanni said, "Cool Cap, don't, please, I'm not worth it—"

"I'm *very*, sorry, Mary. Truly, I am."

Before Tracer could react, a glitter filled the doorway: a servo. It was lobbing a round object at them. As she started to pour, she saw that the object was a portable g-unit. She just had time to wonder what the Cube thought it was doing when—

It was a short-range unit, set at 10G, and it managed to stifle most of the blast's force.

The hull was holed, though.

Neither of the bodies was ever recovered.

We nose into the Canopus system late in March 3295. To determine a more accurate date will be impossible for some years because you can't define the borders of a system until you've plotted all the orbits of all the bodies in it ... The nearest planet is still 200 million kilometers sunwards, but in our neighborhood, comets loiter and dust dances and junk readies itself for the long jaunt around its ellipse.

I've found the Landers a world. Through the scopes it looks beautiful: cotton candy swirled over a ball of beige and topaz. It is a little smaller than Earth, but as if to compensate, its density is a bit greater. Initial estimates place its gravity somewhere in the vicinity of 1.08G. Since I have to decelerate anyway, I throw on the ramscoop, and brake at 10.8 meters/sec^2. This shuts down the shipboard g-units. Residents of odd-numbered Levels either move out, or live on their ceilings, but the crowding and the inconvenience are temporary.

Long-range spectroscopy reveals oxygen, carbon dioxide, and nitrogen in the atmosphere; it also shouts "Water on the surface!" Radar mapping is difficult, though: the atmosphere absorbs, diffuses, and diffracts. I think I see plains, oceans, and four major, monstrous mountain chains. Perhaps a third of the world's surface area is land.

Strange tides splash down there—the planet has four moons, one twice as massive as the one I grew up beneath, another close to that size, and two moonlets, much smaller, though very close.

But I can't start making plans because first I have to have a showdown with the Landers—and it isn't of my making.

Clustered in their headquarters, the former 12-SW Common Room, is a grimmer-faced batch of mayflies than I've seen in a long time. Ivan Kinney is their spokesman. Uncomfortable in his role, he must have accepted it under duress. He stands behind a long Formica table, fidgeting with the wires, cutters, prototype survival kits, and non-lethal electric stun poles that clutter its surface.

"Iceheart," he says gravely, "it's time we got this straightened out."

"What?"

"The matter of your consenting to your cannibalization."

"I thought we'd finished that a long time ago."

"No." He scratches his head, then shakes it. He doesn't glance at the others for support—he just cracks his knuckles and goes on, "We've figured it out, and we can't see us surviving without the material in you."

"Forget that," I say. "You don't get it."

"We have to have it."

"All right." I am about to lie, but they'll never know. "I won't part with my body, and you can't survive without it. Therefore, rather than condemn you all to death, I'll bypass the planet. We're already heading into the system, so it's too late to skip the whole thing entirely, but I can slingshot around the sun. Maybe next time we pass a habitable world, you won't be so greedy. It shouldn't be more than a couple hundred years."

Having heard me out in head-bowed silence, he raises his eyes. Their blue irises are dark and determined. "We thought you'd say that—but we'll give you a chance to change your mind. As your monitors have probably told you, we posted a squad outside the door of the corridor to your vault. Let them enter and detach you from the circuitry."

I laugh. "Who'll run the ship?"

"We've built a replacement." He gestures to the far corner, where squats a bulky but competent unit I helped them design ten years ago. Should it be installed in my place, it will do the job—without my originality or sense of humor, perhaps, but the

Landers don't enjoy those attributes anyway. "We'll move it up to your vault once you're out."

"Sorry," I say. "I refuse."

He shrugs; it is beautifully nonchalant. "Then we'll have to attack you and *seize* control."

"Take me twenty seconds to knock every one of you out."

"Afraid not." He opens a survival kit and extracts a transparent plastic hood. "Recognize this?"

"I should. I did the chemistry on it." It is a selectively permeable membrane, worn shiny side out. Oxygen can osmose into it; carbon dioxide can permeate out. My gas would eddy against it in vain. "And I presume all of you have them?"

"Exactly." He smiles like a chess-player who's worked his opponent into a tight, but not fatal, corner.

I bring up a rook: "Of course, it wouldn't take my servos more than—" nanosecond pause for the calculation "—three minutes to take them all away from you—which means that within two hundred seconds—"

"Sorry." He holds up the electric-shock pole. "We discovered something about this—they'll not kill a large mammal, but they sure will scramble the innards of a servo. One touch—sprxt! Useless."

"Hmm." And I manufactured 100,000 of them, too ... I should have seen what it would do to my minions, but ... "Mind if I test that?"

"Be my guest."

I roll a servo through the doorway; Kinney swings around, pole at the ready. I feint. He dodges. The table wobbles and tools fall off. I reach. He pokes. With a shower of sparks, the servo dies.

"Impressive," I say. Calculating the time needed to design an immune device, and then the time it would take to produce enough to demask the Landers, I realize that if they have three unopposed weeks ... "I'll bet you think you've got me over a barrel."

The smile on Kinney's long face widens slightly; a millimeter more of teeth shows white and shiny. "We think," he says, mildly, "that you'll see the advantages of cooperation."

"Of suicide, you mean," I snort. "But I don't. See, you will have one helluva time trying to cut me out of the circuitry if you have to work in five-G. I can turn those g-units back on up there, you know."

"The nice thing about computers," he says tangentially, or so I think, "is that they're so predictable ... We figured you'd say that. Check the service corridors between three two five and three two six, and the ones leading into your core—notice the people? And the equipment?"

I look. In each of the four corridors, scores of workers press against the inner hatches. Oxy-acetylene torches, braced against floor and ceiling so that shifting gravity won't budge them unless it rips the decks out, stand bare-snouted and ominous. Each worker carries a survival pack and a stun-pole; looped around his waist, a tool belt contains wire cutters and crowbar to pry up plating. "Damn," I say, annoyed with myself. "I thought they were maintenance crews."

"We've calculated," says Kinney modestly, "that the torches, operating without guidance, can cut through your hatches in less than ten minutes. Of course, there are no g-decks beyond them—but the core does hold the cables to *all* the g-decks. The g-units everywhere will shut down eleven, twelve minutes after I give the signal. For that long, Five-G is tolerable. We'd rather not have to do that—the ship isn't designed for Zero-G, and things would float around until we patched up the wiring—but we will if you don't drop out of the circuitry."

"As you probably know," I counter, "I have tremendous exhaust fans—and if you give the signal, if even one of your men unholsters a bolt-cutter—I'll switch them on. You say I have ten minutes? I can slash atmospheric pressure to forty-eight percent of normal in that time, and the vents will stay open until you've repaired all the wiring. Even if you work at top speed, it'll take you another twenty minutes to splice the wires, and then you still have to schlep your replacement computer upstairs, and get it on-line ... tell me, Kinney, do you enjoy breathing vacuum?"

His face has gone pale; his eyes are robins' eggs in a snow-bank. His knees shake. His voice, though, is admirably level. "You'd term everybody aboard if you tried that."

"Uh-huh."

Somebody in the front row twitches his head, and Kinney seems to draw strength from it. "No," he says, "no," and this time confidence buttresses his tone, "you'd not be able to do that—surely you're programmed against it."

The only order that affects me—and I'm not about to tell *him* this—is that I have to land people on a habitable world in the Canopus system. But trimming off all the mayflies wouldn't jeopardize the mission: I have plenty of sperm and ova in the DNA banks, thousands of vats in which to grow them ... Aloud, I say, "Try me."

"Goddammit, you're just a machine! You can't go around killing humans!"

It is time to tell them. "I'm not a machine, although all my body and most of my data-centers are. I am—or was—a human being. Have you ever heard of a brain-puter?"

The listeners gasp; Kinney recoils as though he's just taken a blow. "I—" his throat, hoarse, fails him. He clears it. "I can't believe that," he says at last. "It's a ... a gambit, that's all."

"Please study the display screen."

The heads turn to the right wall, to the large screen hung in its middle. The camera scans my central unit—tall, box-like, wheeled, with wires and tubes running in, out, and all around. A servo stands in the vault with it (it is *never* unguarded), and I move that to the unit. Its claw unlatches the cabinet door. In the plastic case within floats my brain—me. It looks remarkably obscene.

"My God!" chokes Kinney. His right hand shields his jugular.

"Now, do you begin to understand why I defend myself? Do you see why I will not allow you to use me for housing?"

He recovers quickly, I'll give him that. "But look," he placates, "we'll not *kill* you—we'll just go on using you ... or—" he is flustered "—I suppose you might not like that; we'll give you your freedom—your unit there has wheels and all, we could attach a motor, you could—"

"You can't *give* me freedom, Kinney—I already have it. I am not going to surrender it. I am also not going to trade my body for a one-half horsepower motor. I *like* what I am now. I intend to remain this way. Now, will you please act like reasonable beings, or—"

"Jesus." He is groping for a solution which won't involve killing. Give credit where credit is due: mayfly culture has come a long way. Now that they understand my nature, they are willing to look for a better resolution.

"You people," I break the tomb-like silence, "must have spent a long time getting that plot ready."

"Three years," replies Kinney absently. "Since BJ ..."

"I never picked up on it—why?"

"It was all done in bleepspeak." He demonstrates, and at last I know why some mayflies seemed so verbose. "Or notes passed surreptitiously in eyeless rooms. Everything down to the last detail ... but we weren't onto, we didn't have any idea—"

"I see." I pause for thought. They really want my body—

more, they are honestly convinced that they have to have it to survive.

Under these circumstances, setting them down would be ... well, not quite tantamount to murder, but awful damn close ... They have psyched themselves into a position where a self-fulfilling prophecy could ruin them all ... I can't just let it happen.

"I have an idea," I say.

"Huh?"

"Look—we're penetrating above the plane of the ecliptic, but with a few course changes and fly-by, we can drop into it. There's an asteroid belt. I can scoop up material—come to think of it, I could do that after I've dropped you off—no, better before. I scoop it up, and once we're in orbit, I fashion it into the housing my hull would have provided. How's that?"

They wrangle for a while—a long while; some will be bitching about it years after I've gone—but a few sly remarks to the effect that the material will be a millennium younger, and presumably less subject to metal fatigue, carry the day. They agree. Kinney signals the invaders to disperse. I dispatch servos to collect stun poles, promising to return them when the Landers go down. (And meanwhile getting to work on a design immune to electroshock.) Together we work out the course changes that will swoop us through the asteroid belt on a mining trip.

And a nerve-shattering jaunt it is—while the belt isn't as crowded as the Santa Monica Freeway used to be, the kinetic energies involved are significantly higher ... even though I'm decelerating, and the ramscoop (which gathers both fuel for the engines and small asteroids for the settlement) clears out the area immediately ahead, new rocks whistle in from the sides. I am too big to be agile. My eyes and ears strain to their outer limits to detect incoming traffic. Virtually all my time is devoted to constant recomputations of my flight path ... stop, start, reverse engines, swivel, quick! Long blast, short burp, fusion furious about menacing meteoroids, pinholed! Servos slap seals on bulkheads; Landers chew fingernails completely off (wish I had some; could nibble a few right now). Jolt! Jounce! Spin ... and we're out of the danger zone, with two hundred million tons of rock in the hold.

We orbit Canopus XXIV for six months before the probes tell us its atmosphere is safe, its native microbiota too different to be dangerous, and its dry lands apparently uninhabited by intelligence. While the explorations continue, I smelt the metallic harvest into modular housing with ablative bases.

At last Ivan Kinney decides to go down. I shut off the g-units to provide oG. The core hatch on 321-2 North ratchets into the bulkhead; pressurized oxygen spurts the landing craft along the 321-2 North Service Corridor. It stops between the two airlocks; 120 gamblers—some eager, some scared silly—climb into it. The outer hatch cycles open; another gust of oxygen thrusts the aluminum needle into space, where it orients itself and spreads its wings.

"Sure you know how to fly that, Ivan?" I radio.

"Spent twenty years on the trainers," he flashes back. "If I'm not onto it by now, I never will be."

75,000 pairs of eyes burn through the portholes to watch the long, thin vessel head toward the penumbra, and dip into the night side. A great sigh goes up as it is lost to sight, but the radars show their sightings on the display screens. The vigil continues. The air grows smoky. Muscles everywhere tense as the telemetered altimetry readings melt into single digits. I open the speech circuits and we all hear:

"We're down!" Kinney's voice is almost overwhelmed by shouting, cheering, and piercing wolf whistles.

"What's it look like?" I query.

"Flat. Some kind of plant life, similar to grass, all around us, stretching to the far horizon ... which is jagged, serrate; must be mountains ... Jesus, it feels funny to be here ... the ground is hard, we're going to go out and take a look ... goddamn, I just can't believe we made it."

The rest of the mayflies cheer. And cheer. And cheer.

They're all down, now. 68,912 of them. 575 landing crafts' worth; I only have 77 left. They dropped one at a time, and their flights were interspersed with supply drops. Eighteen months, so far, and there's a lot left to do.

The Travelers are helping to manufacture what the fledgling colony would have had if I'd surrendered myself. We figure another three years, maybe four ... it would be more predictable if the parachutes didn't fail on occasion....

And now we're leaving, having beamed a final, farewell message to Canopus Colony that was heard by a couple radio operators, a handful of tape recorders, and Sangria. They're busy down there; they don't have time for sentimental good-byes.

The eyes up here are dry, too, even though six thousand eight Travelers' noses are flattened against the portholes as Canopus XXIV recedes. They've gotten used to its presence, to the large, warm solidarity of it—it'll be a while before they see its like again.

The colonists won't miss us. They've got their four moons, which kept us from competing for their attention at night. They've got their housing and machinery, more of it than they can use, so they should be psychologically prepared for our absence. They've also got Sangria the F-puter, who has a duplicate of everything in my banks.

So it's off to the asteroid belt again, where we'll reap enough ore to fashion 100,000 FTL engines and replenish our depleted resources. From there ... we haven't laid a course, yet.

But I know one thing.

I'm going to go talk to some aliens.

ABOUT THE AUTHOR

As the author of ten published novels and over seventy published short stories and articles, Kevin O'Donnell, Jr. had a devoted following of readers. One of his most popular and beloved works  is the McGill Feighan series, a fast-paced and fun science fiction romp.

Kevin was an active contributor to the Science Fiction and Fantasy Writers Association. He chaired SFWA's Nebula Award Committee, ran SFWA's *Bulletin*, and served as Chairman of SFWA's Grievance Committee, where he fought unceasingly for the rights of authors in an era of growing Internet piracy and corporate disregard of personal copyrights. As a result of these activities, he received the Service to SFWA Award.

Kevin spent much of his teen years in South Korea, where his father was Country Director for the Peace Corps. His interest in Asia and language skills led him to take his degree at Yale in Chinese Studies, where he met his wife Kim, with whom he was happily married until his passing in 2012. An avid gardener, O'Donnell delighted in raising bonsai, vegetables, and assorted plants.

WordFire Press is pleased to bring the works of Kevin O'Donnell, Jr. back into print for a new audience.

IF YOU LIKED ...

If you liked *Mayflies*, you might also enjoy:

Caverns

by Kevin O'Donnell, Jr.

Taylor's Ark

by Jody Lynn Nye

Captain Nemo

by Kevin J. Anderson

OTHER WORDFIRE PRESS TITLES
BY KEVIN O'DONNELL, JR.

Bander Snatch

The Journeys of McGill Feighan
Caverns
Reefs
Lava
Cliffs

War of Omission

Our list of other WordFire Press authors and titles is always growing. To find out more and to shop our selection of titles, visit us at:
wordfirepress.com

 facebook.com/WordfireIncWordfirePress

 twitter.com/WordFirePress

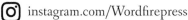 instagram.com/Wordfirepress

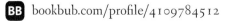 bookbub.com/profile/4109784512

Printed in Great Britain
by Amazon

73360454R00210